THE
SEARCH
PARTY

Also by Hannah Richell:

Secrets of the Tides
The Shadow Year
The Peacock Summer
The River Home

THE
SEARCH
PARTY

HANNAH RICHELL

**SIMON &
SCHUSTER**

London · New York · Sydney · Toronto · New Delhi

First published in Great Britain by Simon & Schuster UK Ltd, 2024

1 3 5 7 9 10 8 6 4 2

Simon & Schuster UK Ltd
1st Floor
222 Gray's Inn Road
London WC1X 8HB

Simon & Schuster: Celebrating 100 Years of Publishing in 2024

Simon & Schuster Australia, Sydney
Simon & Schuster India, New Delhi

www.simonandschuster.co.uk
www.simonandschuster.com.au
www.simonandschuster.co.in

A CIP catalogue record for this book
is available from the British Library

Hardback ISBN: 978-1-3985-2795-9
Trade Paperback ISBN: 978-1-3985-2796-6
eBook ISBN: 978-1-3985-2797-3
Audio ISBN: 978-1-3985-2799-7

Map designed by Jill Tytherleigh

Typeset in the UK by M Rules
Printed and Bound in the UK using 100% Renewable
Electricity at CPI Group (UK) Ltd

For my mum and dad,
Gillian and John Norman

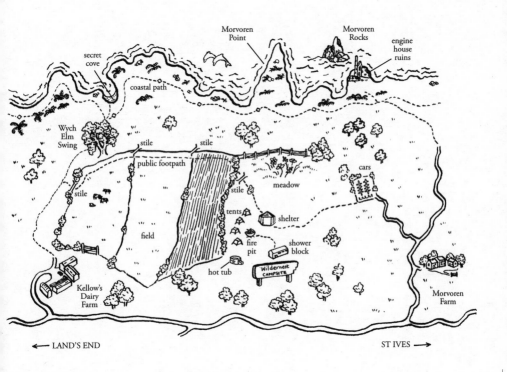

CHARACTERS

The Kingsley Family
Max
Annie
Kip (12 years)

The Davies Family
Dominic
Tanya
Scarlet (16 years)
Felix (14 years)
Phoebe (6 years)

The Miller Family
Jim
Suze
Willow (14 years)
River (13 years)
Juniper (9 years)

Kira de Silva
Fred O'Connor
Asha (5 months)

Josh Penrose – local surfer and Wildernest handyman
John Kellow – local dairy farmer and the Kingsleys' nearest neighbour
Clare Davies – Dominic's ex-wife

Devon & Cornwall Police
Detective Inspector Sue Lawson
Detective Constable Lee Barnett
Family Liaison Officer Patricia Haines

PROLOGUE

The girl stands in the grey morning light, her feet perched at the crumbling cliff edge. Below her, waves smash against jagged rocks, granite shards rising like decaying teeth from the foaming sea. At her back are fear and despair, and his words, urging her on.

She tries to distract herself with the details around her. The roar of the ocean. The gusting wind ripping at the bracken. The small, white flowers growing at her feet. The loud, too-fast thump of her heart. Only it's impossible to focus; she can't seem to fix anything in her mind. Nothing can compete with his voice – all his ugly words bearing down on her. *Do it*, he says. *What are you waiting for?*

The ledge shifts beneath her toes. A fragment of earth crumbles and falls, vanishing into the swirling water far below. Carried on the wind, a bird cry rises high and mournful. She lifts her gaze and sees a gull turn in the sky above. Free.

Do it now. His voice is louder, closer. Goosebumps rise as if his words curl through the air and graze the back of her neck. *What are you waiting for?*

There is no escape. Nowhere else to go.

She closes her eyes and unfurls her arms, stretching them wide as if she too has wings to rise and join the bird hovering above. With a final breath, she launches out into the void. Fall or fly – she no longer cares.

DOMINIC

Sunday afternoon

He has no idea how long he's been sitting there. There's no clock in the room, just a table, three chairs and a single, narrow window set high into the wall – too high to offer anything but a glimpse of the blank grey sky outside. It could have been twenty minutes since the police ushered him in and asked him to 'wait here, please'; it could have been far longer. Dominic knows in moments of heightened stress that seconds can feel like minutes and minutes like hours, though the vending machine cup of tea someone brought him cooled ages ago. He also knows that every time he thinks about what might be happening outside this room, he feels a painful constriction in his chest, a tight band pressing vice-like against his lungs, making breathing hard.

He would be more help out there. Not shut away in a hospital consulting room, sitting in his damp clothing, waiting to answer questions – questions he's certain he won't have the answers to. But the two detectives had been

3

insistent – he was to assist with their enquiries. Almost, he thinks, as if they suspect him of something.

The door opens and Dominic springs from his chair. 'Any news?' he asks, his eyes darting from the lead police detective in her grey suit to her burly, blond colleague just behind.

'Nothing yet I'm afraid, Mr Davies,' she says. 'Take a seat please.'

Dominic hesitates. The last thing he wants to do is sit. 'I think I'd be more use—'

The detective raises her hand. 'We've got a team scouring the site now. As soon as we know anything – anything at all – we'll be sure to let you know. Right now, Mr Davies, we need you to take us through everything you can remember.' She gestures towards his chair, before pulling out her own with a screech, slapping a thin, cardboard file on the table between them. The second officer takes his seat, his huge frame swamping the small plastic chair. He opens a notebook and uncaps a pen.

Dominic eyes the chair with frustration. He wants action and consequences, not talking and note-taking, but sensing the resolve rising off the female detective, he takes the seat.

Lawson, he remembers. DI Sue Lawson. She'd introduced herself earlier. Her younger colleague, the rosy-cheeked young man with the bleach-blond hair and shoulders that would be better suited to a muddy rugby shirt than a starched police uniform, is Barrett. No, Barnett. DC Barnett.

Lawson nods and Barnett starts the recording device resting on the table between them.

'To reiterate,' states Barnett, clearing his throat, 'your participation in this interview is entirely voluntary. You can leave at any time, though of course,' he adds, 'the more information we can gather about the weekend's events, the more successful we are likely to be with our investigation.'

'I've already told you,' says Dominic, 'it's not me you need to talk to. It's that kid. He's got something to do with it, I know it.'

Another nod from Lawson. 'As I said, we'll be talking to everyone involved.'

'They're always making excuses for him, but trust me, there's something wrong with that boy.'

'Mr Davies,' DI Lawson leans forward and fixes him with her level gaze, 'I hear your concerns. I know how worried you must be.' Her eyes, he notices, are an intriguing colour, grey like sea pebbles, an almost perfect match for the streak running through her short, dark hair. 'But I'm afraid we do urgently require your assistance. We'd be grateful for your *full* cooperation.'

There's a part of Dominic that can't help wondering if they are deriving some small pleasure from this. It can't be every day they get to interview someone off the telly. This whole incident will no doubt provide a flutter of excitement at the station. *Guess who we had in the chair today.* God forbid this should reach the press. He should probably call Barry. Give him the heads-up in case the tabloids come sniffing for another salacious Dominic Davies story. They'd certainly raked him over the coals a few years back, around the time of his divorce. He frowns,

5

glancing between the two detectives. 'Do I need to call my lawyer?'

'Would you *like* legal representation?' Barnett glances up from his notepad, pen poised.

It's like falling into one of those gritty crime dramas, Dominic thinks, the kind Tanya loves to watch on a Sunday night, curled up on the sofa in her pyjamas with a glass of wine in her hand and her phone on her lap. He's always thought them silly – overblown and too predictable – and yet here he sits, in an airless interview room with a recording device on the table between them, blinking its red light like an evil eye. 'No,' he says, 'of course I don't need my lawyer. Let's just get on with it.' He folds his arms across his chest. 'What do you want to know?'

Lawson leans back in her seat and nods again at Barnett to continue.

'It was a reunion amongst friends? Four families meeting up for the May Day weekend?'

'Yes.'

Barnett checks back through his notes. 'And there were fifteen in your party?'

Dominic considers this for a moment, counting in his head. 'Well . . . we were sixteen, if you include the baby.' He reaches for the plastic cup in front of him before remembering it's cold and undrinkable. At the sight of the brown film floating on its surface, he slides the cup away.

'You were all invited to stay at Wildernest?' Barnett is consulting his notes again. 'The site belonging to Max and Annie Kingsley, located out beyond the Cape, near Morvoren Point?'

'That's right. I'd just wrapped filming on the latest series of the show, so it was good timing. *Star Search*,' he adds. 'You've probably seen it.'

Barnett nods but the female detective maintains her inscrutable stare. Dominic can't hide his smile. He knows her type. Wants to pretend she's above reality TV. Doesn't like to admit she's one of the ten million viewers tuning in religiously each week, cheering on her favourite contestants, texting her votes.

'No matter,' he says, with a small wave. 'Max and Annie had invited us for the bank holiday to road-test their new "glamping" business.' He lifts his hands and emphasizes the apostrophes. 'You know the sort of thing. All the rage: save-the-planet, sustainable eco-tourism. Max's dream.'

'I understand the Kingsleys had relocated to Cornwall last year, with their son?'

He nods. 'To tell you the truth, none of us quite believed it when they announced they were leaving London. We were supportive, of course. You have to be, don't you? It's not exactly the done thing to tell your friends that you think they're making a terrible mistake.'

'Why did you think it a mistake?'

Dominic lets out a sharp laugh. 'They'd spent years building up their architectural firm, making it a success. Only last year they won a prestigious RIBA award for the "Grand Designs"-style makeover I commissioned from them on my pad. It was a big deal. It got a lot of press.' He looks at the officers in turn, but Lawson still refuses to give an inch. 'Anyway, they did a great job. Knocked out the back of the entire house and built on a huge glass extension. Very cool. Very minimal. But it wasn't just the fact they were giving up successful careers,' he adds. 'They had their own place, right on Clapham Common ... a good school for Kip ... London at their feet, and they were throwing it all away to move to the sticks to do what?' He throws them both an incredulous look. 'Set up a camping business?' Dominic shakes his head. 'It seemed madness to me. But I suppose they had form for springing big life decisions on us all.'

'What do you mean by that?'

'Well, the kid. The adoption.'

'By "kid", you mean their son, Kip?'

He nods, glancing from one police officer to the other, waiting for them to delve further, but Lawson, to his irritation, doesn't bite. 'How about you take us back to Friday. I gather you set out from Hertfordshire around lunchtime?'

'Yes, we left Harpenden at one.'

'We being ...?'

'My wife Tanya and my kids, Scarlet, Felix and Phoebe.' Dominic stretches his legs out in front of him, notices the rip in his trousers and the mud-caked hems, and quickly folds them back again.

'Everyone was happy about the trip?'

He shrugs. 'I suppose there was some resistance, but I really don't see how that's relevant.'

Lawson eyes him. 'We're simply trying to build a clear picture of the weekend. Given the trauma you've all faced and the questions that still need to be answered, we need to be as thorough as possible.'

'Personally, I thought the invitation sounded fun,' he says, addressing Lawson, holding her gaze. 'After the pressures of filming, I was looking forward to some downtime with old friends, a long weekend in the great outdoors. I assumed the kids would love it too, but you know how it is with teenagers these days.' He glances between them. 'The merest hint of a few hours without Wi-Fi and panic sets in.'

DI Lawson nods. 'Carry on, Mr Davies. This is helpful.'

Dominic narrows his eyes. 'You said you're talking to everyone?'

She nods again. 'We've sent an officer to the farmhouse. Family Liaison.'

'Good,' says Dominic. He can't help wondering what the others will say, how their stories might intersect, how their words might corroborate or contradict. All he can hope for, he supposes, is that when all is said and done, twenty years of friendship still counts for something. 'Good,' he says again, raising himself in his chair, tilting his chin, flexing his hands out of the tight fists he hadn't realized he'd formed, 'because I'm sure you'll find we *all* did things this weekend that we regret.'

DI Lawson maintains her level stare, those impenetrable grey eyes boring into him. Dominic is annoyed to find he is the first to look away.

SCARLET

Friday afternoon

If a weekend had ever been designed to ruin someone's life, then it was surely this one. It was bad enough that she was missing Harry Taylor's seventeenth birthday party, but squished in the back of her dad's midlife crisis SUV, jammed in beside Phoebe's booster seat, listening to the tinny hip hop thud emanating from Felix's headphones, with nothing ahead of them but a snaking line of traffic and the promise of three days camping in the middle of nowhere, Scarlet felt a hot rage bubbling inside her.

School was out. She knew it without even checking the time, because her phone had begun to buzz with a near-constant stream of notifications about party arrangements, outfits and gossip, none of which Scarlet could join in with. She eyed her dad in the rear-view mirror. 'I just don't understand why you're forcing *me* to go,' she said, unable to contain her simmering fury a moment longer. 'I could've stayed home.'

'I've already told you why,' said Dominic, meeting her gaze. 'We're going to support Max and Annie. They worked so hard on our wonderful renovation. It's our turn to show up for them.'

'But I could've gone to Mum's . . . or Lily's.'

'As I think I stated last night,' Dominic said, 'if you'd proved yourself to be a little more trustworthy in recent weeks, Tanya and I might have considered it. But this is *my* weekend with you and Felix,' he continued. 'I see little enough of you both as it is. There will be other parties, Scarlet. Sometimes you have to put family first.'

Scarlet scowled through the back window, watching the cars in the middle lane disappear behind them as her father accelerated down the fast lane. It was so unfair. There were so many inconveniences to having divorced parents, but nothing quite as annoying as the constant juggle of weekends between her mum and dad, the back-and-forth she and Felix had endured these past seven years since Tanya had arrived on the scene, and which only seemed to grow more intolerable now that her own social life was *finally* getting interesting. Her dad just didn't get it. He still thought of her as his little girl, but she wasn't. She was sixteen, virtually an adult.

Of course there would be other parties, she wasn't stupid, but there wouldn't be another seventeenth for Harry Taylor, the boy who just two days ago had sent her a string of messages, asking if she'd be there. There wouldn't be another black-tie party in a garden marquee, with uniformed waiters circulating with fancy little canapes, a smoke machine, a proper DJ and, by all accounts, enough vodka jelly shots to get the whole of Year Twelve completely off their faces.

'It'll be fun,' Dominic continued. 'There'll be a barbecue and a campfire. Nice coastal walks. A beach. Everyone's going. All the other kids will be there.'

Scarlet met his gaze again in the mirror. 'That's my point, Dad.' She gave an exaggerated shudder. 'I want to hang out with *my* friends, not a load of annoying little kids and that oddball, Kip.'

'Scarlet, *be nice*.'

She rolled her eyes. 'Now you just sound like a slogan on a sexist T-shirt. Telling a girl to "be nice" totally plays into the hands of the patriarchy. You're telling me to ignore my own feelings to please someone else. Besides,' continued Scarlet, warming to her theme, 'since when were you into "being nice"? You've built a whole career on being the brutally honest "expert". I don't think anyone could argue that you come across as particularly "nice" when you're judging your contestants on *Star Search*.'

'You have to admit,' said Tanya, with a small smirk Scarlet caught in the reflection of the wing mirror, 'she's got a point.'

'Thank you,' said Scarlet, throwing her a nod of satisfaction. 'See, *Tanya* gets it.' She was surprised. She couldn't imagine Tanya being down with her feminist ideals. Frankly, it was rare for Scarlet and Tanya to agree on anything. Scarlet liked to set herself in opposition to most things involving her stepmother, but she wasn't going to pass up an opportunity for validation against her father.

'That's a TV show. A job. It's not real life.'

'So why's it called "reality TV"?'

'There's nothing real about reality TV, darling. You're smart enough to know that. And as for *being nice*, that has nothing to do with gender,' said Dominic, adopting a patronising, world-weary tone. 'It's about being a decent human being. I'd say the exact same thing to Felix if he was acting like you.'

'Tell me then,' Scarlet continued, leaning forward in her seat, 'since when did "everyone else is going" become a reason for us to do something? Wasn't it you who asked me just two weeks ago when I got in trouble at school, "If everyone else jumped off a cliff, would you jump too, Scarlet?"' She mimics him well, slipping into his smooth, broadcaster-approved voice.

'You're getting too clever for your own good, young lady.'

'She's not *that* clever,' said Felix, lifting a headphone to join the conversation. 'If she were, she wouldn't have been excluded for ten days for having weed in her school bag.'

Scarlet leaned across Phoebe and thumped her brother hard on the arm. 'Shut up. What would you know?'

'I know enough to know you don't take drugs into school, dumbass.'

'Settle down you two. You'll wake Phoebe. Anyway, no one's jumping off any cliffs. This is just a long weekend with some of our oldest friends.'

'Newsflash Dad: all *my* friends are going to Harry Taylor's birthday party.'

There was a short silence. Scarlet decided it was time to

land her trump card. 'Anyway, I'm not the only one who's dreading it. Tanya doesn't want to go either.'

Tanya turned in the front passenger seat to stare at her. 'What?' A telling pink flush bloomed on her cheeks.

Scarlet shrugged. 'I heard you – on the phone last night.'

Tanya frowned. 'You shouldn't eavesdrop on other peoples' conversations.'

'See.' Scarlet threw a triumphant look at her dad. 'She's not denying it.'

Tanya turned back to her father. 'I didn't say I didn't want to go.' She wrestled for the right words. 'Not exactly. It's just – it's camping, isn't it? Hardly the most relaxing break.'

'It's not camping. It's *gl*-amping,' Dominic insisted.

'Changing two letters on a word doesn't make sleeping outside and peeing in a stinking portaloo any more *gl*-amorous,' muttered Scarlet.

'They're *your* oldest friends,' Tanya said, after a beat. 'I don't have the same history with them to draw upon. All your stories about your university days, the student radio shows you did together, the parties . . . I suppose, sometimes, I feel like a bit of an outsider.'

'You shouldn't. They see how happy you make me.' Scarlet watched as her father reached for Tanya's hand, pulling it into his lap, the huge diamond ring on her left hand catching the sun falling through the windscreen, refracting back at her like a strobe light. 'You had a good time at Kira's fortieth last year, didn't you?'

Tanya raised her eyebrows and let out a dry laugh. 'Are we remembering the same weekend?'

Scarlet leaned forward, sensing gossip.

'We don't need to worry about a repeat of that,' Dominic said. 'Kira's in a completely different place now. A new man. A baby. It's all change, from what I hear. Even better, you won't be the newcomer to the group anymore,' he added. 'Kira's boyfriend should be the one feeling nervous. You're an old timer now.'

'Less of the old, please.' Tanya pursed her lips, seemed about to say something else before sensing Scarlet's craning interest from the back seat. 'Well, we'll see,' was all she said.

Dominic lifted Tanya's hand to his lips. 'I know it's not quite the May Day weekend you would have liked. I'll take you somewhere more luxurious in the summer. But we're going to have fun. I promise.'

Scarlet was about to interject with another sarcastic comment when a wall of red brake lights flared on the motorway ahead. Dominic cursed under his breath and slowed the car until it came to a halt. Phoebe stirred in her booster seat, her blue eyes opening and blinking at the sudden shock of daylight, taking in her surroundings before leaning back against the headrest of her seat.

'Hello sleepy,' Scarlet said.

'Are we nearly there?'

Scarlet shook her head. 'Not yet, but could you please have a word with Bear. He's been snoring *so* loudly.'

Phoebe threw her a drowsy smile and adjusted her teddy tucked in the crook of her arm. 'Bear doesn't snore.'

Scarlet gave her a wink. It was hard to maintain the intensity of her fury when confronted with Phoebe's sweet face. There were so many shitty things about having divorced parents, but one of the few good things about her dad meeting Tanya was her surprise half-sister.

Throughout Tanya's pregnancy, Scarlet had maintained a solid level of disgust at the idea of her dad becoming a father again, but as soon as he'd dragged her to the hospital on that first reluctant visit and placed the baby in her arms, as soon as she had gazed down into Phoebe's red, screwed-up face, seen the dimples in her cheeks and felt her tiny hand curl around her little finger, holding on as if for dear life, all her anger and protest had fallen away. Whatever feelings she had about Tanya and her parents' messy divorce, she had come to accept her half-sister's presence as something inevitable and welcome.

'*Wild Things?*' Phoebe asked, addressing the car.

'Oh god, Pheebs, not again,' protested Scarlet, and even Felix, usually so affable and laid back, let out a deep groan. They had heard the audio book countless times on car journeys, but its appeal never seemed to wane for Phoebe.

'Sure thing, sweetie.' Tanya fiddled with a cable, connecting her phone to the car stereo.

Scarlet fell back against the seat and scrolled through the latest messages on her phone. The last was from Lily.

OMG. You should've heard Caitlin in tutor group today.

Scarlet typed a quick reply. *What??? Tell me.*

She could see Lily was online. Scarlet waited, impatiently watching the 'typing . . .' status blink.

She told everyone she was going to get with Harry tonight.

Scarlet's insides clenched. Caitlin was one of the prettiest girls in their year. If Scarlet wasn't there, maybe Harry would go for Caitlin. She chewed her bottom lip as she typed her reply. *No way! Bitch. She knows I like him.* 🏩

Don't worry, I've got your back. I'll stick to him like glue, remind him of you every five minutes.

🪦. *This sucks. Wish I was there.*

Me too. ☹ *I'll send photos.*

As the intro music for Phoebe's audio book began to play through the car speakers, Scarlet threw down her phone in disgust.

'All I'm asking,' said Dominic, attempting a last-ditch effort to mollify his captive family, 'is that we try to have some fun … that you're open to new experiences and making some memories this bank holiday.' He grinned at Scarlet in the mirror. 'I bet you a tenner I'll be driving you back on Monday evening kicking and screaming.'

Scarlet turned back to the window with another eyeroll and made a mental note to claim her money on the return journey home.

ANNIE

Sunday afternoon

Annie sits huddled at a long table beneath the hexagonal-shaped wooden shelter in the centre of the campsite. Her arms are wrapped around her body, but her eyes are fixed on the shifting horizon, the oppressive grey sky and the windswept green fields sliding away to meet the distant churn of the ocean. Overhead, the festoon lights and tattered bunting, decorations she had tacked to the timber struts only a few days ago, flap dismally in the breeze. The pizza oven stands redundant. The fire pit is a heap of black soggy ash. A washing bowl of dirty tin cups and plates sits abandoned to one side; one forgotten wet sock hangs off the back of a chair. Around her shoulders lies a knitted blanket that someone has retrieved from one of the nearby bell tents. A cup of tea is pushed towards her. She takes it in both hands, grateful for its warmth, then winces at her first sip, surprised by its sweetness.

'I didn't know if you took sugar,' says the woman,

sliding onto the bench opposite. She is young and petite, her dark, curly hair tied back in a ponytail. She wears small, round glasses, a navy rain jacket and beige cargo trousers. Everything about her radiates calm practicality. 'I thought it might help. I'm guessing you haven't had lunch.'

Annie shakes her head. She couldn't have eaten, even if she'd tried. 'Have they found anything yet?'

The police officer pushes a loose strand of hair from her face. 'Not as far as I know.' Seeing Annie's shiver, she adds, 'I think they're almost done here. We'll get you back up to the farmhouse as soon as we can, but perhaps we could get started?'

Annie nods. The woman had introduced herself as a Family Liaison Officer when she'd arrived earlier with the other uniformed police officers, but like so many details of the past hours, her actual name escapes her. It's as if the storm has come along and jumbled everything, tossed it up, blown it into nonsensical order; Annie's mind is struggling to pin all the details of the weekend back into place. Patricia, she remembers with sudden relief. That's it. A good, no-nonsense, let's-sort-this-out kind of name. DC Patricia Haines.

Annie knows it's essential that they talk. She wants to help. She wants this to be over – for all of them. Most of all, she wants to get her side of the story across, before any of the others can skew the facts, turning them into something ugly and untrue.

'As I mentioned earlier,' says DC Haines, pulling out a notebook and pen, 'I work in family liaison and I'm here to support all of you.' Her voice is calm and low. Annie imagines her practising her tone in training sessions, getting it pitch-perfect. 'I need to go through some information with you, ask you some questions. I want you to tell me anything – big or small – that you think might be helpful to us, given the current . . . situation. Is that okay?'

The situation.

Annie still doesn't fully understand 'the situation'. Do any of them? She keeps asking herself, how could one weekend spiral so dreadfully out of control? How could one small spark start this terrible blaze, threatening twenty years of friendship? Annie clears her throat. 'Of course. Anything to help. I feel awful,' she sighs, 'so responsible. Max and I both do.'

She sips the tea, noticing as she does how her nails are bitten almost to the quick. Though perhaps the hit of sugar is helping, for her nerves do seem a little less jangled. She thinks of Kip back at the farmhouse, of his pale, haunted face, and feels a thread of resolve return. 'It was just supposed to be a bit of fun,' Annie says, lifting her gaze to meet the police officer's. 'We thought we'd invite them here to trial our glamping site before we officially open to the public in a few weeks.'

Haines nods encouragingly. 'By *them* you mean the three other families?'

'Yes. Jim and Suze. Kira and her new partner, Fred. Dom and Tanya. With all the kids, we were quite a gang.'

'One of the PCs mentioned you had Dominic Davies staying this weekend.' The woman's tone remains neutral, but the slight lift of her eyebrows betrays her interest.

Annie nods and manages a rueful smile. 'The one and only.' Over the past few years, as Dominic's notoriety had grown with his role as the acerbic judge on the UK's latest reality TV craze, it had become impossible to ignore the ripples of curiosity their friend generated wherever they went: the elbow nudges, stares or knowing smiles. The bravest ones approached him for autographs or selfies, or to talk about the show, wanting to tell him what he'd got right or to harangue him when they thought he'd been too tough on a contestant. He was known for his 'hard truths', as *he* liked to call them, but *Dictator Dom* was how some of the more salacious tabloids had labelled him. Like Marmite, the public seemed to either love or hate him, but to his friends, the ones who had known him before the fame or the fortune, he'd always just be 'Dom'.

'How did you all meet?'

'There were five of us at university. Dom, Jim, Kira, Max and me. We met in our first year at UCL. We'd all got roped in to helping with the student radio station at fresher's week. As you can probably tell,' Annie gestures self-deprecatingly at her figure, 'I've never been particularly sporty, so I was looking for something creative to get involved with.'

'Sounds fun.'

'It was. I was general dogsbody for a while, making tea, cleaning the studio, but I worked my way up to host an afternoon folk session that absolutely no one listened to. Dom and Jim were more successful. They hosted "The Davies & Miller Show", a subversive, late-night show that gathered a following with the post-clubbing crowd. Kira had a popular underground trance session going by our third year.'

'What about your husband?'

'Max was less keen on the spotlight. He helped out on the production and promotions side. By the end of our first year, despite our differences and our varied degrees, the five of us had become firm friends. We found a student house together and that was it – friends for life, I guess you could say.' She stops, takes a breath. 'Sorry, I'm babbling, aren't I?'

'You're fine.'

'Max says I talk a lot when I'm nervous. What was your question?'

'I was asking how you all met. So, you and Max were a couple, even back then?'

'Not at first. Friends, to begin with.' She gives a small smile. 'Max and I both studied Architecture. We hooked up towards the end of our third year and have been together ever since.' Her smile widens. 'We like to think we're the glue that keeps everyone bonded. We've all known each other for two decades now.'

'That's special. Old friends.'

'Yes. Over the years we've attended each other's weddings, christened babies, climbed career ladders, consoled and cheered each other on. Like all friendships, things ebb and flow. Two years ago, Dom asked Max and I to redesign his home in Harpenden. We weren't sure about mixing business and friendship, but Dom gave us free rein and it was a fun last project before we moved down here.' Annie stops and considers her words. 'If I'm honest, besides our work project for Dom, things between us all had drifted. You know how it is, busy lives and young families taking up more space ... It's hard to stay as connected.'

DC Haines nods. 'Life happens.'

'Exactly. That's why Max and I thought this bank holiday would be the perfect opportunity to get everyone back together. We thought it would be fun to show them our new venture and get the kids out in the fresh air. Our last catch-up had been an adults-only affair at a swanky boutique hotel in the Cotswolds for Kira's birthday. Dinner at a Michelin-starred restaurant.' She raises her eyebrows at the police officer.

'Max figured we'd all got a little soft, a little too urbane since our uni days. He sensed we were all pulling in different directions, so we thought a weekend getting the old gang back together and doing something more ... grounded might help. He began to refer to this weekend as the great "rewilding project". He figured we'd all benefit from stripping things back, getting outside, reconnecting with nature – with each other. Of course,' she adds, throwing Haines a grim look, 'we had no idea how it would turn out.'

'Indeed.'

'This is just ...' Annie waves helplessly around her, feels her tired eyes burning again with the sting of tears, 'it's just unimaginable.'

Behind DC Haines, the flaps to one of the bell tents are drawn and a uniformed officer emerges. Annie peers at the sealed evidence bag in his hands, a mobile phone visible within. She swallows.

Haines pushes on, as if eager to distract. 'I understand you adopted a son – Kip – around six years ago?'

Annie nods. She sees DC Haines studying her and wonders if the police officer is a mother too. She wonders if she can understand the sweet agony, the love and the terror, that comes with parenthood. Wonders if she can have any idea what caring for a kid like Kip, with his own unique set of challenges, can bring. Mothering, she's learned, is a constant blade twisting in the heart.

'Take your time,' says the policewoman, reaching into her jacket pocket and pulling out a packet of tissues, offering them to her.

'I'm sorry,' she says, lifting her glasses to dab at her tears, 'it's been ... a lot. Is there any news yet? Anything from the hospital?'

DC Haines shakes her head. 'We've got an experienced team out searching the cliffs. Everything that can be done *is* being done.' She seems to think for a moment. 'Why don't we focus on the weekend? Take me back to Friday. Everyone arrived in the afternoon, and that first night, everything went smoothly – as planned?'

Annie frowns. 'I suppose so. We had a barbecue and a few drinks, lit a bonfire. The kids were playing games. It was pretty idyllic.'

The police officer waits a beat. 'Nothing ... *untoward* happened that first night?'

Annie glances across at the abandoned fire pit, the remains of the bonfire now a heap of wet ash. One of the log seats has toppled onto its side. A sack of kindling spills across the grass. Someone has already told her. She can hear it in the woman's voice.

'Kip didn't mean anything by it,' she says. 'It was an accident. An accident that got blown out of all proportion. The grown-ups had been drinking – some of us more than others,' she adds pointedly, 'and I'm sure that played a part.'

'Had Mr Davies been drinking?'

She nods. 'If you ask me,' she says, fixing her gaze on DC Haines, 'it was Dom's reaction that was most worrying. He'd been acting a little off since his arrival. He seemed tense, you know? I assumed it was his work.'

The policewoman doesn't say anything.

Annie bites her lip and shrugs. 'All I'm saying is perhaps, if Dom had held his temper in check, things might have gone down differently. But Dom's . . . well . . . Dom. He can be the proverbial bull in a china shop.'

'Mrs Kingsley, I'm sure you don't need me to tell you that time really is of the essence. I have to speak to everyone involved, so if there's something you want to tell me about Friday night – anything at all – now is the time.'

Annie sighs. All she wants to do is race back to the farmhouse and gather her boy into her arms and whisk him away somewhere safe, away from all the suspicion and trauma, but to do so would only invoke more misunderstanding and vitriol. She knows she is Kip's best hope now.

Sensing Annie's defences crumbling, DC Haines pushes again. 'Go on,' she says, her face neutral. 'I'm listening.'

25

MAX

Friday afternoon

Max stood beside Annie near the communal wooden shelter, eyeing the huge pile of dry firewood teetering in front of them.

'Is it big enough?' she asked.

Max laughed. 'It's huge! They'll see the flames over in St Ives.'

'I think it should be bigger. It needs to last the whole evening,' Annie said, staring doubtfully at the bonfire.

'Any more wood and it'll burn all weekend. We're supposed to be an eco-friendly operation, remember?'

As they surveyed the pile, Josh emerged from the off-road buggy and dragged the last branches from the back of the trailer. 'Nice work,' called Max. 'Thanks mate.' He turned back to Annie and pulled her closer. 'What's going on? You don't seem yourself. I thought you'd be more excited to see everyone.'

She shrugged. 'I am excited. I just want everything to be perfect.'

'It is – it will be – and if it isn't, it doesn't matter. They're our friends. They're not going to judge us.'

Annie threw him her best *don't-be-so-naive* look. 'Of *course* they're going to judge us. You saw their faces at Kira's fortieth last year, when we told them we were moving down here.'

Max shook his head. 'That was just . . . surprise. They were pleased for us.'

He turned to his wife and tilted her face gently towards him. Behind her familiar red-framed glasses he could see the doubt in her hazel eyes. 'Look around,' he urged. 'Look at what we've built.' He nodded at the six bell tents standing pristine-white in the May sunshine, the gentle slope of the wildflower meadow running down to meet the rocky headland and the sea beyond. In the centre of the space stood the wooden shelter, a communal meeting and dining area that he'd built with Josh from old shipping timbers. It cast a dark shadow, beneath which stood a well-stocked camp kitchen and a long, rustic wooden table and benches, as well as a large brick barbecue just waiting to be lit. A little further away he saw the wood-fired hot tub they'd imported from Sweden and an attractive, solar-powered shower block with a sedum roof set into the brow of the hill.

He couldn't help a surge of pride when he took in all they had accomplished in such a short space of time, and not without its complications. Planning permissions. Drainage. Business permits. Difficult neighbours. Family issues.

Max's gaze fell on Kip, sitting on a striped deckchair

over near one of the tents. He watched the boy sort through a pile of slender sticks, selecting some, rejecting others, careful, methodical. 'We're in the right place for us, and for Kip. He's doing so much better here, don't you think?'

Annie pursed her lips but didn't answer.

'As soon as everyone arrives,' Max continued, 'they'll see what we've built and understand exactly what we've done and why we've done it. How could they not?'

Annie glanced up at the blue sky, cotton clouds racing each other on the far horizon, the breeze tugging at the bunting. 'Do you think the weather will hold?'

Max shrugged. 'I caught the tail end of the forecast. It could be a little mixed tomorrow, but it's nothing we can't handle. I've asked Josh to stick around and help out, if we need him. I thought an extra pair of hands might be useful.'

Annie threw him a relieved smile. 'Thank goodness for Josh.' She squinted across at the tents. 'What *is* Kip up to? Is that . . . a knife?'

'My penknife. I showed him how to use it.'

'Max!'

'He's twelve, love, certainly old enough to manage a penknife. This is why we came, remember? To give him a different kind of life, away from the city. We wanted him to experience more freedom.'

Annie shrugged. 'I didn't mean knives! It was bad enough when you let him drive the buggy.'

'Stop worrying. This weekend will be good for him – good for all of us.'

'And what about our *friendly* neighbour?'

Max winced. 'Kellow will come round. We couldn't have known how that journalist would spin her article. Or how he'd react.'

'*"Grand designs, glamping and glamorous celebrities heading for Morvoren Point."*' Annie grimaced. 'We should've guessed what she was up to when she kept steering the interview back to Dom's Harpenden project. It's obvious now that she was more interested in writing about *him* than our rewilding plans.'

'You can't say she hadn't done her research,' Max shrugged. 'I thought it would be a good way to introduce ourselves to the local community, a little early publicity for the business. I didn't see the harm.'

Annie rolled her eyes. 'Only she made it sound like we'd be hosting wild *Great Gatsby*-style parties for the rich and famous every weekend.' Annie twisted the cuff on her linen shirt. 'No wonder Kellow's nose is out of joint.'

'It's not as if I haven't tried to walk him through the plans. He won't listen.' Seeing her worried frown, he pulled her towards him. 'There's nothing he can do, Annie. It's with the council now. And what we get up to on our land this weekend is none of his business.' He wrapped his arm around her shoulders. 'Relax, Annie. This is everything we dreamed of. Remember? It's time to enjoy it.'

It was frustrating to witness her anxiety. He wanted to remind her of all those nights they'd lain awake in their London house, listening to neighbours and sirens, worrying about Kip's struggles at school, about their demanding clients, the plans and permits, the escalating building costs. He wanted to remind her of the awful, creeping exhaustion that had begun to suffocate them both, the dawning realization that their life in London – the one they had worked so hard to create – was no longer what they wanted.

Did she not remember as vividly as he did that early summer night last year, when they had walked back across Clapham Common after a gruelling face-to-face with the staff at Kip's school, the two of them still shaken and bristling from the suspicion and fear they'd seen in the teachers' eyes, the damning assessment they'd been offered of their son's "problems". Did she not remember how he had stopped right there in the middle of the park and said, 'What are we doing, Annie?' And seeing her confusion, he'd added, 'I don't mean this,' he'd said, gesturing to the path ahead of them. 'I mean what are we *doing*? With our lives. Our jobs. Our son.'

Annie had turned to him. The faltering evening light falling through the trees had cast a long shadow, making her usually open and easy-to-read face strangely inscrutable. 'I don't follow.'

'Look at us. We're putting all our energy into lavish building projects for our clients. The rest of our time goes on Kip, trying to help him navigate his issues and get him through a one-size-fits-all school system that doesn't seem to give a stuff about him. Don't you ever wonder why we're fighting so hard? I'm exhausted, Annie. Disillusioned. I just want to ... I don't know ... take a step back ... breathe ... look at the ocean ... put my hands in the earth and reconnect with what's important – with you – with Kip.'

'We could take a holiday?' she'd suggested. 'Go away this summer. Somewhere nice?'

But Max shook his head. 'That's not what I mean. I don't want a quick fix. A band-aid. I don't want the best, most wholesome moment of my week to be the ten minutes I spend queuing up for organic veggies and artisan coffee at an overpriced farmer's market. I want the real thing. I want to change things. I want to get out of the city. I want to feel creative again. When was the last time you picked up one of your paintbrushes, Annie, and just painted something for the hell of it? When was the last time I forgot about client deadlines and let myself feel truly inspired? I'm sick of it, love. I want a different life.'

That had been the start of it. The planning, the research, the endless online searches for a plot of land that might offer them everything they dreamed of. Then had come the courting of buyers for their architectural firm, the estate agents trawling through their stylish terrace murmuring enthusiastically about the extended designer kitchen, the south-facing garden and the wonderful light, until everything had been sorted, the contracts signed, the 'SOLD' sign erected outside the house, the boxes packed and it was entirely and thrillingly far too late to back out. They were leaving their old lives to set up something new in the wilds of north Cornwall.

Max knew they had found the perfect spot as soon as they'd viewed it: Morvoren Farm, a shabby stone farmhouse with eight acres of wild Cornish land sloping away to meet the rugged coastline. The farm hadn't been worked in decades, and situated on a remote northern peninsula, surrounded by nothing but rolling fields, sky and ocean, with their only neighbour an old Cornish dairy farmer located a couple of miles away, it offered the perfect escape.

'What does Morvoren mean?' she'd asked the agent, the sun glancing off his shiny blue suit as they'd stood at the peeling front door looking out towards the headland.

'It's Cornish for "sea maiden".'

'Sea maiden? You mean ... "mermaid"?'

He'd nodded. 'There's a rich history of mermaid legends around these parts. Old wives' tales of beautiful maidens luring sailors and fishermen to their deaths. Back in the day, there was a spate of tragedies amongst the workers in the old tin mines, which only added to the folklore. More recently, a sad case with a kid out on the cliffs. The peninsula has long been associated with mermaid sightings and unexplained deaths. Stuff like that keeps the mythology alive. Keeps people talking. Keeps the tourists visiting.' The agent had grinned, as if he'd just realized that dwelling on the dark folk tales of the place might not be the greatest sales pitch. 'Of course, all this talk of mermaid sightings would have absolutely nothing to do with the seal colony off the coast here. They inhabit a small, rocky island offshore. It's part of a protected marine reserve.'

Annie bent to touch a cluster of white flowers growing at the doorstep. 'These are pretty.'

'Don't pick them,' warned the agent. 'It's sea campion. Also known as dead man's bells round here. They say it brings death, if you pick it.' He'd drawn a finger across his throat and pulled a gruesome face, before grinning broadly at them both. 'Let's get you inside before I put you off completely.'

'We'll run it as an eco-friendly smallholding all year round,' Max had said, plotting with Annie on the drive home. 'Organic. Sustainable. We'll only have to open the glamping business for six months of the year. The rest of the time will be ours. Coastal walks. Wild swimming. The farmhouse we'll get to, in time. I'd like to keep bees and goats. You can paint. Perhaps we turn one of the barns into an artist's space? We could run workshops and retreats, invite some of our creative contacts down from London. Think of the opportunities, what we could fuel? We'd be pretty self-sufficient within a couple of years.'

'But it's so much land. How would we manage?'

'That's the beauty of it. We'll rewild what we don't need – return it to its original, ecological state. Let nature take its course. It's a proper wilderness out there, Annie. Somewhere we can create a home – a safe place for Kip. A place to nest.'

'That's what we should call it,' said Annie, a small smile playing across her face. '*Wildernest.*'

It had been hard work. Far more than they'd antici-pated; a minefield of logistics to navigate – both practical and financial – and months of physical labour to prepare the glamping site. They'd found that local builders and contractors were hard to source, but when Max had come across a local lad, Josh Penrose, out on the head-land one day and fallen into conversation with him, he'd sensed the young man's interest in their project and his hardworking spirit and offered him a job there and then. Together they'd battled the last of the work; everything from digging out a septic tank to laying the tent slabs. He'd been a godsend; Max didn't think they'd have been anywhere near ready to host their friends for a trial weekend without him.

Standing in the meadow, Annie pressed herself into his warm chest. He felt her take a long, steadying breath. He knew her. You couldn't be married to someone for sixteen years, go through all the challenges they had, and not know how her mind worked. He knew she'd be thinking of the extra towels she'd been fussing over that morning, mentally reminding herself to check that there was enough of the local handmade soap in the shower block. She'd be wondering if her directions had been clear enough, and where they had put the matches for the bonfire. She'd be thinking that maybe it would be wise to take Kip aside for one final, bolstering pep talk before the other kids arrived. He knew her thoughtful, busy mind – and he loved her for it. He gave her a squeeze and murmured into the top of her head, 'It's going to be a perfect weekend, you'll see.'

As he held her close, the low hum of an engine carried towards them over the rise of the meadow. 'Too late to back out now,' he murmured, lifting one arm from her shoulder to wave at the battered combi van bouncing down the hillside towards them, three tangle-haired blonde children hanging out of the back windows. 'The Millers are here.'

JIM

Sunday afternoon

It's not easy to operate the vending machine. Jim wouldn't have bothered with the effort for a packet of crisps, but he missed lunch and the painkillers he's been given are doing strange things to his head, making him woozy and faint. Once he's grappled with the awkward spring-loaded flap at the bottom of the machine, and wrangled the crisp packet apart using his teeth and his one good hand, he tries Suze's number on his mobile in another feat of dexterity. He hopes to hear her warm, reassuring voice, but the line cuts straight to voicemail. Of course. No signal back at the glamping site. How could he have forgotten?

He slumps onto one of the plastic chairs in the hospital waiting room and shoves crisps into his mouth. Suze wouldn't approve. High in salt and artificial flavourings. But this is his thing. He eats when he's stressed, anything he can put in his mouth, and usually the worse for him the better. Living through this hellish weekend has demanded all the junk food he can inhale, before he can get back to the others and hug the ones he loves.

'Mr Miller?' The receptionist waves at him. 'They're ready for you.'

He is shown into a small office. Jim is surprised at how basic and dreary it is. There's nothing slick or hi-tech about this operation. It's just him, two police officers, some missing ceiling tiles and an ancient-looking tape recorder whirring on the table.

They don't waste any time. They introduce themselves as Lawson and Barnett and tell him they're conducting a first round of interviews as part of their enquiry. The female detective in the grey suit eyes his sling. 'Looks nasty. You okay?'

He nods. 'Waiting for an X-ray.'

'How did you hurt yourself?'

'I slipped.' He hesitates. 'It was pretty treacherous out on the headland last night.'

She holds his eye and Jim tries hard to maintain his level stare but fails.

'Okay, we'll come to that in a bit. How about you start by telling us about the mood of the group when you first arrived? Any notable issues? Tension? Red flags?'

Jim frowns. He wasn't expecting this. 'The mood of the group? We'd just arrived in paradise. The mood was good.' He notices crisp crumbs on his T-shirt and brushes them away. Is he misremembering anything? It's important to get the details right. There's a lot at stake.

'We were the first to arrive,' he tells them. 'I was surprised. It was a long drive from Brighton. Max had warned

36

us they were way out in the sticks, but the unsealed track went on for so long and was so hazardous in places that I remember Suze and I started to worry that the old van wouldn't make it. We passed the farmhouse first, and then a little further on we saw Annie's hand-painted sign for 'Wildernest', so we knew we were in the right place.'

He smiles at the police officers. They stare back. The woman gives him a nod to continue and so he thinks a little harder, tries to draw the memory of their arrival more clearly in his mind.

He'd barely had time to pull on the handbrake before the kids had flung open the doors and bolted, desperate to escape the confines of the van. The three of them raced across the meadow, streaks of rainbow-coloured clothes, trainers thudding across the grass, their blonde hair bouncing wildly as they ran towards a cluster of circular tents standing dazzling white in the afternoon sun, waving at Max and Annie, who stood waiting beside a large, hexagonal-shaped wooden shelter.

Suze was next, swishing across the grass towards Annie, her hemp dungarees catching on the long grass, silver nose-stud glinting in the sun, the stack of wooden bangles jangling on her wrist. Jim stood watching her as he stretched his arms above his head to release the tension of the drive.

'My god, Annie. This place!' Suze called, her arms opening to meet Annie's embrace. 'It's too much.'

'Welcome to Wildernest.'

A hint of the sea carried towards him on the breeze as he joined the others, slapping Max on the shoulder before pulling him into a manly hug. 'Good to see you, buddy. I see you've gone for full assimilation with the grizzled seadog look,' he added, gesturing at Max's new, bushy, salt-and-pepper beard.

'It suits you,' said Suze, rubbing it affectionately with her hands before kissing him effusively on both cheeks.

'I see you're still wearing that shirt,' Max parried, tugging at the faded hem of Jim's Beastie Boys T-shirt.

'He'll be buried in that T-shirt,' said Suze. 'And those awful shorts.'

'I don't think I've ever seen Jim wear anything but baggy shorts,' added Annie, laughing.

'That's not true. If you remember, I pushed the boat out and wore jeans to your wedding.'

Annie smiled as Jim kissed her on the cheek, before he turned and breathed deeply, gazing around at the peninsula to where the headland slid away to meet the distant sea. The landscape was a riot of jewelled blues and greens, bursts of yellow, white and pink wildflowers dotting the coastal fringe. 'I can't think why you wanted to give up commuter trains, traffic jams and city smog for this hellhole,' Jim joked. After the endless stretch of motorway and the cramped van, the space, the colour and the fresh mineral tang in the air was intoxicating. He lifted his trucker's cap and ran his hands through his damp hair. 'It feels like we've arrived at the very edge of the world.'

Suze threw her arms wide. 'This place has a great energy, guys, I can feel it. It's positively humming with good vibes. And that wooden shelter, lovely. Did you build it, Max?'

He nodded. 'It's where we can gather – to cook, eat,

socialise, huddle.' He adds ruefully, 'If the weather turns on us.'

'I love it! I can feel a sunrise yoga session tomorrow morning right here, if anyone's up for it?'

Jim nudged his wife. 'Sunrise? Bit optimistic. You know what we're like when we get together.'

Their three kids were already scouting the campsite. Willow, River and Juniper called out in excitement as they discovered the hot tub, the fire pit and the stash of outdoor games. 'There's an archery set!' River called. 'I'm definitely having a go.'

'What on earth are you feeding them?' marvelled Annie, watching the children roam.

'What *aren't* we feeding them?' Suze replied. 'It's like a plague of locusts sweeping through the kitchen each day. River's almost as tall as Jim.'

'Mate, that's not your cue to dust off the short-arse jokes!' Jim warns Max. 'I get enough of that at home.'

'And can you believe Juniper will be ten this summer?' Suze threw a mournful glance at her youngest. 'My baby . . . double digits!'

Willow, a freckle-faced, long-limbed fourteen-year-old in a yellow sundress and striped leggings with a wild cloud of blonde curls echoing her mother's, appeared at Suze's side and threw a companionable arm around her mother's shoulders. She grinned at Annie, silver train-track braces glinting in the sun. 'Where's Kip?'

'He's right over—' Annie pointed towards the row of striped deckchairs, then frowned. 'Oh. He *was* there just a moment ago.' She glanced at Max.

'We'll find him,' said Max. 'He won't have gone far. Probably just feeling shy. How about we give you a quick tour of the tents in the meantime?'

They followed Annie down to the nearest of the six bell tents and waited as she unzipped the canvas door, releasing the heady scent of warm, trampled grass, before she stood back with a nervous smile, allowing them to enter. 'Each tent is similar inside, just a few differences,' she called, 'but as you're first, you can choose which one you want. We thought some of the teenagers might like to share?'

'Mum! Dad! There's proper beds.'

'And a wood burner.'

'It's like our own little house.'

Jim followed the kids inside and smiled.

'I'm sleeping here.' Juniper, their youngest, was already jumping up and down on a huge four-poster bed, beaming her wide grin, blonde pigtails flying, while River and Willow sprawled across the two day beds draped in colourful blankets and cushions.

'Wow.' Suze exchanged an impressed look with Jim. 'This is gorgeous.'

'It's like a tardis.' The tent felt huge, its high-domed roof supported by a central wooden pillar, blonde wooden struts fanning out like a huge parasol above their heads. As Max took him through the design, and detailed how they had secured the structures, Suze and the girls exclaimed over the colourful Moroccan rugs, the fairy lights and lamps hanging from rustic hooks, the wildflowers in the striped Cornishware jug on the scrubbed wooden table.

Suze admired a painted dresser with its enamelware, mugs and candles while Jim explored a separate tented area pitched off the back, which housed a small kitchen area with a cool box, sink and a gas stove.

'Goodness. It's so well appointed. Look, even heating,' said Suze, pointing to the wood-burning stove that had been vented out of the tent roof, the wicker basket beside it filled with logs and kindling. 'I thought we'd be roughing it.'

'Is it okay?' Annie asked, as they stepped back outside.

Jim squeezed Annie's arm. 'It's wonderful, the height of luxury compared to the camping holidays we take in the old van. You guys will be overrun when you officially open.'

'Do you think the others will like it? Kira's bringing her baby and then there's Tanya.' Annie raised her eyebrows. 'I don't imagine *she's* done much camping.'

Jim saw the two women exchange a smirk. 'Now, now, ladies.'

'It's perfect,' Suze said. 'Just enough of the great outdoors to make the men feel like action heroes, fresh air and freedom for the kids, deckchairs and booze for the rest of us.' She turned to study the horizon, one hand raised to shield her eyes. 'Can you get down to the sea from here?'

'Yes. You can take a trail across the farmland to the cliffs, then it's a scramble down to a secret cove. We'll show you, but let's get you unpacked first.'

They were pulling bags and boxes of supplies from the van when a sleek, white SUV cruised down the hillside and the Davies family emerged, stretching and blinking in the bright sunshine. First Dominic, with his designer stubble and boyish good looks, the sleeves on his chambray shirt rolled up to reveal tanned forearms. Then his son, Felix, already tall and broad-shouldered like his dad, mirroring the same strong jawline, and the same dark, wiry hair. The boy wore expensive-looking hi-tops, a skate T-shirt and sported a huge pair of headphones round his neck.

'Someone's doing all right for themselves,' said Jim, eyeing the gleaming Porsche with Dom's personalized plate.

'Looks like a gas-guzzler to me.' Suze sidled up beside Annie, a mischievous look in her eyes. 'How is it that the rest of us seem to age, but Dom looks younger every year?'

'He's either stashed a portrait in the attic or I'd say he's been getting a little cosmetic assistance.' Annie discreetly mimed a syringe with her fingers.

Suze rolled her eyes. 'That stuff is poison. Literally. You're injecting botulism into your face.'

'I guess that's the pressure of life in the public eye for you.'

'You ladies have no idea of the modern beauty standards us men are forced to conform to,' joked Jim, flicking his hair from his face before feigning a bodybuilder's pose, leaning down to kiss the half-hearted bicep on his left arm. 'The struggle is real.'

Phoebe appeared next, refusing to let go of the brown teddy in her arms as she was helped out of the car by Felix. She rubbed her eyes and looked around, a slow gap-toothed smile creeping over her face when she saw the tents. She was followed by Tanya, looking immaculate in tight, white jeans, designer sunglasses and towering, heeled espadrilles. 'She knows we're camping, right?' Annie muttered, tugging at her own loose linen trousers. 'It's right about now I regret giving up the diet and the hair dye.'

'Stop it,' said Suze. 'You look amazing. I like the natural look on you. The grey suits you.'

Annie shrugged. 'I can barely remember the woman I was in London, all those schmoozy client lunches and networking events. It's this place. The wildness of it chips away at you, strips away all the superficial layers.' She turned to them both, smiling. 'Who am I kidding? Perhaps it's simply my age. I can't be bothered to make the effort anymore!'

'Talking of effort, I've told myself I'm going to try really hard with Tanya this weekend,' Suze breaks into a sly smile, '. . . but if she starts calling us "the WAGs" again, I won't be held responsible for my actions.'

Jim grinned. 'Should I remove the sharp implements from the tents?'

Suze adopted a pious look. 'I'm going to be on my best behaviour.'

'Oh, I certainly hope not,' said Annie. 'Where's the fun in that?'

Scarlet was last to emerge from Dom's Porsche, her long, dark hair swinging down her back. She wore an oversized hoodie and a tiny mini skirt, her black Doc Martens kicking up small clouds of dust as she stalked around the car, holding her mobile phone high overhead. She rounded on her dad. 'Nothing,' she said. 'Not a single bar.'

Dominic held up his hands. 'How could I know that?'

Jim grinned at Suze and Annie. 'Here's trouble.'

Annie intervened. 'I'm sorry, Scarlet. I should have warned everyone, there's no mobile coverage down here. To be honest, it's one of the things we like about it.'

Scarlet stared at Annie as if she had just sprouted a second head.

'Our internet will be connected at the farmhouse next week. We've had a nightmare getting a provider all the way out here,' she shrugged.

'I'm sorry,' said Dominic, stepping in. 'Scarlet's forgotten her manners. She's missing a party this weekend, so emotions are running a little high. You know what it's like at their age. If you're not snapping and chatting and tiktokking 24/7, your life's not worth living.' He mimed a pouting selfie.

Scarlet let out an embarrassed sigh. 'Dad. Stop.'

'How's the extension?' asked Max, coming over to greet Dom, shaking his hand. 'Still standing?'

'Still standing ... and still the talk of the town,' he added with evident pride. Seeing Jim, Dom's face shifted into an even wider grin. 'All right, big man?' He threw a friendly punch at his stomach.

Jim, tensing just a little too late, emitted a low groan. 'It's been a while.'

The two men clapped each other on the back. 'If I didn't know better,' said Dom, throwing Jim a searching look, 'I'd say you've been avoiding my phone calls.'

'Nah mate. Just busy, that's all.'

'I can't wait to hear all about it over a beer.'

Jim nodded, grateful that the attention had already moved on to Annie and Suze, who were greeting Tanya with a more polite exchange of hugs and air kisses.

'Who's the hunk?' Suze nodded at the strapping young man who had emerged from the shower block, tool-box in hand.

'That's Josh,' said Max. 'He's helping out around the place.'

Suze exchanged a look with Annie. 'Must be hard gazing at that all day long.' Seeing the men's faces, Suze gave them all an innocent smile. 'What? I was talking about the stunning view.'

'Don't worry,' grinned Max, 'We'll introduce you.'

'Josh!' Annie beckoned the lad over and as they chatted, Jim sized the kid up. He looked to be in his early twenties, good-looking, the outdoorsy type, a full sleeve of tattoos running down one muscled forearm and dishevelled, sun-bleached hair falling into his eyes. Jim couldn't help sucking in his belly and tensing his grip as they shook hands. Suze, noticing, caught his eye and smirked. Josh turned to greet Dominic.

'You're the guy . . .' Josh said, trailing off, an obvious crimson flush creeping above the neck of his T-shirt.

Jim turned to wink at Suze. It still amused him to see the effect Dom had on others.

'I think he's a bit star-struck,' she whispered.

'Yes,' said Max, jumping forward, 'he's "the guy off the telly". Our *famous* friend.'

He said it jokily, with exaggerated emphasis, but the moment stretched awkwardly between Josh and Dominic, until Dominic conjured a dazzling, toothpaste-white smile and held out his hand. 'What can I say? It's me.' He gave what Jim knew to be a well-rehearsed self-deprecating shrug. 'I take it you watch *Star Search*?'

Josh seemed to gather himself, shaking the hand Dominic offered. 'Yeah, I've seen it.'

'Let me guess,' he threw a knowing glance at the assembled group, 'you're a budding singer?'

Josh shook his head. 'Not me – my sister.'

'Well we'll have to get her on the show, eh? I've been known to pull a few favours here and there. Though I can't promise an easy ride.' He pressed a hand to his chest. 'It's my job to say it how I see it.'

Scarlet, standing nearby, muttered, 'Cringe,' under her breath.

'I don't think anyone could accuse you of not telling the contestants *exactly* what you think,' said Suze pointedly.

'Ah, and here's young Kip.' Dominic turned to greet the boy who had materialized beside Annie. 'Good to see you, son.'

Annie gave Kip a gentle nudge of encouragement, but the boy remained a step behind his mother, his feet fixed to the ground. The outdoor lifestyle didn't seem to have rubbed off on the kid in the same way as it had Annie and Max. He was still pale and skinny, knobbly knees jutting from twiglet-thin legs, thick black hair falling over his eyes as he pushed the bridge of his glasses back up his nose.

'You've grown since we last saw you. What are you

now? Ten? Eleven?' Dominic pressed for a response. 'Don't be shy, son. I don't bite.'

Jim felt the group squirm at Dominic's intense focus. They all knew about Kip's challenges. Dom was like a steam train, pushing too hard.

Annie took a step forward. Jim felt her desperation to shield Kip from the attention. 'He's twelve,' she said, speaking for him.

There was another awkward pause.

'Will you show us your archery set, Kip?' It was River, offering Kip an escape. 'It looks sick.' Jim felt a swell of pride at his son's efforts to help.

'Yeah!' said Felix, pushing forward. 'I want a go.'

Annie gave Kip another gentle nudge. 'Go on, Kip. Why don't you show the boys?'

'Do you think that's safe?' Tanya threw a worried glance at Dominic, but it was Josh who stepped forward.

'I'll supervise, if you like?'

Max nodded his thanks and there was a collective release of tension as Josh followed the boys to the far edge of the field where the target had been set up.

'He seems like a nice lad,' said Jim, watching as Josh lined the boys up at a distance from the target and ran them through some basic safety instructions.

'Josh? Yes, he's been a lifesaver helping us keep the site on track. He's good with Kip too. We've been home-schooling since we moved down here. It suits Kip better, but it does mean he spends more time on his own. It's good to have a young man around, a positive role model for him.' Max cleared his throat. 'We think this weekend might be a little ... overwhelming for Kip. He still has a tendency to clam up when he's nervous or frightened. But we're working on it,' he added.

'Don't you worry, we'll have him out of his shell in no time,' said Dominic.

Annie frowned. 'It's about small steps,' she said. 'Kip needs to go at his own pace.'

They all watched as Josh demonstrated how to hold the bow, before he stepped back to let River take aim at the target. River flicked his long hair from his eyes, focused on the bullseye and released the arrow, sending it wide. He shot two more without success, shrugged amiably and handed the bow to Felix who had already stepped forward for his turn. 'You want to get that boy a haircut,' suggested Dom, nudging Jim in the ribs. 'Then he might be able to see the target.'

'It's his choice. He likes it long,' said Jim. 'Suze and I don't care.'

Dominic's face revealed exactly what he thought of that. 'Go on Felix,' he shouted, turning his attention to his own son. 'No, not like that! Drop your elbow. Pull it back. Now aim.'

Felix threw an irritated glance at his father before re-focusing on the target. He missed the first two shots, but his third grazed the second ring of the bullseye.

Dominic shook his head.

Scarlet, who had drifted closer to her father, stood watching, her eyes fixed on Josh.

When it came to Kip's turn, the boy thudded three arrows in swift succession into the target, the last meeting the bullseye square in the middle. Josh reached out to high-five him.

'He's quite the sharpshooter,' said Jim, throwing a surprised look at Max.

'Just takes a bit of practice, Felix,' called Dom. 'You'll be just as good by the end of the weekend.'

Jim and Suze exchanged a knowing glance. Dom's competitive nature was a longstanding joke between them all. He could turn barbecuing sausages into a sport.

Kip retrieved his arrows and handed the bow to River, before making his way back towards the deckchairs.

Jim reached out to squeeze Annie's shoulder. 'Don't worry. The boys will all be firm friends before the weekend's out.'

As the first beers were pulled from a cool box, a bottle of Prosecco was popped open and a playlist hooked up to a Bluetooth speaker. Kira's red Citroën appeared on the crest of the hill. The sun grazed the horizon as she stepped from the car with a weary smile, hugging her friends, introducing everyone to a red-haired man in jeans and a blue sweatshirt who had emerged from the passenger seat to join her. 'Everyone, this is Fred. And this,' she said proudly, gesturing to the baby in his arms, 'is Asha.'

The whole gang crowded around the new arrivals. Fred looked a little younger than the rest of them, one of those rangy men, lean and strong-looking, with an angular jaw and a firm handshake. Probably the type to pour himself into Lycra on a Saturday morning before hopping on an expensive bike, Jim thought. He peered down at the sleeping infant curled like a dormouse against Fred's chest, two rosebud lips parted in sleep, eyelashes resting like feathers against her olive skin. 'God, are they always that small? You forget.'

'She's lovely,' breathed Annie. 'How's it been?'

Kira nodded. 'Good. Exhausting. The full emotional rollercoaster.'

Annie smiled. 'Motherhood suits you. You look great.'

She did. Kira had always been gorgeous – half Sri Lankan, half proud Yorkshire lass – petite with straight black hair and flawless brown skin. Yet there were signs of transformation too, in the shadows beneath her eyes, and the rumpled denim shirt and leggings she wore, in contrast to her usual, edgy style. Jim saw a new softness in her face, recognized a quiet pride that hadn't been there at their last catch-up. He squeezed her arm. 'We're really happy for you.'

Annie turned to include Fred. 'It's lovely to finally meet you. Congratulations. Asha's adorable.'

'I wish I could take some credit, but she's all her mother.' He spoke with a soft Irish lilt, patting Asha's back as he grinned round at them all. 'Lucky for Asha.'

Kira shook her head and Jim wasn't sure if he imagined a flicker of tension passing between them. No doubt a long drive from Leeds with a baby in tow would test anyone's relationship. Jim nudged Fred. 'I bet you could do with a beer.'

'You're not wrong.'

'Yes, you must be tired,' said Annie. 'We've opened the wine and there's food if you're hungry.' She turned and gave Kira another hug. 'We're so glad you decided to come.'

'I won't lie. We nearly didn't, but my maternity leave is flying and I'm due back at the surgery next month. It felt like now or never.'

'You're in the far tent. I hope it will give you a little privacy.'

'It'll be grand,' said Fred, hoisting a bag of nappies onto his shoulder, 'though I hope for your sake's it's sound-proofed. Asha has quite the set of lungs on her.'

'You haven't heard the rest of us yet,' joked Jim.

The older boys were roped into transporting Kira and Fred's luggage – duffle bags, a box of supplies and all the extraordinary paraphernalia that comes with a five-month-old baby – while Fred wrestled with a complicated pram wedged into the back of the car. After they had settled into their tent, everyone gathered at the long table beneath the wooden shelter for dinner. Max had invited Josh to stay on for some food and he entertained the younger kids by juggling apples and vanishing coins behind ears. Even Scarlet looked a little impressed, though she remained seated on the wooden bench, swinging her dark hair from side to side, intermittently standing to stalk about and check for bars on her phone, before throwing it down again in disgust.

Jim stood beside Annie and Suze, a can of beer in his hand, and watched as Max lit the bonfire, the dry tinder catching quickly, crackling and spitting and sending spirals of golden sparks shooting into the darkening sky as a flock of oystercatchers wheeled high overhead.

'You okay, love?' Suze was studying him.

'Great,' he said, fixing his smile. 'Never better.'

It wasn't easy to fool Suze. She had a way of reading him. She always had. Ever since they'd first met at the youth centre in Brighton, she'd displayed a canny intuition when it came to Jim's inner workings. He hadn't believed in love at first sight until he'd seen her that very first time, sitting cross-legged amongst a circle of teenage boys, leading them in a challenging discussion about substance misuse. It was her warm manner with the kids, her easy smile and her pretty heart-shaped face that had done it. For three agonising weeks he'd wrestled to pluck up the courage to ask her out, but in the end, she'd beaten him to it. Brushing past him one night as he'd waited to lock up the centre, she'd turned to him, her silver nose stud catching the light falling from the streetlamp outside, and said, 'Seven o'clock at the Tempest Inn tomorrow night. See you there?' He'd nodded, still speechless. That was Suze in a nutshell. Straightforward, intuitive, proactive.

Standing beside her at the bonfire, he could see she didn't look entirely convinced by his answer, but before Suze could press him, Annie beckoned her over to the shelter. Jim watched his wife grab a handful of cutlery, heard her loud, easy laugh at something cheeky River had said. Her unruly curls slipped from the colourful scarf piled on her head, her green eyes sparkling under the festoon lights, the laughter lines on her face creasing at River's joke.

His gaze shifted to Tanya. She either hadn't heard the joke or hadn't understood it. She reached down and absentmindedly flicked at something on her white jeans with one long, red nail before taking a tentative sip from her tin cup. She looked as if she'd rather be anywhere else.

'Someone should make a toast?' suggested Kira.

It was Dominic who stepped forward, always the one with the voice, the one to take centre stage. He faced them all, backlit by the bonfire. 'Max, Annie, I know we all secretly thought you were mad to give everything up to move down here.'

Jim saw Annie throw Max a pointed look. *See,* it seemed to say.

'But none of us could resist your invitation. Twenty years of friendship counts for a lot.' He beamed round at them all. 'There's not much we wouldn't do for each other. So let's raise our glasses to old friends ... new additions,' he gestured to Fred holding Asha in his arms, 'exciting business ventures ... and make this a weekend to remember.'

Jim is pulled from the memory of their cheers rising into the night by the throbbing in his left arm. The pain has intensified since he started his interview with the police and he winces as he tries to roll his shoulder, shifting in his seat. 'What is it they say?' he asks the two police officers sitting across from him. '*Careful what you wish for?*'

What he wishes for right now, more than anything, is a spliff to take the edge off, but he can't see the police being particularly cool with him kicking back and rolling a joint here on the table.

It's unnerving to remember how they had all been with each other, how it had felt as they had stood around the fire with their glasses raised in a toast. Max beaming at them all with pride, Annie hovering at his side. Kira leaning across to kiss the baby in Fred's arms. Tanya, looking awkward, with young Phoebe pressed against her legs as Scarlet threw surreptitious daggers at Dominic. Suze leaning her head on his shoulder as the other kids scampered about in the darkness beyond the firelight. And young Kip, of course, a little apart from them all, standing quiet and pale in the shadows.

He shakes his head. It's as if the traces had been there all along – signs and hints of what was to follow. And in recalling those earliest moments together, Jim can't help wondering, too, if they will ever reunite as such a group again. The more he remembers, the more he thinks it highly unlikely. Some things you can't ever come back from.

KIP

Sunday afternoon

Kip is in his bedroom when he hears the low hum rising over the headland. He's been asked by his parents to stay in his room and wait, though he's not entirely sure what he's waiting for. All he knows is that he'd rather be there, tucked away upstairs, than down amongst the visitors, in all the babble and confusion.

He's liked this room since the first day they moved here. It's tucked away at the far end of the house, wide and white, with creaky floorboards, a low beamed ceiling and a small arched window looking out towards the headland. There are striped curtains and a large bed with soft cotton sheets decorated with anchors and boats. In one corner stands a desk with a lamp, in another a bookshelf filled with all the books Annie and Max have given him in the six years he's been living with them. Beside the books is a tall stack of yellow *National Geographic* magazines that Max now subscribes to for him, ever since he'd caught him engrossed in an issue in their work reception a few years back. On certain nights, when the tide is high and the wind is blowing in the right direction, he can lie in bed and hear the waves breaking in the bay.

The very best thing about this room, though, is that this one is all his own. He doesn't have to share this space with anyone. Even Max and Annie knock before they enter. It's a far cry from the chaotic, cramped spaces he remembers sharing in the foster homes he'd stayed in, and before that, the stinking old sofa he had slept on, in his old life, with his old parents.

He is lying on the bed when he first hears the noise. It is a low rumble, like a dog's warning growl, building gradually to a steady drone. He limps to the window on his twisted ankle, assuming, at first, that it is another police vehicle bumping up the track to the farmhouse. But the track is clear and as the sound grows louder, he realizes it's not coming from the road, but the sky.

He looks up and his eyes go wide as a red-and-white helicopter swoops low over the house, the glass pane of his window shaking in its peeling wooden frame, the grass outside flattening, the vibration of the rotor blades echoing in the hollow of his chest. He can read two words printed in black capitals on the chopper's side: HM COASTGUARD.

Kip watches as it flies over the farmhouse, heading north towards the cliffs. A strange, surging nausea grows in his belly as the helicopter gradually fades to a distant dot on the horizon.

At the knock on his bedroom door, he turns to find Annie standing in the doorway. Her face is pale and there

are dark circles under her eyes. 'Did you see the helicopter?' she asks. He can see she is trying to find a smile.

He nods.

'Quite something, eh?'

He nods again. His ankle is throbbing, so he moves to
sit on the edge of the bed.

'I wanted to let you know I'm back from the campsite.
Would you like a drink? Something to eat?'

He doesn't answer. He is looking at the pens and notepad she holds in her hands.

'Oh these,' she says, glancing down. 'The police officer,
Patricia, thought you might like to do some drawing.
Pictures . . . of anything . . . whatever's on your mind while
you wait for us.' She enters the room and places them
tentatively on the end of his bed. 'Only if you want to.'

He doesn't think the woman who showed up earlier in
her blue coat and ponytail looks very much like a police
officer. Family Liaison, he'd heard her say, which didn't
sound very exciting, but then she didn't exactly look the
type to chase after baddies and handcuff robbers. She
looks more like the women who visited him in his foster
homes, the ones who came from the council, sipping tea,
talking in low voices to his carers, while throwing sad
smiles across the room – smiles similar to the one Annie is
currently trying to muster. 'I hope we won't be too much
longer,' she says. 'The police are talking to Kira next. You
sit tight. Your dad and I are handling things,' she adds,
before leaving the room.

Alone again, Kip looks back to the window where
the helicopter has now been replaced by two seagulls,

swooping across the yard, tussling over a scrap. He's always liked seagulls. He read in one of his magazines that they are one of the few birds that can survive at sea by drinking saltwater, that they teach their young how to steal food, and how to smash shells on rocks to get to the creatures inside. Kip thinks seagulls get a bad rap. They might pinch your chips, but they're just hungry. You can't blame a creature for trying to survive in the wild. It's simply doing what it has to do. It's like that science guy said, the one they learned about in primary school: survival of the fittest. Or perhaps when it came to gulls, survival of the sneakiest.

As he watches the seagulls and hears their possessive cries echoing across the yard, another cry comes to Kip's mind, a sound that echoes in his mind whenever he closes his eyes; a sound he really doesn't want to think about. He blinks hard and turns away from the screeching gulls.

His fingers are trembling as he reaches for the box of pens. He finds the black one and draws a dark square in the centre of the first sheet of paper then fills it carefully, over and over, the tip of the pen pressing so hard that it threatens to tear right through the sheet. As he scribbles, voices rise up through the floorboards. He can hear the low murmur of the officer in the glasses, followed by the sound of someone crying. Annie, he thinks. Or maybe Kira.

He stops drawing and leans back, staring at the black square for a very long time. It takes him back to that place, to the sound of the ocean beating against the cliffs, the damp, crumbling stone, the sobbing, pleading sounds she had made, the hot press of metal in his fingers, the warm gush of blood. Fragments come back to him in a sickening, looping carousel. He lies the paper on the bed beside him and closes his eyes, breathing deeply. *It's done*, he tells himself. *There's no going back now. He must stay quiet, otherwise everything will change. Again.*

It's only as he is placing the lid back on the pen that he realizes there are still traces of blood beneath his fingernails – no longer red but now a grimy brown–black, almost as black as the ink drying on the page. He knows they haven't made the discovery out on the cliffs yet, but it won't be long now. He'll need to be ready when they do.

KIRA

Sunday afternoon

'I promise we'll keep this as brief as we can, Dr de Silva,' says DC Haines, shifting the sheaf of papers she has laid out on Max and Annie's kitchen table. Kira glances round at the thick, whitewashed walls, the boxes piled high over in one corner, the cluster of dirty mugs standing by the old, cracked sink. Damp raincoats hang on the backs of chairs; muddy boots are scattered by the back door. Yesterday, the room had felt full of promise, the walls echoing with laughter and banter. Today, the atmosphere is cloying and oppressive.

'Thanks. It's just she's a bit fussy.' Kira jiggles Asha in the carrier on her chest, rocks her back and forth, hoping she will settle. 'This is the first time I've been away with her. I won't be attempting it again in a hurry.'

'She's cute. How old?'

'Five months.'

'Busy times ahead.'

'So everyone tells me.'

'Let's get on, shall we? I wanted to ask you about the incident around the bonfire on the first night. Friday.' Seeing Kira's glance at the kitchen door, she adds, 'What you tell me will be treated in the strictest confidence.'

Kira nods, a sense of dread rising. She wonders who has told the police. And why? 'I may not be the best person to ask . . . I wasn't involved, not directly. Fred and I were mere bystanders.' Asha gives a little cry on her chest and Kira lowers her head and breathes in the sweet scent of her baby, grateful suddenly for her proximity – her safety. She knows now how lucky she is, how she mustn't take a second of it for granted.

There had been a moment on Friday night, as they had gathered round the bonfire, the heart of the fire smouldering neon-orange, sparks circling into the black sky, Fred's arm slung around her shoulder and Asha asleep on her chest, when she had been glad that they had made the effort to come. She'd been pleased that she had fought against her instinct to abandon the trip, when earlier on the Friday morning, standing in the hallway of her Leeds terrace, surveying the mountains of baby kit they had to squeeze into the car and thinking about navigating the journey to Cornwall and the three days ahead – the introductions, the questions, the apologies – she'd almost turned to Fred and said, 'Let's sack this whole thing off.'

Since Asha's birth there had been phone calls, cards and presents sent, but this weekend was her first face-to-face reunion with them all in over a year. Over a year, and still she hadn't been sure she was ready. But standing beside the bonfire, Fred's face lit up in the dancing orange light,

Asha sleeping peacefully on her chest, she'd told herself she hadn't anything to worry about. It was fine. Fred was slotting in brilliantly. Asha was, so far, keeping to her routine. These people were her closest friends and none of them were any the wiser. Everything, she had thought, was going to be okay.

'Just tell me what you remember,' urges the police officer, sliding her round glasses a little higher up her nose.

Kira sways in her chair, soothing Asha with the motion of her body as she casts her mind back. 'Well . . . I suppose everything was going great until that man arrived.'

'That man?' The officer frowns.

'Yes. After dinner. Jim was playing some old school tunes on a speaker Max had brought down from the farmhouse. The kids were running wild, excited by the freedom of the place. I think it's fair to say the adults had consumed a fair bit of alcohol.' She hesitates. 'I wasn't really drinking, of course. I'm still breastfeeding. But some of the others were . . . letting their hair down, shall we say? We'd all had a long drive and it was a bank holiday.'

'Go on.'

'Everyone was having a good time, but then this man seemed to materialize out of nowhere and you could feel the atmosphere change instantly.' Kira gives a small shiver.

In retrospect, it had been odd the way he'd emerged from the shadows. Almost as if he'd snuck up on them all or been watching them for a while in the dark.

Fred was the first to spot him, nudging her leg and

whispering, 'Who's that?' He nodded at a tall, stooped man in a long, black coat making his way around the bonfire, heading straight for Max.

She shrugged. 'No idea.'

The man's face was weathered, old and furrowed, as if beaten over many years by the elements, and his hair was stringy and grey. He was accompanied by a huge Rottweiler straining on a chain leash. Before he had even offered a greeting, he'd thrust himself between Max and Jim and launched into a furious tirade. 'I don't know what you think you're playing at,' he said, 'but I know you don't have the permits to open your campsite.'

Max, visibly startled, took a step back. 'Hello, Kellow. Come to join us for a drink?' He held out the bottle of wine in his hands.

The man ignored the offer. 'You have no right to do this.' His finger jabbed at Max's chest, emphasizing his point. The dog sat at his feet, its muscled chest shining like coal, jowls drooling, dark eyes flashing in the firelight. 'You *emmets* have no respect for the way things are done round here.'

'Why don't we talk about this like civilized adults? Can I get you a glass?'

'You can't open without the official council approvals.'

The finger jabs increased, but Max stood his ground. 'Not yet, no, but we're expecting them any day now.' Max sounded remarkably measured, conciliatory even, but the intruder's already red cheeks flared a deeper crimson. 'And not that it's really any of your business, but we're not open yet.'

The man turned pointedly, a sneer on his face as he took in the tents, the cars, and the gathering around the bonfire. 'You expect me to—'

'This is a private party on private land.' Max cut him off. 'It's really no concern of yours.'

'It is my concern when you ship in a load of tourists to maraud around the place, trample all over my fields and disturb my livestock.'

'I don't believe our friends have done any such thing, and nor will they. If they leave *our* land, they'll be keeping to the public paths and recognized rights of way. In fact, I believe the only one trespassing right now is you.'

The man muttered something unpleasant under his breath.

Max took a step forward. 'I've been patient, Kellow. I've listened carefully to your concerns these past few months and tried to reassure you. I know change is hard, but I promise you, we have nothing but good intentions for this place. I'm sure in time you'll come to see that. Now, if you don't care to join us for a drink, could I politely ask you to stop this ridiculous intimidation attempt and leave us to enjoy our night in peace?'

The man had no reply. With an indignant snort, he turned on his heel and disappeared into the darkness, the dog at his side.

'Goodness, what a horrible man.' Kira turned to Annie. 'Are you okay?'

Annie nodded. She looked upset but seemed to be trying to gather herself.

'What's an emmet?' Jim looked confused.

'It's Cornish slang for tourist. It's meant as an insult. To remind us we're the outsiders here.'

'Charming.'

'It's a shame,' said Max. 'He's the closest thing we have to a neighbour round here.'

Annie nodded. 'As soon as he got wind of the fact we weren't farmers, that we had plans to set up a glamping business, well, that was it. He didn't want to know.'

She turned to Kip. 'It's okay. He's gone. You needn't look so worried. Max handled it.'

'And quite brilliantly, I might add,' said Jim, clinking his beer against the wine bottle in Max's hands.

They tried hard to banish the soured atmosphere. Jim opened more wine and the kids played hide and seek in the dark, streaking their faces with earth, like commandos. When it all began to get a little too *Lord of the Flies*, Annie produced a bag of marshmallows to toast over the fire and gave Fred the task of dishing out the treats fairly.

'Have we any toasting forks?'

Kip, standing beside Max, took a step forward. He was clutching a pile of long thin sticks. 'Kip found them all. He's spent half the afternoon whittling them for everyone,' Max said with a hint of pride.

It was obvious the boy had gone to some trouble. Each stick had been cut to the same length, carefully trimmed and sharpened to a fine point. 'Nice work,' Fred called to Kip, as the boy solemnly handed out the sticks.

'Careful,' Tanya warned. 'They look sharp.' She turned to Kira. 'I'm not sure the sticks are a good idea.'

Kira shrugged. She couldn't see the harm. How else

would they toast them? 'Scarlet, are you going to join in?' Kira had spotted Dom's eldest sneaking a generous glug of vodka into a cup of orange juice before settling on the log beside that young surfer guy Max had helping about the place. She sat tossing her hair, sighing and pouting. When Kira called to her, Scarlet rolled her eyes. 'Fine,' she said huffily, 'if I have to. It's not as if there's anything else to do round here.'

Kira met Dominic's gaze over the bonfire. They shared a knowing smirk. He had trouble brewing there.

Scarlet approached Kip and took the stick he offered, Kip colouring slightly as she threw out her begrudging thanks.

'That means there's two marshmallows each,' said Fred. 'Perfect.'

As the treats were handed out, Kira saw Phoebe, unable to wait, cram her first into her mouth. The kids settled around the bonfire. River and Felix, with experience from past scout trips, threw out bossy instructions. 'You want to aim for the orange embers at the heart of the fire.'

'Not too close, Phoebe, or it will burn,' River warned.

Kip was silent, settling onto the log beside Phoebe, jamming the first of his marshmallows onto his stick, the other resting beside him on the log. Phoebe, leaning in too close, let out a shriek as her second marshmallow slid off her stick into the fire. 'Oh no!' she cried. 'It's gone!'

'Never mind, try again. Be a little more patient,' suggested Tanya.

'I don't have any more.'

'Everyone had two.'

Phoebe frowned. 'Oh yeah,' she said, noticing the marshmallow lying beside her on the log.

An orderly calm fell over the gathering as the kids worked intently on their treats, licking sticky fingers, blowing on hot marshmallows. Kip went to pick up his second marshmallow and Kira saw his pale face, cast in the flickering light of the bonfire, shift to a puzzled frown. He looked around, checking the trampled grass to see if it had fallen, then nudged Phoebe. He pointed to the empty space between them, but Phoebe merely shrugged back at him, the picture of innocence, and turned away, her cheeks, Kira noticed, suspiciously plump, the little girl chewing frantically.

'Oh dear,' said Kira. 'I think there's been a mix-up.'

Kip wasn't fooled. He gave Phoebe another nudge, this time more firmly. Phoebe turned her shoulder away and Kip stared at her, his face growing red, his eyes glittering with tears. He opened his mouth, as if to shout, but no sound emerged.

Annie, watchful as ever, stepped up behind her son and placed a hand on his shoulder. 'It's okay,' she said, 'just an accident. We'll buy some more tomorrow.'

But Kip wasn't pacified. He let out a strangled moan and shrugged her off. Kira saw his knuckles clenching white around his sharpened stick.

Tanya came forward. 'Is everything okay?'

'I think, perhaps,' Annie started tactfully, 'Phoebe took one of Kip's marshmallows – by accident, I'm sure,' she added.

'Are there any more Kip could have?' Kira asked, trying to help.

Fred shook his head. 'That was the last of them.'

Kip glared at Phoebe, and Phoebe, perhaps reassured by her mother standing at her back, poked out her tongue.

Before anyone could intervene, Kip lunged for Phoebe. He barrelled into her and the two children tumbled off the log and thumped to the ground in a clash of sticks and a tangle of limbs. An awful, high scream rose into the air.

'Oh my god!' yelled Tanya. 'Get him off her!'

There was a loud *crack* as one of the sticks broke underfoot. Kip was yanked up into the air by the scruff of his sweatshirt. The boy seemed to fly, hauled backwards in Dominic's strong grip. An awful choking sound left Kip's mouth, his fingers grasping at the tight collar of his sweatshirt, his feet kicking out in panic.

'You little—!'

'Get off him, Dom!'

Asha let out a wail from the baby sling. Kira tried to shush her, but it was as if the infant sensed the disturbance and her cries rose in pitch.

'Owwwww!' Phoebe screamed. 'My eye. My eye.'

'What did he do? Let me see.'

'Dominic! For god's sake, put him down.'

It was chaos, a storm of noise and activity as the group encircled the two children, Tanya pulling Phoebe up into her arms, trying to prise the girl's hands from her face, Max launching himself at Dominic, attempting to drag him off Kip.

Released suddenly from Dominic's grip, Kip fell to the ground, and scrambling up, made a run for the safety of

Annie, hiding behind her as the two dads faced off. 'For fuck's sake, Dom,' Max gestured at Kip, 'you've hurt him. Look at his neck.'

'He attacked Phoebe.'

'Show me, baby. Just let me see,' Tanya crooned to Phoebe. 'Oh my god,' she said, turning to Kira, 'there's so much blood.' Her hands were covered with it, a panic-stricken look on Tanya's face. 'I think it's her eye.' As she stood there helpless, the blood dripped from her hands onto her white jeans.

Kira handed Asha to Fred before crouching down on the other side of the little girl. Please, she thought, don't let it be her eye. 'Phoebe, sweetheart,' she said, her voice low and calm, 'will you let me see?'

'Let Kira see, sweetie. She's a doctor. She can help you.'

Asha was fussing in Fred's arms, still crying loudly.

Kip jammed his hands over his ears and closed his eyes, letting out a low, guttural moan.

'He went for her like a fucking wild animal. I swear, if he's hurt her . . .' Dominic growled.

'Come on, man,' said Jim, taking him by the arm, trying to steer him away. 'Let's all be cool.'

Slowly, Phoebe peeled her hands away from her eye. 'Can someone shine a torch over here please,' Kira asked.

A phone was held up, the camera flash illuminating Phoebe's bloody face as Kira leaned in to assess the injury. She dabbed at the tears and blood and snot with a hand-kerchief and let out a long breath. Phoebe whimpered quietly. 'It's okay. There's a cut on her brow. Looks nastier than it is.'

'No thanks to that boy,' growled Dominic. 'She could have lost her eye.'

Kip was still whimpering, making a strange sort of keening noise, rubbing at the red burn mark on his neck where his T-shirt had chafed his skin. Kira saw the other kids standing nearby in the dark, their faces fixed and wide-eyed. Felix nudged River and leaned in to whisper something. Kira followed their gaze, her heart sinking as she realized what they were smirking at. A tell-tale dark patch bloomed on Kip's cargo shorts. He had wet his pants.

'Kip attacked her.' Dominic looked around at the group. 'You all saw it.'

'What I saw,' said Max, his voice like ice, 'was a grown man attacking a young boy.'

'He went for her. Intentionally. He used his stick as a weapon.'

'Dominic! You can't possibly think—'

'Please, everyone. Calm down,' said Suze, trying to intervene. 'Is there a first-aid kit?'

'Yes, in the camp kitchen.'

'River, will you run and fetch it please.'

The argument was derailed by Phoebe wheezing and coughing, followed by the sudden, urgent search for her asthma inhaler. When she had calmed, Kira cleaned the wound above her eye and covered it with a plaster. 'There, all better. It looks way worse than it is. Faces can bleed a lot.'

'Come on, buddy,' said Max, throwing a protective arm around Kip, 'you're still shaking. I'll take you back to the farmhouse and get you cleaned up.' Max refused to look at Dominic. He turned to Annie. 'I think it's best he sleeps somewhere he feels safe tonight,' he added pointedly.

'Fine by me,' muttered Dominic. 'I think we'll all feel safer if he's up there tonight.'

Max didn't say anything else. He took Kip by the hand and marched him away into the darkness.

After she'd been patched up, Phoebe seemed more bothered about being sent to bed before everyone else. 'None of the other kids have to go to bed yet,' she whined.

'None of the other kids have had a nasty shock like you,' replied Tanya.

'But I don't want to go. It's dark.'

'It's way past your bedtime.'

'But that bad man's out there. The one with the dog. What if he comes and gets us when we're sleeping in our tents?'

'Don't be silly, Pheebs. I'll stay with you. I'll read to you for a bit.'

Their voices trailed away into the darkness, the torch from Tanya's phone arcing across the grass, until moments later Kira saw their tent light up from within, a single glowing dome on the periphery of the campsite, the blurry silhouettes of mother and daughter just visible inside.

The rest of them, relieved to have averted major disaster and a potential hospital dash, tried to return to the jolly mood from earlier, but the tension around the bonfire remained palpable. Kira saw how the group had fractured into two distinct factions. Annie stood on the far side of the wooden shelter, one side of her face lit by the bonfire flames, the other in shadow as she talked with Jim and Suze, gesturing fiercely once or twice towards the spot where the altercation had happened. It was obvious how upset she was. Dominic remained on the other side of the fire pit, sitting with her and Fred, a beer bottle in his hand. He seemed transfixed by the leaping flames. Kira wasn't sure where her own loyalties lay exactly, but she knew it wouldn't be a good idea to leave Dominic sitting on his own in the dark while he stewed. 'I'm glad she's okay,' she said, turning to him.

'Yeah.' Dominic had taken a long swig from his beer bottle. 'No thanks to that bloody kid.'

She knew Dominic had a temper, but she had never seen this side of him before: the growling, protective grizzly bear of a father.

'It doesn't matter what anyone says, there's something not right with that boy,' Dominic muttered, his body still rigid with tension. 'He should've been made to apologize. If he was my kid,' he continued, 'I'd find a way to make him talk. All this "*Oh he can't speak when he's nervous . . .*" rubbish. What's that about then?'

He was, she knew, looking for allies to back him after his set-to with Max. She felt the gentle press of Fred's foot against her own, a gesture of solidarity or warning, she wasn't sure. Annie, at least, was some distance away, far enough not to have heard.

'You're a doctor,' Dominic continued. 'You must have an opinion. Max and Annie pander to him, don't you think?'

'I don't know,' she admitted. 'I don't have all the facts,

72

but it presents like selective mutism. It's a recognized behavioural disorder.'

Dominic let out a snort. 'God, we'll medicalize any-thing these days.'

'It's not a choice, Dom, but a response. It's not easy adopting an older child. Those early childhood years are important – incredibly formative. It can't be easy for Max and Annie, navigating such uncertain terrain.'

'Exactly my point. What do we really know about the boy? There's nurture ... and then there's nature. I saw the look in his eyes when he went for her, and I'm telling you, there's something wrong with that kid. I don't want Phoebe anywhere near him.' Dominic took a long swig from his bottle.

'I think that's a bit rough,' said Kira gently. 'You can't write a child off like that.'

'Kids'll be kids,' added Fred carefully. 'Luckily every-one's okay.' He rose from his seat. 'I think I need another beer. Anyone else?'

Dominic shook his head.

Kira threw Fred an envious look. What with the heightened atmosphere around the fire, if there was ever a moment to resent her breastfeeding sobriety, it was this. It couldn't be easy for him – a new face in such a well-established group of friends. She had the past – solid ground to stand upon – but she still would've liked a glass of wine to take the edge off the night. She didn't begrudge Fred his Dutch courage.

She watched from across the fire as Fred topped up Suze and Annie's drinks then turned up the tunes. Jim performed some dodgy breakdancing moves in a pretend dance battle with Fred, making Felix and River snort with laughter. Willow and Juniper ran across to join the dance party, the two girls spinning and twirling, Juniper copying her big sister's moves. As the night deepened, a loud splash came out of the darkness.

'Guess the hot tub's open,' said Dominic.

'That's probably Fred. He's always one of the first to throw himself into things.'

'An Irish toy boy, eh?' He nudged her. 'Nice work, *cougar*.'

Kira rolled her eyes. 'He's thirty-two. It's not *that* big a gap. It's the same as you and Tanya, only reversed, right?'

Dominic nodded. 'True. He seems like ... quite a character.'

The way he said it didn't make it sound like he totally approved, and Kira felt a flash of annoyance. She hadn't judged him when he'd left Clare, had she? Hadn't said a word about his choice in Tanya, his younger, materialistic, bleached and botoxed second wife. Couldn't he, as her friend, just be happy for her? 'He's a good guy,' she said, sounding more defensive than she'd intended.

'How did you meet?' Dominic asked, picking at the label of his bottle.

'At a work conference last year. He sells medical equipment. I was in the market for a new blood pressure monitor.'

'Who said romance was dead?' Dominic took a swig from his bottle. 'He seems good with Asha. Very hands-on.'

'Yeah,' she softened, 'he's a good dad.'

She stared into the fire. He *was* a good dad. All of her

worries when they'd first found out that she was pregnant – that they hadn't been together long enough, that it was too soon for him, that he was too young, that he wouldn't be ready for such a huge life change – had so far proved unfounded. Sure, Fred drank a bit too much and certainly no one could deny he loved a party, and his footie, spending every weekend playing five-a-side or cheering on his beloved team, but that didn't mean he wasn't good for her – good for Asha. So far, he'd proved to be nothing but steadfast.

'You seem like a great mum, too,' added Dominic. 'Not that any of us would've doubted it. I'm happy to see you so content – you know, after last year . . .' he trailed off. 'It's as if the universe heard you that night and gave you exactly what you wanted.'

Kira nodded, her gaze fixed on the dying flames of the bonfire. 'Yes, I suppose so.' She hesitated. 'I've been wanting to apologize for what happened at my fortieth. I was in a bad place and the things I said to you all – the things I did . . .'

Dominic held up his hands. 'We don't need to go there. I think we all understood.'

She nodded. 'Thanks, but just for the record, I *am* sorry. It took a fair amount of courage to come along this weekend and face everyone.'

Dominic turned to her in surprise. 'Kira, we've been friends for years. Surely you know us all better than that?' He held her gaze. 'It's in the past. If Fred's the guy for you, then that's great. We're all happy for you.'

Kira nodded and fell silent. Unspoken words lay heavy

on her tongue until another flurry of shouts and whoops arose in the darkness, followed by more splashing. 'Isn't it lovely that the kids can run so free here,' Kira said, seizing the moment to steer the conversation onto safer ground.

'I can guarantee they won't be so lovely tomorrow morning. Scarlet's a nightmare on less than eight hours,' Dominic sighed. 'She's become such a stroppy teen in recent months.'

'It's her age. The hormones. She needs to test the boundaries – test herself.'

Dominic gave a hollow laugh. 'Yes, you think having babies is hard, just you wait. First you wrestle with the toddler tantrums. Then it's the cut-throat world of school selections and driving them to every playdate, party and sports fixture going. Then you hit the teenage years and you're up all night waiting for them to come home, worrying about teenage pregnancies, car accidents and overdoses. Being a parent is just one long litany of fire-fighting and damage control. You and Fred have all this to look forward to.' He nodded towards Asha, sleeping peacefully against her. 'I wish I'd known how good I had it when they were that age and couldn't run amok. I haven't even held her yet,' he said. 'May I?'

Kira hesitated. Sensing her reluctance, he backtracked. 'I don't have to. Don't want to wake her.'

'No,' said Kira, 'it's fine.' She released the sling and he took her carefully in his arms, rocking her gently. 'Hello Asha. Aren't you beautiful? Who does she look most like, do you think? You or Fred?'

Kira gazed at her daughter's face. 'Fred says she's all me.'

'Lucky girl. She'll be a beauty then.'

Kira watched Dominic with Asha, saw how carefully he held her in the warm crook of his arm, and felt that tugging sensation of love and gratitude that often came whenever she had the rare opportunity to regard her daughter from a distance. How lucky she was to have this, finally. 'You know, if the reality TV gig ever stalls, you could always go into politics. Making toasts, shaking hands and holding babies seems to come pretty easy to you.'

Dominic was still chuckling as Fred reappeared, wet hair dripping onto his hoodie, a damp towel wrapped around his waist. 'I tried, but not even my epic break-dancing and hot tub belly flops are going to get this party started. I think it's time for bed. You coming?' he asked, turning to Kira.

'Surely not?' Dominic protested. 'I thought you medical types were renowned for your hardcore partying.'

'I'm pretty sure Asha and I will be having another little party at 3am, so technically you could say I'll be the last one standing.' She held out her arms and took the baby from Dominic, before following Fred to the farthest edge of the campsite where their tent loomed ghost-white in the dark.

'Well that was quite a night,' Fred said, once they were safely inside, the flaps zipped up behind them. He hopped round behind her, wrestling with the laces on his train-ers. 'I wasn't sure we were all going to make it through "marshmallow-gate" unscathed.'

'Mmmmm ...' she said, gazing down at her daugh-ter's peaceful form, one chubby cheek rosy from where

77

it had been pressed against Dom's chest, her little mouth parted in sleep. She felt a rush of love so strong it almost floored her.

'Man, that guy is intense.'

'Who? Dom?'

'Yeah. The way he lunged for poor Kip, I thought he was going to deck him.'

'He was worried for Phoebe.'

'But did you see the boy's face? He was petrified. I felt for the little fella.' Fred pulled his hoodie over his head, got stuck somewhere inside it, stumbled against the bed.

'Dom was scared too – he was acting on paternal instinct. It could've been a lot worse.' She was a little surprised at the surge of protective affection she felt for Dominic. Fred had only just met him. It was easy to judge someone you didn't really know.

'Exactly. *Could've*. But wasn't.' Released from the sweatshirt, Fred's face re-emerged, his damp hair sticking up at crazy angles, dressed in nothing but wet boxers.

'You went in like that?'

He shrugged. 'Couldn't be bothered to find my swimmers. Dominic overreacted. Big time. I think he knew it, too. Just couldn't back down. He's like that on his TV show. When he gets the bit between his teeth he can really lay into the contestants. It's brutal.'

'You don't understand.' Kira gazed down at Asha. *She* understood it. The thought of any physical harm coming to her daughter made her feel ill. 'Dom was acting on pure primal instinct. As a parent you'll do anything to protect your baby.'

Fred hesitated. 'And I wouldn't know about that?'

Something in Fred's voice made her turn. 'What? Oh, no. That's not what I meant.'

'It's what you said. Is that what you think?'

'No. I didn't *mean* anything, Fred.' She kicked herself for her clumsy choice of words. 'I'm tired. It came out wrong.'

Fred stared back at her.

The bell tent, which had seemed so generous in size on their arrival, seemed to have shrunk around them. 'Let's not argue. You know that's not what I meant. You've had a few drinks and I'm tired. You're amazing with Asha.'

'But I'm not, am I? Her biological parent, I mean.'

Kira didn't answer.

'And while we're on this subject,' Fred added, 'why did you let them all think that I am? It was bloody awkward, Kira. I didn't know what to say. Why haven't you told them I'm not Asha's dad?'

Kira sighed. 'Because in my head you are. I thought you'd be pleased. It makes it easier, doesn't it?'

'But they're your friends? Why lie?'

'I didn't lie. They just assumed.'

'And you didn't correct them?'

She shrugged. 'I went to ground after my birthday. I couldn't face them for a little while. When they heard I'd met someone, they were so excited. Then came the baby news. They were just happy for me. For us. It all merged into one.' She narrowed her eyes at him. 'Fred, what is this? Are you trying to start a fight?' She turned her back on him, lifting Asha carefully and laying her in the travel cot. 'Maybe I don't want them to judge me. Maybe I don't want them to think less of me – or think Asha means less because of the way she was conceived.'

'Given they're supposed to be your closest friends, I'd have thought you could be honest with them.'

Kira sighed. 'Or maybe, I don't know, it's actually none of their business? Why does it have to be such a big deal? So they think you're her biological dad – so what?'

Kira, still bristling from the argument, fussed with her washbag, searching for her toothbrush. Having peeled off his damp boxers, Fred collapsed naked onto the bed with a sigh. 'It's comfier than I thought it would be.'

'You might want your PJs? It'll get colder later.' She dug about in the holdall she'd packed for her and Asha, searching for her own pyjamas.

'But I've got you to keep me warm.'

She turned then and he grinned up at her, that same crooked smile that had undone her the very first time they'd met.

'You know the best way to sort out a disagreement, don't you?'

She ignored him, glancing about the tent. 'Where's your bag?'

'I dunno. Outside under the awning? I can't be arsed. I'll find it in the morning.' Catching sight of the sensible flannelette pyjamas in her hands, Fred groaned. 'You've got to be kidding! Winter thermals? Babe, it's not that cold.'

Kira didn't feel warm. Away from the dwindling bonfire, the night had taken on a distinct chill, but then she hadn't drunk as much as Fred.

'Forget about the bag. Come here.' He beckoned her towards the bed.

'We might wake Asha. The others could hear us. They're not *that* far away.'

She dimmed the lamp beside the bed and checked on Asha one last time. Fred lay sprawled naked on his side, his eyes closed and his chest rising and falling in deep rhythm. She studied him for a moment in the low light, the thatch of wiry hair on his chest, the taut flatness of his belly, the definition in his arms and, despite herself, felt a twinge of desire grip her. She laid her pyjamas to one side and slid in naked beside him, wrapping herself tightly around his warm body.

'Hello . . .' he murmured, reaching for her.

She heard the clink of bottles, tents being zipped and unzipped, the low murmur of voices, protestations and a shout of laughter followed by the cry of an overtired child . . . one of the Miller kids, perhaps. She shut out the sounds and submitted herself to the sensation of his hands on her skin, their bodies moving together quietly in the dark. When she came, she pressed her own hand to her lips to silence her cry.

Fred fell asleep quickly, still naked on top of the covers. She threw a blanket over him, not wanting him to wake cold in the night, then shimmied into her pyjamas. She thought sleep would come quickly, but it took some time to drift off, long after the other campers had fallen silent, long after Fred had started snoring, his soft reverberations lifting from the mattress beside her. It felt like mere minutes when she startled awake again.

Disoriented but alert, she lay motionless in the pitch black. The wind had picked up, the canvas billowing and flapping gently. With the distant sound of the ocean washing onto the shore and the tang of salt drifting on the air, it was if she'd woken on a boat. She assumed it was Asha who had disturbed her, hungry again, but her daughter, perhaps sedated by the sea air, was still asleep.

Kira lay still, ears pricked, when she heard it. A sound – a shuffling noise, then a low thump near the entrance to their tent. She stiffened, held her breath, her ears straining.

It came again. Soft shuffling, a dragging, like something being pulled across the ground. She lifted her head off the pillow. It was an animal. A fox, a badger, some creature innocently sniffing out their presence. They were the ones trespassing – encroaching on this wild land. Of course there would be wild things out there, investigating and scavenging.

In the darkness she saw a glowing circle of light glance off the far side of the tent. A torch, playing across the canvas. 'Hello?' she called softly. Was it one of the others, lost or disorientated, perhaps seeking the toilet block in the dark?

The light went out, like the flick of a switch. She craned in the dark and heard the soft rasp of something brushing against the canvas. The fabric seemed to give a little. Then she heard it again, the soft pad of footsteps on the timber porch outside – or perhaps not footsteps but paws, she reminded herself. 'Fred,' she whispered.

Fred's only reply was a spluttering snore.

Kira stared wide-eyed into the dark, her skin prickling,

braced for the sound of the zipper being pulled, or worse, the glint of a knife ripping through the canvas, all those teenage slasher movies she'd watched through splayed fingers at sleepovers decades ago coming back to her in a rush. She remembered little Phoebe's protest as she'd been hauled off to bed: *But that bad man's out there.* She shivered, her ears straining in the dark.

But there was nothing. Only the soft shifting of the tent in the breeze.

Slowly, her heartbeat regulated in her chest and her breathing calmed. How silly. They were in the middle of the countryside sleeping under thin sheets of fabric. Of course there were strange noises. The light could've been from one of the kids from the other tents, messing around with a torch.

'Fred?' she whispered again. 'Are you awake?'

He didn't reply so Kira curled into him, pressing herself up against the warmth of his back, burying herself under the quilt, trying to take comfort in his solid presence. Sleep, she willed herself. She'd be up again at first light with Asha. Like the spring fledglings waking with open, hungry beaks, the relentless cycle of it all would start again and lying ahead of her was a day with all the hoops and hurdles she must navigate – the pitfalls she must avoid. It would be easier to keep a clear head if she was rested. Slowly, she drifted back into a fitful sleep.

TANYA

Sunday afternoon

Tanya sits in a plastic chair beside the hospital bed listening to the steady beep of electronic machines, the low murmur of voices, the soft tread of nurses passing back and forth beyond the cubicle. After the last forty-eight hours, it's a relief to be sitting in the Royal Cornwall Hospital in Truro, under a warm, solidly constructed roof, surrounded by competent people going about their jobs with calm efficiency.

She's wearing the white jeans she'd travelled down to Cornwall in on Friday – her other clothes too wet and dirty now – and a navy fleece belonging to Dominic. The expensive herbal tang of his aftershave rises off the collar, but the scent of it isn't as comforting as she once found it; rather it makes her feel light-headed, a little claustrophobic. She tries not to look at the rust-coloured stains on her jeans, stains from Phoebe's run-in with that kid and those wretched sticks. It's hard to believe that was less than forty-eight hours ago.

It feels as if she's lived a lifetime – aged a lifetime – since then.

The cubicle curtain glides back and a nurse appears. Her dark hair is scraped up into a high ponytail and she sports dramatic, arched eyebrows that appear to have been drawn on, as if with a thick marker pen. 'How's the patient?' the nurse asks, moving about the bed, checking the drip standing to one side and the monitor display.

'No change.'

'Poor thing. It could take a while. She lost a lot of blood. It's not uncommon for the human body to shut down after experiencing a serious trauma. She's protecting herself. Healing.'

'But she'll be okay, won't she? The surgeon mentioned there could be organ damage.'

'She's in the very best place. We'll know more when she wakes.' She throws Tanya a sympathetic look. 'You've been here a while, haven't you? Can I get you anything?'

Tanya shakes her head. 'I'm fine.'

'The police have asked to speak with you as soon as possible.' Seeing Tanya's expression, she pats her arm. 'Don't worry, we're holding them at bay for now. Doctor's orders.'

She leaves, her thick-soled shoes squeaking away down the polished floor and Tanya stares once more at the ugly stain on her jeans. Phoebe's high-pitched scream echoes back to her, that awful blood-curdling howl that had pierced the darkness. It's a sound that haunts her, reverberates in her heart in a way only your own child's cry can.

Looking back now, it's possible to see the episode

around the bonfire as a warning for what lay ahead. A portent. She's always trusted her gut – always believed in listening to her intuition. She should have listened to what it was telling her that night. She should have insisted that they pack up there and then, that Dominic drive them home to London the very next morning. Maybe then they could have avoided everything that lay ahead.

She reaches out and takes the hand lying on the sheet in front of her, tries not to look at the ugly, red-raw marks encircling her wrists, instead pressing the back of her hand to her warm lips. 'I'm so sorry,' she murmurs, gazing at the pale, bandaged face resting on the pillows, at the oxygen mask, the tubes and the liquids and the machine wheezing up and down, monitoring and mending, trying to make everything better. 'I'm so very sorry.'

SCARLET

Saturday morning

'What the—?' Scarlet woke to a brilliant light, the kind she suffered on those mornings when she was late for school and her mother marched into her bedroom and unceremoniously flicked on the overhead light.

Peering through screwed-up eyelids, she caught glimpses of blinding white canvas walls, tin mugs hanging on an old, cottagecore dresser, and her brother, Felix, stretched out on a camp bed, one arm flung over his head, his mouth wide open as if catching flies. 'Gross,' she sighed, sliding back beneath the covers. Everything smelled grassy and damp, like washing left out in the rain. 'Oh god,' she groaned, burrowing a little deeper. Another day in hell.

She groped for her mobile, hopeful Lily's promised messages might have found a miraculous way to her phone overnight, but her handset was dead. The battery had given up overnight. There was no way they could stay in touch now, not even if she hiked to the highest cliff on the headland and picked up a bar of elusive 5G. Tears pricked her eyes at the injustice of it all. While her friends were back home living their best lives, she was stuck here, in a minging tent, in the middle of nowhere, with her snoring brother for company.

There were several reasons she was desperate to message Lily, and it wasn't just to find out how last night's party had gone down, and whether Harry Taylor had missed her – had said anything about her, anything at all.

She wanted to download to Lily about the clusterfuck of an evening she'd endured. She wanted to tell her about that kid going batshit crazy over one marshmallow and attacking Phoebe and her dad losing his mind – and all the adults taking sides like little children.

To be fair to Kip, Phoebe could be a pain. Scarlet had been sitting across the fire from it all as it kicked off. She'd seen her little sister screw up her face and stick out her tongue at Kip with that triumphant look, even if no one else had. It didn't justify his attack, but she knew it wasn't quite as black-and-white as her dad was making out.

Most of all, she wanted to send Lily the photo she had taken surreptitiously the previous night. The one of that guy, Josh, shirtless in the hot tub, with his tattoos and his sleepy Ryan Gosling eyes. Lily would go mad for him. He was her type to a tee. While Scarlet was into boys like Harry, clean-cut and well dressed, Lily liked the bad boys. Older guys, with stubble and tattoos, a little rougher around the edges.

Felix and River had been the ones to suggest the hot tub, but by the time Josh had taken the cover off, fetched the wood and got it to the right temperature, the boys had lost interest and run off into the night. Tanya was back in the tent with Phoebe and the rest of the adults were split around the bonfire, huddled in groups. Her dad was bitching with Kira, completely oblivious. She'd eyed Josh. 'Seems a shame to waste it,' she'd said, in a voice she'd hoped sounded suitably offhand and flirtatious.

'You want to go in?' Josh had hesitated. 'I can leave it uncovered for you, but I think you should check with Max or Annie first.'

She'd nodded and disappeared to her tent, slipping into the cute, black thong bikini she'd persuaded her mum to buy her for summer and one of the fluffy white bathrobes hanging up in the tent. Returning to the hot tub, she'd swiped an open bottle of white wine from the trestle table under the pavilion and tucked it beneath the robe before sashaying back to Josh.

'Did they say it was okay?' Josh had asked.

'Yeah,' she lied, 'as long as I don't go in on my own. You'll have to join me.'

Josh had looked about awkwardly. It was just the two of them. Scarlet, emboldened by the vodka she had already drunk, grinned and slipped her robe off her shoulders, wielding the wine bottle in one hand as she climbed the steps to the tub. She'd let out a sigh as she sank down into the water. 'Oh my god, it's so warm. You have to come in.'

Josh hadn't looked entirely comfortable. 'I dunno.'

'It's not safe for me to be in here on my own,' she added with a mischievous smile. She'd lifted the wine bottle and taken a swig, trying not to let her eyes water too obviously as the alcohol burned the back of her throat. 'You've already got your boardshorts on. Come on.'

With a sigh, Josh had slipped off his sweatshirt and then his T-shirt, revealing his muscled chest and the dark ink scrawled up his arm. He'd climbed up quickly and slipped into the tub, wading across to take the seat opposite her. Steam rose off the water between them. In the dark, his eyes glinted at her like a cat's. It felt like a scene from a movie, she'd thought. Lily would be so impressed. She'd offered him the bottle, but he shook his head. 'Nah, I'm good, thanks.'

'Where do you live?' she'd asked, tilting her head to one side, lifting one leg slightly so that her knee rose out of the water.

'I've got a caravan inland. Near my dad's place.'

'Nice.' She didn't fancy the idea of a caravan, but each to their own. She supposed it went with the surfer vibes. She'd reached across and touched his arm. 'What's the A stand for?'

He'd looked down at his sleeve of tattoos, to the ornate letter A that was inked near his elbow. 'Amber.'

Scarlet frowned. 'Your girlfriend?'

'My sister.'

Scarlet had grinned, feeling pleased, and swirled the water around with her hands. She knew her body looked good in the bikini. Her boobs had grown a whole cup-size last term. She looked at least eighteen, Lily told her, in full make-up anyway. Maybe even nineteen. 'What's she like, your sister?'

He hesitated. 'Smart. Talented. A little shy. Heart of gold.'

'Do you get on?'

'Mum died when we were little. It was the three of us after that ... Me, Amber and Dad. We've always been close.'

'Sorry about your mum.' Scarlet tilted her head. 'So are you alike, you and your sister?' She knew she was hammering him with questions, but short of going back to the tent and listening to Tanya read to Phoebe, this was the best entertainment going.

'Not really,' said Josh. 'Dad's always called me an "outsider". I love the ocean. Surfing. Beaches and big skies. Amber's the "insider". She's all feeling and emotion, everything internalized. She'd stay in her bedroom all day writing music and daydreaming, you know?'

'I bet you have dreams. Looking after annoying tourists at a campsite probably isn't your life's grand ambition? Am I right?'

Josh gave a low laugh. 'I always imagined I'd go travelling. I fancy tackling some of those famous surf breaks around the world ... Australia, California, Indonesia. But that's on hold for the moment.'

'Why?'

'Dad's been having some tests. I need to be here for him.'

'Sorry,' said Scarlet. 'That sucks.'

He shrugged. 'Family first. Dad was always good to us. After Mum ... well, it wasn't easy, but he was always there.' Josh gave a small, sad smile. 'He doesn't ask for much, to be fair. He's a quiet man. Likes his routine. Porridge in the mornings. An armchair facing the sea. Fish and chips on a Friday night in front of the TV. On

Saturday mornings I collect his local paper from the newsagents for him and he reads it cover to cover. He falls asleep with it spread across his lap – every time.' Josh's smile broadened at the thought, his angular face softening. 'Simple pleasures. That's Dad. He always put family first, so it's the least I can do for him now.'

Scarlet nodded, but inside she couldn't help thinking that the picture Josh had painted sounded incredibly dull. 'I can't imagine growing up in a place like this. It's so ... empty.'

Josh raised an eyebrow. 'Empty? You're kidding. This place is raw and wild and real. Not like a city where everything is artificial and crammed in.'

'But it's so quiet. What do you do for fun?'

He shrugged. 'You make your own fun. To me, a city would be anything but fun. So overwhelming. People packed in and jostling for space. The idea of that frightens me.'

'Funny,' said Scarlet, in a tone that made it clear she found it anything but, 'because I've felt the exact same thing about being here. All the space, the unpredictability of the landscape. It puts me on edge. I know where I'd rather be. But of course,' she added quickly, in case she'd offended him, 'you've got your dad. I get it. Family first,' she added, parroting back his words.

She'd eyed him through the steam. With his wet hair slicked back he'd looked more handsome than earlier. A selfie with him on her socials would put the wind up Harry and give Lily something to drool over. She'd been wondering how to broach the idea, wondering if she could retrieve her phone from the bathrobe pocket without ruining the moment, when a voice called out to them through the darkness. 'Well you two have certainly got the right idea. Room for one more?'

It was Kira's bloke. Fred. Scarlet had been annoyed. She didn't want anyone else joining them. Especially not this loudmouth Irish dude who seemed a little too enthusiastic about everything, a little too try-hard.

Without waiting for an answer, Fred had stripped off and clambered up to join them, entering with a whoop and a loud splash. He was as pale as a worm with a hairy chest and legs, wearing nothing but his pants. Gross.

He'd drifted across the tub, brushing her leg as he passed, before settling on the seat beside Josh. Scarlet had sunk down a little further into the water. Josh was one thing, but she wasn't going to give this sleaze the chance to gawp at her boobs.

Noticing the wine bottle in her hands, Fred had smirked. 'You want to go easy, young lady. White wine hangovers are the worst.'

'My dad lets me drink,' she said. It was kind of true. Half a glass of wine at Sunday lunch counted. Patronizing wanker. What did he know?

She'd taken another swig then offered the bottle to Josh. Josh declined again, to her disappointment, but he passed it on to Fred who seemed to consider it for a moment before shrugging and taking a big swig. 'Purely medicinal,' he'd winked at them both. 'Drink enough and I won't need my special stash of pills to help me sleep through Asha's crying tonight.'

Scarlet rolled her eyes. Poor Kira. How on earth did such an intelligent woman get saddled with this loser?

She'd listened to the men chat for a while, growing increasingly irate as they'd lost themselves down a tedious rabbit hole about football transfers and premiership rankings that she had no interest in. She might as well have not been there. Fred had come along and ruined everything.

'I'm going to get out,' she'd announced, hoping to prompt a reaction from Josh, but the two men had carried on chatting, and feeling a little foolish, she'd stood and clambered back down the steps. At the bottom she turned, hoping to find Josh admiring her figure, but it was Fred who was watching her, a slight smile playing on his lips. Perv, she'd thought, slipping the bathrobe over her shoulders.

After that, she hadn't known quite what to do. Common sense had told her she should return to her tent, before her dad caught her wandering about in the dark in her bikini, but she'd lingered in the shadows, warmed by the wine, not quite ready to give up on her idea of a photo. Finally, as the two men had stood, she'd seized her chance. As Josh moved across the hot tub and reached for the steps, she raised her phone and took the photo.

She hadn't looked at it until she was safely in her tent. There she had pored over it from the warmth of her bed. It really was the perfect shot. Josh, with his slicked-back hair and his tanned, muscled torso emerging from the steam, dripping wet. All she had to do now was get it to Lily – somehow. Fucking camping. It really was so incredibly uncivilized.

Outside the tent, she could hear the morning stirrings of the other campers. It sounded like the Miller kids chatting quietly in the next tent. A little further away she heard Kira's baby cry, then stop. A tent was unzipped. Soft footsteps padded across the grass. Scarlet tried to ignore the noises by burrowing deeper into the bed, until a loud crack, sounding alarmingly like a gunshot, echoed over the campsite. 'What the hell was that?' she asked, sitting bolt upright.

Felix stretched and opened his eyes. 'Dunno.' He yawned and adjusted his duvet. 'Get any sleep?'

'No.' She threw herself back against her pillow with a sigh. 'You were snoring like a train.'

'I see your mood's not improved.'

'I see your face hasn't improved either.'

Felix reached for one of his dirty socks and threw it at her. She dodged just in time. 'If you're so miserable here, why don't you go home?'

'Trust me, Felix, if I could, I would, but short of magic shoes or a helicopter, I can't see how I'm going to get there.'

'You could hitchhike?' he suggested.

Scarlet considered this for a moment. 'That would be fine, apart from the axe murderers and the rapists.'

Another loud crack rang out over the campsite. Scarlet jumped.

Felix shrugged and closed his eyes. 'It's almost like you're not trying, Scar.'

Scarlet pulled the duvet over her head. There was no way she would be leaving the warmth of her bed this early, and not just because of the dull white wine headache she could feel building behind her eyes. Nor the threat of gunshots ringing over the meadow. If she couldn't leave the campsite, she would stay in the tent and sleep for as long as was humanly possible. The quicker the weekend passed in a comatose state, the better as far as she was concerned.

As she sank into the pillow, another loud crack echoed in the air. Crazy. She'd take a nice, civilized provincial town over this war zone anyday.

MAX

Sunday afternoon

The afternoon is tilting towards evening, the sun sliding earthwards when Max finally sits down to talk with DC Haines. He has just taken a sandwich up to Kip in his bedroom. After all the turmoil and the exhaustion, the sight of their boy, pale and anxious, sitting on his bed scribbling pictures with a set of felt-tip pens almost broke his heart. It was the sheer innocence of it that killed him, that made him wonder if they'd made the right decision, if he shouldn't march down there and release what he held so tightly in his chest – the things he didn't yet understand and that frightened him more than he cared to think about. But then Annie's voice had come back to him. *Not yet, Max. Not until we know.* He had given Kip the gentlest pat on his shoulder. 'I'm here for you, buddy. Whenever you want to talk. You know that, right?'

Kip had given a little nod, his gaze fixed on the pen in his hand.

Max had waited. 'Everything's going to be okay.'

He hoped it was the truth. 'Whatever's happened, we've got you.'

Max was praying that he was right, that the promises he was making could be kept, when something made him hesitate at the bedroom door and glance back. He saw Kip reaching for the sandwich, tearing it into rough quarters, leaving two on the plate, before surreptitiously sliding the other two into the front pocket of his hoodie. Max's heart sank. Kip was doing it again. He'd have to mention it to Annie.

Back in the kitchen, he takes the seat Kira has only recently vacated, feeling oddly like a visitor in his own house. He knows there's a lot to go through, that the police are working as fast as they can, but he can't believe how long it's taken them to get to him. 'Any word from the hospital?' he asks, watching as the policewoman turns to a clean sheet in her notebook. She looks tired too, strands of hair falling from her ponytail, her face pale and pinched.

'Not yet, I'm afraid.'

'It's just with the police vans down at the site and the helicopter earlier . . .?' He trails off.

'I understand your concern, Mr Kingsley, but I have no new information to share at present. What would help, if you don't mind,' she says, throwing him a weak smile, 'is if I could ask *you* a few questions.'

Max swallows his frustration. 'Of course. Whatever I can do to help. We all want answers as much as you do.'

'I'm sure.' She holds his gaze just a moment too long, before turning back to her notepad. 'I'm trying to track the movements of your group across the weekend. Your wife mentioned that everyone had breakfast together at the campsite on Saturday morning?'

'Yes.'

'That must have been awkward, given the incident around the bonfire the night before?'

He sighs. It was probably naïve to assume the misunderstanding between the kids wouldn't have come up. 'A little, but everyone had slept. Tempers had calmed.'

'Would you say *you* have a fiery temper, Mr Kingsley?'

Max frowns, surprised at the question. 'Under the right circumstances, I suppose. Don't we all, if certain buttons are pushed?' He runs his hands through his thick hair, leans back in his chair. 'I won't deny I was still furious with Dominic when I went to bed, but by the morning I could see that it was important we put the incident behind us, that we re-set – for the sake of the kids, and the rest of the weekend.'

'You weren't upset, still?'

'Maybe a little.'

'Just a little?' Haines looks at him with thinly veiled surprise. 'A grown man roughs up your twelve-year-old son and it's just water under the bridge?'

'No. Not exactly, but I knew Dominic wouldn't apologize. It's not his style. You've probably seen him on that TV show?'

She nods.

'So you'll know he's a blunt instrument. He hams it up for the cameras, but he's made a successful career from his plain-speaking.'

'Some might say he's a bit of a bully,' Haines suggests lightly.

'Well, yes, he has been known to get a little carried away ... heavy-handed, even. He is, fundamentally, a good guy, but he just doesn't back down. It's his ego. I know from experience that you have to let things slide with him. I figured it was best to try to forgive and forget.'

'And how did Mr Davies seem to you on Saturday morning? Do you think he had forgiven? Forgotten?'

Max sighs. He remembers Dominic sitting at the head of the long table quietly nursing a tin mug of coffee, his eyes hidden behind dark Wayfarers. To the untrained eye, he still looked like the Dom that Max had greeted over the years, after any other big night out. The same Dom he had lived with at university, seen slumped at a breakfast table, wearing his hangovers like a badge of honour. But Max knew Dom. He could see the tension in the rigid set of his shoulders and his clenched jaw. 'Dom was a little bristly,' he tells the police officer, 'but that's his way. He's always played the alpha of the group, and we've always indulged him. Mostly, I put his grumpiness down to a hangover.'

'How was Phoebe?'

'Phoebe was fine, totally fine, playing happily with the other kids. Besides the bandage on her face, you'd never have known anything had happened. It really was just a scratch.'

'And Kip?'

Max bit his lower lip. 'Shaken. I'd talked to him up at the house after the incident. I'd told him that what he'd done was wrong, that there's never an excuse for physical violence. I asked him to try to put himself in Phoebe's shoes, to see things from her side. I could see he was sorry. I suggested he try to join in with the other kids more, but it's hard for him, with his "difficulties".'

'Could you explain what you mean by "difficulties"?' asks Haines, zeroing in on his words.

Max kicks himself. He hadn't wanted to get into this, but now he's opened the door and the woman is sitting opposite him with that inquisitive look on her face, he knows he'll have to continue. 'Look, I'll be honest. We knew early into the adoption process that Kip had some behavioural issues. We were told we would have more luck – that the process would move more quickly – if we were open to adopting an older child. Most couples want babies. Newborns. We heard it time and time again. But it didn't matter to us. We just wanted to be parents. It was that simple.' He shrugged.

'Kip was six when he came to live with us. He'd spent over a year in foster care, and prior to that, from what little we've been told, his family life had been . . . chaotic. We weren't privy to everything, but we understood from the social worker that he'd been exposed to substance abuse issues, domestic assault, withholding of food . . . that sort of thing. I'm sure you've seen it a hundred times over in your work.'

She nods. 'Sadly, yes.'

Max swallows and takes a moment to compose himself. Even just thinking of those earliest days with Kip brings a storm of emotion surging back. Six years ago and it still feels like yesterday, gazing into the rear-view mirror at the skinny little boy sitting in the back seat of their car staring silently out of the window as they had driven him home from his foster carer's suburban terrace. He could still remember the way Kip had trooped upstairs and sat quietly on the edge of the bed in the room they had freshly decorated for him, his head bowed, his dark hair falling into his eyes, one small suitcase still shut tightly resting at the end of the bed, as if he were afraid to open it, afraid to show any sign that he might – this time – be staying somewhere for good.

They had taken painstaking care to help him settle, doing everything gently, allowing Kip to go at his own pace; trying not to smother him with their affection, their desire to be the best parents they could be, their wish to somehow make up for all the hurt he had already experienced in his short life; trying not to want him to *be* anything other than exactly what he was: a fragile, broken-hearted six-year-old boy.

He remembers all of his and Annie's anxious, late-night conversations in bed. *Do you think he misses them? Do you think he'll be happy here? Do you think he likes us? Do you think we can be everything he needs us to be?*

After the pain of their fertility issues and the trauma of their failed IVF attempts, becoming a father through adoption – a path so different to any Max had ever imagined – held many layers of complex emotion. Not just the love and the gratitude that finally something had gone right for them, but also the fear that Max himself might not be enough, might be found wanting of this incredible gift they had been entrusted with. He remembers how they'd reassured each other that all it would take was love and patience. That in turn they would earn Kip's trust – his love. It would just take time.

It hadn't been easy. There had been the many evenings they had lain awake listening to Kip's night terrors, the careful, respectful distance they had given him, while trying to show him they would never be a threat to him, and perhaps the worst day of all, when Annie had discovered the food he had been secretly stashing beneath his bed – half sandwiches, rotting fruit and bags of crisps he'd been hiding – security, they'd realized, in case they too ever forgot to feed him or punished him with starvation, a fact that had made Annie burst into inconsolable tears when she'd realized the extent of what he had suffered.

Sometimes the process of helping Kip feel at home with them – feel like family – was overwhelming, and while Kip six years on still wouldn't call them 'Mum' or 'Dad', the one thing Max had known without a shadow of a doubt from his very first night in their home, was that he was going to try his very best to love and protect their little boy with the fiercest, truest love any father had ever felt. Whatever Kip's needs might prove to be, Max knew it was on him to do whatever it took to fulfil them. He wasn't going to let him down, not like every other adult Kip had encountered. He wouldn't give up on him.

'Mr Kingsley?' The police officer brings him back to the farmhouse kitchen. 'You mentioned Kip's "challenges"?'

He swallows, tries to compose himself to answer her question. 'It took time for Kip to learn to trust us, to know that he was safe. We expected that. But sometimes, even now, his emotions will overwhelm him. In certain situations – anything stressful or frightening – he'll withdraw. He simply shuts down, stops speaking – can't speak. It's debilitating for him and it affects his relationships with others. The therapist we took him to in London suggested he suffers from an anxiety disorder called "selective mutism".'

The police officer is looking up with interest, her pen poised over the notebook. 'Could you give me an example?'

Max nods. 'Kip was going quite well at primary school until his last year, when a couple of kids took against him. There was some bullying . . . kid's stuff . . . you know the sort of thing. Unfortunately, Kip stopped talking overnight – just like that. There was one teacher who didn't understand . . . who seemed to think he was being rude. She lost patience with him and, we later found out from some of his classmates, grabbed him by the arm and shook him. Unfortunately, Kip responded in . . . a rather *physical* way.'

'What do you mean by that?'

'He doesn't like to be touched by people, particularly people he doesn't know well. It's taken Annie and I a long time to build up to hugs and affection with him. Unwelcome or uninvited physical touch seems to trigger something in him. From what I understand, when the teacher grabbed him, he lashed out in panic. I don't believe he truly knew what he was doing,' he adds quickly.

'Lashed out? Meaning?'

'He punched her. He gave her a black eye.' Max, seeing the woman's surprise, feels a surge of anger. Everyone was so quick to judge when really they knew nothing about Kip, nothing at all. 'Annie and I didn't feel the school handled it well. We weren't happy with their approach. They focused more on punishing Kip than they did on working with the teacher or tackling the triggers for his behaviour. It's one of the reasons we decided to move down here. We're home-schooling him now. It's a new beginning for all of us. Kip's a great kid,' he insists, hating himself for how desperate he sounds, how much he wants her to understand and agree. 'He's just . . . a little different.'

'Would you say, Mr Kingsley, that your son has a propensity to physical violence?'

'No,' says Max adamantly, horrified at where the conversation has led them. 'That's definitely *not* what I am saying. Not at all. Kip is a child. Children don't always have full control over their impulses, do they? For a boy with Kip's experiences, I imagine having even a single marshmallow taken from him would've been triggering. But an adult? An adult should have control. Dominic's reaction was over the top. His aggression has pushed Kip right back. But as I said,' he adds hastily, clearing his throat, 'come Saturday morning, I thought it best we all just move past the incident. Let it lie.'

Let it lie. He wonders if the Family Liaison Officer can tell that he's lying. He wonders if she can sense how he is papering over the cracks, hiding the deep fissure that had opened up overnight in his and Dominic's friendship. Because the truth was, that when he woke too early on Saturday morning, before he'd even opened his eyes, he was reliving that moment by the fire pit – Dominic's awful lunge for Kip, the way he had hauled him up by the scruff of his shirt, the fear he'd seen in his son's eyes, the humiliating damp patch blooming on his shorts. Remembering it all, Max had felt hot fury rise up in him like acid.

'You're going to have to let it go,' Annie warned him, rolling across their bed, putting her arms around him. 'We invited them all here. The weekend will be ruined if you can't move past this. You're going to have to try, for all our sakes.'

'How can you forgive him? He hurt our son.'

'I'm not sure I have, yet. But it's going to be the longest long weekend if we can't at least try.' Annie stroked his arm lightly. 'You have to remember, none of them can possibly understand what he's been through. You were adamant, remember? You wanted him to start with us with a clean slate. No sad history. No judgement. You didn't want any of them to know about his past.'

'Because I didn't want them to judge him.' Max swallowed. 'I didn't want them to judge us.'

'But what if that was a mistake? If they knew, perhaps they'd tread more gently? Perhaps Dom might have tempered his outburst last night?'

Max turned to meet her gaze. 'And what if knowing only made it worse – made everyone more angry, more suspicious? Do you really want to take that risk?'

Annie sighed. 'I don't know, love.' She lay back against the pillow. 'We'll deal with it as best we can. We always do. He's our son. We love him. We'll help him through.'

They had driven back to the campsite in the buggy as a threesome that morning, the trailer bouncing behind them filled with cartons of fresh milk and orange juice, Annie with two large boxes of eggs balanced in her arms. Jim was clowning around with the kids throwing a frisbee in the meadow, so Max steered Kip to sit in a deckchair beneath the shelter, as far away as possible from where Dominic sat alone, ominously quiet, as the others bustled around. Suze, looking fresh-faced and wholesome in her loose yoga clothes, her curly hair tied up in a scarf, colourful bead earrings swinging from her lobes, unpacked a cloth bag containing a glass jar of granola and two loaves of dense-looking bread. 'All homemade,' she said proudly.

'Impressive. I can barely find the time to make beans on toast these days,' said Kira, her white shirt unbuttoned as she fed Asha.

'All right, little man?' Jim asked Kip, throwing him a friendly smile as he passed.

Kip nodded and Max gave Jim a grateful nod. At least someone was making an effort.

'Suze and I thought we heard gunshots earlier this morning,' Jim said lightly. 'Is there a shooting range nearby?'

Max frowned. He felt Annie's frustrated glance in his direction. 'No. No range. That would be our friendly neighbour, Kellow, again. He likes to shoot at the wild rabbits. Says it's necessary pest control.'

'How cruel,' Suze sighed.

Annie nudged his shoulder. 'Of all the weekends,' she murmured. 'Nothing like making his presence felt.'

Max squeezed her arm. 'Come on now, we don't know he's doing it to wind us up.'

'Don't we?' Annie shook her head. 'Where are Tanya and Scarlet?' she asked, addressing the rest of the group. 'Will they be joining us for breakfast?'

'Scarlet's getting herself ready, so we'll probably see her sometime this afternoon. Tan's having a lie-in,' said Dominic.

'Course she is,' muttered Suze, clattering a pan onto the open stove a little more loudly than was entirely necessary.

'I don't want to rain on anyone's parade,' Max announced, 'but we should make the most of the sunshine this morning. I caught the tail end of a weather report back at the house. We might see a front moving in from the north.'

'No way. Look at that sky.' Kira raised her sunglasses and gazed about. 'It's picture-perfect.'

'The weather can change fast on the coast,' Annie warned.

'Exactly,' said Jim. 'It might miss us completely.'

Max shrugged. 'All I'm saying is don't pack away your raincoats just yet.'

As the smell of frying bacon lifted into the air, Tanya emerged from the nearest bell tent.

'Look at you,' said Annie, in obvious astonishment. 'That's quite a dress.'

Tanya glanced down, tugging at the clinging floral fabric. Her slim, brown legs were bare, her feet clad in suede ankle boots. 'Thanks. It's Balenciaga.'

Suze stared at her blankly.

'The weather's so nice I thought a summer dress . . .' Tanya trailed off.

'You look as if you're headed to a fancy garden party, not camping here with us. Tea?' Suze waved a pot at her. 'Or there's some turmeric chai I brewed earlier, if you'd rather?'

'I'm more of a coffee person first thing.' Tanya flicked her hair. 'I asked Dom to put our Nespresso machine in the back of the car. I thought there might be somewhere to plug it in?'

Suze laughed, then stopped herself when she realized Tanya wasn't joking. 'Yes, you could do that. Or there's a cafetiere over there? Might be easier?'

Tanya gave the coffee pot a long, hard stare before she helped herself, pouring milk from the carton into her tin mug just as Fred appeared, loping up from the far end of the campsite, his tall frame clownish in Kira's flannel pyjamas, dark sunglasses and a pair of yellow welling-ton boots, his red hair sticking up at funny angles from his head. A pink towel hung casually over his shoulder. He stopped to high-five the kids as he passed them in the meadow.

'Here's one fit for Glastonbury.' Suze poured tea from the large earthenware pot and handed the steaming mug to Fred. 'You look like you could do with this.'

'Thanks.' He slurped from the cup before turning to Kira. 'Babe, I can't find my bag anywhere.'

'I told you last night, I thought I saw it under our tent porch. Did you look?'

He nodded. 'Not there.'

Kira frowned. 'And you checked the car?'

'Yep.'

Kira turned to the others. 'Does anyone remember carrying a blue rucksack to our tent last night?' She was met by blank faces and shrugs.

Fred frowned. 'Shit. Maybe we did leave it behind.'

'*We?*' she asked pointedly.

'I suppose with the pram and all the clobber in the hall,' he scratched his head, 'it's entirely possible I overlooked it. Guess I'll be borrowing clothes and using your toothbrush for the rest of the weekend.' He downed his tea before wandering off towards the shower block.

Jim put his fingers to his mouth and let out a piercing whistle, a signal for all the kids to come. Almost immediately, the table beneath the wooden shelter descended into a free-for-all of bowls and plates and cutlery, jugs of milk and bacon sandwiches.

Seeing Kira struggling to butter a piece of toast, Tanya offered to hold Asha. Max watched as she lifted the baby and cooed down at her. 'She's so precious,' Tanya said, smiling, delighting in the baby's reaction to the faces she was pulling. 'All big eyes and chubby cheeks. Reminds me of Phoebe at that age. Almost makes me broody again.'

Max glanced across at Dominic. On a normal day he knew they might have exchanged an amused look, but Dominic turned away, still sullen.

Kira jammed a slice of toast into her mouth and held her arms out for Asha. 'It's okay,' she mumbled, 'I'll take her.'

'So,' said Annie brightly, 'plans for today?'

'I'm dying to see inside your farmhouse,' Kira said.

Max saw Annie's frown and knew exactly what she was going to say. 'It's a mess. I'm ashamed to say we still haven't unpacked half our moving boxes. All our time and energy has been spent getting Wildernest up and running.'

'You could show them the plans for the farmhouse that we've drawn up?' he suggested. 'They're not approved yet, but you'd get a good idea of the project.'

'I'm in,' Suze declared. 'Tanya, how about you?'

'A WAGs jaunt?' she asked, sipping her coffee. 'Sounds fun, only I thought I might head into St Ives.'

There was a moment's silence.

'Are you sure?' Even Dominic looked a little surprised.

'Parking will be a nightmare,' warned Annie. 'A bank holiday weekend brings the tourists flocking.'

Tanya shrugged. 'I've always wanted to visit. Seems silly to come all this way and not go.'

'Is this about what happened last night, Tanya?' Suze asked, the only one brave enough to say what they were all thinking. 'Can't we leave all that silliness behind us?'

'No,' said Tanya, just a little too quickly. 'Of course it's not about that. You know me,' she smiled brightly, 'I just love shopping.'

The awkward exchange was interrupted by a high shriek rising from the shower block. Dominic leapt in his chair. 'What the—'

Seconds later, Scarlet came racing out of the low building, her long hair wet and plastered around her shoulders, her body only just covered by a small white towel.

'What is it, Scarlet?' Dominic called.

She didn't answer, but ran for the nearest bell tent, her cheeks flaming red.

'Probably a spider,' laughed Felix. 'I saw a huge one in there earlier.'

Max's heart sank. 'I meant to warn you guys about the lack of locks on the shower stalls. They're coming next week. I think Fred might've just given Scarlet a bit of a surprise.'

Dominic frowned. 'Should I go check she's okay?'

Tanya patted his shoulder. 'Stay here. I'll go. She's probably embarrassed.'

Suze turned her attention back to the arrangements. 'So if Tanya's taking herself off on a jolly, that leaves the dads in charge here.' She turned to face the men. 'You guys don't mind, do you?'

'Sure,' said Jim. 'We'll babysit.'

Annie and Suze exchanged an irritated glance. 'Technically, it's not "babysitting" when they're *your* kids,' corrected Annie. 'It's *parenting*.'

'Look,' said Kira, pointing to the sky as a huge flock of brown birds rose off the headland, swooping low over the meadow before massing into a single, shifting form that soared away inland.

'Wow,' breathed Suze. 'Beautiful.'

'Shearwaters, I think,' said Max, holding his hand up to shield his eyes as he watched them fly away.

'Where the hell are they going?' Jim turned to them in amusement.

'St Ives, from the sound of it,' answered Dominic drily.

'So, we're decided? We'll all rendezvous back here this afternoon.'

Jim clapped his hands together and everyone fixed

112

bright smiles on their faces, trying to pretend that the tension still simmering between Dominic and Max didn't exist.

The sound of the phone ringing in the farmhouse kitchen breaks Max's account of the morning gathering. It pulls him back to the table, to where the police officer scribbles his recollections in her notebook. 'Should I get that?' he asks, as if it isn't his own phone, in his own house.

He's hoping it will be Tanya calling from the hospital with an update, or perhaps Josh, asking if he should come in for work tomorrow, but it's neither. 'It's for you,' he says, holding out the handset to the policewoman.

Max hovers, eavesdropping on the one-sided conversation, trying to glean some sense of what might be going on. Haines gives a few terse answers, scribbles some notes before saying goodbye and replacing the handset. Her face, when she turns back to him, is sombre.

'Has something happened?' he asks, unable to feign disinterest.

'There's been a development,' she says.

Max waits but she doesn't seem to want to expand.

'DI Lawson is heading this way now,' she says after a long moment. 'I'm sure she'll speak to you all in due course.'

Max nods. He glances at the open pages of her book. It's hard to read her writing upside down, but his eyes land on two letters written in capitals and circled in neat, black biro. *DB*. The initials don't mean anything to him, but the next two words do: *Morvoren Point*.

Seeing his interest, Officer Haines flips her notepad shut and tucks it away.

'Shall we continue?' Her voice is bright, but Max isn't fooled. There is a steely edge in her tone, a new grim set to her jaw. The police have found something. Something bad.

THE POLICE

Sunday afternoon

'What's the DB's location?' Lawson asks, zipping up her windcheater, before striding out towards the stationary helicopter settled like a bird of prey on the headland.

'The coastguard spotted it on the cliffs below,' says the leader of the search and rescue crew. 'It's not going to be an easy retrieval. We've got a team assessing the descent now, before we rope up.'

'We'll need to get a move on,' she says, checking her watch. '5.40pm. We've got three hours until sunset.'

Lawson strides to the cliff's edge, Barnett close behind. She peers over and sees the body below, snagged between two shards of granite, like a fish caught in the jaws of a yawning mouth. The rescue worker was right. The high tide from the storm and the huge swell still moving across the bay will make it a difficult recovery.

They stand back, watching as the area is sealed off, and the team finally begin their descent. There is a fair amount of swearing from the unit as they abseil their way down the rockface to meet the coastguard's boat bobbing in the cove. Carefully, the body is extricated from the rocks, the team maintaining a respectful silence as it is raised on a stretcher back to the top.

As the body comes into view, one of the newer members of the team moves away and retches into the nearby bracken. The pathologist, a tall woman dressed in white, steps forward. She bends over the body, her face impassive as she appraises it with her keen gaze, noting the devastating wounds and deep lacerations, testing the rigor mortis status with her fingers.

'Anything obvious leaping out at you?' asks DI Lawson, joining her colleague beside the body.

'My best guess? I'd say they've been dead around twelve to fifteen hours. I can narrow that down with the autopsy.'

'And the injuries?'

'You don't need me to tell you those head wounds would've been catastrophic.' She points to the caved-in skull, the hair matted with blood. No one could survive trauma like that.'

'Consistent with a fall?'

'Yes, I'd say so. The head's cracked open like eggshell.'

The pathologist leans over the cliff edge and points to the treacherous, jutting shards of rock and the tall granite stacks below. 'Anyone going over the edge here will pinball off the rocks, so all the injuries could very well have occurred in the fall.' She frowns. 'It's just this one.' She points to the victim's torso. 'I could be wrong, but it looks more consistent with a stab wound.'

Lawson frowns, eyeing the blood smeared across the victim's top.

'One thing I do know – I'm going to need dental records to provide a formal identification.'

Lawson studies the victim's hands. Smooth. Line-free. Young. Too young to die.

As they lift the corpse from the stretcher and seal it into a body bag, the supervising technician reaches out with a gloved hand and gently tucks a fold of blue sweatshirt fabric inside the bag, before the zipper is pulled over the shattered face. Lawson gives a wave and the stretcher is carried to the helicopter waiting up on the headland.

As the chopper starts its engines, blades beating the air, Lawson spins in a slow circle, surveying the site in full. She sees the crumbling stone ruins in the distance, the overgrown path winding away across the clifftops and, standing amongst a clump of sea campion and thrift fluttering in the gusts from the helicopter's rotor blades, a small wooden cross perched a short distance from the ledge. 'Let's get the area sealed off. I want a fingertip search. No stone left unturned. No one uses the coastal path until I say so. Someone get in touch with Haines at the farmhouse again. Tell her to apply a little more pressure. I don't care how tired, how emotional or how bloody famous they think they are. Someone knows more than they're letting on.'

'You think this is linked to the gathering at the campsite?' Barnett asks, turning to his boss.

She regards him with a grim look. 'Without a shadow of a doubt.'

TANYA

Sunday evening

Tanya's head jolts forward, the sudden movement waking her from a fitful sleep. She has been sitting in the same hunched position in the visitor's chair for what feels like hours, and her shoulders and back are stiff, her eyes gritty. She stands and stretches, checks for any signs of wakefulness from the bed beside her before leaving the curtained cubicle.

Her reflection in the bathroom mirror is a shock. She is pale and drawn, black mascara smudged beneath her red-rimmed eyes adding to the deep, violet shadows already there. She splashes cold water onto her face, scrubs at her armpits with a damp paper towel and tries to comb her hair with her fingers, noticing the chips in her Shellac manicure. It's a pitiful attempt to improve her wretched appearance. The toll of the weekend is etched plainly on her face.

Back in the corridor, she slides coins into a vending machine for a cup of coffee before following a looping maze to the front entrance of A&E. The automatic doors glide open and expel her out into a car park where the light is starting to fade, the sun sliding down behind a bank of tall trees. The wind, calmer now, tugs at their branches, making them bend and wave. Spring leaves are scattered across the grey asphalt like confetti and over by the roadside she sees a one-way sign lying toppled on its side, the only indications of the wild storm that had passed through the night before. After the sterile environment of the hospital, she welcomes the slap of fresh air on her cheeks.

An older man, hunched and skinny, knobbly knees visible beneath his flapping hospital gown, stands just outside the doors, still hooked up to his drip as he puffs greedily on a cigarette. Tanya moves away from his drifting smoke and leans against the wall to sip her too-hot coffee and check her phone. The battery is on its last red bar. There's nothing from Dominic, which must mean he is still in with the police. Not that she'd want to speak to him anyway.

She scrolls through her phone and tries Max first, whose number goes straight to voicemail. Annie's phone rings and rings. She imagines her sitting at the farmhouse, ignoring her name as it flashes on her screen, until she remembers there isn't any mobile phone coverage up at the farm.

Trawling back through old emails, she eventually finds Annie's last message with the directions to Wildernest and the landline number for the farmhouse at the bottom. The phone rings twice before it connects. 'Oh my god, Tanya,' says Suze, breathless with relief. 'We've been worried sick. How is she?'

'Still unconscious.'

'Do you know anything yet?'

'Nothing.' Tanya closes her eyes, suddenly frightened by all the possibilities that lie ahead. 'How is everyone there?' she asks. 'Are the kids okay?'

'They're fine, I promise. They're being complete troopers. I've fed them and settled them in front of a film, that Pixar one about the robot. It was the only thing they all agreed on and that I thought would be safe, nothing triggering, you know? We saw helicopters and sniffer dogs earlier,' she adds. 'A whole team of them out on the cliffs. It was like something out of a movie.'

Like a movie, yes . . . or perhaps a nightmare. She'd like to wake up now, please.

Suze continues, talking fast, relaying as much as she can. 'There's a Family Liaison Officer from the police here. She's interviewing everyone. Max is with them at the moment.'

'The police are here too. They want to talk to me,' says Tanya, 'but the doctors have told them to wait, for now.'

Suze goes quiet. 'It's just unbelievable.' She hesitates. 'Have you spoken to Dominic?'

'No.' Another silence. What is she supposed to say?

'I'm so sorry, Tanya.'

Tanya bites her lip. She doesn't want sympathy. She doesn't want to be pitied.

'I keep asking myself how something like this could have happened? What we all missed? We all feel so guilty.'

Tanya feels a surge of irritation at the use of 'we'. 'I have no idea what's gone on yet, but one thing's clear in my mind: someone knows *something*. The police will find out.'

Suze is silent. Tanya's words hang between them, like a threat.

'I'd better go,' says Tanya, suddenly wanting to get off the line, wanting to be back at the bedside where she belongs, 'my phone's about to die.'

'Tanya ...' Suze adds quickly, before she can hang up, 'we're all so sorry. I hope you know that. You take care, okay?'

Tanya's eyes are filling with tears as she rings off. She leans back against the solid brick wall of the hospital and brushes at her face, staring up at the shifting sky, trying to focus on something other than her profound fear that everything is now fundamentally broken – irreparably so. She reaches for the scarf hanging around her neck, dabbing at the tears, pressing her face into the soft silk. It is, she realizes, the same scarf that she'd bought just twenty-four hours ago in St Ives.

Could it really only be yesterday that she'd walked the winding streets of the seaside town, brushed shoulders with the milling tourists, inhaled the scent of lattes and buttery pastry, ran her fingers across rails of Breton-striped tops and summer dresses? It didn't seem possible that her shopping jaunt remained so sharp in her memory – so tantalizingly close – when absolutely everything else seemed so nightmarishly muddled.

As she tries to compose herself, the automatic doors

slide open and expel a young girl and her mother. Tanya watches them walk hand-in-hand across the car park, the little girl with her braided pigtails safely shepherded to a waiting vehicle. Her phone buzzes in her pocket. Checking the screen, she sees Dominic's number flashing. She watches it, frozen, waiting for it to go through to her voicemail. He is close by, somewhere inside, but the thought of talking to him, of facing him right now, is too much.

What had Suze asked her just now on their phone call? *What signs did we miss?*

Tanya shakes her head. What a question. She knows Suze was referring to the weekend, to the escalating events, the shock of all that's happened. But if she were to apply the same question to Dominic – to her marriage – she knows she would weep.

DOMINIC

Sunday evening

Dominic is in a furious mood as he stalks the hospital corridors. Ever since the police had rushed away mid-interview, to investigate an 'important development', he's been hoping to find Tanya. Lawson had asked him to wait in the interview room, but he was damned if he was just going to sit there like a naughty schoolboy on detention. He needed to speak with Tanya. He needed to see his child.

He'd tried Tan's mobile first, but when she didn't pick up, he'd slipped from the interview room and navigated the corridors of the ward until he'd found the right curtained cubicle. He stood for a very long time, watching the steady rise and fall of her chest, listening to the terrifying hiss and beep of the machines surrounding her, praying that she would wake at any minute and throw him that cheeky smile he loved so much. It tore him apart to see her like this.

Although Tanya wasn't there, there were signs that she

had been – her denim jacket slung across the back of a chair, a packet of tissues, a lip balm and a half-drunk cup of water on the bedside table.

He wanders the corridors, checks the nurses' station and is about to head outside to scour the hospital grounds when he sees the detectives returning through the automatic glass doors, DI Lawson striding into the hospital reception with a resolved expression, DC Barnett right behind.

'Mr Davies,' Lawson says, frowning to see him there. She indicates that he should turn and follow. 'We're ready to continue now.'

'What was it?' he asks, glancing between the two of them. 'Anything important?'

'If you don't mind,' says Barnett, ushering him down the corridor, 'we'll talk in private.'

Back in the interview room, Barnett presses the red button on their recorder and kicks off the questions. They aren't wasting any time. 'Whose idea was it that the kids should go off on their own?'

Dominic, back in the hot seat, looks from Barnett to Lawson and narrows his eyes, resentful of the accusation lurking in the question. 'We didn't *decide* that they would "go off on their own". It was just one of those things. The kids were pestering us, as kids do, and we agreed that they could go.' He waits. 'Did you talk to the boy? Was that where you went?'

He knows he is coming over as aggressive, but what did the police expect when they left him waiting for such an unfathomable amount of time? It was enough to drive a sane man demented. 'Look, I really don't see how any of this is helping. At a time like this, I should be with my family.'

'Of course, Mr Davies. We understand your frustration.' Barnett is using his amiable, nice-guy voice. 'Everything that you tell us helps to build a picture of the events of the weekend. It's important that we track exactly what happened out there so that we can bring justice to whoever is responsible. I'm sure you want answers just as much as we do.'

Dominic regards the junior constable through narrowed eyes. He doesn't look much older than Scarlet, with that bum fluff sprouting on his chin and the pink shaving rash rising near the collar of his shirt. He turns to Lawson, hoping to appeal to her feminine sensibilities. 'I'd really like to talk to my wife.'

Lawson leans forward in her chair and fixes him with a hard stare. 'Mrs Davies has said that she doesn't want to see you right now. Do you have any idea why?'

Dominic's cheeks redden. 'She's upset, naturally. After everything that's happened . . . who wouldn't be?'

'Indeed, though some might say traumatic events such as these would bring a family together. It seems curious, her desire to avoid you.' Her words hang pointedly in the air between them.

'I can't speak for my wife. You'll have to ask her about that.'

'We certainly intend to.' She gives Barnett a nod, the signal to continue.

Barnett clears his throat. 'Returning to Saturday, we

understand the dads were left in charge of the kids – all the children bar Scarlet, who went shopping in St Ives with her stepmother.'

'That's right.' Dominic folds his arms across his chest and lifts his chin. 'Annie, Suze and Kira went up to the farmhouse, leaving us chaps in charge.'

'So, to my earlier question,' says Barnett, 'whose idea was it that the children went off on their own?'

Dominic casts his mind back. It was such a blur. Was it Jim's idea? Was it *his*? From the jumble in his mind, a moment comes back to him, around midday, when the sun still slanted across the peninsula, the clouds just a bank of grey far out at sea, and he, Jim and Fred sat slouched in deckchairs near the fire pit. The kids were throwing a frisbee in the meadow. Max was off somewhere with that Josh lad, sorting out a problem with the septic tank system, the mere mention of which had been enough to keep the other three men firmly ensconced in their seats. The last moment of relative calm, Dom realizes, before it all went to utter shit.

There was no denying that things had still been tense between him and Max, though Dominic felt sure it would be fine, as soon as Max and that kid apologized. Dominic had watched Max and Josh head away up the slope, Josh hesitating for a moment, turning back to stare in their direction, before disappearing behind the shower block. 'Is it just me,' he asked, 'or is that lad kind of intense?'

'Which one?' asked Fred.

'The one with the tattoos. Josh.'

Jim shrugged. 'Maybe he's a bit overawed. Some people get like that around "famous" people. I mean, who can blame him? You are utterly *dazzling* in the flesh, Dom. Though that could just be your new veneers.' Jim made a show of pretending to be blinded, pulling his cap down over his eyes.

Dominic leaned over and punched him on the arm, almost tipping him from his deckchair.

Still laughing as he righted himself, Jim reached into the top pocket of his shirt. 'Guess what I've got.' He revealed a fat reefer, rolled and ready to be lit.

Dominic shot a glance in the direction of the kids. 'Shit mate, don't let them see that.'

Jim's laugh was a soft, deep rumble. The sound reminded Dominic of long ago when the two of them would sit up into the small hours after their late-night student radio show, passing a bong back and forth at the kitchen table in their flat, playing tunes and creasing each other up with inappropriate jokes and outlandish stories.

'They're miles away.'

'I don't know ... with this hangover I might just pass out.'

Fred nodded. 'I don't have the stamina. Not since Asha.'

'Ah, those early years,' Jim sighed, pocketing the spliff before lifting his trucker's cap and spinning it backwards, resting his hands on his head. 'You're in the thick of it now, Fred, but trust me mate, it gets easier.'

Fred grinned. 'I took Kira out last week to celebrate the one-year anniversary of our first date. A main course each, half a bottle of red wine and we were home and in bed by nine. Crazy times.'

'Hangovers are no fun when you've got to be up at the

crack of dawn with a baby,' agreed Dom. 'Parenthood changes us.'

'Just you wait. In a few years you'll have hair loss and an expanding waistline to contend with. The dad bod gets us all eventually.' Jim patted his beer belly with pride.

'Speak for yourself,' bristled Dom. 'We haven't *all* let ourselves go.'

Fred pressed at one of his forearms, studying the pink flush on his pale skin. 'I'm not sure my delicate Irish complexion can take much more of this sun. If you'll excuse me gents, I'm going to take the opportunity for a little lie down, while the ladies are otherwise engaged.'

Jim and Dom waved Fred away, watching as he crossed the dusty meadow to his tent, stopping halfway to lob a misthrown frisbee back to Willow. 'Do you think we should join in with the kids?' Dominic asked.

'Ah man,' said Jim, opening one eye, 'they're fine. We don't need to hover over them every minute. Kids need their freedom.'

Dominic frowned. 'I wasn't suggesting we hover over them.' He resented the implication. 'My kids find *plenty* of ways to test the boundaries.' He looked around then lowered his voice. 'Scarlet was busted at school with a bag of weed in her rucksack. Dope at school! They excluded her for two weeks.'

'She's all right. She's just bucking against the system. That's what teenagers do. Look at us. We had our own share of wild times, didn't we?' Jim winked at him.

'That was different. We were older, living away from home. Scarlet's sixteen, still a kid.'

Jim shrugged. 'They grow up fast these days. You need to relax, chill out a little.'

Dominic stared at Jim. Could there be anything more infuriating than being told to *chill out* by one of life's greatest slackers? There was a time, back when he and Clare had still been married, when they had joked between them that it was Jim and Suze's kids they'd need to watch. 'Those poor kids, saddled with their hippy names . . . and all that airy-fairy forest school and free-range parenting. You wait,' he'd told his ex-wife, 'they'll be off the rails. Pot heads and teen pregnancies.'

'Or they'll go the other way and rebel against their parents completely,' Clare had suggested. 'They'll be big pharma CEOs and fossil fuel execs by twenty-five.'

It occurred to him, for the first time, that maybe Jim and Suze had been having their own private conversations, laughing at their parenting style and joking about how *his* kids would turn out. The thought made him cross.

His take had always been that kids needed rules. Kids should hear 'no' just as much as they heard 'yes'. That was his motto. Though sitting in the sunshine, watching Jim's kids playing frisbee in the meadow, he couldn't see anything wrong with the Miller brood. They looked like charming, confident, annoyingly wholesome youngsters. More to the point, he hadn't heard a single whine for an electronic device come from them since they'd arrived. He scratched his chin. Maybe there was something in what Jim was saying?

Sensing Dominic's shifting mood, Jim smiled. 'That's it, man. You just need to breathe. Life's good.'

'What do you think of Kira's new toy boy?' Dominic asked, keen to change the subject.

'Fred? Seems like a nice enough guy. It's good to see Kira happy. Quite the change from last year,' he added. A thoughtful look passed over his face. 'You remember how she was at her birthday last March.'

Dominic shrugged. 'I guess turning forty is as good a reason as any to let your hair down.'

'If that's what you want to call it,' said Jim with a smirk.

They both knew Kira had done more than let her hair down. Dom could still recall the sight of her knocking back cocktails at her birthday dinner, the tearful, impromptu speech she had given standing at the head of the table, swaying as she'd lambasted them all. 'Motherhood's changed her.'

'I guess we've all changed. Twenty years of friendship. It's inevitable, don't you think? I read somewhere recently that the cells in our bodies renew every seven years.'

'If that's the case, we're different people – literally – from when we all first met.'

'Yeah, I'm almost onto my third incarnation!'

Dominic shook his head. 'There goes that theory. You'll never change, mate – forever Peter Pan, living for the good times.'

The words, as they left his mouth, sounded harsher than he'd intended. He squinted in the sunshine at Jim. It was the first time all weekend that it had been just the two of them. Now was the perfect time to bring up the loan. 'So,' he asked, careful to keep his voice casual, 'you haven't been avoiding my calls?'

'Course not.' He noticed that Jim didn't quite meet his eye.

'How is the business coming along? I was half expecting you to bring the truck down here this weekend.'

Jim shrugged and took a long swig of his beer. 'It's getting there, mate. These things don't happen overnight.'

Dom felt a prickle of frustration. Jim owed him more explanation than that. 'You were full of it last year when you pitched the idea to me. You wanted to be up and running by the summer. How far off are you?'

'I hit a few bumps. The truck needs more work than I anticipated.' Jim closed his eyes and leaned back, his face angled towards the sun.

Dominic frowned. Was that it? Was that all he was going to give him? A huge, fifty-thousand-pound-sized favour, and Jim was going to dismiss him like that?

It had been just the two of them drinking coffee in the hotel bar the morning after Kira's fortieth birthday dinner, when Jim had asked him for the money. 'This is it, Dom. I'm telling you,' he'd said, 'a sure-fire money-maker. I was at WOMAD last year and you wouldn't believe the queues for the food trucks. It's the perfect business model for me. It combines all my favourite things: street food, music, travel. I've already found a van. Two young guys in Brighton are selling it on. With some TLC, I reckon I can have it roadworthy in no time.'

Dominic had eyed his friend with a healthy dose of scepticism. 'What does Suze think of all this?'

'She's been on at me for ages to find something I can

throw myself into. Her yoga and wellness studio ticks over nicely, and now the kids are older I don't need to be at home as much. I can still do the youth work freelance,' he'd added hastily, 'in the winter, when the bookings are slow. But my heart would be in the food truck.' He'd drained his cup, setting it back on the table before giving Dominic a searching look. 'This would be something that's all mine.' He'd drawn an imaginary sign. '"Jimbo's Burritos". All I need is a starter loan – a helping hand to get things off the ground. What do you say?'

Dominic had looked around at the hotel bar. The tasteful, abstract monotone prints adorning the wallpapered walls had seemed to shift and morph with his hangover like a psychoanalyst's nightmare. He'd turned back to Jim, aware of the weight of his friend's expectation. 'Fifty grand, you say?'

'Paid back with five per cent interest over three years. I've worked it all out.'

Dominic had rubbed his chin, reached for his espresso and taken a sip.

'Plus beers, burritos and VIP festival passes on the house whenever you want, my friend.'

Dominic had settled his coffee cup on the table between them. 'We're right in the middle of this renovation. Tanya's got expensive taste. She's been fussing about marble floors and frameless glass.' He'd tried to draw Jim into the joke of it, rolling his eyes, but Jim had just sat there, hopeful, staring back at him. 'Have you tried the bank?'

Jim's laugh had been short and dry. 'As if they'd back a loser househusband like me. Come on, man. This could be life-changing.' Jim had thrown him a pleading look. 'Help a mate out?'

Three days later, Dominic had transferred the full amount into Jim's bank account and Jim had emailed his thanks, asked if they could keep it between them. *No need to bother Suze with the details, okay?*

They had barely spoken about the truck – about anything very much – since. Whenever Dominic had phoned, Jim had ducked his calls. Dominic knew he was owed an update, perhaps even a first repayment on the loan. Only it seemed Jim was yet to show any signs of launching his 'sure-fire money-maker' and he sure as hell didn't seem to want to talk about it.

Dom glanced around at the glamping site, at all that Annie and Max had created in a few months, and felt his irritation rise. He used to find Jim's slacker persona charming, but these days his friend's 'easy life' attitude grated. It was all well and good living like a kid in your twenties, but they were adults now. Jim should know better.

And so should Dom. It wasn't as if Jim didn't have form. Dom knew the sort of man he was from their earliest university days. *We'll deal with it manyana, my friend.* It was always Jim, egging him on, pulling him from his assignments, tempting him out to hear some band or try a new club night. Privately, Dom had thought it a miracle that he'd scraped through his sociology degree. Jim had hopped around from job to job ever since, giving up a small-bit broadcasting gig at a local radio station, before abandoning his efforts to launch an indie record label to focus instead on his youth work in Brighton. Meeting Suze was arguably the best thing ever to happen to him. He supposed it was Suze's woke 'throw-your-arms-around-the-world' principles that allowed her to endlessly see the good in him.

When their kids had been born, Jim and Suze had decided that he would be the one to stay at home while Suze focused on her plans for the wellness centre. Personally, Dominic would never have sacrificed his manhood like that, and of course, it was obvious now that Jim was paying a hefty price. For here they were in their forties and while the rest of them had forged ahead with careers, families and homes – had really made something of themselves – Jim still seemed to bumble along in the same old scuffed Converse and baggy shorts, with little to show for his efforts bar his brood of tangle-haired children, an increasingly matted beard and a crumpled pouch of tobacco in his back pocket.

Dom regarded Jim, slumped in his deckchair, trucker cap propped backwards on his head. A tinge of sunburn was beginning to bloom across the bridge of his nose, sweat patches spreading out beneath his arms. 'Mate,' he said, a hint of steel in his voice, 'I'm going to need a little more than that. Maybe I should I talk to Suze? Ask her about the repayment schedule?' He knew it was a low blow to threaten to involve Suze, but he had to do something. 'Do you even have a launch date?'

Jim opened his eyes and turned to him, a look on his face the likes of which Dom had not seen before. It wasn't just the sun reflecting in Jim's eyes, it was something hard and flinty, uncompromising. 'It's funny your sudden interest in schedules and dates,' Jim said quietly, his smile not quite meeting his eyes. 'I'd have thought you'd have your own dates and timings to be worrying about.'

Dominic's hand tightened on the arm of his chair. What the hell was he on about? Why was Jim dicking around, being so cryptic?

'Daddy!' Phoebe, leaving the other kids in the meadow, ran to his chair and tugged on his sleeve. 'Daddy!'

Dom pulled his gaze from Jim. 'What is it, sweetheart?' He lifted her onto his lap. She held the brown smudge of her teddy nestled in the crook of one arm.

'Everyone's going to the rope swing.'

She delivered it as a statement, though the question was written plainly on her face. Dominic nuzzled her neck, just below her earlobe, avoiding Jim's eye.

'Stop, Daddy! It tickles.'

Yesterday's plaster was just starting to come loose on one corner of her brow, revealing the red gash above her eye. 'Who's everyone?'

'All the kids. Can I go too?'

'I don't know, Pheebs ... where is it?'

She shrugged. 'Across the fields. You can come?'

Dominic eyed the horizon. A thin, high haze of cloud, like a sheer veil, was drifting across the sun. The air around them felt still and heavy. He ran his finger under his collar. 'You can't go anywhere in those flip flops,' he said, pointing at her feet. 'You'll need trainers.' He knew he was stalling, but she was off, sprinting across the meadow, disappearing inside their tent.

Jim was still staring at him, a strange, intense look on

his face. 'What?' Dominic asked, uncomfortable under such scrutiny.

'It hasn't even occurred to you, has it?'

'What? Just spit it out.'

'Didn't you hear what Fred said just now? He as good as admitted it. He said he and Kira celebrated the anniversary of their first date *last week.*'

'And?'

'Well I'm no obstetrician, but how exactly is that supposed to work?' He waited for Dominic to catch up. 'Asha is five months old.'

Dominic frowned.

His silence seemed to spur Jim on. 'If they only met a year ago, there's no way Fred can be Asha's father.'

Dominic's mouth had grown suddenly dry. He tried to swallow and felt something stick in his throat.

'I can't help but wonder . . .?' Jim lifted his hands and made a show of counting backwards on his fingers. 'She was a November baby. So Asha was conceived in . . . early March?' He threw Dominic an innocent look. 'Remind me, when did we all get together for Kira's birthday?'

Dominic felt winded, as if all the air had been punched from his lungs. He tried to draw breath but the air around him felt too thick and soupy, as if it might choke him. If he could've moved, he would've launched himself out of his chair and wiped Jim's sly smile from his face, but he was pinned in place, paralysed by fear. He cleared his throat. 'I think you've been smoking a bit too much of that weed, mate. You've well and truly lost it.'

Jim rubbed at his beard. 'Have I?'

136

Dominic's mind was racing, churning through dates and possibilities as Phoebe ran back to them, her feet now clad in purple Velcro trainers. 'Pleeeease Daddy,' she implored, giving him her best puppy dog eyes. 'Can I go? Can I?'

Dominic couldn't think straight. His mind was whirling, a rush of nausea rising in his throat. Jim had got it wrong. He had to have got it wrong.

'Hey guys!' Jim called, drawing the attention of the older kids, assembling purposefully by the fire pit. 'You'll look after Phoebe, won't you? Help her with the swing?'

'Sure, Dad.' River brushed his hair from his eyes and gave them both a thumbs-up.

'Juniper, you hold her hand?'

Juniper, hopping around the fire pit in a bright tangerine-coloured T-shirt and denim shorts, turned and grinned. 'Okay, Dad!'

'There you go,' said Jim. 'The bigger ones will watch her. Safety in numbers.'

'Daddy?' Expectation beamed from Phoebe's round face. He saw the dimples in her cheeks, the faint constellation of freckles that had broken out across the bridge of her nose and felt his heart expand with unbearable emotion. It was hard to formulate coherent thought. The kids were right there and Jim was a loose cannon, shooting his mouth off with his wild theories. Dominic needed to get everyone out of earshot. All of them. 'Fine. Go,' he said, releasing his grip on Phoebe. 'Make sure you take your inhaler with you,' he added.

She grinned and patted the pocket on her corduroy dungarees. 'Got it.'

He wanted to add, 'and stay away from *that boy*,' but he swallowed the words, watching as she ran across to join the bigger kids, her feet kicking up small clouds of dust. At the fire pit she stopped and turned back to him with that adorable gap-toothed grin, her bear dangling from one hand. 'Thanks, Daddy.'

Dominic eyed Felix, his stoop-shouldered boy getting so long and lanky. Just yesterday he'd noticed the first, downy hairs sprouting on his son's chin, the bulge of a bicep on his arms. 'Hey Felix, keep an eye on your sister.'

Felix turned away but not before Dominic had seen his son's eye roll. 'Stop worrying, Dad. We'll be fine.'

'Be back for dinner,' called Jim. 'Bring us a bison. We're barbecuing.' He thumped his chest with his fist and deepened his voice. 'Dads make fire. Dads cook meat.'

The older ones cringed at Jim's caveman impression, but they were all smiling as they traipsed down the sloping meadow towards the wooden stile.

Jim didn't waste any time producing the spliff, lighting it with a zippo, inhaling deeply, but Dom was still struggling to process Jim's bombshell. He turned to Jim with growing irritation. 'How'd you square that with your health-nut wife?' he snapped, nodding at the joint.

'She's not a health nut. She's a wellness coach and a yoga teacher.'

'Same thing. If sugar is the devil, surely smoking weed isn't far behind?'

'This is natural. Mother Nature's bounty. Suze still dabbles, when the kids are safely tucked up in bed.' He was already up and heading to the cool box, where he retrieved two cans of pale ale from the chest, fizzing them open, handing one to Dom before settling back into his deckchair with a satisfied sigh. He took another deep inhale on the spliff, before offering it to Dom.

Dom eyed it for a moment, before accepting it from Jim's outstretched hand. Maybe it would help. He took a couple of drags then passed it back, fixing Jim with a stern gaze. 'If you've got something to say, you may as well come right out with it.'

Jim shrugged. 'All I know is that I left you and Kira looking rather cosy that night . . . and if you remember, Suze and I had the room next door.' He threw his hands in the air. 'Let's just say it wasn't my greatest night's sleep.'

'You're talking shit . . .' Dom shook his head. Fuck. This couldn't be happening.

'Has it really not occurred to you at all – the timing of it?'

Dominic swallowed. 'No. Because it's absurd. Kira and I . . . we . . . we didn't . . .'

Dominic couldn't finish his lie. Fear and anger pulsed through his veins. Jim was supposed to be his best friend. He was supposed to have his back. 'So what is this? A threat? If I don't tell Suze about the loan, you won't tell Tan what you *think* you know about me and Kira?' Dominic tried to laugh, to show how preposterous it was.

Jim took another drag on the spliff and exhaled a perfect smoke ring. It rose and vanished in the hazy sky. 'All I'm saying is that there are worse things Tanya could be worrying about than furnishings for your fancy renovation.'

So there it was. Spelled out at last. Jim believed he had something over him, and he was sure as hell going to use it to his advantage. Dominic's fists clenched until his knuckles blanched white. 'This sounds awfully like blackmail.'

'I prefer to think of it as an honest conversation between friends.'

Dom sighed. 'What do you want me to say? Yes, Kira and I had sex. But it was just once. That's all. And Asha? Come off it.' He shook his head. 'The timing might seem a little ... uncanny, but that doesn't make me her dad. Does it?'

He regarded Jim, hoping to see agreement in his face, but Jim wasn't looking at him. He was staring over his shoulder. Behind Dom came the sound of a throat clearing. Dom turned and found Fred standing behind his chair, the colour leaching from his face. Fred gestured half-heartedly at his empty seat. 'I thought I'd left my phone . . .' He gave up trying to explain. He threw Dom a disgusted look before he turned on his heel.

'Fuck,' said Dom, spinning back to Jim. 'You stupid, fucking fuck.'

TANYA

Saturday, midday

It had annoyed her, more than it should've done, that Annie had been right about the parking. She and Scarlet circled St Ives in Dominic's Porsche, creeping through the near-gridlocked one-way system, sliding past whitewashed cottages, art galleries, boutiques, bakeries and cafés, until they found a postage-stamp-sized car park settled on a bluff overlooking the ocean.

'There's no spaces,' Scarlet wailed.

'Someone will leave soon. Keep your eyes peeled.'

Scarlet laid her phone back in the cradle where it was charging, her feet up on the dash. 'Look,' she said, nodding her head at the sky.

Tanya followed her gaze. Above them the sky was turning a strange orange colour, the sun filtered by a shimmering sea haze. Further out, a dark bank of cloud gathered, a mass of grey cumulus, huge and peaked like a distant mountain range rising over the ocean. 'Looks a little ominous.'

'Do you think it'll rain?' Scarlet sounded hopeful.

'It might not come this way.'

'But if it does, do you think we'll go home?'

Tanya shook her head. 'I doubt it. Your dad seems hellbent on fulfilling all his Bear Grylls fantasies.' Seeing Scarlet's weak smile, she decided to seize the rare atmosphere of solidarity that had sprung up between them. 'I'm glad you decided to come with me. I mean, I know it's so that you can charge your phone and message your friends,' she added quickly, 'but I've been thinking it would be nice if you and I spent a little more time together.'

Scarlet nodded noncommittally.

'And I'm sorry about your run-in with Fred in the shower block. I know it was awkward, but it was probably just as embarrassing for him as it was for you.'

'I was washing my hair, shampoo in my eyes, and when I opened them he was just standing there, door ajar, staring at me.'

'Max explained about the locks. Maybe next time you could hum really loudly, so we all know you're in there?'

Scarlet shook her head. 'There won't be a next time. I'd rather stink all weekend than risk being ogled again by that pervert.'

Tanya frowned. Scarlet's damning assessment of Fred seemed rather harsh. The poor man had appeared just as mortified as Scarlet, after the incident had come to light. She decided to change the subject. 'This party last night, it was important to you, wasn't it?'

Scarlet nodded slowly.

'A boy?'

Tanya felt Scarlet's sideways gaze land on her, a brief moment of assessment, before another small nod.

'That's a shame,' said Tanya lightly. 'Still, you looked like you were having a good chat with Josh last night at the bonfire,' she added, giving her the lightest nudge. 'He's pretty cute. A bit old for you, mind. Not sure your dad would approve.'

Scarlet shrugged. 'Don't be ridiculous. It's Harry I like.'

'We'll be home on Monday.'

Scarlet let out a strangled sob. 'But it's only Saturday. He'll have forgotten all about me by Monday.'

Scarlet's distress brought back memories to Tanya of the unique agony of time as a teenager, how a single day could pass in soul-crushing slow motion, how everything good and exciting always seemed to be on the distant horizon, just out of reach, freedom and life steeped in delay and frustration.

'There!' said Scarlet, pointing towards the white reversing lights of a Mini Cooper.

Tanya squeezed the car into the space as Scarlet snatched up her mobile and turned it on, smiling as the screen lit up, the car filling suddenly with the chiming of a steady stream of notifications.

'Doesn't sound like he's forgotten about you,' said Tanya.

Scarlet wasn't listening. She was scrolling through her apps, swiping photos and videos, tapping 'likes' and sending emojis with startling efficiency. Over Scarlet's shoulder, Tanya glimpsed images of leggy girls in short mini dresses, pouting and posing for the camera. There was one of a tall, good-looking boy in a tuxedo, his dark hair flopping into his eyes, another of Scarlet's best friend Lily, looking extraordinarily provocative in a thigh-skimming white dress, all push-up bra, and glossy pouting lips, waving a bottle of champagne at the camera. Scarlet clicked on a video clip and a group of girls came to life under flashing disco lights, arms thrown about each other's shoulders as they shouted the chorus to a song. 'Looks like fun. I'm sorry you had to miss it.'

Scarlet didn't reply. She angled the screen away and kept swiping, two small red dots beginning to burn on her cheeks.

Sensing that their moment of connection was over, Tanya reached for her handbag. 'Do you want to come with me or shall we catch up later? We could meet in an hour at that cafe we drove past, the one with the red-check tablecloths?'

'Sure,' said Scarlet, barely glancing up from her screen. 'See you there.'

It didn't take Tanya long to discover that it was best to give in to the momentum of the crowd. Rather than fight her way through the packed cobbled streets, she submitted to the flow of tourists, like a tide dragging her along. She found it a relief to be away from all that grass and sky, back in relative civilization, surrounded by the buzz of a crowd, her senses enlivened by the scent of ground coffee, the sight of pastries piled high in bakeries, the promise of pretty new things displayed in shop windows.

She braved a couple of busy boutiques, bought a brightly coloured silk scarf and a big bag of fudge for the kids to share, knowing the high sugar content would annoy Suze, before following the winding lanes down to the harbourfront, where a flotilla of tethered fishing boats jostled on the water. A breeze had picked up and the mountainous dark cloud Scarlet had noticed seemed to have drifted closer. A seagull eyed her fudge, then rose from the wall, flapping and shrieking, wheeling away across the grey slate rooftops.

Tanya, feeling the shift in temperature, wrapped her new scarf about her shoulders and walked the promenade, past a group of young men in matching Hawaiian shirts seated at a pub table crowded with pint glasses. They fell silent as she passed by, one of them throwing out a comment about her 'great arse' that she knew she was meant to hear. Tanya felt a small surge of triumph. She had never understood why some women got so uppity about compliments. She'd never minded the male gaze. She'd never been one of those women who felt belittled or objectified. Instead, she tucked the comment away with a sense of triumph. She worked hard for her 'great arse'.

It was a shame Dom wasn't with her, to witness their appreciation. She knew the kind of man her husband was. She knew his vanity, his wandering eye, his desire to be admired, envied even. He'd have taken a certain possessive pride in seeing Tanya coveted by other younger men. And she, in turn, would've taken pride at being seen with Dominic, at the nudges and knowing glances exchanged by strangers as they passed by. *Did you see who that was?*

They'd met just as he was making the jump from radio to TV, when she was working as a hair and make-up artist and he was still mostly known as a voice over the airwaves. Over the course of twelve weeks, as they'd filmed the first successful season of *Star Search*, she'd styled his hair, evened out his fake tan, concealed the shadows under his eyes and powdered the shine on his forehead. The chemistry between them had been undeniable. It seemed all but inevitable that they would find themselves in a taxi together on the way home from the wrap party, detouring to a hotel, where they spent their first night together.

If she was honest, Tanya knew that Dominic's fame had deepened her attraction. And the fact that he was married? Well, that just made the early days of their affair all the more illicit and exciting. It wasn't something she was proud of. It was just how it was. There were only so many attractive and successful men in the world. Some of them might already be taken, but so what? If it had been a happy marriage, he never would've strayed. Clare shared some of the blame. She should've taken better care of him.

They'd moved in together after a national tabloid had revealed their affair in a sensational spread. Clare had kicked him out that very weekend, and Tanya had moved into the bachelor pad he'd rented in Fulham just two weeks later. It had been surprisingly easy to force his hand. Dom never knew that it was Tanya who had tipped off a paparazzi, revealing the location of their secret, late-night dinner date, carefully orchestrating a passionate clinch on the street outside the Mayfair restaurant. But had anyone found out, she'd have told them that she felt no guilt. She had simply taken steps to speed up what she knew was inevitable. She and Dom were meant to be together.

The only time she'd ever felt a hint of doubt was when she went home – alone – to visit her parents. She didn't like taking Dom back to Chelmsford. She didn't like to think of him in her parent's pebbledash terrace, sampling her mother's bland cooking, suffering her father's tedious small-talk about his career as a local councillor. But she also couldn't bear the concern she saw in her mother's eyes. 'He seems very charming,' she'd said, 'but all this fuss in the papers . . . and his poor wife. Are you sure, love? You know what they say: once a cheater, always a cheater. No one ever thinks well of the "other woman".'

Tanya didn't want to entertain her mother's anxieties. Some might consider her a 'homewrecker', but she didn't care, not really. What she and Dom had was special. If she'd had to step over others to get what she wanted, so be it. She wasn't one to feel ashamed.

The hazy sun was a distant memory and Tanya was shivering by the time she arrived at the café. She huddled at a table in the corner, warmed her hands around a flat white and waited, flicking through a stack of glossy magazines to pass the time. After half an hour, when Scarlet hadn't appeared, she called the girl's mobile, bristling as it rang through to voicemail. Where was she? Why wasn't she answering?

Unsure what else to do, Tanya returned to the car park and, finding Dom's Porsche empty, punched out another message. Scarlet's phone was charged. She had a signal now, so the girl had no excuse. It wasn't as if the car interior held any clues either. All she saw were small signs of Dom. His breath mints. A cluster of petrol receipts. A pair of designer sunglasses. A handful of small change.

Beyond the windscreen, the sky was now a bank of heavy, leaden clouds. Spray lifted off the cliffs, carried on the stiffening breeze in great gusts as white caps raced towards the shore. As she gazed at the horizon, a figure caught her eye, a silhouette hunched on a bench on the furthest tip of the headland, long, dark hair streaming in the wind. Scarlet. She'd been there all along. Tanya swallowed down her irritation. Teenagers really were the most selfish creatures.

She slammed the car door and hurried across to the bench. 'Where've you been?' she called. 'You were supposed to meet me. I was worried.'

Scarlet lifted her head. Closer now, Tanya could see the black mascara streaked down the girl's blotchy face. Her eyes were red, her mouth downturned. The sight of her distress caught Tanya by surprise. 'What is it?' Tanya slid onto the bench beside her. 'What's happened?'

Scarlet shook her head, clutching her phone a little tighter to her chest.

'You can tell me. Did something happen?'

She let out a shuddering sigh, the wind tossing her long hair like a mane. 'It's Lily,' she said. 'Lily and Harry.'

She held up her phone and Tanya saw an image on the screen, of Scarlet's best friend pressed up against the good-looking boy in the tux. Lily's arms were thrown around his waist and their faces locked in a passionate, open-mouthed kiss.

'She *knew* how much I liked him. She told me she'd keep an eye on him. But *this*?' Scarlet wailed. 'Some friend.'

Tanya drew the devastated girl into her arms. The ache of first love, the painful sting of betrayal. 'Oh Scarlet. I'm sorry.'

Scarlet pushed her away and kicked angrily at a tuft of grass. 'This is all Dad's fault. If he hadn't made me come away, Harry would never have got with Lily. I never wanted to come on this stupid weekend.' Scarlet sniffed and wiped her nose on the sleeve of her oversized hoodie. 'I could get the train home. I checked the timetable. They leave St Ives every hour.'

'And how would you pay for that?'

'You could help me?'

Tanya shook her head. 'What would I tell your dad when I return to the campsite without you?'

'So maybe I'll hitchhike. Take my chances with the rapists and murderers,' she added.

'Over my dead body.'

Scarlet gave her a pleading look, but Tanya knew she couldn't do it. She couldn't help Scarlet. Dominic would never forgive her.

Another strong gust swept over the promontory and whipped Tanya's scarf, almost sending it flying. She eyed the massing clouds and shivered. 'Come on. We should get back to the others.'

Scarlet shook her head. 'I don't want to go back. I want to go home.'

'I know. Me too. But we can't, love. Not yet.'

Tanya stood and without any other real options,

Scarlet followed her back to the car. 'At least you might have got one wish,' said Tanya as she reversed out of the parking space.

'What's that?'

Tanya nodded at the sky. 'That storm. It's heading right for us.'

KIP

Sunday evening

Kip is lying on his bed, Annie stretched out on her back beside him, the two of them staring up at the ceiling as the low sound of the TV drifts up towards them from downstairs. Annie turns her head to look out the window. 'It's a beautiful sunset,' she says. 'They often are, after a big storm.'

Kip follows her gaze and sees the dramatic vista – shades of violet and grey streaked with orange – framed by the window.

'I'd like to paint it,' she sighs. 'When all of this is over, I'll get my oils out. I'll start properly, like I've been meaning to.' She turns on the pillow to face him. 'Are you sure you don't want to come down and join the others?'

He shakes his head.

'I'm here for you, Kip. Whenever you're ready. Whatever you want to tell me, I'll still love you.'

Kip lies very still. He wants to believe her, but he knows from experience that the words adults say are cheap. Easy to say, much harder to mean.

This is for the best.
You can stay here as long as you like.
You're safe.
I'm not going to hurt you.

All lies. Kip had learned from a young age never to trust the things adults told him. He'd done a pretty good job of it too, until he'd come to live with Max and Annie. But six years on, he still remembers all too well how a home can disappear, ripped away so quickly, like a tablecloth in a magician's hands. He knows how a hungry belly can eat away at you from the inside, what anger pumping through your veins and warm blood on your hands feels like. He wants to trust Annie, wants to tell her everything that races through his mind and sets his heart pounding, but he doesn't trust that her love is strong enough. He doesn't trust that she won't rip it away when she hears the truth.

Annie sighs. 'I suppose I'd better see if anyone needs anything.' She rises from the bed and walks towards the door, stopping halfway across the room to look around at the sheets of paper scattered about the floor. 'You've been drawing?' She bends to retrieve the sheets nearest her feet. 'May I see?'

He imagines launching himself off the bed and tugging the drawings from her hands, shielding them from view, but he knows it would be rude, so he nods and lies very still as she studies the first picture.

'That's a lovely tree.' She peers more closely. 'It looks like the one where you and Max built the swing?'

He nods.

'It's very good, Kip.' She shifts the papers and studies

the next one. 'The cliffs, and the sea. Lovely. And what's that you've drawn there? A stick?' She frowns. 'A cross?'

He nods.

'And all that red?'

He doesn't reply and her frown deepens, a flush appearing on her cheeks. He feels her gaze slide in his direction, before glancing away. She swallows, then lays the sheet of paper on top of his chest of drawers and heads to the door, pausing with her hand on the knob. He can tell Annie wants to say something – ask something. But she doesn't. She leaves, without another word.

Kip lies back against the bed and closes his eyes. He wonders what Annie was going to say. He wonders if she is thinking about his pictures. He wonders when she will figure out how it all fits together.

There weren't many places you could hang a swing on their land. It was one of the things he'd first noticed when they'd moved to Cornwall, how few trees there were. Not like in London, where his bedroom window had looked out over the tall plane trees of Clapham Common. Max had explained it to him, when they'd first arrived on the peninsula, how the high elevation of the land and the strong winds blowing off the Atlantic stunted a tree's growth. The few trees he did find – straggly hawthorns and hunched rowans dotting the coastal headland – reminded Kip of stooped old men, or twisted umbrellas, blown inside out by the wind. But they had found one beauty, a single wych elm, just off the trail leading down to their tiny, secret beach. It was thriving, against the odds, in the sheltered 'V' of two steep cliffs.

The elm grew at a lurching angle, but it had a branch strong enough to take the weight of a swing and a steep drop below that made launching off an exhilarating, heart-in-the-mouth affair. Last winter, Max had let him skip a morning of home schooling and they had hiked across the fields, carrying the rope and the carved wooden seat between them, stringing it up and testing it together.

Kip was the only one who knew the way, so he'd had no choice when the other kids said they wanted to see the swing. He wasn't thrilled about the idea of going off with them all – about sharing his special place – but a small part of him hoped that if they went, Scarlet might come too. He'd been disappointed when he'd realized that she was going to St Ives instead.

She'd been kind to him that morning. After breakfast, as the others had cleared the breakfast table, she'd seemed to make a point of seeking him out. 'I'm sorry about what my dad did to you last night,' she'd said.

He'd wanted to look at her, but he found he couldn't lift his eyes from his lap, or from the glimpse of her smooth, brown thigh he could just make out in his peripheral vision.

'It was obvious Phoebe stole your marshmallow,' she'd added. 'She can be pretty annoying sometimes.'

He hadn't been sure how to respond, wasn't entirely sure that she wasn't pulling his leg, tricking him in some way. But as she'd risen from the bench, he'd finally lifted his head, his gaze following her and the swing of her long, dark hair as she'd headed back to her tent.

Felix and River tried to make it look like they were

leading the swing expedition, but Kip knew he was the leader. The two bigger boys jostled in front, but they kept glancing back, looking for Kip's gestures and nods to show which way to go as the six of them wove across the fields, slinking like a pack of wolf cubs trailing the scent of prey.

Max's words still echoed in Kip's ears, the advice he'd given to him in private back at the house after the marsh-mallow theft. *Try to be a good friend. Put yourself in their shoes.* This was his chance, to show them he could be part of their gang; that he wasn't as useless as they all seemed to think he was.

There were three fields to traverse before they met the steep coastal track leading down to the shoreline. Max had told him that he was allowed across the fields, as long as he didn't stray off the public footpaths. What Kip wasn't expecting, as he drew up to the third stile crossing, was the herd of milk-heavy cows milling beyond the fence line. They had gathered at an old water trough across the field, their tails swatting lazily at flies. 'What are you waiting for?' Felix asked, butting up behind him. 'It's just a few cows.'

'Look at the baby ones,' said Juniper, tugging at one blonde pigtail. 'They're so cute.'

Kip didn't like cows. It wasn't just the pungent manure-stink of them. There was something about their huge, bloated bodies, their dangling udders and their black-coal eyes that put him on edge. At this distance they looked harmless enough and Juniper was right, the calves did look quite cute, but still he hesitated.

'Come on,' said Felix, jostling him from behind. 'Get a move on.'

Kip clambered over the stile and waited for the others to join him before traipsing through the stubby grass littered with yellow buttercups and dandelion seed heads. The majority of the herd seemed more interested in grazing than the intruders loping across their field, but Kip noticed a couple of cows raise their heads, watching their progress as River and Felix attempted to steer each other, giggling, towards wet cowpats the size of dinner plates.

'It's not the cows you need to worry about,' said Felix, lowering his voice. 'It's the farmer who owns them. I heard he roams around at night with his big black dog, looking for children to murder and feed to his pigs.' Felix let out a loud, porcine snort.

'Shut up, Felix!' Willow was indignant. 'You'll scare the younger ones.' Willow carried some authority, as the eldest girl present. She adopted a school teacher's tone, admonishing the boys, but Felix wasn't going to be bossed by a girl.

'I'm right though, aren't I, Kip?' Felix nudged Kip.

Kip, caught between backing up Felix in his outlandish story and reassuring the two younger girls, hesitated. He felt Felix's sharp elbow prod his ribs again and gave a quick, non-committal nod.

Juniper and Phoebe stared at Kip with wide eyes. Willow threw her hands up in disgust. 'Boys!'

Once they had made it safely past the herd and over the far stile, they came to a fork in the footpath. One branch disappeared left, winding through an overgrown thicket of gorse and brambles, the other led right, a stony path zigzagging down the steep terrain towards the sea far below. Kip nodded right and they started down the slope, the older ones pushing ahead, Willow and Felix jostling for the lead. 'We'll take turns,' Felix called back to the others with authority. 'Everyone gets the same amount of time on the swing.'

Kip thought that sounded fair, but the declaration only seemed to create a sense of urgency, spurring all the kids on, their trainers thudding down the path, trampling bracken and wildflowers as they went. Kip, noticing that Juniper and Phoebe were falling behind, hung back. Phoebe held her bear protectively in the crook of her arm, a thread of sticky weed trailing from the hem of her blue dungarees.

It was Felix who arrived first. Kip saw him come to a standstill beside the old wych elm, peering around, before his hands rose in a gesture of dismay. 'Wait! What?' he cried.

Willow drew up behind him. 'What is it?' She followed his gaze, then let out a long sigh. 'Oh.'

Kip hurried forward.

'Where's the swing?' The two older boys turned to Kip, an accusatory look in their eyes.

Where the rope swing had once hung, there was now nothing. No wooden seat drifting lazily in the breeze. No rope. Not even a branch. Just a splintered stump of a limb shining stark white on the old tree, where once had been a strong branch. Kip leaned over the edge and saw the broken branch and swing lying in a tangled heap in the gulley below.

'What's happened?' asked Juniper.

'Did it break?' Felix turned to Kip, seeking answers.

'Maybe it was the wind?'

Kip didn't know what to say, he was too busy trying to control the fierce emotion rising in him. His swing had been destroyed. He didn't want to cry, not in front of the other kids.

'It's okay, Kip,' said Willow, moving closer, reaching out to touch his arm. He flinched and took a step backwards. Willow held up her hands. 'It's okay.'

But it wasn't okay. It wasn't okay at all. This was his place, something he and Max had created together. Just the two of them.

A confused discussion began amongst the other kids. Willow wanted to go back. Felix disagreed. In the commotion, Phoebe started to wheeze.

'Where's your puffer?' asked Felix.

Phoebe shifted her bear into her other hand and withdrew the inhaler from her pocket. She took a deep breath of the medication before capping it and shoving it back into her pocket.

'Let's go back,' said Willow again, still trying to assert herself.

'No way,' said Felix. 'We spent most of yesterday cooped up in the car.' He turned and pointed to the track winding down the gulley. 'Where does that go, Kip? To the beach?'

Kip nodded.

River smiled.

Willow shook her head, her face a picture of worry. 'I don't think so.'

'Dinner's not for ages,' said Felix.

'And if you remember correctly,' added River, flicking his hair from his eyes, 'they gave us strict instructions to stick together.'

Willow chewed her lower lip, clearly torn. 'The weather doesn't look so good.'

Looking out to the horizon, Kip saw she was right. An eerie orange haze seemed to have settled over the sun, while further out at sea the sky was darkening, clouds rising like smoke belching from an invisible volcano.

'Even more reason to go now. If it starts raining, we'll be stuck playing boardgames in the tents all afternoon,' added River.

'What about you, Phoebe?' Felix was studying his sister. 'We can take you back if you *really* want to go?' It was obvious that this was the last thing Felix wanted to do. 'But if you come to the beach, we can look for shells and poke around for crabs?'

Phoebe eyed the others. She gripped her bear a little tighter under her arm. 'I love shells.'

Willow sighed and turned to Kip. 'You'd better lead the way.'

Kip stared at their expectant faces and felt torn. He didn't want to get in trouble again, but he didn't want to disappoint the kids either. *Put yourself in their shoes.* Well he knew where their shoes wanted to go. With a small nod, he turned and led them down the trail towards the beach.

ANNIE

Sunday evening

Annie is making tea in the kitchen while the police officer sits quietly at the table, going through her notebook. It already feels like the longest day, but it doesn't look like it's going to end any time soon. A little earlier, the coastguard helicopter had flown back over the house, its blades beating low and loud. 'Do you think they found anything?' Annie asks lightly, her back still turned as she stirs a teabag round and round.

'I'm sure DI Lawson will update you all, as soon as she's able.'

It's not much of an answer.

An empty bottle of rosé stands on the windowsill near the sink. Annie glances at it and feels another surge of guilt. 'It seems awful now,' she murmurs, 'to think we were up here talking about renovation plans and making dessert when the kids got into trouble.'

DC Haines tilts her head. '"We" being all you ladies?'

'No. Just me, Suze and Kira. Tanya had made other

plans. We invited her to join us,' she adds quickly. 'We've always tried to make her feel welcome, but that's Tanya all over. She seems to want to keep herself apart.' She hesitates, wondering if she sounds judgemental. 'I'm sure it's not easy infiltrating a group that have been friends for years. We were all really fond of Dom's first wife, Clare, but that's how it goes with divorce, isn't it? Eventually everyone has to pick a side. I still meet Clare for coffee once in a while, but it isn't the same.' Annie moves across to the table with the tea and slides one of the mugs over to Haines before pulling out a chair. 'We try to put the effort in with Tanya, knowing how important she is to Dom, but there's only so much you can do, don't you think, when it's not reciprocated?'

DC Haines opens her notebook to a fresh page and picks up her pen. 'You okay to carry on?'

Annie nods. It doesn't seem she's got much choice.

'So, to Saturday afternoon. Three of you were up here at the farmhouse, and Tanya had gone to St Ives, so that left the four men at the campsite. How long do you think you left them for?'

'Oh, I don't know exactly.' The colour rises in Annie's cheeks as she remembers Suze going to the fridge and retrieving a second bottle of wine, a hard-to-resist glint in her green eyes, bangles jangling as she'd popped the cork. 'I don't know about you two,' Suze had said, 'but I'm in no rush to get back.' Kira hadn't even been drinking really, just a small glass of wine with lunch, so between her and Suze they must have been going for it.

DC Haines is silent, waiting for Annie's answer.

'We walked up to the farmhouse around midday. We made a salad for lunch and went over our drawings for the renovation. I decided to make tiramisu for the evening meal. We were chatting so much, time got away from us. I suppose we were gone around three hours. Maybe longer.' Regret washes over her. 'Honestly, none of us thought the men would let them go off like that. We certainly wouldn't have been gone so long if we had. But that's the beauty of hindsight, isn't it? I suppose we all wish we'd done things differently.'

'I'm sure,' murmurs Haines.

Annie remembers how she hadn't been able to find the Marsala wine she needed for her recipe. They'd had to rummage through the last of the unopened packing crates, until Suze uncovered a box scrawled with the words 'blender & booze' in fat, black marker pen on the side and eventually Annie had found it, buried near the bottom.

'Well, it's certainly different to your last place,' Suze said as she resettled herself at the kitchen table and began to grate a block of dark chocolate. 'Is there anything you miss about your old home?'

'You mean other than my soft-close German kitchen cabinets, the underfloor heating and my Scandi pendant lights?' Annie took a large gulp of rosé. 'I know it's rather neglected, but it's got good bones.' She looked about and saw the dated kitchen through her friends' eyes: the stained Formica worktops, the tap dripping into the cracked enamel sink, the cupboard doors hanging off their hinges. It was a world away from the sleek basement kitchen extension they'd added to their

London townhouse. 'It's got potential though, don't you think?'

'If anyone can turn this place around, it's you two,' said Kira. 'I wouldn't know where to start, but you and Max are so good at this stuff.'

'How about you and Fred? How are you both adjusting? Parenthood can be a shock, and you two have hit the ground running. How long have you been together now?'

Kira smiled. 'We celebrated the one-year anniversary of our first date last week.'

Suze raised her glass. 'Congratulations. You know, it wasn't that long ago we celebrated your fortieth birthday, when things were *very* different.'

Kira blushed. 'Not my finest hour. I blame those espresso martinis Dom ordered.'

Suze reached out and squeezed Kira's arm. 'We just felt bad for you. You were so upset, wondering if you'd ever meet the right person ... if motherhood would ever happen for you. That speech you gave at the dinner table ...'

Kira covered her face with her hands. 'Oh god.'

'But look at you now!' interjected Annie. 'A beautiful baby girl. A lovely man. A successful career. You've got it all, Kira.'

Suze frowned, the block of chocolate falling still against the grater. 'Hang on, you said it's been one year? Since you met Fred?'

Kira looked between her friends, her face shifting, her smile faltering. 'I meant ...' she hesitated, then gave a little shrug, 'yes. One year.'

'But Asha's five months old.'

Kira didn't quite meet Suze's eye. 'Yes.'

'So ... forgive me for being dense, but how does that work?' Suze waited, watching as Kira shifted awkwardly in her seat.

'I was going to tell you, but it just never seemed to come up. Fred's not actually Asha's father.'

Annie saw Suze's mouth drop wide open and knew her own expression mirrored similar surprise.

'It's really not a big deal,' Kira added, seeing their faces.

'How did we not know this?'

Kira shrugged. 'Perhaps no one thought to ask. Everyone just assumed. Fred was on the scene when I told you all about my pregnancy. The two sort of got wrapped up together.'

Annie shook her head. 'Sorry, I know I'm being a bit slow, but you're telling us that you were already pregnant when you met Fred?'

'Yes,' Kira nodded. 'Though I didn't know it at the time. We met at a medical conference last spring, started dating soon after. It was pretty ... intense.'

Suze grinned at Annie. 'She means shagging. They did loads and loads of shagging.'

Annie sighed and reached for her glass with a smile. 'Ah ... I remember the days. Just.'

Kira blushed, but she was laughing. 'Yes, all right, there was *a lot* of sex.'

Suze raised her glass. 'Bravo.'

'We were together a few weeks before I suspected I might be pregnant. I assumed the baby was his, we hadn't been particularly careful. I took a pregnancy test and told him that night. I didn't know how he'd react, but he was brilliant. We agreed it was a bit quick, but he said it was fate. He was keen to be a father, just as much as I wanted to be a mum.' She hesitated, tucking a loose strand of dark hair behind her ear.

'Go on,' urged Suze, taking another slurp of wine. 'This is better than Corrie.'

'It was only at the first ultrasound that we discovered I was further along than either of us had realized.' She gave a small resigned sigh. 'I'd had no idea. My periods were never particularly regular, but still, you can imagine the shock. There were some pretty heavy conversations – we even talked about splitting up – but in the end, Fred decided to stick by us both. He wanted to be Asha's dad. He said her paternity was a non-issue for him, if he was going to be the one raising her.' She shrugged again. 'So here we are.'

Annie frowned. 'But if Fred's not the father . . .?' She let her question hang.

Kira twisted the stem of her empty wine glass between her fingers. 'God, I wish I was drunk right now.' They waited. 'Don't judge me, please, but it was a one-night stand. Just a random fling – nothing that was ever going to go anywhere.'

'A patient?'

'God! No! I'm not *that* bad.'

'Wow.' Suze let out a breath of air. 'O-kaaaay. So, is *he* involved – the real dad?'

Kira's eyes flashed. 'Fred's the *real* dad. He's the

one holding her, feeding her, pacing the house at night with her.'

'Of course . . . I didn't mean . . . I just wondered if the other man knew, if he was involved in some way?'

Kira shook her head. 'No. He doesn't know. I haven't seen him since. What was I going to do? Call him up out of the blue and tell him I was keeping his baby? I didn't see the point. Fred and I had already decided to raise the baby together.'

'But don't you think you *should* tell him?' Annie felt uncomfortable. Memories of her multitude of IVF appointments, painful self-inflicted injections, the hormonal rollercoaster she had ridden, the emotional turmoil she and Max had gone through, came flooding back. Becoming a parent was a serious business. Not something to be undertaken lightly, or stripped away from someone without care and consideration. What if this man had wanted a baby as much as Kira? As much as she and Max had wanted one?

Kira shook her head again. 'It's no different to using a sperm donor, as far as I'm concerned. It's not as if I need anything from him. I have a good career. I have Fred.'

'But ethically speaking? Sperm donors sign contracts and waivers. They understand what they're doing.' Annie shifted in her seat. 'The man you slept with has no idea he's fathered a child.'

'I knew I was going to keep the baby as soon as I found out I was pregnant. I knew I'd do it on my own, no matter what, but Fred's agreed to be my partner in this. You said it yourself just now, Suze: I've got everything I wanted.

Why would I rock the boat and introduce a third party?' She lifted her chin. 'Someone who probably doesn't care anyway?'

Listening to her, Annie felt a flurry of emotions. Kira sounded convincing, yet something still didn't sit right for her. Why hadn't she told them all this from the start? Was she embarrassed? Did she think they would judge her for a one-night stand? They were her friends, and they, more than most, had known how deeply she had longed for a baby. Surely Kira knew they would never begrudge her the happiness of becoming a mother, unless she too felt deep down that she had done wrong by someone?

Annie watched Kira as she adjusted Asha in her arms and offered the dummy that had fallen from her smacking lips. Perhaps Kira was right. As long as Kira was happy, what should it matter to the rest of them? She could certainly relate to the sharp sting of childlessness – the way it ate away at you, pushed you to do things you had never considered before. Maybe, Annie realized, her own discomfort lay buried in something more deeply rooted, in that tiny part of her that stung with jealousy to hear how easily Kira had fallen pregnant.

'Tell us at least that the shagging hasn't stopped?' Suze asked with a smirk.

Kira smiled. 'Let's just say pregnancy agreed with me.'

Asha let out a high wail and began to fuss against Kira's chest.

'Let me take her?' suggested Annie. 'I won't smell of milk. I might be able to calm her.' Annie gathered the baby into her arms and sat for a moment, pressing her face to the top of Asha's head. 'Mmmm, that baby smell. Someone should bottle it.'

'My ovaries ache just looking at her,' said Suze with a sigh.

Annie felt a twinge of longing. 'I can't deny I some-times feel robbed to have missed out on the early years. I would've loved to have known Kip as a baby. It makes me wonder what we missed.' She swallowed. 'What it did to him. How we could've changed things for him, if we'd been given a chance to be his parents ... you know ... earlier.'

Suze reached over and squeezed her hand. 'You're doing such a great job. You and Max are terrific parents. We all see that.'

Suze's validation struck like a tuning fork at the cham-ber of her heart. She rose from the table, tears pricking, distracting herself with the box of sponge fingers.

Before Kip, Annie had been convinced that she could offer everything a child needed. Love, affection, stability, support. She'd felt certain that she and Max were well equipped to raise a child. They had sailed through the adoption process, filed endless papers, met with social workers and support groups, attended assessments and hosted home visits. They had armed themselves with all the information and research they'd felt necessary. When the longed for phone call had finally come, telling them that they had been matched to a child, she knew they were ready.

Their first meeting with Kip had taken place in his foster home. They had sat on a sofa drinking tea, watching as Kip played quietly with seven grubby plastic bricks, over and over, sticking and unsticking them into the same configuration. As she'd talked with his foster parents, Max had slipped down onto the floor and pulled a few more bricks from the bucket until gradually, silently, the two of them had built a high tower – one with windows and turrets and an impressive crenelated roof.

Watching them play together, Kip's small, pale hands fumbling over the bricks, following Max's gentle guidance, his eyes seeking validation and encouragement, Annie was convinced that he was meant to be their son. She'd felt it deeply, certainly, just as she'd felt, watching Max, that he was meant to be a father. She was confident any issues that arose from Kip's challenging start in life – issues their social worker was keen to impress upon them – could be overcome together, with love, patience and time.

Six years ago. She had been so naïve.

Blinking back her tears, Annie returned the box of sponge fingers to the table and took another swig of her wine.

'How is Kip adjusting to life down here?' Kira asked, oblivious to Annie's emotional turmoil. 'It's a big change for him too.'

Annie gathered herself. 'To begin with, it was great. *He* was great. The move seemed to release some pressure.' She thought for a moment, wondering how much to say, wondering if Max would mind her being so candid. In the end, it was the sight of her friends' sympathetic faces that urged her on. 'We haven't really told anyone, but Kip was having some struggles ... at school. There was a bit of bullying ... a violent outburst. I know teachers these days are overworked and stressed out with exams and government targets, but Max and I felt they lacked the skills to handle the situation properly.'

'That sounds ... challenging,' said Suze carefully.

'Have you sought professional help?' Kira asked, standing and jiggling a fussing Asha in her sling.

'We took him to a therapist. They wanted to give us a "diagnosis". Max and I didn't really understand – a diagnosis for what? For being a little bit ... quirky, withdrawn and sensitive?' She laid her whisk down on the kitchen table, dabbing at a dollop of mascarpone that had landed on her sleeve. 'Who wouldn't be those things, given the start he'd had in life?'

'Yes, that's the problem these days,' agreed Suze. 'Everyone wants to slap a label on anything remotely challenging or different. Fifty years ago, he'd just have been Kip, that shy little boy who didn't like to talk to strangers. Doctors these days are so quick to throw disorders around like easy-fix plasters.' Suze stopped abruptly, realizing what she'd said. 'No offence, Kira.'

Kira shrugged. 'None taken. To a degree, I think you're right.' She turned back to Annie. 'But Kip does present with some particular symptoms that I can see might benefit from specialist support.'

'God, don't let Max hear you talking like that,' said Annie. 'He baulks at the idea that Kip might have "special needs". He's adamant that he just needs the right support, from us. If we love him enough, care for him enough, then we can see him through this. We can come out the other side.'

'What about you?' asked Kira, gently. 'What do you think?'

Annie shrugged. 'I feel as though I'm failing him. Moving down here was supposed to make him feel more comfortable – safe even. Now I can't help worrying that we've run away from the problem. That we might be making it worse by shutting him off from the world. He's so . . . withdrawn. Sometimes I look at him and just want to know what he's thinking. Sometimes I worry that he'll always be a mystery to me.'

Suze raised her glass. 'Welcome to the wonderful world of parenting.'

Annie swallowed. She doesn't continue with the words playing on her lips. She holds back her deepest fear: that maybe she can never be enough. That maybe it's her fault; that Kip senses something lacking in her, something holding her back. That maybe nature had never intended for her to become a mother to her own biological baby because there was something wrong with her.

She loved Kip. They both did. Fiercely. That was never in doubt. But what she'd learned these past six years was that parenthood meant loving another person so wholly, so unconditionally, that the pain they felt became your pain, their wounds your wounds. She hadn't expected being a mother to be so damn hard. She hadn't expected their love to be tested so fully.

There had been nights when she had lain in bed, Max sleeping peacefully beside her, when she had felt suffocated by the emotion, as if she couldn't breathe, her airways choked with it. Nights when she had wondered if they had been wrong to undertake such a huge responsibility. On those harder days or weeks, when Kip reacted or shut down, shut them out completely, she'd found herself wondering about the two people who'd made him – not his parents, she couldn't call them that, not after what they'd done. She and Max were his parents, the ones who loved and nurtured him. But she couldn't help wondering what legacy he might carry. She wondered if the time would come when she would ever truly understand this complicated boy who had entered their lives. Because no matter how much she loved him, she still wasn't entirely sure she *knew* him. Sometimes she wondered if she ever would.

These were the things she couldn't tell her friends. These were the things she would never say out loud – not even to Max – the things she hated to admit, even to herself, but it didn't mean she hadn't thought them. It didn't mean she hadn't wrestled with those moments when she'd wanted to turn to Max and say: *this is too much. I can't do it.* Even just thinking it brought her shame.

Wanting to shift the mood, Annie cleared her throat and tried to steer them onto a more familiar topic as she began to assemble the layers of the tiramisu. 'So ... what do we all make of Tanya's decision to go shopping? Should we be offended she chose St Ives over us?'

'She couldn't get away fast enough.'

Kira shrugged. 'I'm relieved, to be honest.'

'Who wears *Balenciaga* on a camping trip?'

'I've been wondering . . . do you think those are her real boobs?' Kira was all wide-eyed innocence. 'They look suspiciously . . . perky.'

Suze snorted. 'No one's boobs look like that after having a kid.'

'Mine *never* looked like that. Maybe I should get a reduction,' said Annie, jostling her breasts up and inwards with her hands, staring down despondently at her cleavage. 'At this rate mine'll be round my knees by Christmas.'

They were interrupted by a knock. Josh's head appeared round the back door. Annie, still holding her breasts, dropped her hands hurriedly, her face flushing red.

Josh averted his eyes. 'Sorry to interrupt, ladies, but it looks like there's some weather heading our way. I'm driving back to the campsite to check on the tent guy ropes. Would you like a lift?'

Suze raised one eyebrow at Annie. With her back to Josh, he couldn't see her mouth, '*So hot.*'

Annie tried to hide her smile. 'If you can wait two minutes while I finish the dessert, I'm sure we'd love that.'

'He is rather lovely to look at,' agreed Kira, as soon as Josh had ducked away.

'I'm not sure we should be objectifying the employees,' said Annie with mock indignation. 'I mean, yes, of course, he is undeniably handsome . . .' she trailed off.

'Undeniably,' agreed Suze with emphasis.

'Oh stop it. He's young enough to be one of our sons . . . and such a nice lad. He looks after his dad, you know? And I've only ever heard him say lovely things about his sister. That's rare for siblings, right?'

'You just keep talking, Annie,' smirked Suze. 'I'm calling "shotgun".'

Out in the yard, they scrambled giggling and breathless into the vehicle. Josh waited for Annie to take her seat, before passing her the dish of tiramisu to balance on her lap. Kira slid in beside her, with Asha nestled safely in her sling. Suze, as negotiated, commandeered the front, beside Josh.

It was only in the fresh air, with the wind smacking her full in the face, that Annie realized how much time had passed, how much wine she had drunk, and how dramatically the weather had shifted in the few short hours they had spent inside. The sky was no longer blue, but hung dark and forbidding overhead. A salty breeze tugged and snapped at their clothes and there was more than a hint of rain in the air.

'How do you think the guys got on without us?' Suze yelled over the drone of the diesel engine.

'I'm sure they've handled everything beautifully,' said Kira.

Annie felt a small tremor of disquiet, but forced the smile back onto her face. 'Have you even met our husbands?'

KIP

Saturday afternoon

Kip led the way as they picked up their pace down the rocky cliff path towards the cove below. The closer they got to the beach, the sharper the mineral scent of the sea and the rougher the terrain grew, until the winding track finally levelled out and they began a strenuous clamber over boulders, huge tangles of driftwood and stinking, blackened kelp to reach the strip of sand beyond. Seeing Phoebe struggle with the final obstacles, Felix returned to help his sister over the rocks.

Down on the beach, with the towering spires of the granite cliffs at their backs, it felt as if they had arrived in their own private amphitheatre. Kip turned his face to the sky. The sun had vanished completely, overwhelmed by a mass of grey cloud, and the wind gusted across the sand with a strength they hadn't noticed higher up in the sheltered gulley.

The change didn't bother them. Set free, and filled with the excitement of their illicit adventure, the kids ran and screeched across the beach, their exhilarated screams and whoops mingling with the startled cries of the gulls they chased. Felix and River raced each other along the ocean's edge, whirling glistening strands of seaweed over their heads like lassoes. Phoebe and Juniper clambered on the rocky fringe, picking clusters of wildflowers, pink thrift and white sea campion, before joining Willow by the rockpools where they crouched over the shivering water, poking at snails and molluscs and darting translucent fish. A crab was caught then released.

Wandering towards the girls, Kip's eye was caught by something glinting silver at the edge of a sandy pool. He crouched and saw it was a knife, its stout wooden handle caught in a tangle of weed, the metal blade flat and corroded with age. It looked like a shucking knife – the kind he'd seen fishmongers using on oyster shells and scallops at the harbourside market Max sometimes took him to. He lifted it and brushed the sand from the handle. It felt good in his hands, sturdy yet light. He swiped it through the air a couple of times then tested the blade against the pad of his thumb.

Kip knew you could sharpen dull blades, but he wasn't sure about rust? Maybe he could polish it up, make it like new again, make it his. The weight of it in his hand reminded him of what it had felt like to wield Max's penknife, the control he'd felt whittling the willow sticks, the importance he'd felt to be entrusted with Max's special tool and the praise he'd received for a job well done. Until Phoebe had stolen his marshmallow and ruined everything.

In his old house, the one with the green-swirling carpet and the sagging red sofa that smelled of cigarettes and worse, the house he'd lived in with his other parents – the ones he didn't see anymore – you didn't get treats like biscuits or marshmallows. You didn't get very much of anything. There were no trips to the supermarket to fill a big trolley. No plasters for scratches or grazes, no kisses for cuts and bruises. No piles of clean, folded laundry. No books on shelves. No warm radiators or well-fitting shoes. No one reminding you to go to school. Meals were infrequent. Forgotten. Sometimes for days.

Left alone at home, Kip would scavenge through cupboards for forgotten traces of food: the dregs in a cereal box, the end of a loaf of bread, crumbled crackers, a wrinkled apple at the bottom of the fridge. When the milk ran out, the baby would scream and scream – until she didn't.

He didn't like to think about her very much. It was hard to separate the good thoughts – the ones of her baby fingers curling round his, her smiling and gurgling, lips smacking at a bottle, or curled asleep in her cot like a squirrel, one fist tucked beneath her chin – from the ones that came after. Alone in the house with her endless crying, her stinking nappies, unable to quiet or comfort her, no matter what he tried. The sight of her lying on that filthy red sofa, still and lifeless, her skin a strange, mottled blue. He shivered. It was best, he'd found, not to think about her at all. Best not to think about what had happened in *that* house.

Last night, he'd watched the kids around the bonfire, clamouring at Fred, snatching for their marshmallows, groaning that they only got two each. Everyone had been crowding in, faces looming, ghoulish and hollow-eyed in the firelight. For Kip, a treat like a marshmallow, even just one, was something precious, something to be savoured, and when he'd realized his had gone, when he'd seen Phoebe's puffed-out cheeks and her gleeful scorn as she'd stuck out her tongue, it had felt like a mist descending. A buzzing had begun in his limbs, an electricity surging through him, as if rising from the ground, firing through the soles of his shoes to take hold of him. Then he'd lunged.

The flames. The sticks. The shouting. Phoebe's screams. The chaos had exploded around him, that man's hands on his T-shirt, lifting him up, the pain at his throat, his angry words hissing and spitting in his face. But the worst sound of all, the one that had made him blind with fear and rage, was the sound of the baby, Asha's crying rising in the dark. It had propelled him straight back to that house with its green carpet, awful red sofa and the blue-skin baby. He hadn't been able to stop it. He'd felt the warm release of his bladder, the liquid trickling down his leg, pooling in his trainer as the other boys watched on with horrified amusement.

Kip's fist squeezed around the gritty wooden handle of the knife as he remembered his shame. With a knife like this, people would think twice about the way they treated him. He rubbed at the red mark on his neck. They'd think twice about taking his stuff, shouting at him, grabbing him, hurting him.

'Hey Kip!' It was Felix, calling from across the sand,

head tilted, beady eyes fixed on him. 'What've you got there?'

Felix was already marching towards him, but Kip didn't want to share his treasure. He knew Felix or River would take it, claim it as their own. This was his find – his alone. He slipped the knife into his shorts pocket and turned his back on the boy, stalking away towards the rockpools.

'You want to go play with the girls?' jeered Felix. 'Suit yourself, *weirdo!*'

He didn't join the girls. Instead, he perched on a ledge overlooking a rockpool and watched the surging waves for a while, the way they rose up and raced each other to the shore, smashing onto the sand with a foaming roar. He'd never seen the sea until he'd come to live with Max and Annie. Now, it felt like his special place. A place where he could think and breathe. A place where good things happened. A place where secret treasure could be found.

His mind drifted to Scarlet and the way she had spoken to him earlier that morning, the smooth, tanned skin of her thigh, and how, when she had leaned towards him, he had caught the floral perfume rising off her long dark hair, hair he'd had the sudden, inexplicable urge to reach out and wind tightly around his fingers. She was very pretty – like one of the avatars from his favourite computer game. Thinking about her made his heart stutter in his chest.

It was Phoebe who interrupted his thoughts, coming across to show him her own treasure. She crouched in front of him and opened her palm to reveal a crushed white flower nestled amongst a handful of small dusky-pink shells and one solitary mussel, its purple casing crusted with white barnacles. 'I'm going to take them back to show my dad.'

Kip frowned. Phoebe had picked the little white flowers Annie had warned him about. And the shells – the shells belonged here. He knew you shouldn't take things off the beach. A knife was different – that was manmade. But natural things, they were supposed to stay put. He wanted to tell her to leave them behind, but instead he just nodded.

Phoebe tilted her head up at him. 'Why don't you talk?'

Kip shrugged.

'Don't you want to?'

Kip felt a fizzing sensation on his tongue, letters dancing haphazardly, refusing to form. He shrugged again then turned away.

The sky was now as dark as pencil lead, the waves beating furiously against the shore, spewing white foam onto the sand. Feeling uneasy, Kip hopped down from the rocky ledge and nudged Willow, pointing to the threatening sky.

Willow followed his gaze. 'Yeah,' she agreed, 'time to go.'

It was a struggle to round everyone up, but eventually the group began the obstacle course back over the rocks, weary legs stumbling on boulders and slipping in the mossy stream trickling down the ravine as they climbed the winding path back up the cliffside. They all took it in turns encouraging Phoebe, who had begun to flag. 'I'm thirsty,' she said, licking her lips.

'Don't whine,' said Felix. 'We're all thirsty – and hungry.'

It seemed to take forever to reach the wych elm and

by the time they arrived at the stile leading to the cattle field, spirits were flagging. Kip stopped at the fence and frowned. The cows had moved. They had left the water trough and were closer now, sheltering from the wind beside a hedge, where they blocked the footpath.

'We'll just have to go through them,' said Felix, climbing over the stile. 'No big deal.'

'Is that rain?' asked Juniper. 'I think I felt a spot.' Kip could see she was shivering, her orange T-shirt and shorts no match for the breeze, her bony knees knocking as she rubbed at her goosebumps.

'I don't want to go near the cows,' said Phoebe quietly.

'What are they going to do?' asked Felix. 'Squirt you with milk?'

Kip frowned. Sometimes Felix sounded so much like his dad.

'Come on,' urged Willow, a worried frown creasing her face. 'We can't stop now.'

River was the first to launch himself over the stile. He flicked back his long hair and strode confidently towards the milling cattle, Felix close behind. The others climbed over in turn. 'There's nothing to worry about,' Felix shouted over his shoulder, 'see, they're just cows.' He made as if to run at the herd, his arms outstretched, and a few of the nearer cows reared out of his way.

Willow helped Juniper and Phoebe over the stile, then turned to Kip. 'Coming?'

He headed up the rear, just behind Phoebe as she tripped across the uneven ground, her trainers dragging through the long grass, her bottom lip clamped between her teeth as she plodded on, braced against the wind. The space between the two of them and the others gradually opened up. Kip glanced at her out of the corner of his eye. Couldn't she move any faster? He was sick of her now. Sick of looking after her – looking after them all. He just wanted to be back at the campsite. Better still, back at the farmhouse. Away from everyone. Kip hunched his shoulders, his fingers tracing the rusty blade in his pocket as he trudged on, his eyes fixed on the milling cows. Nearly there.

It wasn't exactly clear what happened next, but as Felix and River drew closer to the herd, a trio of more frisky-looking heifers trotted forward. Felix let out a shout, which sent them veering away, but from his position behind them all, Kip saw more of the cows turn and, with nostrils flaring, start a steady trot forward. The herd, as if obeying a silent signal, began to assemble and move as one.

Kip opened his mouth, wanting to shout some kind of warning to the others, but all sound was lost when he saw what they had missed when they had crossed earlier: it wasn't just cows and calves grazing in the field, but another animal, this one much larger, with a huge muscled neck and two pointed horns that stood silhouetted against the dark sky.

Kip saw the bull's eyes flash white as the animal tossed its head, before lowering his horns to the ground and starting his charge.

They moved fast for such cumbersome beasts, the herd gathering and streaming towards the children in one fluid mass, the bull now somewhere in their midst, its horns just visible every now and then amidst the flow of cattle. Kip, still a little behind with Phoebe, felt the tight breath of air trapped in his lungs finally release from his throat and with it came a single word.

'Bull!' he yelled, unsure whether they would even hear him over the cattle stampeding across the field.

Kip saw Felix's head turn. He saw the boy's mouth open with shout of surprise before the kids disappeared in a cloud of dust and thundering hooves.

JIM

Sunday evening

The X-ray of Jim's arm shows a clean break in the mid-shaft of the humerus of his left arm. The doctor tells him that he's been lucky – it won't require surgery. A nurse, matronly and unsympathetic, gives him gas to suck on as the doctor realigns the bone and sets his arm in a cast. 'Plenty of rest,' the doctor orders, 'and keep up with those painkillers.'

'Thanks Doc.'

'Linda here will take you back now. Sorry that we had to interrupt.'

The nurse returns him to the same bland interview room where he first chatted with Lawson and Barnett. He waits a few minutes before the police officers re-enter and settle once more at the table. 'Let's talk about Saturday afternoon,' says Lawson. No preamble. No niceties. There is a different energy about them both – an intensity that makes Jim think something has changed.

Jim leans back in his chair. 'What do you want to know?'

'When did you realize there was trouble with the kids?'

'Max came and found me. He'd noticed the rain clouds coming in and wanted some help packing away the outdoor games. There were balls and cricket stumps, the archery kit and frisbees scattered all across the meadow.'

'What time was that?'

'I guess around four ... maybe four thirty. I confess, it was a bit of a shock it was so late. I had no idea where the afternoon had gone.'

Jim watches as the police officer makes a careful note. The dull ache is already building again beneath his cast. 'After we'd tidied up, Max suggested he and I go check on the kids. I could see he was starting to worry, but we didn't get a chance to set off because right then we heard the buggy approaching. Josh was at the wheel, with Annie, Suze, Kira and the baby. Annie had a dish of something balanced on her lap and it was obvious from their laughter and flushed cheeks that they'd had a good time up at the house. I'm telling you now,' he adds, annoyed to hear the defensive note enter his voice, 'we weren't the only ones who'd kicked back a bit over lunch.'

Jim took the dessert dish from Annie before offering his hand to help them off the buggy in turn.

'Well this all looks surprisingly calm and ordered,' said Suze, looking pleased and surprised. 'Where is everyone?'

Jim glanced at Dominic's tent. He hadn't seen him at all since their conversation about Kira and the loan when Dominic had stormed off. Guilty conscience, Jim had thought. He felt bad about Fred though. He'd gone to find him to apologize for their gaffe, tapping lightly on the canvas entrance to his tent, but there had been no answer. Instead, Jim had settled back in his deckchair with his headphones on and watched the clouds building on the horizon, drifting and merging, forming impressive grey peaks, the bunting fluttering overhead as he waited for the women and kids to return and some kind of normality to ensue.

'What have you done with the kids? Don't tell me they're all in the tents?' Her smile faltered. 'You didn't let them have iPads, did you?' She turned and rolled her eyes at Kira.

'No iPads. Only wholesome, outdoor fun. To be honest, Max and I were just thinking of going after them.'

Annie threw him a quizzical look. '*After them*? Where are they?'

'Don't worry,' said Max, jumping in. 'They're at the rope swing. They'll be back any minute.'

Annie frowned. 'Dominic's gone with them?'

'No ... uh, he ... he went for a lie down.' Jim saw the women cast their gaze over the empty beer cans on the long wooden table, the exchange of knowing glances. He realized how it must look. 'We put the older kids in charge.'

'What time did you ask them to be back?'

Jim scratched his head. 'I'm not sure we did specify an exact time.'

Annie lifted up her hands in exasperation. 'You guys. Have you even seen the sky? We've got rain coming this way.'

Josh, who had been unhitching the trailer off the back of the buggy, raised his head. 'I could go, if you like?'

Annie gave him a grateful look. 'That's kind, Josh.'

But Josh didn't need to go anywhere because at that moment Jim spotted a flash of orange at the far end of the meadow. 'Look, it's Juniper.' She was closely followed by Willow. 'See, no drama. They're coming back.'

A moment or two later the two older boys emerged from the hedge line. Juniper broke into a sprint as she neared the shelter, though she was red in the face and panting so hard they couldn't understand a word she said, at first. 'We had to run for it . . . they chased us.'

'Slow down,' said Max. 'Take a breath.'

'Who chased you?' Suze asked, moving towards her youngest, seizing her hand. 'What's happened?'

'There was a bull. It charged at us. It was a stampede.'

'What?' Suze's voice was a squeak. 'A bull?' She threw a concerned glance at Annie. 'That can't be right.'

'The footpath does lead through Kellow's fields. But I can't believe he'd put a bull in there.' Annie threw Max a worried glance. 'He wouldn't, would he? It's a public right of way.'

Max frowned. 'I certainly hope not. Not without proper signage to warn the public.'

The two older boys arrived next, joining the others at the shelter. Both were out of breath, their cheeks flushed.

'How was the swing?' asked Jim.

Felix and River exchanged a glance. 'No swing. It was gone.'

'What?' Max stared at them in alarm.

'*We* didn't do it,' said Felix hastily. 'It was already

destroyed when we got there. Looks like the branch had snapped, maybe in the wind?'

'What have you been doing all this time?' Annie looked around at the kids, baffled.

Felix snuck another look at River. 'Kip took us to the beach.'

'What?' The adults exchanged alarmed glances.

'You went to the beach? Alone? I'm not sure that sounds terribly safe.' Annie rounded on Max. 'Weren't you guys supposed to be in charge?'

Max threw his arms in the air. 'Hey, don't have a go at me. Josh and I were sorting out the septic system. I left Jim and Dom with the kids.'

Dominic, hearing the disturbance outside, emerged from his tent and came over to join them. Jim noticed how he avoided his gaze completely, his glance drifting to Kira with Asha in her arms, his eyes lingering on the baby, before he turned back to the rest of them. 'What's going on? Where's Phoebe?'

Annie frowned. 'Yes, where's Phoebe? And where's Kip? Why aren't they with you?'

The four children swapped puzzled looks. 'They were right behind us,' said Felix. 'I swear.'

'You saw them, didn't you, Willow?' River was staring at his sister.

Willow frowned. 'I heard a shout ... saw the bull. I grabbed Juniper and we started running.'

'They're still out there?' Dominic rounded on his son. 'Felix, I *told* you to look out for your little sister.'

'There was no time, Dad. I had to run.'

'Jesus. What if they've been trampled?' Fear made Dominic's voice rise in pitch.

All of Felix's boyish bravado disappeared in the face of his father's anger. 'Sorry. I didn't know ... it wasn't ...'

Max turned to Dominic. 'It's okay. If they were behind the others, then they'll have turned back.' His calm voice didn't hide the fear in his eyes. 'If it's the field I think it is, there's a trail back up to Kellow's farm. Kip knows the route. He'll bring Phoebe home the long way round.'

'So, what you're saying is that if she's not been trampled by stampeding bulls, she's out there alone – with Kip? The same kid who nearly gouged her eye out yesterday!'

Kira laid a hand on Dominic's arm. 'Dom,' she said. 'Come on.'

'There's no need to rehash that,' snapped Max. 'We'll go right now and check the field. They might be waiting for us on the other side.'

'Should I come too, Dad?' Felix asked.

'No, I think you've done enough.' Felix's cheeks flamed a deeper red. 'The last thing we need is you lot wandering around again,' he added, softening a little at his son's crestfallen face. 'Stay here.' Dominic spun on his heel and set off across the meadow in the direction the children had come from.

Jim exchanged a look with Max and the two of them followed, having to increase their speed to catch up with him at the fence. As they drew near, they saw Dominic point back over their heads towards the crest of the hill. Jim turned, hoping to see Kip and Phoebe emerging on the horizon, but instead he saw Dominic's Porsche bumping down the hillside towards the campsite, bright white against the darkening sky.

'Christ,' said Dominic, shaking his head. 'We'd better get this sorted – and fast. Tanya's going to kill me.'

MAX

Sunday evening

'I didn't want Kip out there alone and responsible for
Phoebe any more than Dominic did. But not,' he adds
with insistence, 'because I had the same worries as Dom.'
Max eyes DC Haines, sitting across the table from him in
the farmhouse kitchen. He hopes she is getting a fair representation, an accurate account from everyone. 'I trusted
Kip. He might only be twelve, but I knew he could find his
way home. I'd shown him the area, told him to stick to the
footpaths and trails. Simply, I didn't think it was fair for
him to be alone and responsible for a six-year-old. That's
why it was important we found them.'

'So you, Mr Davies and Mr Miller formed a
search party?'

'Yes, of course. We left right away.'

Dom had set the pace. He'd set off at a furious charge,
only turning to wait for them at the first stile. 'Did you
hear that?' he'd asked.

Max shook his head. Jim shrugged.

191

'I thought I heard a cry.'

The three men stood at the stile and listened. They heard nothing but the gusting wind rising up off the bluff and racing across the fields, the distant thump of the ocean smashing into the headland. A crow, wheeling on the breeze, let out a high *caw-caw-caw.*

'Just a bird,' reassured Max. 'No need to panic.'

He laid a hand on Dom's shoulder, but Dom shrugged it off. 'Let's go.'

Dom climbed up onto the stile. 'Phoebe!' he called, cupping his hands to his mouth. Then louder, 'Phoebe!' There was no answer. He jumped down on the other side and indicated with an impatient gesture that Max should lead. 'Come on.'

There was no sign of the children in the first two fields and at the stile into the third field, they hesitated. 'There are the cows,' said Max, pointing. 'We should be all right if we keep to the hedge, but keep your wits about you.'

'I didn't know . . . cows . . . would do that,' puffed Jim.

Dominic ignored him. There was a strange energy crackling between the two friends Max couldn't quite place. He looked back to check if Jim was all right and saw the sweaty sheen on his forehead. 'You okay?' He appeared to be struggling with the pace.

Jim nodded. 'Seriously though, I thought cows were docile things, just wandering round chewing grass all day long.'

'They can be protective of their calves. And bulls, of course, are different. Far more aggressive.'

Dominic spun to face him. 'Don't you think you should

have warned us? I never would have let the kids go off on their own like that if I'd known about the bull.'

Max raised his hands. 'I had no idea. I've walked this route for months now and I've never seen a bull before.'

'I don't understand,' said Jim, 'if it's a public footpath, how can that be okay?'

'It's complicated. There are all sorts of convoluted agricultural rules, but you're right, the onus is on the farmer to protect the public. If he's put a bull there without warning, well it's bang out of order. Let's get the kids back safely and I'll go up there later to have it out with him, I promise.'

'I'll join you,' added Dom, through gritted teeth.

Max was annoyed to feel so attacked, but Dom's worried frown also brought a rush of guilt. Of course he was anxious. His six-year-old daughter was out there in an unknown landscape. Kip knew the area. Max felt sure he would be okay, but it was different for Dominic. He could sense something huge bubbling up in the man, ready to explode. 'You mustn't worry. Kip's with her.'

Dom didn't reply. His silence spoke volumes.

'They'll be fine,' said Max firmly, but one glance at the threatening sky saw him pick up the pace. A heavy veil of rain was falling out at sea. It wouldn't be long before it was on them.

'Maybe they got it wrong,' said Jim, eyeing the herd. 'Maybe in all the excitement they just imagined the bull.'

The wind gusted across the grass, carrying with it now the strong scent of cow manure. Max looked about the open grassland, hoping at any minute to see Kip and

Phoebe coming towards them. He wasn't sure if it was the change in the weather or the fear rolling in his belly, but the scene, once pastoral and innocent, had taken on a sinister, oppressive quality.

Back at the campsite, it had seemed ludicrous that a herd of cows could have given the kids such a fright, but facing them now, reminded of their immense bulk, their heavy hooves like sharpened flint, Max realized how they might have spooked the children.

'Oh shit.' Jim stopped in his tracks and pointed at the herd. 'I guess they weren't making it up.'

Max turned. Several of the heifers had shifted to reveal a huge, thick-necked bull, all sinew and muscle, standing in their midst.

'Do you see him?' Jim whispered.

'Uh-huh,' said Max. 'No sudden moves, chaps.'

Dominic didn't say a word, though his face was set with something Max couldn't quite read, fear or fury, perhaps a combination of the two, as they continued their stealthy progress along the hedgerow, dodging fresh cow pats and thick tufts of grass, until they came to the stile on the far side. Dominic climbed up and turned back to scan the flat field stretching behind them. He shook his head. 'No sign. They're not here.'

Max was relieved. His greatest fear – the one he hadn't dared voice – was that they would find Kip and Phoebe lying injured in the field. At least they hadn't been trampled.

'So, where are they?' Dominic asked, jumping down and turning to Max with a challenge. 'Phoebe! Kip!' His calls were met by silence.

'Guys, over here!' Jim crouched and pulled something from the long grass beneath the stile.

It took a moment for Max to realize what the blue object balanced on the palm of his hand was, though Dominic's face turned ashen at the sight of it. 'That's Phoebe's inhaler,' he said. 'She knows she's supposed to keep it with her. Pollen can play havoc with her asthma, and if she gets stressed ...'

The three men fell silent. Max turned his face to the ocean, feeling the slap of the Atlantic breeze against his cheeks, green bristles of ling and bell heather shivering at his feet. In a different situation, in a different mood, Max wondered if his friends would have been captivated by the impressive landscape, if they would have appreciated its vast wildness, its elemental force in the same way that he did; right now, through their eyes, he could only see a myriad of dangerous pitfalls and hazards and the gathering storm racing towards them. 'That weather front's coming in fast,' he said.

'Jesus, that's all we need.'

'Look,' said Max, 'there's no need to panic.' He tried to sound as reassuring as possible. 'There's only one other route back to the campsite if you don't go through these fields.' He turned and pointed to the overgrown path leading away from the clifftops. 'That way. You circle back through Kellow's dairy farm and take the lane all the way to our place. They're on tired legs, so they can't be that far ahead of us. We can probably catch up with them.' Seeing Dominic's face, he sought to reassure him. 'Kip knows the way, Dom. Don't stress.'

'Don't stress?' Max could see Dominic was struggling to control his emotions. 'My little girl is wandering about the countryside, god knows where. What were we thinking? She's six, for fuck's sake.' He rounded on Jim. 'This is your fault. I only let her go because you ... you ...' Dominic trailed off, his eyes burning with fury.

'How about we play the blame game after we've found them?' Max snapped back.

Dominic raised his eyes to the sky and let out a sharp breath before turning back to Max. 'Fine,' he said. 'Lead the way.'

They hadn't gone more than a few yards up the trail when they rounded a corner and saw a stooped man in a flapping wax jacket with a long wooden stick coming towards them. 'Kellow!' Max raced forward. 'Hey, have you seen two kids – Kip and a little girl – passing your way?'

'Two kids?' Kellow shook his head. 'You think they came this way?' The farmer frowned. 'I certainly hope not. I told you, I wouldn't stand for you lot coming down here and destroying crops and fencing, stressing my cattle. This is working land.'

'We're not destroying anything,' said Max firmly. 'We're sticking to the public footpaths.'

'They wouldn't be wandering around on their own if it weren't for that bloody great bull you've got in the field back there,' added Dom, fronting up next to Max.

Max felt a surge of irritation at Dom's intervention. 'Let me handle this, Dom.' He turned back to Kellow. 'He's right, I'm afraid. Our kids were chased by your herd – frightened out of their wits by the bull you've put in there.'

Dominic was still bristling with anger. 'Aren't you supposed to put up warning signs? Aren't there rules?'

'You're a fine one to talk about rules, with your illegal camping.'

'Come on,' said Jim, stepping up next to Max, 'we're wasting time. We should get going.'

'You should,' agreed the farmer. 'I'm moving the cows to the barn, as it happens. Don't like the look of that sky. You'd be wise to gather up your kids and get home before the storm hits.'

Max nodded. 'That's exactly what we plan to do. If you see them, do me a favour and tell them to head straight back to the farmhouse.'

The farmer gave a curt nod and let out a piercing whistle. Moments later his huge Rottweiler bounded out of the undergrowth and came to heel at his side.

As the three men moved away down the path, Jim shook his head. 'Well he's truly a delight.'

Dominic turned to Max with a desperate look. 'He said he hadn't seen them. What now?'

'It's a good thing, Dom. If Kellow didn't see them then they must be further ahead than I thought. They might almost be back,' he added, trying to cheer him.

'If any of us had phone reception we could call to check,' he muttered.

Max pulled his phone from his pocket, though he knew it was useless. 'Let's crack on. In an hour's time I bet all this will feel like a crazy, wild goose chase.'

'Yeah mate,' agreed Jim, slapping him on the shoulder. 'We'll get back, complete the head count. Crack open a couple of cans, stick on the tunes and bed in for the storm. The party will be back on track in no time.'

Dominic let out a derisive snort, but Max gave a firm nod and swallowed down the sick feeling rising in his gut. He trusted Kip, he reminded himself, and Kip knew the way back. He'd make sure they both got back safe and sound.

In unison, the three men turned their backs on the coast and the storm racing towards them and began to make their way down the track leading to Kellow's farm and the lane that would circle them home.

ANNIE

Sunday evening

Annie has been listening to Max's account of their field search from the open doorway of the kitchen. Hearing her husband relive those first awful moments of Saturday afternoon has set her nerves on edge.

'You can join us if you like,' says DC Haines, spotting her standing at the door. She gestures to the seat beside Max. 'It might be helpful to hear your side of things.'

Annie nods and steps into the kitchen. From somewhere behind her comes the familiar theme song to a kids' movie, something cheerful and jaunty, out of step with the mood in the house. She pulls out the chair and sinks into it with a sigh.

'You're tired, I know.'

Annie nods.

'Do you want to tell me what was happening back at the campsite while the men were searching for the kids?'

Annie glances across at Max. He gives her a nod. His eyes communicate encouragement, understanding, but she

199

isn't fooled. She knows he is as confused and afraid as she is. She takes a deep breath. 'I had the unenviable task of telling Tanya where they had gone – and why.'

Haines throws her a sympathetic look. 'That can't have been easy.'

'No.' Annie gives a small shudder. 'But someone had to do it.'

Annie remembers how the men had only just left when Tanya emerged from Dom's car, the wind whipping at the fabric of her dress, flashing her slim calves as she reached into the back seat for a paper shopping bag. Scarlet slipped from the passenger seat, and the two of them fell into step as they approached the shelter. Another strong gust sent Scarlet's long hair streaking out behind her and she shrieked, staggering slightly before righting herself and carrying on down the hillside. Annie noticed Scarlet's red eyes. Somehow she looked even more pissed off than when she'd left. Perhaps she and Tanya had argued.

'What is it?' Tanya asked as they drew closer to the communal shelter. 'Why is everyone looking so serious?' She gestured to the sky. 'Is it the weather? Is it time to abandon ship?' You couldn't miss the hopeful note in her voice.

Annie swallowed. She glanced at Suze, then Kira, but they just stared back at her. Kira nodded. She knew, in her role as hostess, that it was up to her. 'We're just waiting for the guys to return. They've gone to get Kip and Phoebe.'

'Gone to *get them*?' Tanya frowned. 'Where did they go?'

'It seems all the kids went on a little expedition, to the

rope swing.' She hesitated. She didn't know how to say it without freaking Tanya out. 'When the others got back, we discovered Kip and Phoebe were missing. Not missing,' she corrected, hurriedly. 'I mean, just left behind. They got separated while crossing one of the fields.'

'We were stampeded by the bull,' added Juniper unhelpfully. She had sidled up next to her mother, an apple in one hand.

'Shhh,' said Suze.

'Stampeded?' Tanya's eyes went wide and began to dart about the campsite. 'What are you all talking about? Where's Dom?'

'He's gone with Max and Jim to find them.'

'I don't understand. Weren't the dads supposed to be in charge?'

'Yes. Yes, they were,' said Suze, jumping in. Annie threw her a grateful look. 'That *was* what we'd agreed. Though it seems Dominic and Jim allowed the kids to go off alone.'

Tanya looked from Annie to Suze and then back to Annie. 'Phoebe's six,' she said flatly.

Annie swallowed. 'Let's not jump to any conclusions. Apparently, they weren't far behind the others. You know how it is with tired little legs?' Annie tried to smile. 'She probably just needs a piggyback home.'

Tanya's look of confusion was shifting to distress. Annie could see it in her eyes and felt a jolt of sympathy. 'Don't worry. I'm sure Dom will return with her at any moment.'

As if in defiance of her suggestion, a huge gust of wind

blasted across the meadow, ripping at the bunting hanging from the shelter and shaking the timber roof above them.

Tanya pointed up at the sky. 'Well, they'd better get back soon. That's coming in fast.'

Half an hour passed in slow motion. Then forty-five minutes. The sky darkened to inky black. Items that could blow away were returned to the tents. Lamps were lit and the solar-powered festoon bulbs were switched on. They swung in the wind like eerie fairground lights against the dark landscape. Annie tried to stay calm, to project a confidence she didn't feel, but the weather was deteriorating fast, the high winds agitating them all. Kira sat with Asha beneath the shelter. Suze kept Tanya company, offering soothing words of reassurance. Josh ran around checking the ropes on the tents and wrestling with tarpaulin sheets, which he laced to the wooden shelter to offer more protection.

'Thank you,' said Annie, throwing him a grateful look.

'Has anyone seen Fred?' Kira asked no one in particular. No one had.

Felix appeared out of the gloom. 'The girls are scared. They're worried the tents are going to blow away.'

Annie didn't know what to tell him. She'd been there when Max and Josh had sunk the huge pegs into the ground, hammered a few in herself. She knew the bell tents were designed to withstand strong winds, but in the face of a mounting gale, she felt less sure that the fixings would hold. She wished Max was there to reassure them all.

'These tents were built to withstand winds of fifty miles per hour.' Josh stepped forward. 'I've checked them all.

Tell them not to worry.' He turned to Annie. 'If you like, I could drive the truck up to Kellow's farm, see if I can spot anyone coming from the road? They're probably walking back that way together?'

Annie bit her lip. 'You wouldn't mind?'

Josh shook his head. 'It's no trouble.'

'Wait!' cried Kira, pointing to the brow of the hill. 'Isn't that Dom coming now?'

A man's outline emerged on the rise above them, followed moments later by another. 'Oh thank god,' said Annie. 'Are the kids with them?'

'Hang on ... yes ... that's Dom and Max ... and is that ... oh ...' Kira said, trailing off.

Annie stared hard, willing the image of Kip and Phoebe to appear skipping along beside the men, but as they marched despondently down the hill towards them, it was obvious that the three men were alone.

Tanya let out a gasp and rounded on Annie. 'You said they'd bring them back!'

'Are they here?' Dominic shouted as he drew closer to the shelter, the wind whipping his words over his shoulder.

Annie shook her head, cold dread seeping through her bones.

'They're not?' Max's face fell, a picture of confusion and fear. 'I felt sure ...'

Tanya ran towards Dominic, meeting him halfway up the slope. 'Where is she?' she yelled. 'How could you? How could you let her go off like that?'

Dominic held up his hands. 'Tanya, I know you're upset but this isn't the time.'

'*You* were supposed to look after her!'

The three men were out of breath, their hair windswept, the first spots of rain darkening their clothes. Jim's face was almost puce with the exertion of the walk. Where the hell were they, Annie wondered? How could they have missed them?

'We should call for help.' Tanya was wringing her hands, looking about at them all, desperation in her eyes. She turned back to Dom. 'Anything could've happened. She's with *that boy*.'

Annie met Max's glance and shot him a warning look that simply said, *don't*. A large raindrop landed on her arm, then another on her face.

Max shook his head. 'We did the full circle, across the field to where the path splits, then back up through the farm and the lane. We saw Kellow. He was moving the cattle. He said he hadn't seen them.'

Annie felt sick to her stomach.

'We did find this though,' muttered Dominic.

Tanya let out a low moan at the sight of Phoebe's inhaler lying in the palm of his hand.

'Okay, let's stay calm,' said Kira, stepping forward. 'We've ruled out a few places, right? Where does that leave? We'll form a proper search party.'

Annie didn't know what to say. The land around them suddenly seemed so vast and wild and perilous. It didn't make any sense. Kip wouldn't just go off like this, not with Phoebe. She couldn't believe it.

As the rain began to fall more heavily, splattering onto the roof of the shelter, the adults moved beneath it.

Someone pulled out an ordinance survey map and spread it across the long table. Someone else fetched a couple of logs from the pile stacked beside the fire pit to pin down the corners that bucked and reared in the wind. As Max began to point and explain the terrain, and the adults' voices began to rise and overlap with urgency, Annie felt her stomach fill with acid as her mind rehearsed all the horrifying alternatives ... shady characters walking the south-west coastal path ... huge waves smashing onto the tiny cove at the bottom of the trail ... a wrong turn onto the vertiginous cliffs. The sinister words of the estate agent who'd shown them around on their very first visit – his grisly tales of mining tragedies, unexplained deaths, a local kid lost on the cliffs – all came flooding back to her. She shivered at the thought.

'Hey,' someone shouted, the voice breaking her train of frightening thoughts. 'Look!'

Annie spun round and saw Felix pointing across the meadow, in the opposite direction that the men had just appeared from, back towards the trail the children had originally taken. She squinted in the faltering light, unsure what she was supposed to be looking at.

Then she saw it: a pale smudge moving against the dark hedgerow, a figure stumbling and tripping. 'Oh, thank god,' she said. She'd recognize those slight, hunched shoulders anywhere. 'It's okay, everyone, they're back,' she called, relief flooding through her like warm liquid honey. 'It's them.'

Kip continued his faltering progress. He was limping, she saw, one arm held awkwardly to his chest. With a low moan, she detached herself from the rest of the group and ran out from beneath the shelter, oblivious to the cold sting of the rain, determined to reach her boy. 'Kip!' she called, almost to him. 'Where've you been? What happened?'

Kip barely had time to give a small, wordless shrug before Dominic raced past her, falling on the boy and grabbing his shoulders. 'Where is she?' he cried. 'Where's Phoebe?'

Annie snatched at Dominic's shirt and tried to pull him off Kip, pushing him aside. She fell to her knees and clasped Kip's face in her hands, searching his eyes. 'What happened?' Her gaze took in the blood smeared across the front of his T-shirt. 'You're bleeding?'

Kip didn't answer. Raindrops streaked his ashen cheeks. He stared down at his shoes. Following his gaze, Annie saw his swollen ankle, puffy and red, and sucked in a breath. She ran her hands over his skinny wet limbs. 'Where else are you hurt? Where's all this blood from?' She was trying to remain calm, trying to coax something from him but Dominic wouldn't wait a moment longer.

He pushed in front of Annie and grabbed Kip, shaking him until his eyes rolled back, flashing white, his teeth clattering audibly. 'Tell us!' he yelled. 'Where is she?'

'Stop it!' Annie cried. 'You're frightening him. He's hurt.'

Kip, with his eyes still lowered to the ground, reached beneath his stained T-shirt and revealed what he had been hiding: a dirty brown teddy bear, soaking wet and covered in sand.

At the sight of it, Dominic let out a roar. 'Where is she?' he demanded, his face almost pressed against Kip's, angry flecks of spittle landing on the boy's cheeks.

'Dominic, he's hurt. He's bleeding, can't you see?'

When Kip did finally speak, his voice was a low, virtually unrecognizable rasp. 'Not mine.'

Annie seized his hands, stared imploringly into his eyes. 'What do you mean? What's not yours? What are you talking about?'

Kip screwed up his face. It seemed to take every ounce of his willpower to conjure his next five words. 'Not my blood . . . Phoebe's blood.'

Annie let out a sharp breath and reared back, as if shoved by the wind.

Dominic let out another wild roar and slapped the boy with a violence that made the other adults approaching from behind gasp and call out in protest. But Dominic didn't seem to hear. He only had eyes for Kip. 'Speak, you little shit,' he shouted. 'I know you can speak. Open your goddamn mouth and tell us what you've done to her.'

'Only he didn't speak,' says Annie, pulling back from the memory, returning to the farmhouse kitchen and DC Haines' shocked face. 'Thanks to Dom, Kip hasn't said a single word since then.'

MAX

Sunday evening

'Kip was curled in a ball on the ground by the time I got there.' He eyes DC Haines, wondering if he is saying too much, but the emotion he'd felt that evening comes rushing back at him like bile. Dominic towering over Kip with his hands in fists. His boy, cowering in the mud at his feet. Annie screaming and pummelling at Dominic's immoveable bulk. As Max had hurled himself at Dominic, his friend had turned, and in the split second before they'd connected, he'd seen the rage burning in Dominic's eyes, caught in the glow of the swinging festoon lights. He'd never seen such wild fury.

Max got the first punch in, the surprise of it knocking Dominic to the ground. Shocked to see his friend go down so easily, Max took a step back, but then Dominic was up, lunging at him, grabbing him around the waist and dragging him down with him, the two men scrapping and flailing at each other in the soaking grass.

'So, Mr Davies attacked Kip, and you hit Mr Davies to protect your son?'

Max sighs. 'Yes.' He rubs his face. 'That's exactly what went down. I never would've thought him capable of something like that, but yes, in that moment he went for him. A twelve-year-old kid.' Max raises his gaze and meets the female officer's steady stare. 'He was in a blind rage. I had to act, to protect Kip. I honestly don't know what would've happened if Scarlet hadn't called out.'

'Mr Davies' daughter?'

'Yes. She was just behind us. She was screaming at Dominic to stop. She looked so frightened. I think it was Scarlet who snapped him out of it.'

Max hadn't known if they were tears or raindrops rolling down Scarlet's shocked face, but at the sight of her standing there in the rain, Dominic had seemed to come to his senses. He staggered up, his chest heaving, his arms hanging at his sides, though his hands, Max noticed, were still clenched in tight fists. Max tasted something metallic on his tongue and realized his lip was bleeding.

For a moment there was nothing but the sound of the two men's loud panting and the rain pelting down onto the canvas tents and the shelter behind them. Then Annie broke the stillness. 'Kip's hurt,' she called. 'Max, help me.' She was on her knees in the wet grass, the rain lashing them both as she ran her hands over their son, trying to assess what was wrong. 'His leg's injured and I think he's bleeding.'

'Stay the fuck there,' Max spat at Dominic, before moving to her side. 'It's all right,' he said, 'Kip, you're all right. We've got you.'

Kip was shaking – with cold or fear, Max wasn't sure. 'He's soaked through. Let's get him into one of the tents.'

'Use ours,' Suze suggested. 'It's closest.'

'Where's Phoebe? Ask him where Phoebe is.' It was Tanya, standing nearby, her face as pale as the ghostly tent fabric standing white against the thunderous sky.

'He knows where she is.' Dominic was muttering, but the violence seemed to have left him. 'He's covered in her blood.'

'Screaming at him isn't going to help. Let's do it this way,' said Annie, imploring Tanya. 'I'll talk to him.'

Tanya reached out and put a restraining hand on Dominic.

Max scooped up the boy and carried him into Suze and Jim's tent, lying him on the bed. The lamp overhead swung in the wind like a searchlight, casting them all in surges of alternating light and shadow. Someone lit another and brought it closer. The rain hammered down on the canvas like a drumroll of unrelenting thunder. It felt, to Max, as if they had fallen into a nightmare.

Kip's face, lit by the glow of the lamp, was pale. His eyes were squeezed shut. 'Kip, love,' Annie said. 'I know you're scared but it's really important you tell us where Phoebe is. Where did you last see her?'

Kip remained silent.

'Get him some water,' someone suggested.

'Kip, please. This is important. She's out there alone. There's a big storm coming. You want to help her, don't you?'

Kip opened his eyes and Max willed him to speak, to say something.

His lips parted.

Come on, buddy, thought Max, help us out here.

But Kip closed his eyes, as if he couldn't bear to see the pain and the fear in their faces.

'Kip, please,' said Max, a hint of frustration entering his voice. 'We need to know where Phoebe is. If . . . if she's . . . hurt?' He hesitated. 'Why is her blood on your clothes?'

Kip shook his head and placed his hands over his ears.

'It's an act! He's playing you both.' It was Dominic, standing at the entrance to the tent. 'Make him tell you!'

'Come on, man.' Jim tried to take Dominic by the arm and usher him out. 'This isn't helping.'

Dominic wrested himself from Jim's grip. 'I'm not leaving this tent until he tells us what happened.'

Kip's eyes opened, his gaze tracking to the entrance of the tent. At the sight of Dominic, he froze, then slowly rolled away to face the billowing canvas wall, curling himself into a small ball, rocking himself back and forth.

'Well done,' said Annie, turning to Dominic, her eyes ablaze. 'You've frightened him to death. How is he going to tell us anything now?'

Max inwardly cursed. He had one job as Kip's father – to protect him. He knew Kip's birth parents were both behind bars, serving sentences for the manslaughter of Kip's baby sister. He knew they'd willingly given him up for adoption. The social workers had told him about the bruises and fractures they'd found on Kip. He could only imagine what his boy had been through. Dominic's violence was a trigger. It would take them backwards, to a terrible place.

A huge gust of wind ripped at the tent as a low rumble of thunder drummed across the campsite. 'Jesus,' muttered Jim. It's getting biblical.'

The flaps to the tent were pulled back and Fred entered, soaked through and shivering. 'Quick, shut the doors,' said Kira. 'Where've you been?'

'I heard shouting. What's going on?'

Kira pulled him to one side and murmured low in his ear.

'I'm going back out there,' Dominic said. 'We must've missed her.'

'If we go out in this, we're at risk of creating an even bigger problem. The cliff paths won't be visible ... the land's unstable ...' Max trailed off, realizing what he was saying.

Tanya let out a low moan and closed her eyes. 'I don't understand.' Her voice was almost a whisper. 'Why does Kip have her blood on his shirt?'

Max glanced at Annie. He didn't have an answer.

'Maybe she's taking shelter somewhere,' Jim suggested, trying to be helpful.

'Shelter?' Dom spat. 'Where the fuck do you think she could be sheltering?'

'Isn't it just fields and clifftops ... the ocean?' Tanya looked frantic.

Dominic gritted his teeth. 'I'm going down to the beach. Maybe we missed something.'

'What about the dairy farm? She could've gone that way? Found a barn? A shed. Maybe that farmer could check for us? Maybe he's already found her? We could call him?'

The thought wasn't particularly comforting. A little girl in the care of gruff old Kellow.

'Where's the nearest landline?' Dominic snapped. 'Our mobiles don't work, remember?'

'The farmhouse,' said Max. 'I'll go right now. Fred, you come with me. We'll call the emergency services and try Kellow too.'

Fred nodded. 'Course, whatever I can do.'

The sky over the headland split with a fork of lightning. Tanya let out another small cry. Dominic tried to pull her towards him, to comfort her, but she pushed him away.

'Suze, why don't you bring the kids up to the house,' suggested Max. 'The storm is upsetting them. At least at the house they'll be warm and dry.'

'I'm not moving Kip,' said Annie emphatically. 'Look at him. He's practically catatonic. I think he should stay here, with me. For now.'

Max winced. He felt torn. It wouldn't be easy to move Kip, but to leave him down here with Dominic?

'I'll stay right by his side. I'm the only one that's going to get him talking,' insisted Annie. 'If we move him to the house and he starts talking, we've got no way to communicate with the rest of you down here. No way to tell you where to look.'

'Fine,' agreed Max, though he didn't feel good about the decision. He gave Jim a look, jerked his head in Dominic's direction and Jim returned it with a small nod of understanding. *Watch him.* 'So Dominic, Tanya and Jim are staying too,' he confirmed, 'in case Phoebe

213

appears. She might see the lights of the campsite and find her way back to us.' Max knew he was grasping at straws.

'I'll stay too,' said Kira. 'In case I'm needed.' Her words hung in the air, all of them aware of what she meant. A trained medic on hand.

'You sure? I'd understand . . .' Max gestured at Asha.

She shook her head. 'She's oblivious, see.' She turned sideways and he saw Asha's sleeping face pressed against her mother's chest. One small mercy.

'Well, I'm not leaving either,' said Scarlet.

'Scarlet,' said Dominic. There was a warning note in her father's voice. 'Do as you're told.'

She shook her head. 'Stop treating me like a kid. I want to help.'

Seeing the fierce look in her eyes, Dominic threw up his hands in exasperation.

'I can stay on too, if you want?' said Josh. 'I could drive you and Fred up to the farmhouse in the buggy, then circle back in the direction of Kellow's farm? It would cover a different area, if Dom's going to check the beach.'

'Thank you,' said Max. 'That's a good idea.'

Suze went to the other tents and began to gather the children, wrangling them into raincoats and boots. Max watched from the covered porch. It struck him that under normal circumstances the kids would be excited to be heading out in such wild weather, jostling and giggling with each other at the adventure, but instead they were quiet, all of them aware of the gravity of the situation.

'Look, I'm not saying it was a perfect plan,' Max says, eyeing Haines. 'I didn't like leaving Kip down there, but it seemed wrong to move him and Annie had made a good point. The most pressing matter was finding Phoebe. We were panicking. Time was of the essence.'

'Just so I'm clear, your intention was to call the emergency services from the house?'

Max nodded. 'Yes, but when we got there, we found the power was out. We have a wireless phone. The handset doesn't work without an electricity connection to the base unit. Honestly, it was a perfect bloody storm.'

DC Haines leans forward in her chair. 'What did you do?'

'It was a no-brainer. Fred and I left Suze and the kids at the house with candles and blankets. We knew they'd be okay. Josh took the buggy as planned. Fred and I took my car. We thought we'd drive as far as we needed to get mobile phone reception so we could raise the alarm. I wanted to call Kellow too, ask him to check his outbuildings.'

'But you didn't make it?'

Max shook his head, miserable at the memory. 'No. We got halfway up the track. The wipers were set to maximum, but they still couldn't seem to clear the windscreen fast enough. If we'd been going any faster, we would've crashed straight into the power line that had come down across the track. I only just had time to slam on the brakes.'

Max shakes his head. 'It was blindingly obvious why we had no power at the farmhouse. Fred suggested we try to clamber over the downed lines and walk to the road, but there were live wires, sparks fizzing and crackling from the exposed cables. It was too bloody dangerous. I couldn't see a way to get around it safely.

'I remember, Fred turned to me. "What the hell do we do now?" he asked.'

Max glances up at Haines in anguish. 'I didn't have an answer.'

TANYA

Saturday evening

The storm wasn't just ripping across the headland, tearing at the shelter and raging at the tents where they strained on their moorings. It felt as though it was inside Tanya. A thundering, shuddering, gut-wrenching maelstrom of emotion. She didn't care what the others said, she couldn't just sit and wait. She had to *do* something.

Grabbing her phone, she slipped out from beneath the shelter and was met by the full force of the wind, tearing at the fabric of her dress, slapping her with cold rain. She hunched her shoulders and forced her way forward, her heeled boots slipping on the wet grass as she began to climb to the crest of the hill.

Maybe, if she made it to the top, back to where they'd parked the cars, she'd be able to pick up a signal and ring for help. It was worth a try. They might all be on different providers. Maybe *her* phone network would be the one with reception. Maybe she'd be able to make an emergency call. If not, she'd carry on along the headland until she could.

The weather was unrelenting, but with each step, she reminded herself that it was for Phoebe. Several times she skidded and slipped, falling to her hands and knees, splattering her dress with mud, her hair plastered to her face. She was soaked to the skin by the time she reached the top of the hill, but she didn't care. Standing next to Dominic's car in the darkness, she pulled her phone from her pocket and held it high above her head, willing a signal to find her. There was nothing. She jabbed 999 anyway, but the line remained dead.

She spun in a circle. Which way to go? The storm had robbed the sky of its fading light, and the landscape, now masked by early nightfall, felt full of danger and uncertainty. Already trembling with cold, she let out a cry of despair. She was no match for the storm.

Defeated, she turned and stumbled back down the hill, towards the dim glow of the campsite below.

'Oh my god, Tanya. You're soaked through.' Kira, shocked at the sight of her, pulled her back beneath the shelter. 'You went out there alone?'

'I had to try,' she sobbed. She gestured down at her ruined clothes, her boots caked in mud. 'I didn't get very far.'

'Let's get you some dry clothes. Scarlet,' Kira called, 'can you run and get a change of clothes?'

Tanya lowered herself onto a bench, shivering uncontrollably, a solitary lamp lighting a small perimeter of dark, as her panic crashed and roared like the world around her. Seeing Phoebe's bear sitting on the table beside her, she snatched it up and pressed it tightly to her. She held it like she held a piece of her missing daughter.

Scarlet returned with Tanya's clothes and she and Kira dressed her like a doll, pulling on the white jeans and one of Dom's fleeces, working their way around the bear, coaxing it from her hands, replacing it gently.

Scarlet hovered for a moment, as if she might reach out for a hug, then seemed to decide against it and took a seat at the far end of the bench, smoothing a long strand of her hair over and over between her fingers. 'I couldn't go to the farmhouse with the others, not knowing Phoebe's out there somewhere.'

Tanya remained silent.

'She'll be okay,' Scarlet said, though the tremor in the girl's voice made it sound more like a question, a question Tanya couldn't answer.

She could only think of those bloody smears across Kip's T-shirt. The sheer cliffs dropping away to the raging sea. That frightening man who had appeared at the bonfire yesterday, his huge black dog and the sound of his shotgun echoing over the hills earlier that morning. She had nothing to give Scarlet in return – no reassurance or affection. She could only think of all the terrible threats that Phoebe might face, out there alone in the storm.

It was Kira who put her arm around Scarlet and let her weep onto her shoulder. Kira who tried to comfort the girl with soft, shushing sounds until, after a time, Scarlet stood and returned to the tent. Tanya watched her go.

It wasn't just Dom that she blamed; a small part of her blamed Scarlet too. If she hadn't been late, if she hadn't had to go and find her on that bench overlooking the sea, hadn't wasted time thrashing over her miniscule teenage problems, she might have returned sooner and been able to prevent this horror, somehow.

'Are you hungry?' Kira was looking at her with concern. 'You missed lunch.'

Tanya shook her head. 'No. I had something in St Ives.' She couldn't remember if this were true or not, but the last thing she felt like doing was eating. Her stomach kept flipping, as if it might disgorge its contents at any moment.

Kira drew a little closer, the baby safely in her arms. Tanya, feeling as though she stood at the edge of a precipice, madness and wild terror within reach, tried to pull her mind from all the dizzying possibilities of her fears. She tried to focus instead on the smallest details around her. The bunting flapping madly in the wind. The spatter of rain on the wooden roof. The sandy grit caught in the damp fur of Phoebe's beloved bear. Its salty, mineral scent when she pressed her face to the toy. The sound of the baby, snuffling and gurgling in her mother's arms beside her.

She turned and looked into Asha's face. The baby's large brown eyes stared back, wide and serious, dark eyelashes sweeping against her bronze skin, the same as her mother's. Mother and daughter, safe, together.

She hadn't known it back then; hadn't appreciated how simple everything had been when Phoebe was still an infant, almost permanently attached to her, like Asha, anchored safely to her mother.

It shook her to remember those early days. The struggle

she had felt. The resentment. After her initial elation to the positive test, her pregnancy with Phoebe had been gruelling. Tanya had been nothing like those women you saw on Instagram, those shiny, glowing mamas-to-be, sipping their green smoothies, tiny, taut bumps encased in expensive yoga wear as they decorated their designer nurseries in tasteful neutral shades and posted excited countdown tickers on their feeds. Instead, she'd been exhausted and nauseous, bedridden for several weeks with sickness, craving sugar and bland white carbs, unable to stomach anything green or nutritious. The shifting and swelling of her body, morphing into something bloated and unrecognizable, had frightened her. She'd felt betrayed. Wasn't her body supposed to be designed for this? Why didn't anyone tell you about the acne, the mood swings, the bloating, the stretch marks, the haemorrhoids and sleepless nights? Was it some kind of conspiracy?

Then came the birth – hours of toil and pain – swiftly followed by the seismic, unrelenting shift of her life, suddenly at the mercy of a smaller, unfathomable being and all the sacrifices that had to be made for her, every single day. Even with the bottle-feeding, the night nurse, and the nanny they'd hired from a prestigious academy to care for Phoebe three days a week so that she could have a little 'Tanya time' and get back into the gym with her personal trainer, she had struggled. The routine had been brutal. She'd longed for this, hadn't she? Clare hadn't had a nanny. Clare had managed just fine with two kids at home. Standing in the kitchen listening to Phoebe wailing on the baby monitor, tears streaming down her face, Tanya had felt sad and resentful . . . a failure. For all her desire to be a mother, the reality, when it came, was a shock.

Emotion rose in her throat, threatening to overwhelm her. She took a breath and pushed it down, fiercely. Get a grip, she told herself, squeezing the damp bear in her arms. There would be time, later, once Phoebe had been found, for blame and recriminations. She couldn't lose it now, not here. She wouldn't allow it. Phoebe was out there, somewhere, and they *would* find her. There was no other option. To even think it was to open the door to an alternative, one that she simply couldn't abide. Every fibre of her being was focused on willing her daughter safely back to her.

'Do you know what I keep thinking?' Tanya murmured.

Kira glanced up and shook her head.

'I keep thinking about what I tell her when we go somewhere new, somewhere busy, like the supermarket or a shopping centre. "If you get lost, just stay where you are. Don't move. I promise I will find you."' She bit her lip. She wouldn't cry. Tears wouldn't help Phoebe right now. 'She's never been anywhere like this before. There's no one out there who can help her. So how can I keep my promise? How can I find her?'

Tanya placed the teddy bear on the table in front of her and gave a small shiver. The temperature was dropping. She checked her phone again, then threw it back on the table. No reception. It was nearly 8pm. Phoebe had dressed that morning in her dungarees and a thin hooded sweatshirt. Nothing to keep her warm or dry. She felt sick at the thought.

And what had she been doing when Phoebe had gone missing?

Shopping. She'd been bloody shopping.

But no – this wasn't all on her, was it? She hadn't left her alone. She'd left her with Dom.

She turned to Kira. 'He didn't want Phoebe, you know.'

Kira's eyes widened. 'Oh, I'm sure that's not—'

'It's true. When we first met, Dom told me explicitly he didn't want any more children. I thought I was okay with it. I thought he'd be enough. But he wasn't. After a time, I realized I didn't want to go through life without experiencing motherhood. You can understand that, can't you?'

Kira nodded. 'I can.'

Tanya reached out to stroke the top of Asha's downy head. The essential 'babyness' of her, those round cheeks and dimples, brought a terrible longing rising in her like a silent howl. 'I forced his hand. I stopped taking the pill. When I fell pregnant, I told him it was an accident, but it wasn't. I wanted a baby.'

Kira looked uncomfortable, but Tanya didn't care. What did it matter now if she spilled her dirty little secrets?

In their earliest years together, Tanya had thought she was fine with Dominic's decision. It was Dominic she wanted – a future with him, whatever that meant, whatever shape *he* decided upon. She didn't particularly want to risk her looks, her figure, her job – for a baby.

Yet a year or so into their marriage, Tanya had felt a shift. She'd caught herself studying women in the park, mothers in activewear pushing plump little babies round

223

in designer prams, or standing in line at the supermarket, cooing at their podgy toddlers slumped in shopping trolley seats. She'd found her gaze drawn to these women with their babies as her gaze had once been drawn by expensive dresses and fancy shoes in shop windows.

Out with her friends, she'd noticed another shift. Their conversations, once so focused on jobs, relationships, holidays and homes had begun to endlessly circle back to their children – their achievements, their mistakes, their adorable ways. Tanya had sat silently, sipping her Prosecco, feeling left out as her friends waxed lyrical about their little darlings.

It was fine for Dominic. He had Scarlet and Felix. He could bang on about *their* accomplishments, bask in the warm glow of his fatherly pride. A private, unknowable piece of his heart would always belong to his and Clare's children. It felt like something Clare held over her. Sometimes, she was ashamed to admit, even to herself, she felt jealous of his affection for his children. She wanted to be everything to him.

But Dominic was a man fulfilled. He was one of 'The Club'. Tanya had begun to feel that it wasn't fair of Dom to ask her to give that up. He was denying her something he already had the luxury of having. Why should Dominic get to have it all? Why should she sacrifice an essential part of herself to make him happy? If he truly loved her, she'd thought, he would want the same for her.

Besides, most men didn't know what they wanted, did they? Not until it was presented to them. On a plate. Of course, they all *thought* they knew what they wanted, but they had to be shown – told even. Men could be so clueless.

It was like when men said they preferred 'the natural look' on women. They *thought* they wanted the natural look, but if you actually gave it to them ... the raw, unwaxed, untanned, un-primed woman in her undone state, they'd be off quicker than a toupee in a hurricane. Men weren't good at looking below the surface of things. They took everything at face value. They saw a pretty woman and didn't realize the 'natural look' they revered was a glossy, blow-dried, artfully made up, toned, tweaked, filtered version. That was the 'natural look' *they* wanted. Not the version where a woman let herself go and let it all hang out. You only had to look at what had happened with Clare to know that.

If Dominic said he didn't want another kid, Tanya knew he *thought* that's what he wanted, but if he was presented with one – fait accompli – she knew she'd win him round. After all, it required no sacrifice from him. It wasn't as if they couldn't afford it. A baby would be a meaningful bond between them. Security. It would establish her, in other peoples' eyes, as on an equal footing with Clare. No longer just the 'homewrecker' – the *second* wife – but the mother of his child. It was a gamble she had been prepared to take.

Only look at them now. Was that what this was about? Fate was punishing her for forcing something that hadn't been meant for her – something Dominic had told her he didn't want. Because if she couldn't keep her daughter safe, then what kind of mother did that make her? Did she even deserve to be one?

'I'm sure Dom doesn't regret having another child,' Kira said quietly. 'How could he?' Kira gave her a searching look. 'He adores Phoebe. He's a devoted father.'

'Where was he today then? Tell me that? Why wasn't he looking after her?'

Kira squirmed, struggled to meet Tanya's gaze. 'He's a great dad, Tanya. He loves his kids. Anyone can see that.'

Tanya turned and stared out into the darkness. They sat in silence, Kira shifting on the bench beside her, until she cleared her throat. 'I'm really sorry,' she said, lifting Asha and giving her a sniff, pulling a face, 'but I think she needs a change.' She threw her an apologetic look. 'Will you be okay here for a moment? Do you want to come with me? Or I can get one of the others . . .?'

'Go.' Tanya waved her away, distracting herself with her phone. She dialled 999 over and over, willing the line to connect, until Dom appeared out of the darkness, wet and white-faced, anguish written plainly on his face. She didn't need to ask if he'd found anything, but he shook his head anyway. 'It's high tide. I couldn't get across the beach. I had to turn back.'

Tanya closed her eyes. She could barely stand the sight of him.

'Aren't the others back yet?' he asked.

She shook her head.

'What's taking them so long?'

'If you'd gone with the kids in the first place, Phoebe would be here with us now. Safe. To think you let her go off . . . with *him*!' She turned away.

'Don't you think I know that? Do you think that's in any way helpful right now?'

A huge gust of wind caught the edge of one of the tarps and lifted it, blowing rain inside the shelter. Dom ran to wrestle it back into position. 'Max and Fred can't be much longer. I'll find out when the police will get here, then go back out there to retrace the kids' steps again. Tanya,' he said, lifting her chin, forcing her to look at him, 'I'll find her. I promise.'

She couldn't answer him, just watched him leave, staying beneath the shelter, a small point of stillness, never once shifting her gaze from the black shadows beyond the small circle of light, as if by the sheer act of willing it, she could conjure Phoebe from the darkness, back safely into her arms.

KIRA

Saturday evening

Kira's hands were shaking as she entered the tent and lay Asha on the change mat, fumbling with the poppers on her sleep suit. The flimsy canvas walls shuddered in the wind, the central pole creaking ominously. Kira glanced about and swore quietly under her breath. What the hell were they all doing out here, in this? It was insanity.

As if sensing her mother's unease, Asha began to grizzle, her chubby arms and legs flailing. Kira wrestled the baby into a fresh nappy and change of clothes, before lifting her to her chest to comfort her. She kissed the top of her warm head. 'See, everything's fine,' she said in a high sing-song voice, rocking the infant. 'You're okay. You're okay. Everything's okay.' She wasn't entirely sure for whose benefit she was singing – Asha's or her own – but gradually, Asha began to calm.

Bearing witness to Tanya's plight had upset Kira deeply. It was a terrible situation. Tanya had seemed so eerily calm. She knew it was shock. She hoped Fred and Max would return soon and tell them that the police were on their way. Time felt twisted and uncertain, but surely enough time had passed to find help? They needed a proper search party. They needed helicopters and dogs and those great big floodlights to illuminate the dark. They needed professionals with calm voices and years of training.

She knew it was selfish to stay a moment longer in her tent than she had to. She knew she should go back to Tanya, but she wasn't ready to return to the reality unfolding outside. She needed a moment to steel herself. She settled on the edge of the bed, holding Asha a short distance from her face, studying her daughter's eyes, her button nose, the dark quiff sprouting from her crown, those two little dimples.

Kira couldn't imagine being without her daughter for a single night. The realization of how precious, how fragile it all was, felt overwhelming. Poor Tanya. It was sympathy that had drawn her to the other woman's side, that had seen her sit on that bench and try to console her. But really, she should have known she couldn't be the one to help her. The more Tanya had opened up, the more she had disclosed how Phoebe had been conceived, how she had manipulated Dom, the more the knife had twisted in Kira about her own deception.

A loud unzipping sound came from the front of the tent. Kira turned, hoping to see Fred but instead saw Dominic's white face appear through the opening. 'Any sign of Fred? Did they phone for help?'

'Nothing yet.' She pulled Asha closer to her chest, protecting her from the burst of cold air. 'I was just about to put Asha down. Come in for a moment?' she said. 'I can't believe they'll be too much longer.'

Dominic shook his head. 'I can't just sit around waiting, knowing she's out there . . . alone.' The last word left his mouth as a sob and he seemed to collapse before her eyes. 'It's a fucking nightmare.'

She laid Asha in the travel cot before drawing him into the tent.

'If I could just talk to Kip . . .' He buried his face in his hands. 'Why was he covered in her blood?'

Kira didn't know what to tell him.

'Do you think he did something to her?'

'Dom, stop. He's a child.'

He raised his head and fixed her with red-rimmed eyes. 'What if Kip's still holding a grudge over the marshmallows. I know it's crazy, but the kid's odd. You can't deny it. Annie and Max, they've hardly spoken about his past. What are they hiding? Do we really know what he's capable of?'

'Dom,' she said in a low voice, 'this is a distressing situation, but think about what you're saying. Do you honestly believe Kip would hurt Phoebe intentionally? That's pretty messed up.'

'I don't know,' he groaned, 'but if Annie and Jim would just let me near him, I'd make him talk.'

She shook her head. 'I can't believe Kip would do anything . . . purposefully violent.' She was trying to reassure him, but in her mind, she was remembering the night

230

before, Kip lunging at Phoebe with that stick in his hand. It was immaturity. A childish reaction. Nothing more. Wasn't it?

'Maybe this is my punishment,' Dominic said, his voice low. He swung his head up and met her gaze. 'For what happened . . . that night.'

Kira froze. 'Dom,' she said, a clear warning.

'Do you think that's what *this* is?'

Kira shook her head vehemently. 'Of course not. This has nothing to do with that.'

Dominic took a step further into the tent. He moved towards the travel cot, his gaze fixed on Asha's sleeping face. Kira felt a deep disquiet come over her as he studied her child. 'That's not how life works, Dom,' she said, trying to offer him reassurance. 'One lapse of judgement isn't the catalyst for every terrible thing that happens in your life from that moment on.'

His gaze lingered on Asha. 'Maybe I deserve this. I'm a terrible husband, a terrible father.'

'Dominic, *no one* deserves this. Not you. Not Tanya. Not Phoebe.'

He lifted his eyes, searching her face, opening his mouth as if about to say something, ask something, but then seemed to catch himself. He made for the exit and she thought he was leaving when he hesitated, turning back to her briefly at the opening. 'Did you tell anyone? About us?'

Kira shook her head. 'God no.'

'Jim?'

'No!

'Not even Fred?'

'No! I kept my promise,' she insisted. 'I haven't told anyone, and I don't intend to.'

He stared at the floor. 'Tanya can't find out. It would destroy us.'

'Dom. Now isn't the time. Let's focus on Phoebe.'

He lifted the collar of his raincoat, pulled his hood back over his head before disappearing into the dark.

Kira watched him go, waiting for her wildly thudding heart to calm in her chest.

That night.

She'd kept their guilty secret locked away ever since her birthday, a night when she'd found the proximity of her friends with their perfect lives talking about their perfect families overwhelmingly grating. There she'd been, staring down the barrel of her forties, still single and aching with her childlessness. She had suggested the Cotswolds week-end away, no kids, just grown-ups, as a bit of fun, so rarely did they get together just as adults – the old gang. She'd thought it might steer things away from the usual pattern of kids' activities and family chatter and at first, it had worked.

It was like old times when the seven of them all met in the hotel bar. But then, over cocktails, Suze, Tanya and Annie had started up with their gently competitive banter about the children, about school issues and sporting achievements and then the chaps had joined in too and Kira had sat patiently for a while, listening to them all basking in their parenthood while she slowly simmered inside. It was *her* birthday. Was it too much to ask for just one night of grown-up conversation and fun?

She'd compensated by drinking far too much, and when

the waiter had presented her with her melting chocolate fondant with 'Happy 40th Birthday' scribbled artfully across the plate in raspberry coulis, she had made the ill-fated decision to give an impromptu after-dinner speech, wobbling at the head of the table as she'd assassinated them, one by one.

'*Look at you all, with your perfect lives, your perfect homes, your perfect children. I used to think we had so much in common . . . that we'd be friends forever, but I'm starting to see that the different paths we've all chosen are changing us. And,*' she added, jabbing her finger at them all, '*not necessarily for the better. I mean, when did you all get so boring? So tedious. When did you all turn into such . . .*' she'd grasped for the right words, '*. . . fucking smug assholes?*'

The stunned faces around the table as she'd flopped back into her seat had said it all.

It turned her stomach to remember how she had acted, how they'd retired to the bar after dinner, their valiant attempts to ignore her brutal take-down and resurrect the celebratory mood, but it was too late, the birthday party had flatlined.

Max and Annie had been the first to make their excuses, declaring that they had to be up early the next morning to get back to Kip, much to Kira's vocal protests. Tanya had gone next, claiming a headache. Shortly after that even Suze had thrown in the towel. She'd bent to kiss Jim on the forehead and whispered – just a little too loudly – that Jim and Dom should please ensure Kira got back to her hotel room safely.

'Why is everyone being so dull?' Kira had complained, flinging herself back against the velvet sofa. 'You're not going to make me drink alone on my birthday, are you?' She'd waved at the barman polishing glasses behind the gleaming chrome bar. 'A bottle of your finest tequila and three shot glasses please,' she'd called. And then, barely lowering the volume, she'd added, 'Maybe I'll get lucky with *him* tonight.'

Dom and Jim hadn't left her. They'd drunk a last shot each while Kira had told them both that they were 'the greatest' and by far the most fun out of all her friends and therefore her absolute 'favourites' until finally, they'd coaxed her out of the bar and escorted her through the lobby, into the lift and back to her hotel room, where she had immediately run to the bathroom and thrown up the cocktails, the tequila, the vintage champagne and her seven-course degustation dinner.

Jim had been worried. 'We can't leave her like this,' he'd said to Dom. 'What if she falls asleep and vomits again?'

'I'll be fine,' Kira had declared, staggering out of the bathroom and stumbling over the small stool in front of the dressing table before collapsing onto her king size bed. 'Go on, both of you, run back to your perfect wives … your perfect lives. I'll be *fine*.'

Dominic had nodded at Jim. 'Go, I'll stay.'

'I'm fine,' she'd groaned. 'Totally fine.'

'You sure?' Jim asked.

Dom had nodded again and closed the door behind Jim. He'd switched on the television and propped himself up on the pile of plush cushions littering the bed, flicking the channels until he found an old black-and-white movie. Occasionally, he'd nudge Kira and remind her to take sips from the bottle of water beside the bed. 'Trust me, you'll thank me in the morning.'

Kira had curled into him with a groan. 'Oh my god, Dom. I fucked everything up, didn't I? I was awful. The things I said.'

Dom put his arm around her shoulder and stroked her hair. 'We're your friends. We understand.'

Kira nodded. 'I just don't get it. I see all the things you guys have. Why can't I have that too? What's wrong with me?'

Dom squeezed her shoulder. 'Forty is hardly over the hill. This is just the start for you. I know it.'

It had felt nice to lie close to someone, to be held, to inhale the scent of aftershave and warm skin. Lying beside him, Dom didn't feel so much like Dom anymore, no longer the friend she had known for twenty years but more 'other', more unknown. She had become exquisitely aware of the gentle back-and-forth movement of his fingers, the slow rise and fall of his firm chest beneath her head. She'd turned to him, intending to thank him for staying, but found as her eyes met his that the words remained locked on her tongue. His eyes were so close, so brown, and those cute dimples she'd never really noticed before . . . In a hazy moment of impulse, she had leaned in and kissed him.

Dominic had remained frozen, his shocked gaze meeting her own, but as she'd gone to pull away, suddenly feeling very sober and a little foolish, he'd said one word. 'No.'

She'd thought at first that he meant *no, I don't want this*. She'd thought he'd meant, *no, I'm a married man*. But then his arms had snaked around her waist, pulling her back into him and their lips had met again, this time his tongue gently probing her mouth.

Neither of them had spoken as she'd peeled off her tights. Neither of them had uttered a word as he'd unbuttoned her dress, or when she'd unzipped his fly and climbed on top of him, or when her hair had fallen across his face, and her hands reached for his, and he had held her hips and groaned in pleasure.

Her desire was overwhelming. Dom had been in her life – been her friend – for twenty years, and yet in that moment he also felt like a complete stranger. Unlike with other men she'd slept with, she found she didn't care about her stubbly legs, her imperfect body or her lack of sexual prowess. She didn't think about what had led them to this place or where it might be going – what he might be thinking. All she cared about was feeling, sensation and pleasure – all her own. And even if she had stopped to consider Dominic, his marriage, and Tanya's feelings, to contemplate the three children he'd fathered and the marriage vows he had taken, she knew that she would have carried on regardless, because in that moment, in that hotel room, she found she only cared about herself, about feeling something other than her own aching loneliness.

Lying beside him afterwards, she'd wondered if it was the very wrongness of it, the terrible, illicit nature of what they had done that had proved to be the most incredible turn-on. Dom had form. He'd messed his girlfriends about at university. He'd cheated on Clare with Tanya. It wasn't a huge surprise to her that he might stray again. But Kira had always been the good girl. She'd always done the right thing – everything that her parents, her friends, her society had expected of her.

Her father had drummed it into her from an early age that she would have to work a little smarter, fight a little harder. As a young boy arriving from Sri Lanka in the sixties, he'd had to overcome prejudice and privilege to become one of the country's top civil engineers. 'Kira,' he would tell her, perched at the end of her bed at night, 'there are people out there who won't believe in you, who won't see anything but your surname, your gender or the colour of your skin. You must work for what you want. You must be proud of who you are – of your heritage. Mine and your mother's. You are the perfect blend of us both. You straddle two worlds. It's a strength. Don't let anyone stop you from achieving your dreams.'

She'd rolled her eyes as a teenager when he'd tried to repeat his little pep talks, but she'd done as he'd asked. She'd studied hard at school and even with all the partying and the evenings spent at the radio station with Jim and Dom, Max and Annie, she'd focused on her studies and passed her medical exams with flying colours. She'd risen to be the youngest partner at her GP surgery. But for what? What had she worked so hard for?

She sat in her office, day in day out, listening to patients complain about their misshapen moles and their ingrown toenails, their STDs and their menopause, their swollen tonsils and their high blood pressure. Some days she felt like nothing more than a walking prescription pad. Who cared for her and her needs? When would life give her what *she* wanted? It wasn't so extraordinary – a fulfilling career, a partner to share her life with, a child to love. It wasn't much to want, was it? So why, when everyone else around her seemed to breeze through life so easily accumulating partners, weddings and children, had these things evaded her?

'Oh god.' Dom, lying beside her, had groaned and rolled away.

She didn't know if he'd meant *oh god, that was incredible* or *oh god, what have we done?* She didn't really care.

For a little while they'd lain side by side on her hotel bed, both of them quiet and contemplative, until the inevitable apologies began. 'Sorry. I'm so sorry. I shouldn't have done that, Kira.' Regret seeped from him, rising from the bed and filling her hotel room with its claustrophobic weight.

She knew he was worried that he'd taken advantage of her – poor, drunk, emotional Kira. She'd considered, briefly, reassuring him, telling him that it was okay, that she had chosen this, that she was the one who had been in control and that it didn't mean anything, truly. But she didn't. She just lay there quietly on the bed offering up her own unspoken prayers to the universe. She had no regrets. Not a single one.

'Tanya can't find out,' he'd said after a while, clearly unnerved by her silence.

'She won't.'

'I mean it. We can't tell anyone.'

'I don't intend to.' She'd turned back to him and squeezed his hand. 'This was a one-off. A secret. Between friends. Okay?'

That was how they'd left it, him skulking out of her hotel room back to Tanya, and Kira rolling over and falling asleep, a small smile playing on her lips.

A few weeks later, she'd met Fred at a work conference and the whole sordid night with Dominic had been pushed from her mind.

A huge gust of wind tugged at the tent, pulling Kira back to the present. Her eyes darted to Asha, still sleeping, blissfully unaware of the tempest raging outside. Something about the way Dom had studied the baby just now had made her uneasy. The lingering, searching look. Had she imagined it?

It was the tension in the air, their fear for Phoebe rubbing off on them all, she told herself, yet something still niggled. Had she been foolish to think she could come away on this weekend with Asha and Fred, without any repercussions?

She leapt as the tent doors opened with a loud ripping sound, a cold gust of air swirling into the space, Fred stepping through, dripping wet.

'God!' said Kira, her hand to her chest. 'You made me jump.'

Fred shook himself. 'There's a power line down across the lane. No phone or internet. No access to the town.'

Kira felt a chill seize her. 'So no help's coming?'

Fred shook his head. 'We need to find another way.'

'We're trapped.'

239

He zipped up the doors behind him and shrugged off his coat. There was a strange, set look on his face. 'Looks like it.'

'My god. I can't bear to think of Phoebe out there in this.'

'It's bad, Kira.' Fred sat on the edge of the bed and ran his hands through his wet hair.

'You're dripping onto the bed. Do you want to get out of your coat?'

Fred didn't move.

'Fred?'

He turned to meet her gaze. 'When were you going to tell me about Dom?'

'What?'

'Kira, I *know*.'

Kira's stomach plunged. A guilty flush rose on her cheeks.

'She's his, isn't she? Asha's his.'

She wanted to deny it, but one look at Fred's face told her she couldn't lie. 'How?'

He shrugged. 'Does it matter?'

Shit. Had she given something away? Had he noticed something in the way they'd interacted around the bonfire last night? Thoughts raced through her mind. 'This doesn't change anything. It doesn't have to make any difference to us.'

'Kira! It makes all the difference.'

'Why? You've known as long as I have that you're not her biological father. Why does this alter things?'

'Why?' He gave a hollow laugh. 'Because you told me Kira had been conceived on a random, one-night stand

240

before we met. But Dom's not some stranger you hooked up with, never to be seen again. He's one of your best friends.'

'It *was* a random one-night stand. It just happens to be the case that I already knew the guy.'

'Kira, don't you see how shady this is? Why didn't you tell me, when we did that first dating scan, when we realized she wasn't mine?'

Kira dropped her gaze. She remembered the shock of it. The two of them at the hospital, excited and hopeful, her hand squeezed tightly in Fred's as the technician ran the ultrasound wand over her abdomen taking measurements, the surprised look on her face as she'd turned to them both. 'Well it looks as though you're a little further along than you thought, Kira. Your baby's dating at sixteen weeks. Congratulations.'

Fred had turned to her with a frown. 'Sixteen?'

Kira, still holding his gaze, had felt her chest compress with panic.

There were some heavy conversations to be had. Fred's shock had morphed to disappointment as Kira had shared vague details about the random one-night stand she'd had just weeks before she'd met him. No one important, she'd told him. A Tinder date. No one she intended to see again.

They'd agonized about what to do, even talked briefly about splitting up, but in the end, Fred had decided he would stick by them. He wanted to be with Kira. He wanted to be the father to her baby. If he was to be the one who would raise her, he could get past it. They could still be the family they'd dreamed of.

'Will you tell him?' he'd asked her.

'Why complicate things? Our baby has everything she needs right here.'

It wasn't the best start, but they had worked hard to put the issue behind them. Until now.

Fred shot her a dismayed look from the bed. 'You asked me to come on this weekend so that I could get to know your friends. I've spent the last twenty-four hours getting acquainted with Dom, trying to ingratiate myself with him. Only it turns out he's Asha's biological father. Don't you think you should have told me? Don't you see how this makes me look?'

'It doesn't make you look anything.'

'You're wrong. It makes me look like a fool.'

'I don't understand why you're getting so upset. It's not as if *he* knows about Asha.'

Fred shook his head. 'I wouldn't be so sure about that.'

Kira fell still. She remembered the way Dominic had stood over the cot earlier, gazing at Asha, the unspoken question in his eyes. Her heart sank.

'You need to talk to him.' Fred sounded weary.

'No way.'

'Kira, he's her biological parent. It's the right thing to do.'

'So now you're claiming the moral high ground? You didn't think Asha's father should know about her when we talked this all through before. Why now?'

Fred raised his hands. 'I suppose it's one thing considering all of this with a hypothetical stranger. It's another to meet the guy and know that you've been keeping this from him. It's huge.'

'You want me to blow up my friend's marriage, just to ease my guilty conscience? That's nice of you.'

'It's not about being "nice". It's about telling the truth. You're lying to all your friends. I was uncomfortable with you keeping the fact I'm not her biological father from them, but I was prepared to go along with that because I assumed you didn't want them to judge you – or Asha. Easier to say she was conceived in a loving relationship than on a random one-night stand. I get that. But this is different. It wasn't a random one-night stand. And worst of all, you've been lying to me. It makes me feel less – like we're not the partnership I thought we were. That you don't see me as her real dad.'

Kira's eyes flashed. 'You are the *real* dad.'

'Well, what about Asha? What if she wants to meet her biological father one day? What will you tell her?'

'I don't know. I figured by then . . .'

Fred shook his head. 'We need to think about Asha.'

'Now you want to lecture me about my daughter's needs?' The words were out of her mouth before she could stop them. That painful, singularly possessive word she'd always been so careful to avoid. *My* daughter.

Fred's face fell. To deflect, she pushed deeper. 'Perhaps this isn't actually about Asha – or Dom. Perhaps this is about you, Fred?'

'What?'

'If you're looking for an easy way out, if you've had enough of us – of me and Asha – you could just say. You don't have to go through this whole charade of moral indignation and outrage.'

Fred gave her a long, hard stare. 'You think that's what this is? You think that little of me? Of my bond with Asha? You think I'd just walk out on you both now?'

Kira shrugged and turned away to hide her reddening cheeks. She'd overstepped the mark, but she couldn't unsay it. It was her defences kicking in, her desperate need to build her protective walls.

Fred studied her, his eyes glittering, dangerously close to tears, or anger, she wasn't sure which. 'Is that what you want? Do you want me to go?'

Kira felt her resounding 'no' bubbling up from within, but pride kept her from speaking.

'I don't understand you, Kira. Why let me walk into this weekend blind? Do you have that little respect for me? I thought you were starting to truly see me as Asha's dad. That we could be a proper family. I thought you felt that too?'

'I thought . . . I thought . . .' She couldn't find the words.

'Do you have feelings for him?'

She shook her head. He couldn't be further from the truth but that angry, stubborn streak that ran through her, that voice that told her that this was how things always ended for her, that she couldn't rely on anyone, that she had to do everything on her own was screaming at her. Somehow, she'd known all along that she couldn't keep him. It was only a matter of time.

Fred threw up his hands in exasperation. 'Your silence is immensely reassuring, Kira. Thanks.'

She watched with a sideways glance as he bent to kiss Asha where she lay in the travel cot. He straightened her blanket then turned and left the tent, zipping his jacket as he stepped out into the raging storm.

'Where are you going?' she called but he didn't reply. Either he hadn't heard or he didn't care to answer.

God, it had been awful. Leaning back in her chair in the warm farmhouse kitchen, Kira pulls her mind from their shitstorm of an argument and eyes the police officer. She hasn't relayed the details of their fight. Some things had to remain private. It was bad enough that she and Fred had fought so spectacularly. She didn't need to air these distractions and trash someone else's marriage at the same time. No matter what Dominic thought, their sordid night together was wholly unrelated to the events of the weekend. So instead, she's given DC Haines a simple precis of their movements, of Dominic and Fred's comings and goings and of the group's dismay to find themselves completely cut off from the outside world. 'Fred will tell you the same,' she adds, 'if you need anything corroborated.'

'Well that's the thing, Dr de Silva. My colleagues are keen to talk to Mr O'Connor, but we're having trouble contacting him. He's not answering his phone.'

Kira sighs. 'And there I was thinking it was just me Fred wasn't speaking to.'

DC Haines frowns. 'You haven't spoken to Mr O'Connor since he left you in the tent last night?'

Kira squirms on her chair. 'No.'

'And you don't know where he was going?'

Kira shakes her head. 'If you must know, we had a bit of a fight. The stress was getting to us all. He stormed off.'

The officer shoots her a troubled look. 'And that was the last time you saw Mr O'Connor?'

She nods.

'May I ask, do you or Mr O'Connor own a blue canvas rucksack?'

'Yes, I gave him one for Christmas last year. Why?' Kira doesn't like the sudden turn in questions.

DC Haines reaches for her phone, opens an email and clicks on a file attachment, angling the screen towards her. 'Do you recognize this?' She swipes through a series of photos.

Kira leans forward in her chair. 'Yes, that's Fred's bag – or one just like it.' She peers more closely at the images. The rucksack appears to be lying on its side in the corner of a gloomy room, somewhere like an old barn or a shed. She can see it is unzipped, spilling items of clothing she is more than familiar with. Striped socks. The ridiculous elf pyjama bottoms she'd bought him last Christmas. A favourite Liverpool T-shirt. 'Those are Fred's clothes, but I don't think I recognize those other things.' She peers more closely at a roll of gaffer tape, wire cutters and a white pill bottle gleaming in the light of the camera flash. 'Those could be the sleeping pills we sometimes take. I get them on prescription. Doctor's perk.' She glances up with a guilty look. 'Just sometimes. We take it in turns if Asha's having a bad night. No point both of us being shattered the next day, right?' She glances at the officer, confused. 'But I don't understand. I thought we'd left this bag at home. Where was this photo taken?'

The woman doesn't answer Kira's question. She simply switches off the phone and makes a note on her pad.

'Is Fred okay? I mean, should I be worried?'

'One last question. Can you remember what Mr O'Connor was wearing when you last saw him on Saturday night?'

'I don't know. It's all such a blur. A jacket and probably a hoodie? He didn't have many clothes with him, not after the bag went missing.'

'Do you happen to recall the colour?'

She shrugs. 'Green, perhaps. No, blue. I think blue.'

'Thank you, Dr de Silva. You've been very helpful.'

Kira studies the woman's face and finds nothing to comfort or allay the sudden, all-consuming fear sweeping over her. Where was Fred? And what the hell had he done?

JIM

Saturday evening

It was like battling through a wind tunnel to reach the tent, one foot in front of the other as gusts of rain blasted his face, the taste of sea salt heavy on his tongue by the time he reached the entrance. 'Only me,' he said, shaking himself off. 'How's Kip doing?'

Annie, looking relieved to see him, beckoned him in. 'He hasn't stirred. He's completely shut down.'

'Has he said *anything*?'

Annie shook her head. 'What time is it?' she asked. 'I've lost track of everything.'

'Nearly ten.'

She leaned across and straightened the blanket over Kip, laid her hand on his shoulder. 'Kip?' she said softly. 'Can you hear me?'

Jim cleared his throat. 'Obviously we don't want to stress the little lad, but as far as any of us know, Kip was the last one to see Phoebe. If he could just give us some indication as to where we should be looking . . .'

248

'Trust me, I'm trying.' She sighed. 'Kip, love,' she said gently, leaning into the curve of her son where he lay huddled beneath the blanket, 'Kip, can you hear me?'

Kip didn't stir and the only reply was the heavy splatter of raindrops on the canvas roof above them, the violent shudder of the tent. She turned back to Jim with a defeated look, then glanced with apprehension at the entrance as the sound of raised voices carried towards them.

Jim unzipped the door a fraction and peered out into the darkness. 'Oh hell,' he muttered.

'Is it Dom?'

He nodded. In the distance he could see Max and Dominic beneath the dimly lit shelter. Dominic was gesticulating furiously. After another heated volley of words, Dom spun on his heel and made right for them. 'He's coming,' he warned Annie.

Annie seemed to physically brace herself, adjusting her position on the bed to shield Kip as Dominic ripped open the canvas door and pushed straight past Jim. 'Has he said anything?' he demanded.

'I'm trying, Dom. But you barging in here isn't helpful.'

'I've walked all the way to the beach and back and there's no sign of her, so I'll tell you what would be helpful. If that little psycho would just—'

'Mate. Stop.' Jim stepped between them.

'Hey,' Dominic yelled, looking past Jim and Annie, gesturing at the bed, 'hey, Kip! I know you can hear me. I'm telling you now, if you've done anything to Phoebe – anything at all – you'll have me to answer to. You got that?'

'Enough,' said Jim, fronting up to Dominic. 'You've

said your piece. The more you frighten the kid, the less likely he is to talk. Don't you understand that?'

Dominic threw up his hands in frustration. 'Why is everyone protecting the reprobate? If he was my kid, I'd make him talk.'

For a moment it looked as if Dominic might lunge at the bed. Annie rose to her full height, blocking his way, a fire in her eyes Jim had never seen before. 'You need to leave,' she said, her voice low and forceful. 'You need to let me handle this.'

Dominic held her gaze, then spun wordlessly on his heel.

'Where are you going?' Jim called.

Dominic turned back to him, his face twisted with distress. 'Haven't you heard? Help isn't coming. Not now. We're completely cut off. She's my daughter. I have to do something. I'm going to search along the cliffs.'

Jim turned back to Annie. 'Shit, that's all we need.'

Annie looked aghast. 'It's too dangerous. He doesn't know the paths. One wrong turn . . .'

Jim nodded. 'I know. I'm going.' He zipped his raincoat and stepped out into the storm. 'Dominic,' he called. 'Wait up!'

SCARLET

Saturday evening

Scarlet watched her father stumbling about the tent in his sodden clothes, gathering up torches and batteries. 'Should I come too?' she asked.

'Stay here,' he said, turning to her, his face grave. 'Don't go anywhere, do you hear?'

She nodded.

'Try not to worry,' added Jim, pulling the hood of his raincoat tight over the peak of his cap. 'I'll go with your dad.'

Watching them disappear into the storm, Scarlet felt, amidst her overwhelming sense of helplessness, a small pinch of relief. She knew it was dangerous for them to go searching, but someone had to do *something*. They couldn't just sit around and leave Phoebe out there alone.

More out of habit than any real hope, she reached for her phone. The screen showed no new notifications and when she opened her message feed, she saw it was still stuck on the last photo download she'd received in

St Ives, the photo of Lily with Harry. She stared at it for a long moment, felt the pain of it all over again, like pressing on a new bruise. She didn't know who she'd contact now, even if she could speak to someone. It was always Lily who she'd call in her hour of need, but she didn't know if she'd ever be able to speak to Lily again. She threw the phone down, watched it bounce off the bed and onto the floor.

The sound of someone behind her made her jump. She turned, expecting to see her dad or Jim, giving a little shriek as a tall, hooded man entered the tent. 'Oh,' she said, her hand on her chest. 'You scared me.'

Fred pushed his hood away from his face and stared about, wild-eyed. 'Is your dad here? I need to talk to him.'

'No.' She scooted back on the bed and reached for one of the cushions, holding it across her chest, painfully aware of being alone with the man who just hours ago had seen her completely and mortifyingly naked. 'You just missed him. But if you want to apologize for this morning,' she added, sounding prim, 'you can apologize directly to me.'

He frowned, pretending he couldn't remember. He didn't fool her. His face broke into a thin smile of under-standing. 'Shit. Yes, sorry. That was embarrassing, wasn't it? No hard feelings?'

He was *smiling*? He thought it was *funny*? There was a bottle of vodka in his hands – half empty. She watched as he unscrewed the lid and took a swig before holding it out to her. 'Want some?'

Scarlet hesitated. 'No thanks.'

'Ah, go on. It's good for stress.' His dark eyes glittered in the lamplight. 'Takes the edge off.'

She wasn't sure she wanted to, but she shrugged and took the bottle from his outstretched hand, took a swig and felt it burn all the way down the back of her throat to her stomach where it sloshed like liquid fire. She passed it back. 'Thanks.'

He didn't say anything for a moment. There was a weird look on his face. Scarlet adjusted the cushion on her lap, wishing he would leave. 'You're a very pretty girl,' he blurted.

Scarlet frowned. She didn't know what he expected her to say in reply. 'Thanks. I guess.' She tucked a loose strand of hair behind her ear.

'Do people say you look more like your Mum ... or your dad?'

'I – I don't know.'

'I haven't met your mum, you see, so I can only see your dad.'

Scarlet nodded.

'You're all good-looking kids, aren't you? You *Davies* kids.'

He said it with a strange emphasis. What a creep. Scarlet wished she hadn't accepted the vodka. It was burning in her tummy and now this dude was trying to crack onto her.

'You with your little dimples.' He reached out and pressed her cheek with a cold finger.

She turned her face away. 'Where's Kira?' she asked, her voice high. 'Won't she be looking for you?'

He shrugged. 'Kira's gonna do what Kira's gonna do. I don't have any say in that.'

Fred held her gaze a moment longer before he turned and left the tent, melting away into the dark, leaving Scarlet with the sensation of his cold finger pressed into her cheek and the vodka burning in her belly. As he hadn't had the courtesy to zip up the flaps behind him, Scarlet stood and made her way across the tent to close them. Standing by the porch, she could make out Tanya's hunched frame sitting beneath the rain-soaked shelter. Josh, who she'd seen return a little while ago in the buggy, was handing her a steaming mug and a blanket, which he lay over her shoulders. Seeing Scarlet watching, he gestured that he would join her, and moments later he dashed through the rain, another blanket in his arms. 'Here,' he said, 'don't get cold.'

'Thanks.' She took the blanket from his hands and buried her face in it, breathing in the scent of damp wool. 'Were you okay out there?'

'It's pretty wild. I went as far as I could, until I had to turn back. Didn't want to risk the buggy getting bogged. Sorry. I tried my best.'

'Do you think that farmer could be involved? He looks like a paedo.'

Josh shrugged. 'He's a moody old git, but I can't believe . . .' he trailed off. Neither of them seemed to want to think about Phoebe in the hands of a strange man. 'Was that Fred I just saw leaving?'

Scarlet nodded again.

'What did he want?'

'No idea. He gives me the creeps. I'm sure he was hitting on me just now,' she added, hoping to stir a little jealousy in him. 'I don't know what Kira sees in him.'

Josh peered outside. He looked as if he was about to leave.

'They'll find her – won't they?' she asked, suddenly desperate for company and reassurance.

'Yeah, I'm sure they will.'

'Do you think Kip did have something to do with it?'

Josh frowned. 'He's always seemed like a good kid. But I guess you can never truly know what's in someone's heart.'

He didn't sound reassuring. Not in the slightest. 'If anything's happened to her . . .' she trailed off. He still looked as if he might leave, as if he were timing his departure with the fierce wind and the rain splattering across the campsite, so she reached out and laid her hand on his arm. 'Stay for a minute, will you? Just in case Fred comes back.'

To her relief, he nodded. 'Sure.'

As he turned to face her, she saw the lamplight shining orange in his eyes, the high angle of his cheekbones and felt a shiver run through her body. He was a good-looking guy. Perhaps even better-looking than Harry Taylor. She'd wasted too many tears on that boy already. Josh wasn't a boy. Josh was a man. For one wild moment she allowed herself to imagine walking into a party with Josh. Someone sexy, and older. That would show Harry – and Lily.

She moved back and perched on the bed. 'I feel like I'm going out of my mind.'

Josh leaned against the table and eyed her. 'It's not easy, is it, worrying about family? You guys are all pretty close?'

Scarlet nodded. 'Felix and I fight like crazy, but we love each other. Phoebe's easier to get on with, hell of a lot cuter too.' She bit her lip. 'I've been thinking about what you said yesterday ... in the hot tub. About family coming first.' She knew she'd done nothing all weekend but moan about being with her family, and here they were, torn apart. 'I'd give anything to have us all back together, safe and sound.'

Josh ran his finger along the edge of the table. 'I get that.'

'I mean, imagine if it was your sister out there. Amber, right? Imagine if she was out there? Lost and in danger.'

'Yeah,' he nods. 'I'd be going crazy.'

A gust of wind ripped at the canvas tent, making it billow and flap. Scarlet shivered. 'I hope Dad's okay.'

Josh tilted his head. 'You look like your dad. Same eyes.'

'Yeah, everyone says we're very similar. Both stubborn,' she gave a wry shrug, 'and a little selfish perhaps.'

'Must be strange growing up with a famous dad. Someone everyone knows.'

'That's the thing. Everyone *thinks* they know him, but they don't. Not really.' She turns to him. 'He's not the guy you see on telly. That's just an act. A persona.'

Josh didn't look convinced. 'From what I've seen of him this weekend, he's exactly that guy. He's got quite the temper on him. He was pretty rough on poor Kip.'

Scarlet felt a rush of loyalty. 'You can't judge him for that. You'd be raging too, if Kip had hurt *your* little girl.'

Josh studied her, his eyes fixed on hers, and Scarlet felt another shiver run down her spine. There was an intensity in his face and for one wild moment she thought he might kiss her. She didn't know if she was excited or terrified. 'Yeah,' Josh said softly. 'I suppose I would.'

He made for the door and Scarlet, disappointed to see him go, thought he wasn't even going to say goodbye but he stopped by the exit and turned back to her. 'I made tea for Tanya. Would you like some?'

His eyes were in shadow, dark and hard to read, but she hoped they mirrored what she felt: excitement, fear and perhaps a small tingle of desire ... feelings that had momentarily removed the bigger fear that consumed her. Scarlet shook her head. 'I'm okay.'

'Suit yourself.'

She watched him go, listened to the zipper being pulled from the outside, wishing she could take back whatever it was she'd said that had made him leave so quickly.

TANYA

Sunday evening

Mindful of her request to avoid Dominic, the detectives
have brought her to one of the emergency doctor's consulting rooms, set aside for difficult conversations with family
members. Faded pamphlets about stroke symptoms, high
blood pressure and grief counselling are pinned to a
noticeboard beside them. A box of tissues sits on the table.
The nurse with the severe eyebrows has brought them a
tray of tea before bustling out. 'Don't worry,' she says,
throwing Tanya a sympathetic look from the door, 'my
shift doesn't finish for a few hours yet. I'll let you know if
there's any change in her condition.'

'I appreciate it's getting late and that this probably feels
like treading over old ground,' says the younger of the police
detectives, 'but we'd like to understand what was going
on at the campsite, after your husband and Jim Miller left
to search for Phoebe. Who was there, what the dynamics
were like, that sort of thing?' Barnett waits, his gaze fixed
on Tanya. The two detectives seem to have decided that

the younger man – the one with the blond hair and the kind blue eyes – will lead with the questions. Tanya doesn't mind. The woman – Lawson – strikes her as blunt and a little too severe. She's never warmed to women like her.

Tanya shrugs. 'I'll tell you what I can, though I warn you, I was kind of out of my mind. All I could think about was Phoebe.'

Barnett glances up from his notes. 'Understandable,' he says. 'You must have been deeply concerned for her safety. It was around eleven pm that your husband and Jim Miller went to search for your daughter.'

'I knew it was dangerous, but I didn't care.' She glances up at him from beneath her lashes. 'Someone had to do something. All I wanted was Phoebe back, safe and sound.'

Barnett clears his throat. 'I believe we also had Annie and Max Kingsley, the landowners, with their son, Kip, remaining at the campsite at this time. Joshua Penrose, who had returned from his earlier search, was also there, plus Kira de Silva and her partner Fred O'Connor, with their baby daughter. And your stepdaughter, Scarlet, who had insisted on staying at the tents. The other four children had been moved to the farmhouse, where Suzanne Miller was looking after them?'

Tanya frowns, trying to piece it all together. 'Yes, that sounds about right. I remember Scarlet refused to leave.' She gives a weak smile. 'It's almost impossible to make Scarlet do anything she doesn't want to. She's strong-willed like that.'

'I appreciate you were in a state of deep anxiety, but does anything in particular stand out to you about that evening and the hours that followed?'

Tanya stares down at her lap. 'I've been over this, trying to figure things out,' she glances up at them both in turn, 'to slot the pieces together. I keep trying to understand what we missed.'

'What *do* you remember?' he asks gently.

Tanya hesitates. 'I assumed Kip stayed in the tent the whole time. I didn't see much of Max and Annie – they were with him. I hoped they were trying to coax him to talk – to tell us where she was. Kira went to put Asha down. Josh gave me a blanket. He said I looked cold. Scarlet was in our tent. The lamp was lit. I could see her silhouette. I thought she might be cold, so I asked Josh to take her a blanket too. She'd found out earlier that day that a boy she liked had hooked up with her best friend. She was pretty upset.' Tanya feels a surge of guilt. 'I'm afraid I didn't have the bandwidth to worry about her too. Scarlet's broken heart wasn't high on my priorities. I could only focus on Phoebe. I think I thought if I sat there long enough, if I willed it hard enough, I could wish her home.'

'Let's talk about Mr O'Connor,' says Lawson, leaning forward slightly in her seat. 'Where was he?'

'Fred?' Tanya frowns. She'd been hoping they weren't going to ask about him. 'He was with Kira, settling the baby. At least I thought he was.' She hesitates. What have they asked her for? Anything that stands out? 'Then a little later I became aware of him sitting a short distance from me beneath the shelter. I was startled to find him there. I hadn't heard him.'

'What sort of state was he in, when you saw him?'

Tanya hesitates. 'State?'

'Yes, did he seem upset? Angry? Nervous? Any detail, large or small, could be helpful to us, Mrs Davies.'

'I guess he looked ... upset.' She sees the officers exchange a glance.

'Do you know what he was upset about?'

Tanya nods. She picks at a chip in her nail varnish and a flake comes away and lands on her jeans, blood red against the white. 'I think he'd had a row with Kira.'

'Did he tell you that?'

Tanya swallows and looks about the room. There are no windows and the grey walls seem to press in on her from all sides. 'Not in so many words, but it was obvious.'

'Go on.' He's staring at her with those kind blue eyes and she knows she needs to tell him everything. No matter the consequences. There's too much at stake.

'He was drinking. Vodka. It was the bottle that caught my eye,' she tells them.

The glass shone beneath the festoon lights as he lifted it to his lips, glittering in the darkness. She turned and saw him slumped on the farthest bench, a short distance from the perimeter of the shelter, where the wind ripped at the tarpaulin. She felt sure the driving rain would be pelting his back. 'You're getting wet,' she said, and beckoned him closer.

Fred stood and moved towards her, flung himself down onto the bench opposite. He was soaking, water dripping down his hair onto his face, into his eyes, yet he seemed oblivious. 'Tell me, Tanya,' he said, 'you've known this group longer than me – how long does it take to infiltrate them? How long before you feel like one of them?'

He was on his way to being very drunk. She could see it in his swaying posture, his exaggerated hand movements, the slurring of his words. She shrugged. 'I don't know that I do feel like one of them.'

He nodded, as if this were the answer he'd expected, and leaned in towards her, close enough that she could smell the tang of alcohol on his breath. 'We're the outsiders, then. Us two.' He waved around at the campsite. 'The *outsiders*. Get it?' His laugh sounded forced. Already she was regretting inviting him over. She didn't have the energy for this. She wanted only to think of Phoebe.

'I'll tell you what I find strange about this whole setup,' he said.

'What's that?' She eyed the shadows behind him, wondering if there might be some relief from this intense exchange in the form of Annie or Max emerging from their tent. Or Kira, perhaps, looking for him.

'Doesn't it strike you as odd, this gang of "old friends"?' He made exaggerated quotation marks with his fingers. 'I've seen you, Tanya. I saw you yesterday, sitting back, watching them all. I think you're like me. Observing. All that forced camaraderie. The reminiscences and memories. You know what it makes me wonder?'

Part of her didn't want to engage with his drunken rant, but she found herself increasingly intrigued by his outpouring, how his thoughts echoed many of her own. 'What's that?' she asked.

'I can't help wondering if – after all this time – any of them even like each other.'

Tanya leaned back, taking in what he had said as he took another swig from the bottle then wiped his mouth on his sleeve. 'Except for Dominic and Kira, of course. They like each other – veeerrry much.'

Tanya felt something cold slice through her like a blade. 'What did you say?'

'You must've noticed it. That *thing* between them.' He shook his head. 'And at her birthday too. Right under your nose.' He looked up and seeing her stricken expression, something shifted in his face. 'Oops.' He held up his hands. 'I guess you didn't know either.'

She stared at Fred, the glow of the lightbulbs catching in his eyes, making them dance with fire as the cogs turned slowly in her brain. She 'didn't know'? What didn't she know? 'Dominic and Kira?' She laughed. 'Don't be silly. They've known each other for years. They're just friends.'

'But just how *good* friends are they, Tanya?' He raised his finger at her to emphasize his point. 'That's the question.'

'You're drunk, Fred. You should go and lie down.'

'Yeah, you're probably right. I guess I just thought you'd want to know about your hubby's extra special *gift* for Kira, the one he gave her on her fortieth birthday.'

She studied Fred's face. What was he talking about? She didn't remember the gift they'd bought her. Hadn't they all clubbed together on something – a set of expensive wine glasses, or a decanter? What she *did* remember was the terrible state Kira had been in on her birthday night – so drunk and overwrought that Tanya had lost all patience and taken herself off to bed, hoping Dominic would follow as soon as he could extricate himself from the car-crash of an evening. She had a vague memory of him sliding into bed much later – at god-knows-what-time. And yes, he had been in a strange mood the next morning, but she had put that down to his hangover. 'You didn't even know Kira back then. You weren't there. Why should I believe anything you're saying?'

Fred shrugged. 'Because I know Kira *now*. And I know *Asha*,' he added, taking another long swig from the vodka bottle. 'It's an uncanny likeness, don't you think?'

Tanya gaped at Fred. He'd lost his mind.

'He said it himself last night, didn't he? That charming, impromptu speech at the bonfire? How he'd do *anything* for his friends. Very touching.'

Tanya felt a rush of nausea. 'Are you saying what I think you're saying?' She swallowed. 'You think Asha is Dominic's?'

'Those cute little dimples.' He grinned at her. 'You look like you need a drink.' He offered her the bottle again, but she pushed it away.

'Suit yourself.' Fred stood and made his way out from beneath the shelter into the full force of the storm. He swayed and held out his arms, allowing the wind to hold him momentarily before he turned and melted away into the darkness, leaving Tanya still seated on the bench, frozen in shock.

'That must have been a very difficult conversation for

you,' said the female officer, breaking the silence that had fallen over the interview room.

Tanya nodded. She didn't *have* to give the police the full account of their conversation. She could have spared Dominic the embarrassment, but why should she protect him? He obviously hadn't any regard for her feelings. What did she owe him?

'And then Mr O'Connor just took off, you say? Did you see which direction he went in?'

Tanya shook his head. 'It was too dark. I thought down towards the meadow and the cliff track, the same direction the kids had originally gone, but I'm not entirely sure. To be honest, after our conversation, I felt quite ill. I took myself back to the tent to lie down.'

The police officers exchange a glance.

'What is it?'

'He offered you a drink. Did you take it?'

Tanya frowned. 'No. I don't, I don't think so. I already told you. I didn't want it. I just wanted him to go.'

'I see. And I don't suppose you can recall what Mr O'Connor was wearing, that last time you saw him?'

Tanya frowns. She can't for the life of her think why this might be relevant. 'I'm sorry, I don't remember. A jacket. Or a hoodie?' She thinks a moment longer. 'Blue, I think.'

The male officer turns to DC Lawson and nods. Tanya tries to read the look they exchange but the moment is interrupted by a knock on the consulting room door. It is the nurse with the eyebrows, back again. 'I thought you should know, our patient's regained consciousness.'

Tanya stands quickly, releasing a long breath. 'Oh, thank goodness. May I see her?'

'I'm afraid she was very distressed. She was asking about "Kip".'

'I should've been there.' Tanya throws a glance at the police officers, but Lawson held up her hand.

'Has she said anything else?'

'No, she just kept asking me, "Where's Kip?"' The nurse looks around at them. 'She seemed very frightened.'

Tanya presses her hand to her mouth. 'I *knew* he was involved in this.'

'We'll need to speak with her.' Lawson is shuffling her papers. 'As soon as possible.'

'The doctor had to administer a sedative, something to calm her,' the nurse says. 'She'll need to conduct a thorough assessment before she'll allow an interview to take place. I suggest you come back first thing tomorrow morning.'

Lawson sighs and gives a curt nod. 'Understood. We'll conduct a final interview with Mr Miller, then return in the morning to speak with the girl.'

'In the meantime,' the nurse says, turning back to Tanya, 'we'll keep her calm and comfortable.'

Tanya isn't satisfied. She leans forward in her chair, her gaze jumping from Barnett to Lawson. '*Now* will you do something?' she demands, exasperated. 'You have to bring that boy in. You have to make him talk. None of this will be resolved until you do.'

DOMINIC

Saturday night

They were walking blind, the storm hammering them from every direction. Up on the bluff, exposed to the elements, there was no mercy. It was like fighting in a boxing ring, being assailed by an invisible opponent, hefty blows beating down on them, the rain slashing at them, drenching their clothes, turning the broken, stony ground slippery and treacherous. Jim tripped along behind him, puffing and stumbling, but to Dominic, it felt personal, as if it were just him alone battling the tempest, man versus storm, his desperation pitted against its dark elemental rage.

'Wait up!' Jim called, sliding down the path behind him. 'Or we'll get separated.'

Dominic ignored him, powering on, slipping and skidding along the rocky track. Jim had been tailing him since he'd left the campsite, the beam of his torch swinging just a little behind his own, the thud of his footsteps and his heavy panting at his back. He had no idea how long they had been out there in the dark. Time had lost form, though the weight of his sodden clothes and his physical exhaustion would suggest they had been walking for hours. It felt like this hellish night would never end. His Sisyphean punishment. Surely it would get light soon?

Every so often, Dominic would stop and shout for Phoebe, her name flying away on the wind as his voice grew increasingly hoarse. At some point, in a vain attempt to warm his hands, he shoved them deep into his sodden pockets and his fingers grazed the cold plastic of Phoebe's asthma inhaler. He let out an involuntary sob. What if she was out here, frightened and wheezy? What if she needed those steroids to open her airways and allow her to breathe? At the thought of her distress, at the thought of her lungs gasping for air, her eyes wide, her face and lips draining of colour, he felt an excruciating twist of pain. He wasn't going to stop. Nothing was going to hinder his search for Phoebe; not the lashing rain, nor the thunder rolling in off the sea, nor the pitch black that masked every sprawling root or rock he stumbled over. He wouldn't stop until he'd found her.

He filled with shame at the memory of his distracted farewell to her earlier that afternoon, his focus not on Phoebe but on his own problems, his desire to get her away from the campsite before any of the kids overheard his conversation with Jim.

He ran through them in his head, all the many reasons he was a terrible person – all his many misdemeanours and failures as a man – and wondered if this was it. Was this the reckoning he had always felt, somewhere deep in his gut, was coming for him? The charmed life he had lived he saw now to be so precariously balanced. The material trappings, the high ratings, the courting of TV executives and producers, the bullish judgement and criticism he threw out to unwitting contestants every Saturday night, playing for shock and laughs, for the notoriety.

None of it mattered. It was artifice. He'd give it all up – give up anything that was asked of him – just to have his daughter's hand safely clasped within his own, just to have his family home safe and sound. In his head he offered up his silent plea – his bargain with the universe. The universe could have it all: his fancy car, his career, his house, his fame, his looks. Anything. Just as long as his family were left unscathed.

His anger wasn't reserved for himself alone though. He used his fury against Jim and Max to motivate every one of his thudding steps across the headland. Bloody Jim. With his theories and his blackmail. And bloody Max, too, standing sentry at the tent entrance, as if Dominic were the danger and Kip was the one that needed protection. The kid had returned with her bear, covered in Phoebe's blood. There was no possible explanation in Dominic's mind that didn't end with Kip having done something unspeakable to Phoebe. The fact that no one else – not one of their friends – had backed him up, or agreed that it was time to make the kid talk, skewered him. He knew, had he been allowed in there, had he been given five minutes alone with the boy, that he would have made him spill his guts.

He followed the precarious coastal trail, picked out by

the light of their torches, until the route seemed to dissolve before him, the unforgiving scree and gorse opening out onto a rocky plateau. Dominic cast his torch about, looking for the thread of the trail, but it appeared they had taken a wrong turn. They stood on a perilous headland high above the raging sea. The howling wind seemed locked in competition with the ocean smashing onto the cliffs far below. Out over the water, the black void was torn with a jag of lightning and for a second everything was lit up, the sky cracked in two, the foaming ocean dark and malevolent, seething below, before a split second later they were plunged back into darkness. Dominic's legs shook when the thunder hit.

'Dom, it's not safe up here,' Jim shouted. 'We should get to lower ground.'

Dominic rounded on him, anger surging through his chest. He felt like an instrument, channelling the elemental rage of the storm. 'I don't know why you followed me if you only intended to bitch and moan. If you wanted to stay warm and dry you should've gone and put your feet up at the farmhouse, with Suze and the kids.'

'Come on, man. That's not fair. I'm trying to look out for you.'

'And I'm trying to find my daughter.'

'This is madness,' Jim shouted. 'We've been stumbling round in the dark for hours. It'll be light soon. We should conserve some energy and start looking again then.'

Dominic let out a bitter laugh. '*Now* you're full of great ideas? You know, if it wasn't for you, she wouldn't even be out here. She'd be back at the campsite, safe.'

'If it wasn't for *me*?' Jim seemed to visibly stumble backwards at the accusation. 'How'd you figure that?'

'You were goading me.' Dom stepped forward, jabbing at him with a finger. 'You were threatening me with your nasty little theories. Shooting your mouth off. Leveraging what you thought you knew about me to get out of paying back that loan. Of course I wanted to get her out of there.'

Another bolt of lightning split the sky and in its white light Dominic saw Jim's face, puffy, tired and slack-jawed with shock. In that moment, twenty years of friendship, of camaraderie, of pints in pubs and late-night bonding over music, of toasting each other's weddings and children, of standing shoulder-to-shoulder through life's ups and downs went skittering away on the wind. In that moment, Dominic hated Jim and everything he stood for.

'You know why you've never got anywhere in life?' he shouted. 'It's because you're lazy, Jim. You've got no drive, no commitment to anything – record labels or food trucks. It was never going to happen. Look at you now. Failing even as a poxy youth worker.' Dominic saw the shock in Jim's eyes, but he couldn't stop. The sight of him standing there, drenched and pitiful, had unlocked all of Dominic's pent-up vitriol.

'You've probably got more problems than those kids you're supposed to be helping. I bet they laugh at you behind your back. I bet they feel sorry for you. The fat old geezer, still trying to keep up. Still trying to be relevant and cool.'

Jim gaped at him, but Dominic couldn't stop, not now the flood gates had opened.

'You take the piss out of me for my nice clothes, my car, my public profile, but you're jealous. You've got nothing to show for your life and your goddamn laziness. I wouldn't give a shit, mate, but your "have another beer and forget about it" attitude hasn't just stuffed up *your* life – it's stuffed up mine now too.'

Jim turned away, visibly reeling.

'Yeah that's right. Walk away. Take the easy way out. Just like always.'

Jim froze and turned slowly, fixing Dominic with a glare. 'You want to blame *me* for this? You want to throw out insults and bang on about your "better instincts"?' He rolled his eyes. 'Dom, you're the joke.'

Dominic narrowed his eyes, tensed himself for Jim's rebuttal.

'I may not have thousands of followers on social media, loads of money in the bank, a flashy car or designer clothes, but at least I know what I stand for. I have principles.'

Dominic's laugh was snatched away on the wind, but Jim wasn't finished.

'Not you, Dom. You kid yourself that you're strong. You're a *real* man. But we both know that you're weak. You're the one that sold out to the reality TV machine. You're the one that's become a grotesque TV persona. You want to talk about "better instincts"? I see what motivates you. It's pride and vanity, greed and ...' Jim sucked in a deep breath and spat the last word at him, 'lust.' He drew himself up. 'At the end of the day, I can look at myself in the mirror. I know I'm a good father, a faithful husband. It's more than I can say for you.'

Dominic lunged at Jim with a feral roar, catching him about the waist, sending them both heavily to the ground. For a second or two they lay winded, until Jim jabbed out at Dominic with his elbow, catching him in the jaw. They fought like teenagers, scrapping and flailing at each other, lashing out and lunging, sliding in the mud. Dominic landed two blows that sent Jim staggering. Dominic turned to put some distance between them, but Jim wasn't done with him. He lunged for his ankles, pulling him back down. Dom tasted blood on his tongue, his or Jim's, he didn't know. He felt sickened by the physicality of him, the solid weight of his friend lying on top of him, his hot breath on his face. He shoved him off and Jim sprawled onto his back near the edge of the cliff. Dominic stood and landed three violent kicks, two to his ribs and the last connecting with his arm with an awful crack.

Jim let out a groan and Dominic turned, leaving him writhing in the mud. He didn't bother to look back. He didn't care. In that moment he didn't give a shit about Jim. He staggered away across the dark bluff, repeatedly calling Phoebe's name, as the storm whipped it out to sea.

SCARLET

Sunday morning

Scarlet was woken with a gentle shake.

She rubbed her eyes, confused. It was still dark out, but the rain on the roof of the tent had eased and it sounded as if the thunder had stopped too. She listened. Even the wind had died a little, the tent no longer snapping wildly like a sheet on a washing line, just billowing more rhythmically, in-and-out. The storm was definitely passing. 'What is it?' she murmured, still half asleep until she remembered where she was and what was unfolding and saw who was crouched in front of her. She sat bolt upright and scooted back on the bed. 'What are you doing in here?' She frowned. 'Is it Phoebe?'

He nodded, his face just visible in the dark, his eyes fixed intently on hers.

She gaped at him. 'She's back?'

'I know where she is.'

Scarlet frowned. 'What? Really?'

He placed a finger to his lips then pointed to Tanya,

274

curled on the bed, a quilt over her legs. He gestured for her to follow him.

'I should tell her where we're going.' She was already reaching for her trainers, fumbling with the laces, but he shook his head and returned a finger to his lips.

Remembering Tanya's distress, the pain and worry she had seen etched on her stepmum's face, Scarlet realized it would be better to let her sleep. She slipped out of the tent behind him and quietly zipped the flaps closed.

Outside, the campsite was dark, just the festoon lights swaying eerily over the abandoned shelter, the tarpaulins flapping in the wind. He gestured towards the buggy. Still groggy with sleep, she slid into the passenger seat beside him, squinting as the headlights flashed on, two bright spotlights in the dark, the engine starting with a roar.

She thought they might drive down through the meadow towards the cliffs, but instead he spun the vehicle around and headed up the slope, back in the direction of the farmhouse. Puzzled, she turned to him. 'This way?'

'They're searching in the wrong place.'

Scarlet frowned. 'But she's okay?'

He nodded again, his hands clenching the wheel as he navigated the jolting track away from the campsite. He'd made her nervous earlier, but she felt important now, pleased he had thought to wake her. They had a job to do. 'Look, it's starting to get light.' She pointed out to sea, where a thin grey light teased the horizon. They flew over a particularly violent rut in the trail and she jolted forward in her seat. He reached out and placed one hand on her leg.

'How'd you find her?' she shouted over the diesel roar of the engine.

She waited for him to explain but he'd fallen silent, concentrating instead on navigating the bumpy terrain that emerged at high speed in the headlights of the vehicle. She shivered and wrapped her raincoat more tightly about her body. He pointed down at her feet and she bent and found a tartan-patterned flask tucked into the footwell. 'What is it?' She opened it and sniffed. 'Tea?' She waited for a less bumpy stretch before taking a long slug. It was hot and sweet. 'That's good. Thanks.'

She offered him the flask, but he shook his head. 'Just imagine their faces,' she smiled, 'when we return to the campsite with her. We'll be heroes.'

The track began to narrow until it became impassable, even for the off-road buggy. He brought the vehicle to a halt, climbed down then gestured for her to follow him.

Scarlet nodded. She was weary from lack of sleep, her legs heavy and her mind struggling to catch up with the unfolding events, but her need to get to Phoebe drove her on. If her six-year-old sister could make it all the way out here by herself in the middle of a storm, the least Scarlet could do was go a little further to help bring her back.

The landscape around them began to emerge from the darkness, taking shape in the faint dawn light like a fuzzy polaroid coming into focus. The outline of the headland appeared as if it had been drawn in felt-tip pen against the purple horizon, the scrubby brush and tumbled rock formations coming into view. 'What's that?' she asked, pointing to a high turret just visible against the lightening sky.

'That's the place.' He pointed to a steep, overgrown fork leading off the main path.

Scarlet, cheered at the thought of being so close to Phoebe, turned down the scrubby trail, her footsteps navigating the uneven ground, trying to avoid the overhanging gorse and tangled brambles clasping at her ankles, all the while keeping the stone ruins perched above the raging ocean fixed in her sights. She allowed herself to skip ahead in her mind, to imagine the moment when they returned triumphantly to the campsite, how everyone would crowd round, jubilant and grateful to have Phoebe back safely. Scarlet saves the day! It would make a change from the usual shitstorm that seemed to follow her round.

A sound carried towards her, a chorus, strange and ethereal; mournful voices singing faintly, as if carried towards her across the waves. Tilting her head, she listened, wondering if she was imagining the dissonant wailing. As the gusting wind dropped, so too did the sound. She shook her head. It was the wind, singing across the bluff – or her imagination. Either way, a distraction from the task at hand: rescuing Phoebe. 'Thanks for this,' she called. 'Thank God you found her.'

We're coming for you, Phoebe, she thought. Not long now.

JIM

Sunday evening

'You're telling us that your injury – your broken arm – was caused by "a slip" out on the headland? You're sticking to that story?' Sitting in the interview room at the hospital, DI Lawson's razor-sharp focus rests intently on him. It must be nearly midnight, yet she shows no signs of fatigue.

Jim frowns. He can see she doesn't believe him. He weighs his options. He could tell the truth, but what good would it do to take them blow-by-sordid-blow through his fight with Dom? It wouldn't reflect well on either of them. Besides, now he's been patched up by the doctors, he just wants to get out of there.

He clears his throat. 'Yes. Out in the dark on those rocky slopes it was impossible to navigate every trip hazard, every mudslide. Frankly, I consider myself lucky that's all that happened to me.' He tries to conjure a convincing smile, but it feels forced and ghoulish on his face.

Lawson gives a curt nod. 'Very well. Let's continue, shall we? You found yourself out on the headland at daybreak after you and Mr Davies had decided to ... part ways?'

'Yes.' He doesn't quite meet her gaze. 'We decided we might have better luck if we split up.'

'You must've been very tired, Mr Miller?'

'I was. Battered.'

It had been tempting not to move. He'd lain there on his back in the mud, where Dominic had left him, and studied the shifting sky. Gradually, the relentless black began to fade to graphite grey and the silhouette of a solitary bird soaring overhead appeared in the sky. Watching its arcing flight, Jim realized that the rain had stopped. Day was breaking, at last.

His left arm lay at an odd angle, radiating pain all the way to his collarbone. It felt as if he had been pinned to the ground by a heavy boulder. He knew he should move. He knew he should pull himself up from the wet ground, but exhaustion had claimed him. He had been walking all night, was drenched to the skin, his clothes cold and clammy, and now *this* with Dom.

Dom thought Phoebe's disappearance was his fault. Perhaps it was.

He squeezed his eyes shut. Get a hold of yourself, he told himself, but he couldn't move. A familiar black feeling, thick and cloying, crept over him as he lay and allowed the tears to slide down his face and seep into the mud beneath him. Far below, beyond the bluff, waves crashed against the cliffs, a relentless, hypnotic pounding.

God he was a fool. On so many levels. A fool for where he found himself, damp and exhausted lying spent on the ground. A fool for thinking that Dominic had ever rated him, respected him, *loved* him, even. A fool for following him blindly through the storm. What a metaphor for their friendship that was.

Dominic leading. Jim following.

Wasn't that how it had always been between them? Twenty years and only now do they tell each other what they really think of each other. What a joke.

Only it wasn't a joke. There was a little girl lost out there and if anything had happened to Phoebe ... Jim closed his eyes again. *Was* Dom right? Was it his fault?

It was true that he had been goading him. He'd enjoyed that rare moment of power over Dom, the realization that he knew something his friend didn't. He wouldn't have said anything at all – would have kept the fact he knew what had happened between Dom and Kira secret out of loyalty. But when Fred had dropped that detail about their first date, it had sparked questions about Asha's paternity in his mind. And when Dom had started needling him about the loan, when he'd threatened to spill the details of it to Suze – he'd had enough. Dom had pushed his buttons and Jim had well and truly flipped. Well done, Jim. Another epic failure.

Dominic was right. It came too easy to him. Failure. Over the years he seemed to have got it down to a fine art. The dismal attempt to launch an indie record label. The waning shifts at the youth centre. And now the mess he'd got himself into with the food truck, overpaying for a van that needed significantly more work than he'd anticipated, which now sat outside their house demanding road tax payments and renovations, and that was before he'd even booked a single festival or gig.

He was good at playing the clown – he'd done it most of his life, covering up his insecurities and emotions with his jokey humour. He'd certainly been working hard this weekend to maintain the front, to be the Jim they all expected him to be. But he was exhausted. He couldn't do it any longer. The façade was killing him.

He knew what Suze would say. She'd give him that look – the wide-eyed, encouraging smile, the one he knew she used to motivate her clients – and tell him he was a wonderful father, a loving husband. She'd tell him he was kind and funny and loyal. She'd tell him she didn't care about the jobs, the money or the extra strain it put their family under. She'd try to bolster him by reminding him of all the many things she loved about him. And when that didn't work, she'd get a little stern and tell him to buck up and stop feeling so sorry for himself.

But the truth was, her relentless attempts at positivity and encouragement hadn't been working too well these past few months. And even she didn't know the half of it. She didn't know about the days, after the kids had left for school and she'd left for the clinic, when he simply gave up. She didn't know about the days he climbed back into bed and pulled the covers over his head, only dragging himself up just before her key turned in the lock, where he'd sit at the kitchen table and recite stories about work contacts and meetings and walks in the fresh air to reassure her, even though the real story was often that he'd accomplished little more than several hours lying flat on his back staring at the ceiling, thinking of all the reasons Suze and the kids might be better off without him.

Suze was a powerhouse. He knew she'd be fine without him. She was the woman who'd taken night courses in yoga and reiki, while still working as a counsellor at the youth centre all those years ago. She was the one who'd qualified as a nutritionist while pregnant with River, opening her own wellness clinic just a few months later with a newborn at her breast. She was the one adept at fixing all their issues and ailments, healing bodies and minds. Her achievements dwarfed his tenfold. She just wasn't able to fix him. While she charged about, spruiking healing and wellness, her own husband disintegrated at home in a puddle of lethargy.

Suze didn't know the extent of his depression, just as she didn't know about the fifty thousand pounds he'd borrowed from Dom, which he knew he wouldn't be able to pay back any time soon. He'd kept it all from Suze. His shameful little secrets. Thinking of it made him feel sick to his stomach.

He groaned loudly then dragged himself up, standing gingerly, testing his bruised, mud-splattered legs, feeling the ache of his ribs as he checked for injuries. One of his eyes felt swollen and puffy, and his left arm dangled uselessly. He'd broken something. He was sure of that. He should probably try to make a sling, but he couldn't think what he would use or how he would fashion it one-handed.

His beloved trucker's cap was floating in a puddle. He picked it up and tucked it into his pocket. His torch lay a little further away, still shining a weak beam across the scrub. He switched it off and slid it in his other pocket, eyeing the trail leading away from the bluff, the same trail Dom had taken.

What was the point? Instead, he turned and made for the cliff's edge.

The wind pressed insistently against him. It wasn't as strong as it had been overnight, but there was still a force to it, an intentional surge that meant he had to plant his feet carefully to counter its strength as he crept closer to the edge.

The worst thing, he thought, staring down at the rocks below, mesmerized by the thundering waves, at the way they surged and retreated and swirled with white foam, hadn't been Dominic's violence. The worst thing had been hearing all the terrible things Jim thought about himself acknowledged by his oldest friend. Jim wasn't blind to his own weaknesses and insecurities, but he'd thought he had the rest of them fooled. He'd hoped that, amongst his closest friends, he conjured affection, love and respect. He'd been wrong. Clearly, his faults were as obvious to them all as they were to him.

'You useless piece of shit,' he cried, throwing his self-hatred into the sky. 'You loser.'

He gave up too easily. He was lazy. He'd been nothing but a hindrance to Suze and the kids. They deserved a better man. And now even his best friend had given up on him, and for good reason. He was the one who had been waving the spliff and beers around like an irresponsible teenager. He was the one who'd suggested the kids go off alone. He was the one who had tormented his friend with the secrets he held over him. Jim prodded his injured arm, allowed the pain to radiate through him until he felt dizzy with it. 'When are you going to grow up?' he shouted. 'When will you learn?'

His toes were on the very edge, the water seething and frothing below him. The possibility of the moment made him dizzy. One strong gust was all it would take to unbalance him. If he were to lose his footing, he would be over the edge, falling into the foaming wash below. If the fall didn't kill him, the currents there would hold him down, suck him out to sea. He could disappear, without a trace.

Out on the horizon, a faint light rose off the water, a silver shimmer on the waves and with it, carried on the wind, a faraway sound, high and mournful. A bird, he thought. He stared up at the sky. The clouds were visible now, dark and shifting in the high wind, but there was no bird. Perhaps he had imagined it, but then it came again, a desolate wailing sound carrying across the sea.

Jim turned his head.

He must be imagining it, his sleep-deprived brain playing a trick, because to his ears it sounded like a song. A chorus of unintelligible voices. Plaintive. Human, almost.

The wind dropped and with it the sound faded away. He stood very still, waiting to see if it would come again, but there was nothing but the ocean pounding below.

Disappointed, he turned to leave. But no – there *was* something! Something closer now. Not the strange singing voices he'd heard. Not a bird cry carrying on the breeze. It was a voice. A child's voice – calling for her parents.

Jim took a step back from the ledge, careful now, suddenly aware of his perilous position, of what was at stake. 'Phoebe?' he bellowed as loudly as he could, turning slowly, afraid that he wouldn't be heard over the crashing waves. 'Phoebe!'

For a terrible moment in the silence that followed, Jim thought he must have imagined it, wishful thinking tricking him back from the ledge, but then it came again. A single, plaintive word. The unmistakeable call of 'Daddy'.

'Phoebe!' he yelled. 'It's Jim. Keep calling and I'll find you. I'm coming, sweetheart.'

He stumbled back across the bluff, stopping to listen, trying to trace the sound, following it all the way to where the bluff seemed to split into distinct sections of rock, as if cleaved in two. 'Phoebe?' he called, peering down.

'I'm here.'

He leaned closer and tried to fathom where the sound was coming from. She couldn't be, could she? He ran his hands over the rock and pressed his mouth to the crevice and called her name. 'Phoebe?'

'I'm here.' The voice was weak, but it was definitely her.

'Phoebe, it's Jim.' From what he could tell, she was somewhere below him, as if the earth had opened and swallowed her into a secret fissure, before closing up again. 'Are you hurt?' he called.

There was a moment's pause. 'I'm hungry.'

He smiled at that. 'Hold tight, sweetheart. I'm going to get help. We'll get you out of there as soon as we can. Don't you move a muscle.'

'I want my mum,' she said. Her plaintive voice made his heart crack.

He didn't want to traumatize her by leaving her again so soon, but he had to fetch help. There was no way he could get her out of there on his own – not with a busted up arm. He was going to have to leave her to go after Dom. 'I'll be back. I promise. I'm going to get your dad. Don't move.'

'Don't go!' she cried.

'Just for a little while. Just to get help. Everything's going to be okay, Phoebe. Stay right where you are.'

The sound of her sobs tugged at him, but he forced himself to turn and hurriedly retraced his steps over the clifftop, to where he had last seen Dominic disappearing along the track.

KIP

Sunday morning

Kip lay sleepless in the tent, the first glimmers of dawn brushing the canvas walls, painting them a soft pigeon-grey, his fingers running over the rusty knife nestled in the pocket of his shorts. Annie slept beside him, curled beneath a blanket on the bed. He could see Max slumped in a chair across the tent.

It wasn't the storm that had jolted him awake. From what he could tell, the worst of the wild weather had passed. Instead, it was the distant revving of the buggy that had stirred him.

At first, he'd thought he was safe in his bed at the farm-house, listening to Max setting out on one of his early morning construction sessions down at the campsite. But then the scent of wet grass and the sound of the shifting canvas walls had come to him, and he had remembered where he was and what was unfolding. Phoebe was still missing, and everyone thought it was his fault.

He rolled away from Annie and lay still, watching the

tent transition from grey to off-white as the blade of his shucking knife warmed in his fingers. He knew Max and Annie had stayed with him all night because they were worried – worried that Phoebe's dad would come back again, worried that he wasn't speaking, worried that he wasn't telling them what had happened to Phoebe. They had coaxed and cajoled, pleaded and puzzled, but the truth was, even if he'd wanted to tell them where Phoebe was, he couldn't. He had no idea. He was as stumped as the rest of them.

He'd gone over the afternoon in his mind, replayed it over and over, like he was playing one of his computer games, trying to master a level, always hitting the same stumbling block and crashing out each time. He would reboot, reload and start again. But it didn't matter which way he played it; the hurdles always remained the same. He always struck the same dead end.

He started with the stampede. It had been Phoebe's high-pitched scream that had pulled him from his paralysis. He'd had a split second to make a decision. With the cattle blocking their path forward to the others, there was no way they could proceed. Their only option was to go back.

Kip had reached for Phoebe's hand and tugged her in the opposite direction. She hadn't resisted. She'd allowed him to drag her back to the stile where he'd shoved her unceremoniously up onto the wooden step, before launching himself up behind her. As she went over, Phoebe had let out a cry of pain.

Kip had turned at the top of the stile, hoping to spot

some sign of the others, but all he could see was the herd, stamping and bucking. Phoebe had started crying. She'd sat on the strut of the stile and bawled, tears flooding down her cheeks, a bubble of snot inflating out of her left nostril. A deep scratch was raked across her arm, blood trickling down to her wrist. At the sight of the blood, her crying had escalated. 'It hurts.' She'd pointed to the stile and he saw what had happened. In his efforts to shove her over, she'd caught her arm on an old nail poking from the fence.

Kip had dabbed at her wound as best he could, but when that didn't seem to stem the flow, he'd pressed the front of his T-shirt against it, holding it in place.

'Ouch,' she wailed.

Her breathing had shifted, escalating in pace, shallow and raspy, and so he'd patted his pocket, gesturing that she should do the same. She understood, reached for her puffer and inhaled deeply.

They'd sat for a bit in silence, Phoebe sniffing, wiping tears from her eyes, as they waited for her rattling breath to ease. Beyond the fence he could see the cows at the far end of the field, still agitated and stamping, still blocking the route back to the campsite. He'd gazed at the gaps appearing intermittently between their shifting bodies, searching for a glimpse of the others, but there was no sign.

At least the other kids were on the right side of the field. He and Phoebe had a problem. Even if he could've persuaded her back over the stile, there was no way they could cross again without facing the bull, and they couldn't outrun the angry herd. Which meant there was only one other way back: the longer, more circuitous route through Kellow's dairy farm and along the country lane leading to the farmhouse. He'd glanced up at the glowering sky. He hadn't fancied their chances of making it home before the rain.

Lifting his shirt from her arm, he'd seen that the pressure had helped. The bleeding had eased, but his T-shirt was ruined. He hoped Annie wouldn't be too cross. Reaching for Phoebe's hand, he'd tried to coax her off the stile, but she'd shaken her head and pulled herself free of his grip. 'Don't want to,' she'd said, wiping her nose on her sleeve before folding her arms tightly across her chest. 'I want my dad.'

Kip had felt a surge of impatience. He didn't want to be stuck there any more than she did – and certainly not with her. Phoebe had caused him nothing but trouble since she'd arrived.

He'd moved his tongue around his mouth, felt the stubborn resistance of it, wondered if he could do it again, wondered if he could find the words he needed to coax her along with him. It had been tempting to just leave her there. He couldn't though – could he?

He'd pursed his dry lips, taken a breath and opened his mouth. 'This way.' The words rose from his throat, sounding strange, forced, fuzzy round the edges and not quite right.

Phoebe had looked to where he pointed, to the barely visible track leading in the opposite direction to the beach. She'd sniffed. 'Are there cows that way?'

He shook his head.

She'd seemed to weigh up her options.

Kip took a couple of steps towards the track, then waited, giving her a chance.

Finally, she'd slid off the stile, her feet landing with a thud on the dry ground, and with a rush of relief that they could get moving again, Kip began to push his way through the overgrown hedgerow, holding back a spiky bramble before stopping to check she was behind him.

She wasn't. Phoebe had returned to the stile, and was spinning in a slow circle, studying the ground. She'd looked back at him with lip-wobbling dismay. 'Where's Bear?' She was close to tears again, a flush of pink rising in her cheeks.

Kip had cast his mind back and realized that he hadn't seen her with her teddy for some time. She hadn't had it when he'd grabbed her hand to haul her back through the field of cattle. He didn't even think she'd had it when they'd clambered back up over the rocks leading from the beach.

Phoebe's eyes had widened suddenly with understanding. 'I sat him by the rockpool. I didn't want him to get wet.' Her lower lip began to wobble.

Kip had glanced over Phoebe's head, to where the footpath disappeared down the cliffs to the shoreline. The thought of them both trudging back to the beach, clambering over those boulders, searching for the bear with the wind whipping at them and the threat of rain now heavy in the air, didn't appeal one little bit. He'd shrugged and gestured impatiently for Phoebe to follow.

'No!' Phoebe had looked alarmed. 'I can't leave him. I won't go without Bear.'

Kip frowned. What he wouldn't give to be back at the campsite or, even better, safely tucked in his bedroom playing Xbox, away from everyone else with their noise and confusing games and stupid, forgotten teddy bears.

Phoebe had started to cry again, tears trickling down her grimy cheeks. Looking at her downturned face, her blood-streaked arm, at the Peppa Pig plaster flapping loose on her face, he'd heard the echo of his father's words: *try to be a good friend, Kip.*

If he went back to the beach on his own, he would be much faster. He would reunite Phoebe with her bear and then lead her home. Who knows, maybe Farmer Kellow would take pity on them and give them a lift back to the campsite, though he didn't fancy their chances. With a monumental effort, Kip had opened his mouth. 'Stay. I'll go.'

Phoebe had looked about anxiously. 'Wait here? By myself?'

Kip had patted the stile.

Phoebe bit her lower lip then nodded and Kip, pushing thoughts of his tired legs to one side, had set off back down the coastal path. Just before he rounded the bend he'd stopped to look back. Phoebe was sitting on the wooden stile, her short legs swinging back and forth in the air. She gave him a wave. *Get Bear. Get Phoebe. Get home.* He repeated the refrain over and over in his mind as he turned back to the path and began the climb down to the shoreline below, his feet hitting the ground in time to the beat of those six silent words.

Down on the beach, an elemental shift had taken hold. All traces of blue were long gone, the sky transformed to violent grey, storm clouds massing, the sea a seething, metallic wash. The wind had raced at him, carrying the sting of salt spray, buffeting him sideways, forceful gusts that spat and shoved at him like a bully in a playground. As he'd made his way back along the shoreline, he'd noticed how all signs of their earlier visit had been washed away, their footsteps erased by the rising tide.

A single gull braved the beach, strutting and pecking fruitlessly at what remained of the ocean's scattered treasures. Kip had followed it, scanning the rocks, searching for signs of matted brown fur, a sticking-up ear or the telltale glint of a beaded eye. Eventually, the gull rose with the wind and wheeled away, seeking shelter, he thought; exactly what he and Phoebe should be doing.

There had been no sign of the bear. Kip had wondered if it had been washed out to sea. Given how much trouble Phoebe had caused him already, the thought was strangely appealing. He'd been ready to admit defeat when an image returned to him of Phoebe and Juniper crouched over one of the larger rockpools at the furthest end of the beach, their heads bent together as they'd giggled and poked at something with a piece of driftwood.

The rocky ledge had become slippery underfoot, made treacherous by the sea spray carried on the wind. Kip stumbled, righted himself, then carried on towards the biggest pool, keeping one eye on the rolling waves slamming against the jagged cliffs at the far end of the cove. He'd spotted the bear near the largest pool, slumped beneath a sandy, limpet-encrusted rock, its head drooped low so that he appeared to be contemplating his sad, solitary reflection in the rippling water. With a surge of relief, Kip had clambered closer and grabbed the bear, stuffing it beneath his T-shirt for safekeeping. Mission accomplished. Now he just had to get back to Phoebe and get them both home before the rain came in.

He'd been making good progress across the slippery outcrop when he felt a rock give beneath him, his foot plunging into a narrow crevice, sending him off balance. Falling heavily onto his hands and knees, his ankle, still trapped, twisted awkwardly, pain firing up his leg. His cry had lifted and blown away on the wind.

Kip had taken several breaths, trying to calm himself, waiting for the pain to ease. I'm okay, he'd told himself. Can't stop now. Got to keep moving. *Get Bear. Get Phoebe. Get home.*

Grazed, sore, and with his ankle throbbing painfully, he'd used both hands to free his trapped foot, the effort making his face twist in pain and the tears stream down. He winced as he rolled down his sock to inspect his ankle. It was already swelling, red and puffy.

There was nothing to do but carry on. The storm was moving in. There was no time to waste. He'd limped along the slippery outcrop and across the beach, scrambling awkwardly over the boulders, grateful for the shelter of the ravine as the path wound back up.

Halfway to the stile, he'd heard a shriek rise from somewhere high above his head. He'd stopped and listened, but all he could hear was the panting of his breath, the bluster of the wind and the booming of the waves crashing onto the beach below. Another gull wheeled across the sky, just a bird screeching in protest at the impending storm.

Rounding the last corner, he'd expected to see Phoebe perched on the stile, exactly where he had left her. But she was nowhere to be seen. He'd swallowed, rolled his tongue in his mouth, pursed his lips searching for the sound he wanted. 'Ph-Ph-Phoebe!' he'd called, her name stuttering from his mouth. He'd tried again, a little louder. 'Phoebe! I've got B-B-Bear.'

He'd looked for signs, trying to work out where she could be. The grass was trampled, as though heavy feet had passed by only recently. A clump of crushed dande-lions lay beneath the stile and something in the air felt heavy and expectant, as if someone or something had moved through the space only moments before. Had she got bored of waiting for him? Did she think he wasn't coming back? Had the others come for her and taken her home already?

He'd felt a rush of frustration. He'd told her to wait. He'd gone all that way for her bear, hurt himself in the process, and she'd just left him? Maybe she hadn't cared that much about the stupid toy after all. He had a good mind to leave it right there. That would show her.

As he'd cast about, wondering what to do next, he'd heard a distant lowing sound. Raising himself up onto the stile he'd been surprised to see that the field they had tried to cross earlier was now empty of cows and that the steel gate diagonally across from him had been secured shut. Just beyond, he saw the stooped figure of farmer

Kellow shuffling away, his huge black dog loping at his heel. Kip wondered if he could raise his voice loud enough to call out – to ask if he had seen Phoebe – but he was too far away. He'd never hear him over the din of the cattle ambling towards the dairy farm.

That was it, he realized. Phoebe must've seen Kellow moving the cows and taken her chance to cross the field. Which meant there was, at last, a silver lining for him too: with the field free of cattle, he wouldn't have to limp the long way home on his twisted ankle. He could follow Phoebe.

The scent of rain was heavy in the air. Out on the horizon, the space between the low black clouds and the now oddly violet-coloured sea seemed to smudge and merge. He had to keep moving. The storm was almost upon him.

Hoisting himself gingerly over the stile, Kip had begun his slow hobble across the empty field back to the campsite, wincing as his damaged ankle jarred with each step, trying to focus only on the rhythm of his shuffling walk and the warmth Phoebe's furry bear offered where it pressed against his skin. To distract himself, he'd imagined the reception that would await him, Phoebe's grateful smile as he handed her the bear and the praise he'd receive for finding it, the forgiveness for yesterday's misunderstanding with the marshmallows. As he'd limped his way back, he'd allowed himself a small smile. It was all going to be okay.

Lying in the tent at daybreak, Kip plays the scenes over and over. The stile. The beach. The bear. The return journey. He'd had no idea that Phoebe wouldn't be at the

campsite waiting for him – no idea of the terrifying reception that had awaited him. No idea why everyone had been
staring at him with horror and fear written so plainly on
their faces. When Dominic had seized him, when he'd felt
that man's huge hands grabbing and squeezing, seen his
flashing eyes and heard the anger in his voice, it was as
if he'd been spirited straight back there, to the old, dingy
house he'd once called home, the one with the green carpet
and the red sofa and the terrible memories he tried not to
think about. All at once his words had flown from him,
as if carried away on the encroaching storm.

Kip turned on the bed and glanced across at Max and
Annie. He knew they would wake soon, and that their
questions would begin all over again. But even if he could
find the words to help them, he didn't know what he'd say.
He didn't know where Phoebe was.

DOMINIC

Sunday morning

Dominic was torn. He regretted his fight with Jim. Whatever issues now stood between them, whatever secrets they wielded, he knew they couldn't be resolved with one wild brawl. Remorse gripped him. He knew he should go back and check if Jim was okay, knew he should apologize for the awful things he'd said, for the violence of his outburst, but at the same time he was desperate to press on. Jim was a grown man, but Phoebe was a child and she was out here alone, in heaven only knew what state. He had to find her.

Dawn hovered on the horizon. With the worst of the storm behind them, he had to hope that the chances of finding Phoebe were growing. Maybe the power had been switched on at the farmhouse. Maybe help had been summoned. A professional search and rescue team. Dogs. The full works. Going back now wasn't an option. He wouldn't allow himself to consider any outcome other than the one where his daughter was found safe and well. He had to keep moving – for Phoebe.

Dominic spun in a circle to take in the full, spectacular coastline, trying to determine which way to go. For the first time, in the growing light, he saw the craggy cliffs, boulder-strewn with tufts of hardy bracken and gorse, the surging ocean stretching away to meet the horizon, and the sky above, now a vivid wash of violet and grey with the slightest hint of orange breaking in shards through the dense clouds.

Stepping closer to the cliff edge, he saw something round and black bobbing in the swirling foam far below. He peered and recognized it as distinctly human – a head – trying to stay above the waves. Terror seized him. He stared, watching as the head disappeared, then resurfaced moments later a little closer to the shore. Slick and dark, definitely a head – but not human. A seal. Just a seal, surfing the storm-wash. Relief flooded through him.

Looking east, he saw a tall stone stack rising from the far cliffs. It looked man-made, a chimney perhaps, projecting towards the sky. Dominic frowned. A building, on this remote headland? In the weak morning light, it was hard to judge how far away it was. A mile, perhaps. Could Phoebe have walked that far in the dark? Could she have found shelter there? It had to be worth a look.

His mind made up, Dominic turned and began to navigate his way east along the path, though he had only gone a short distance when he heard a shout behind him. Spinning, he saw a familiar figure stumbling towards him, lop-sided and oddly hunched. Dominic hesitated.

'Dom!' Jim called, his voice carrying on the wind. He waved awkwardly with one arm. 'Dom! Come back!'

Dominic frowned. He didn't want to waste any more precious time fighting.

'It's Phoebe. I've found her.'

Jim led the way at first, the two men moving as fast as they could along the rough track. 'She's trapped below ground level. There must be a seam or a crevasse in the rock, but I can't figure it out. There's got to be a way to get her out.'

Dominic powered on, impatient at Jim's lumbering pace, scrambling ahead and only stopping when Jim called for him to slow down. 'Careful, if there's an open cavity we don't want you falling in too.'

'Where?' asked Dominic, frantic. 'Where is she?'

Jim pointed towards the rocky outcrop. 'She's down there.'

'Phoebe!' Dominic bellowed through cupped hands. 'It's Dad.'

'Daddy!' Phoebe's reply was faint, but it was definitely her.

'Don't move, darling. We're going to get you out, I promise.'

Dominic threw Jim a look. 'Mate, I'd hug you, if I didn't think it would hurt you.'

'We'll do the hugging later. First, let's figure out how we're going to get her out.'

The two men spent an exasperating twenty minutes searching for an access point to the fissure. 'It's no good. We're going to need more help.' Jim was hunched over, holding his damaged arm, his face drained of colour.

Dominic, increasingly frustrated, wanted to tear at the ground with his bare hands. He was wracked with guilt at seeing his friend in so much pain, but he couldn't help him – not yet – not when Phoebe was still trapped. 'I guess one of us will have to go back.' Dominic eyed Jim. He wanted to stay with Phoebe, but he knew he'd be quicker. 'Will you be okay? Can you keep her calm?'

Jim nodded. His face was ashen, but he seemed determined.

Dominic was preparing to leave, dropping his now redundant torch and batteries, when a distant sound made both men pause. He turned to Jim. 'Do you hear that?'

Jim tilted his head. 'Sounds like a radio.'

A burst of static and a man's tinny voice rose up from the path. Then came the thud of boots. Dominic and Jim stood, waiting, until the most glorious sight appeared on the path ahead of them: four search and rescue volunteers in hi-vis jackets and blue helmets hiking towards them. The leader, a grey-haired man with an impressive moustache, held a walkie talkie. At the sight of Dominic and Jim, he raised his arm in greeting. 'Are you the gentlemen from Morvoren Farm? You're looking for a little girl?'

Jim and Dominic exchanged a baffled look. 'Yes. How did you know to come?'

'One of your party walked through the night to raise the alarm.'

'One of our party?' Dom threw Jim a confused look. 'Who?'

'I don't have the details. A young man, I think.'

Jim and Dominic exchanged another glance, understanding dawning. 'Josh.'

Jim nodded. 'Bloody hell. What a hero.'

'I owe that lad a beer.'

Jim looked confused. 'But there was no way off the
peninsula?'

'Yes, we heard you'd been cut off by downed power
lines, but he found a way out on foot. The police radioed
us to come out and investigate. We came in across the
headland.'

'Phoebe's down here,' Dominic said, pointing to the
fissure. 'We've found her, but we have no idea how to
get her out.'

The man moved closer to the rocky ledge. He had a
good look round, then called out to Phoebe, before acti-
vating his two-way radio. 'This is Mike Brown calling
base unit. We're at the northern end of the search zone.
We've located the two men out on the headland and the
little girl. It looks like she's fallen into a mining shaft. The
girl is responsive, though we haven't yet been able to get
to her position or assess for injuries. Over.'

A crackling response came back on the radio. The man
listened intently to the instructions given before turning
back to Dominic and Jim.

'We have to find the adit.'

'Adit?'

'It's a horizontal entrance that leads to a mine shaft.
This area is littered with them. Most of them were
boarded up years ago, but a few remain overgrown and
undiscovered. I suspect your girl crawled into one for

shelter, thinking it was a cave. Either she got lucky and this one leads to a shallow, abandoned shaft, or her fall was broken by something.'

'My god, shouldn't there be warning signs about open mine shafts?'

'Usually there are. Unfortunately, they get damaged in bad weather, or vandalized, sometimes stolen. Kids, you know.' He gave Dominic a pat on the shoulder. 'Best you let us get to work.'

Dominic didn't want to stand back, but Jim pulled him away gently and the two of them sat on a nearby rock and watched in silence as the men unloaded their packs and carefully scouted the area. It didn't take long for a cry to go up from one of the rescuers, alerting the others and drawing them all to a patch of dense scrub partially hiding a dark opening in the rockface. 'You wouldn't see it unless you were low to the ground, like a youngster,' the man called Mike told them, showing them the entrance to the adit.

Ropes and cameras were produced from their kit bags. The lead volunteer radioed back to base and received new instructions. All four men worked busily at the entrance to the adit, before Mike with the Moustache, as Dom now thought of him, came back to address them again. 'We've got a visual on her position. The adit extends horizontally approximately four metres into the rockface before it joins the main mine shaft.' He drew the topography in the air for them with his gloved hands. 'Your girl looks to be five or so metres below the adit.' He wiped his brow. 'She's been very lucky. She landed on a flat outcrop, a ledge which has broken her fall and saved her life. Beyond that, the shaft drops another thirty metres down to sea level. I imagine it's flooded right now, after last night's high tide.'

'Oh god.' Dominic paled at the thought.

'It's going to be a precarious job to extract her. The most important thing is that we keep her calm and still while we work our way down to her.'

Dominic swallowed, sick at the thought of what might've happened – what could still happen.

'I'd say it's a good thing you didn't find the opening and attempt to reach her yourselves. You might not have been so lucky.'

Dominic and Jim exchanged a look.

'Sit tight. We're roping up and lowering someone down to her now.'

Dominic let out a long exhale of breath. 'Thank you,' he said, grabbing the man's gloved hand. 'Thank you, so much.'

TANYA

Monday morning

Tanya waits impatiently on the other side of the cubicle curtain while the doctor finishes her assessment, checking blood pressure, examining dressings and testing vision. She can hear the doctor's shoes squeaking as she moves about the bed, the soft murmurings of her questions. 'Does this hurt? What about this? Now just follow my pen with your eyes. Good.'

'My head is pounding.'

'And your leg?'

'It really hurts.'

'We'll see about a slightly stronger painkiller. You've been through quite an ordeal, young lady. You're very brave.'

'How long will you want to keep her in for?' Another woman's voice joins the conversation. Even though she's known she was coming, hearing her makes the vertebrae of Tanya's spine stiffen. She wonders if she should turn and leave, but then the doctor is pulling back the curtain and suddenly it is too late for Tanya to pretend she isn't standing there.

Scarlet, finally conscious, is lying pale and bandaged in the hospital bed, her mother Clare perched in the seat beside her, the same seat Tanya herself had occupied until very recently. Clare is unmade up, tired and anxious-looking. Her long dark hair is unbrushed and she is dressed in casual sweats – the sort of clothes you grab in a rush when you learn you have to dash from the house to complete a long and frantic drive to your child's hospital bedside. Looking at Clare, Tanya feels like her mirror image. In more ways than one.

The two women exchange a glance, a small nod of acknowledgement, before Tanya's eyes track back to Scarlet.

Scarlet offers her a faint smile and tries to wrestle herself up to sitting. She is too weak and falls back onto the pillow. 'Phoebe. They said . . .'

'Shhh,' says Tanya, taking a step forward. 'Don't you worry. You just focus on getting strong.'

She glances at Clare and is relieved to see warmth in the other woman's eyes.

'Thank you,' says Clare. 'The nurses told me you've barely left her side since she was admitted.'

Tanya nods. 'Of course.'

Clare indicates the second chair on the other side of the bed. Tanya takes the seat and Scarlet surprises her by reaching for her hand.

'You look terrible,' Scarlet says, her voice a dry rasp.

'Thanks a lot.' Tanya manages a faint smile. 'Not had much sleep these past two days.'

Scarlet swallows, then licks her lips. 'Told you we should've gone home.'

Tanya can't help smiling at that.

'The police are back,' says the doctor, reappearing at the end of the bed. 'They'd like to talk to you, Scarlet, as soon as possible. Do you feel up to it?'

Scarlet winces and closes her eyes. A single tear slides down her cheek. She grips Tanya's hand. 'I – I don't know. When I close my eyes all I can hear is the sea. It's like it's stuck inside my head, the waves against the rocks . . . and that strange singing. It's driving me mad.'

Singing? Tanya exchanges a worried glance with Clare. She has no idea what Scarlet is talking about. Perhaps it's the strong painkillers muddling her mind.

Scarlet's eyes snap open again, the fear written on her face. She grips Tanya's hand, her torn fingernails digging into her skin. 'Where's Kip?'

Tanya studies Scarlet for a moment, her eyes glancing over the bloody, broken skin on her wrists. She doesn't know what to tell her, what might be more upsetting. 'You don't need to worry about him. The police are sorting everything out. You're safe now.'

Scarlet sinks back against the pillow and closes her eyes. Tanya exchanges a look with Clare.

'It's okay,' Clare soothes. 'You're okay. I'm here with you. Tanya's here.'

They are quiet for a moment, but Tanya's apology bubbles up. 'I'm so sorry, Scarlet. My mind was on Phoebe. I didn't notice you weren't there when I woke in the tent yesterday morning. I didn't know what was happening.

I'm sorry.' Tanya bites her lip, her eyes glancing between Scarlet and Clare.

Clare gives a small nod. 'I gather you had your own worries to deal with – with Phoebe.'

The doctor clears her throat. 'We can ask the police to wait a little longer,' she says, 'if you're not quite ready?'

Scarlet turns from Clare to Tanya. 'Will you both stay?'

They nod.

To Tanya's relief, Scarlet also gives a small nod. 'Okay, you can send them in.'

KIRA

Monday morning

Kira is feeding Asha in one of the guest bedrooms at the farmhouse when she hears the police detective's car pulling up outside the house. It's still early. The only other sounds she can hear are the first stirrings of birdsong and the distant ocean washing onto the shore. DC Haines hadn't left them until gone eleven last night, so she can't have had much sleep either.

The kids had been tucked up on sofas and mattresses in the lounge, while she and Suze had taken the two spare rooms upstairs. At some point she'd heard Jim return from the hospital in a taxi, the rumble of his voice rousing her. Later, she'd been disturbed by the sound of Max and Annie talking in low voices in the kitchen below. She hadn't slept after that. She had been too worried, thoughts of Fred – of where he could be and why he hadn't been in touch – playing on repeat through her mind.

It's been more than twenty-four hours since they argued

309

and there is still no word from him. Everyone has so much to worry about, she hasn't wanted to throw another thing at them. Fred is a grown man, more than capable of looking after himself, but the longer his silence continues, the more desperate she feels. Where is he? Why isn't he there with them? With her and Asha?

She knows she should've been more understanding. Of course he'd be upset at finding out about Dom like that. She had been too defensive, too dismissive of his feelings, but the truth was she'd never intended for him to find out about Asha's conception that way. She'd thought if he'd met Dom and grown to like him a little, it might have been easier to tell Fred the truth. She'd thought he might've accepted it more easily.

But maybe this wasn't about Dom? What if it was about Fred? What if he wasn't ready for any of this – for a serious relationship with her, for fatherhood? What if he'd been playing – trying them out for size? What if he'd decided, as she had initially feared, that he was too young for such a huge commitment? She had a good few years on him. She wasn't naïve. He didn't need to settle for her and her drama. He could choose anyone – at any time. He didn't need to rush this.

And what if it wasn't that at all? What if he'd gone out there after Dominic in the storm? What if he'd intended to have it out with him and something had happened on the cliffs? These are the scenarios that have kept her awake half the night, stiff with worry and fear.

Asha yawns at her breast. DC Haines' car door slams. There is the soft crunch of the officer's footsteps, followed by the sound of a mobile phone ringing. Kira cranes her head towards the open window to listen.

'Yes, ma'am. Just arrived.' There is a pause. 'No. Not a word.' Another pause. 'Yes. Agreed. The parents are key.' Haines falls quiet before she asks her next question. 'Any ID yet on that body found out on the headland?'

Kira freezes, barely breathing.

'Yeah, I heard. Nasty. Hard to identify someone from one blue hoodie.'

Kira can't swallow. She feels a tight, gripping sensation in her chest and wonders if she's having a panic attack – a heart attack? They are talking about finding someone out on the cliffs. Someone wearing a blue hoodie.

Haines' final words are inaudible as her footsteps disappear round the side of the house. The sound of her knocking at the front door echoes through the house, swiftly followed by Max's footsteps descending the staircase.

Kira doesn't move. She sits instead, with Asha snuggled warm against her skin, and wonders how she let everything get so screwed up. Wonders how long she can remain there in that bed, hoping that if she does, her deepest fears won't come true.

A light tapping on the bedroom door pulls her from her thoughts. Suze pokes her head round. 'Okay?' she whispers.

Kira doesn't answer.

'I wasn't sure if you were awake.' Suze frowns and takes a step into the room, closing the door softly behind her. 'I'm going to rustle up some food for the kids. Are you hungry?'

Kira shakes her head.

Suze eyes her with concern. 'Did you sleep?'

Kira shakes her head again. 'I know there's a lot going on right now, but I'm so worried about Fred. Where is he? Why hasn't he come back?'

Suze frowns. 'You still haven't heard from him?'

'No. We . . . we had a big row.' Kira bites her lip. 'It was pretty bad. He went off in the storm. I was talking to that police detective yesterday and she started asking me questions about him. When I last saw him. What he'd been wearing. She showed me photos of his bag – the one we thought we'd left behind. It looked like it was lying in a weird room, but she wouldn't tell me anything.'

Suze frowns again. 'Did Fred give you *any* hint about where he was going?'

'No. Not a word.' Kira's eyes sting with tears and tiredness.

'What were you fighting about? Would it help to talk it through?'

Kira shakes her head. 'I can't. Not yet. Sorry.'

Suze eyes her carefully but doesn't push.

'There's something else though.'

'Go on.'

'I overheard the detective just now, outside. I heard her say they've found a body . . . down on the cliffs.'

Suze's eyes go wide. 'No!'

Kira, having said it out loud now, feels the full force of her fear rolling through her. 'I didn't hear everything, but she said they were wearing a blue hoodie.' She hesitates.

'Suze, I think that's what Fred was wearing when I last saw him.'

'Oh Kira.' Suze stares at her. 'It can't be him. Can it? I don't know what to say. I mean, why would he be out on the cliffs?'

'He was so angry when he stormed off. What if he got lost or disorientated? What if he went looking for the others? What if he tried to find Phoebe – or Dom – and he fell?' She chokes back a sob.

'Kira, come on. None of us have had much sleep. We're all running on empty. Your mind's leaping to terrifying conclusions but I'm sure if the police had something to tell you, they'd have done it by now.' Suze eyes Kira with concern. 'It could be anyone. A lost hiker. A local ...' She trails off. 'Why don't you come downstairs with me? Sitting up here alone isn't good for you.'

Kira stares at Suze. She wants to believe her, but nothing she has said has eased the terror growing within her. Where is he? Why isn't he there with her?

SCARLET

Monday morning

Scarlet twists the white fabric of the hospital sheet between her fingers, her heart thudding as the two police officers enter the cubicle and pull up their chairs. She stares at the female detective, impressed by her short hair with its streak of silver and her black Doc Marten boots. Unlike the male police officer beside her, she isn't wearing a uniform, which Scarlet knows means she's more important. She looks kind of badass. Scarlet likes that.

She introduces herself as DI Lawson. 'We want you to tell us anything you can remember. Any details, big or small. Can you do that for us, Scarlet?' There is a soft West Country lilt to her voice, but her tone is serious. 'Take it as slow as you need to.'

Scarlet glances between the two detectives. 'What's Kip told you?'

The woman frowns then glances across at her colleague. 'I'm afraid Kip's not saying very much at the moment, so we'd like to hear from you, if that's okay?'

Scarlet bites her lip. Her mum and Tanya have moved back to give the police officers space, but they're still there at the far end of the cubicle, listening.

'It's okay,' says Tanya, giving her a nod. 'Just tell them what you remember. You mustn't worry about getting him into trouble. That's for the police to sort.'

Scarlet frowns. 'I don't care if he gets in trouble. After what he did, he should be locked up for ever.'

'I know. Just tell them the truth.'

'Mrs Davies.' DI Lawson shoots Tanya a look. 'Please.'

Scarlet looks between Tanya and the police. She shakes her head. 'I went with him because I wanted to help. I was only thinking about Phoebe.'

'Go on,' says Lawson.

'He said he knew where Phoebe was.'

Tanya murmurs again from the end of the bed. Lawson ignores her. 'Go on,' she says, addressing Scarlet.

'We took the buggy from the campsite and drove to the headland. We had to walk from there. He had a torch,' she says, remembering how the arc of it had played across the ferns and gorse rustling in the breeze, 'but it wasn't long before the light began to change.'

'Let me just stop you there, Scarlet. Could you confirm who you mean by "he"?'

'She means Kip,' insists Tanya.

'Mrs Davies,' says DI Lawson, a warning in her voice. 'If you interrupt again, I'm afraid I'll have to ask you to leave.'

'No, not Kip,' says Scarlet, looking round at them in surprise. 'I'm talking about Josh.'

'Josh?' DI Lawson raises an eyebrow. 'Joshua Penrose?'

'Yes. He was the one who woke me. He led the way, and I followed.'

Tanya's eyes widen, but she doesn't interrupt again.

'Very well. You can continue, Scarlet.'

Scarlet takes a breath. The room is suddenly very quiet, the younger detective's pencil poised over his notebook, Tanya's and her mother's eyes fixed on her. Fear bubbles up. She grips the white sheet lying across her chest again and squeezes it more tightly. Taking a breath, she returns to her nightmare.

She remembers how she'd kept her eyes fixed on the turret rising off the promontory as they walked. It looked like a chimney – tall and circular – thrusting towards the sky from the stone building perched on the cliff's edge. She was glad Phoebe had found a safe place to shelter from the storm, but the thought of her little sister stumbling across this hazardous terrain at night made her shudder. It was a miracle she was okay.

The sound of the ocean grew louder as they approached the ruins. In her hurry, Scarlet stumbled on the uneven rocks, losing her balance and skinning her knee. She stood and brushed herself off, feeling a little foolish to have tripped, but Josh hadn't seemed to notice. He powered on and she had to race to catch him.

It was the strange half-light, she thought, the early hour and her lack of sleep, but she felt so clumsy, so disorientated, the constant rushing of the ocean to her left, the wind buffeting and shoving her as they drew closer to the looming building, as if her feet might go from under her at any minute. She was afraid one misstep would send her plunging down into the deep, rocky cove below.

Closer, the ruins seemed to rise before them, taller and more forbidding. It made her dizzy to stare up at them. 'What is it?' she asked.

'An engine house. It's a relic from the old mining days, when the tin industry round here was booming.'

It stood almost three storeys high, a monolithic grey stone structure, ancient-looking and bleak. She noticed a small, wooden cross standing nearby at the cliff's edge, tiny white and pink wildflowers growing at its base. Scarlet saw the marker and shuddered. She could only imagine how dangerous mining these vertiginous cliffs would've been.

Josh looped around the back of the stone building and came to a halt outside a metal door. Jarringly modern compared to the rest of the building, it blocked their way. 'The council try to keep people out,' Josh told her. 'It's all protected round here.'

The door might have been designed to keep kids and vagrants out, but it was scarred with graffiti and the padlock swinging on the catch was open. The faint morning light glanced off an assortment of discarded glass bottles and cans scattered near the entrance. Scarlet knew this sort of place – it was one of those abandoned spaces, sought out and reclaimed by kids with nowhere better to go. She'd hung out in her fair share of disused places with friends, the back of skate parks, underpasses, old toilet blocks. Kids were nothing if not resourceful when it came to claiming neglected plots and making them their own. 'She's in here?' she asked.

He answered with a nod, pulling on the heavy door. 'Phoebe,' he called into the dark space, 'I've brought Scarlet with me. Told you I'd be back.'

Scarlet couldn't help her shudder. Phoebe must have been desperate to willingly climb inside such a horrid building. A sheen of sweat prickled on her forehead, that dizzy sensation making her head swim again. From far away came that strange mournful sound, just a hint carried on the breeze. 'Phoebe,' she called, reaching out to steady herself with a hand against the cold stone. 'It's me, Scarlet.'

A scuffling noise came from the interior. 'You can come out now. You're safe. Follow my voice, Pheebs. Can you see the light?' The scuffling noise came again. The darkness was disorientating. 'Phoebe? Don't be scared.'

She turned back to Josh, uncertain how to proceed, but he nodded encouragingly. 'You might have to go in and get her. She wouldn't come to me either and I didn't want to scare her.'

'Pheebs?' she pleaded, her voice echoing through the dark interior. 'Josh, can you shine your torch inside? I'll go in.'

Josh moved closer and shone his torch over her head as she stepped inside, the wavering light bouncing off the dank stone walls and allowing Scarlet to creep forward, her vision adjusting, revealing how the space seemed to open out into one large room, the roof mainly intact, just a few slipped tiles allowing a faint shaft of morning light to fall into the interior. The building carried the heavy scent of damp stone, moss and earth.

She peered into the gloom, trying to find the outline of her sister, felt her vision struggling to focus in the swaying light of the torch. Her legs shook but she pressed on. In the far corner, Josh's torch swept over a bundle of fabric, the blue of Phoebe's corduroy dungarees. Her heart leapt. 'Oh Pheebs, you poor thing.'

Scarlet rushed forward, staggering a little on the uneven floor, reaching for her sister. As her hand met the bundle of wet fabric, Scarlet drew up short. Up close, she could see that it wasn't Phoebe lying huddled in the corner, but a large blue rucksack lying on its side, spilling an assortment of clothes and items, none of which she recognized. A mouse shot out from beneath the bag, disturbed by her presence, darting along the wall before it disappeared into the crack between two stones. Scarlet let out a small shriek of surprise before sinking down to her knees, her head spinning sickeningly. 'Oh my god. I thought . . .' She swallowed, her heart thundering, a rush of nausea flooding her throat. 'It's not her, Josh,' she called, her voice shaky. 'She's not here. I'm coming out.'

She tried to stand, but as she did, her legs gave beneath her. She tried again, desperate to leave the awful room, but found her limbs would no longer obey. She slumped down onto the damp stone floor. 'Josh,' she said, her voice thick and slow. 'I . . . I . . . something's wrong.'

He held the torch, shining it right into her eyes, forcing her to hold an arm up to block its glare. 'Josh, don't . . . I – I can't . . . see.' She tried to crawl towards the open door on her hands and knees, but her body wasn't obeying the panicked signals from her brain. Why was he just standing

319

there? She needed help. 'Josh,' she called again, but this time the torch snapped off, plunging her into darkness.

His silhouette stood in the open doorway, backlit by the dawn light. 'Don't fight it, Scarlet. You've got a handful of sleeping pills coursing through you. Best let them do their thing.'

He sounded calm but she stared at him, the panic and fear growing. What was he talking about? Sleeping pills? Where was Phoebe? Was this all an elaborate hoax? If so, it wasn't funny.

She tried to stand again, but it was impossible. This was no joke. 'My dad . . . he's gonna kill . . . you.'

Josh smiled, his teeth glowing white in the dark. 'Your dad – now there's a topic we could discuss at length. People like your dad have no idea what impact they have on others, do they?' His voice was calm and cold. 'No real understanding of the power their words and actions hold. I've watched him closely all weekend. He's nothing but a bully.'

Scarlet tried to grope her way forward through the dark but the drugs in her system were winning, her eyelids heavy, her head swimming. His footsteps came towards her in the dark.

'I couldn't take much more of his bullshit. I thought it time he learned that any family can be torn apart – even his. He needs to realize that all it takes is a little careless cruelty for dreams to come to crashing down.'

'Phoebe,' said Scarlet, fear surging through her veins. 'What have you done?'

'To Phoebe? No, Scarlet. It's you I'm talking about.'

He grabbed her arm, his fingers digging into her skin, his breath hot on her neck.

'Get off!' she cried, using her last reserves of strength to lash out with her feet, kicking at him, her trainer connecting with his groin, making him groan loudly.

'Goddamn it,' he breathed. He shoved her hard and she fell back, her head colliding with the stone wall with a loud crack, her vision exploding into a burst of white stars. Sprawled on the ground, she reached up to touch her temple, felt warm blood on her fingertips.

'Shit,' she heard him say, the word drifting towards her as if from down a long tunnel. 'Scarlet? Scarlet, can you hear me?'

She couldn't fight it any longer. She fell back against the damp stone floor and let the darkness take her.

SCARLET

Sunday morning

It was a dream. Or rather, a nightmare. It had to be, because when she opened her eyes she was still inside that awful, ruined place – only now she really couldn't move. She could wiggle her fingers and toes, but her hands and feet were bound tightly by what felt like thick strips of fabric or tape.

The light falling through the crack in the roof was brighter than before. Squinting, she could see the pool of blood on the floor fanning out around her head, though the light was like a hammer thumping behind her eyes. Lifting her head off the ground, a trickle of fresh blood began to leak from the wound at her temple. She lay back against the stone floor, too dizzy to move again. 'Josh,' she called, her mouth dry, her tongue still heavy from the sedatives he'd tricked her into drinking. 'Josh, are you there?'

Maybe she was tripping, because beyond the pounding of her head and the slow drip of water trickling down the walls of the engine house, she thought she could hear something else – something very far away. Something that sounded like singing. Eerie. Mournful. Desperate. A chorus of dissonant voices.

And closer still, over the too-loud thump of her heart-beat, she heard something else – something that made the hairs stand up on the backs of her arms. In. Out. In. Out. It was the heavy rise and fall of someone's breath.

He was there, lurking in the shadows, watching her. 'Josh,' she called, fear making her voice tremble.

There was no answer. She groaned. 'Josh,' she pleaded, 'please let me go. Everyone will be worried. They'll be looking for me.'

She wondered if this was true. As far as she knew, everyone was thinking about Phoebe. Would they even notice her absence, given the panic over her sister's dis-appearance? Phoebe. Oh god. She was still out there too – somewhere. Her stomach churned. Was *all* of this on Josh? Was he the reason for Phoebe's disappearance? Was Phoebe lying tied up somewhere, just like her? The thought made her head spin, but it brought something else too. An ember of rage flared in her gut.

She lay very still, letting her anger rise as she listened to the eerie, faraway chorus of voices singing their mournful song and his steady, mocking breath. Why was he doing this to her? What had she done to him? What sort of sick fuck just stood there in the dark watching her suffer?

Until it came to her.

That sound.

It wasn't Josh's breath. It wasn't him she could hear at all.

It was the ocean, relentless and indifferent to her plight, moving against the jagged cliffs below. She was alone in the ruins. Tied up. Trapped. And no one except Josh knew where she was.

She closed her eyes in fear and the strange, sad chorus of those faraway voices sang on as Scarlet gave in once more to the darkness. Josh wasn't there now, but he'd be back soon. Scarlet was sure of it.

KIP

Sunday morning

Kip watched the celebrations from where he lay inside the tent. Peering out through the canvas doorway, he had a clear view of the wooden shelter and everyone gathered around it beneath the heavy morning sky. Max's wooden pavilion had held up well in the storm, but two of the tents furthest away looked a little the worse for wear, lopsided and shaken, like sails torn from their masts. Several chairs had blown across the meadow, the lid of the hot tub was missing, the bunting tattered and torn, yet all in all, the site appeared to have weathered the storm relatively unscathed.

He'd never seen the place so busy. Several of the search and rescue team had stayed behind, allowing Annie to ply them with mugs of tea and celebratory bacon sandwiches as Max bustled around the barbecue. Judging from the volume of laughter and chatter outside, spirits were high.

Dominic had carried Phoebe back to the campsite a little earlier, arriving triumphantly and delivering Phoebe into

Tanya's waiting arms. There had been tears and laughter. Tanya had held the little girl so tightly she had complained she couldn't breathe. 'You had us all so worried. You're okay? You're not hurt?' She'd run her hands over her. 'That's a nasty scratch. We'll get someone to look at that.'

Phoebe had burrowed into her mother's arms. 'I'm hungry. What's for breakfast?'

'You're not in trouble,' said Tanya, 'but we need to know what happened?' Kip saw Tanya's glance in the direction of his tent. 'Tell us, sweetie. Why were you on your own out there? How did you get so lost?'

Phoebe, perching on her mother's lap, with the other campers crowding round, her brown bear tucked in her arms, held court like a tiny empress. 'Kip left me all alone,' she said. 'He told me to stay on the stile. I didn't like it. I was frightened. Then a big black dog came – the one that belonged to the scary man. I thought he was going to catch me. The boys told me the horrid farmer fed children to his pigs. I didn't want to be eaten by a pig.'

'Boys!' Max turned to the other children, alarmed. 'You said what?'

Felix and River exchanged a guilty glance. 'It was just a joke.'

Phoebe, enjoying the attention, continued her tale. 'So I ran. I didn't stop. I ran and I ran. I tried to follow Kip to the beach, but the dog kept chasing me. I could hear it behind me. I saw a little cave and I thought I could hide. I crawled right in, but I could still hear the dog sniffing around outside, so I went further in and then … I fell. Like Alice. When she falls down the rabbit hole.'

Kip noticed Dominic's face. It was a picture of emotion, tears welling in the man's eyes.

'I wasn't hurt, but it was dark, so I felt around and knew that I was on a rock. I remembered what Mummy tells me when we go shopping: if you get lost, just stay where you are. I didn't move. I waited for her to come and find me.'

Tanya leaned in and gave Phoebe a squeeze. 'That was very clever of you.'

'Then it got so dark and so loud. I could hear the wind and the rain outside. I drank some of the water that trickled down, and then I fell asleep.' She tells it simply, matter-of-fact. 'I woke up when I heard shouting. It was Jim. He was the one who found me.'

Tanya threw Jim a grateful look. 'Thank God you did. But what about you? That looks nasty.' She nodded at Jim's arm, now supported in a makeshift sling knocked up by one of the rescue workers.

Jim glanced across at Dominic and shrugged. 'I fell.'

'We should get that checked out at the hospital,' said Dominic. 'I'll drive you, as soon as the track is cleared.'

'You think I'm missing out on the bacon sarnies?'

Suze leaned into her husband, standing on tiptoes to kiss his cheek.

Kip saw Annie move across to Max. She laid her hand on his lower back and murmured something into his ear. They both turned towards his tent and saw him watching from the bed. Annie raised her hand, gave him a smile and a wave. Kip raised his hand in acknowledgement and Annie, encouraged, beckoned for him to join them. He shook his head.

There was talk of taking Phoebe to the hospital too, but Phoebe seemed reluctant to go anywhere, clinging in turn to Tanya and then Dominic like a baby koala. In the end, the paramedics gave her a thorough once-over at the campsite. She had a few cuts – the worst of which Kip knew she'd got from the stile – as well as some large bruises from the fall into the mine shaft, which they assured her would turn a spectacular rainbow of colours before the week was out, but nothing more serious than that. She was, they declared, a little superhero. She had survived her ordeal 'remarkably unscathed'.

'That's my girl,' Dominic crowed, hoisting her onto his shoulders for a victory lap around the camp kitchen, her teddy bear clutched like a prize in her arms.

Kip waited for someone to tell Phoebe that he had been the one to find her bear, how he had injured himself retrieving it from the beach, how he had looked after it and brought it safely back for her – but no one did. In the exhilaration that had come with finding Phoebe, those details seemed to have been forgotten.

'Careful,' Tanya warned as Dominic bounced Phoebe on his shoulders. Dominic grinned, reaching out to include his wife in the celebration, but she ducked away from his embrace.

'Has anyone seen Fred?' Kira was moving through the group, asking everyone in turn, only to be met by head shakes and puzzled frowns. 'I thought he'd be sleeping off a hangover in one of the tents, but I can't find him. I doubt even *he* could sleep through this racket.'

She stood in the centre of the glamping site and turned

slowly. Kip watched as Tanya went across to join her, leaning in close to say something quietly in her ear, something that made Kira's eyes go wide and her face drain of colour. Kip watched as Kira's eyes darted from Tanya to Dominic, her hands flying to the baby sleeping at her chest. She seemed to hesitate, then reached out to Tanya, but Tanya took a quick step back. She eyed Kira coldly before stalking away. Kip watched and wondered. Adults were so confusing. At least kids mostly said what they meant – showed their emotion plainly on their faces. Kids were much easier to read.

After a while, a man in an orange boiler suit and hard hat appeared on the crest of the hill and walked down to the group. He pulled Max to one side for a word and a loud cheer went up as Max confirmed that the farmhouse track had been cleared and the power lines secured. 'We'll be reconnected to the world very soon.'

Annie came to find him, as Kip knew she would. She carried half a bacon sandwich on a tin plate and a cup of milk. 'It's great news about the power lines. Won't you come and join us?'

Kip shook his head. She looked sad, but he couldn't face the noisy jubilation of the group and more importantly, he didn't want to be anywhere near Dominic.

'He's going to apologize to you,' said Annie, as if reading his mind. 'Max and I will make sure of it.'

Kip stayed very still. That was the last thing he wanted.

'You went to get her bear, didn't you?'

He nodded.

'That was really kind of you. Your ankle looks a little

better,' Annie said, reaching out, her hand hovering over his foot, not quite touching.

He nodded again. It still ached, but the swelling had gone down. Kip moved his tongue around his mouth. It felt sluggish, slow, dry, but he knew he'd have to find the words if he was to get out of there. 'Can I go . . . to the house?' he asked. The relief in her eyes as he formed the faltering words made him feel bad. He knew how his silence affected her.

Annie frowned. 'You shouldn't be walking on that ankle. It's too far. Your dad or I will take you later. Have some food first.'

She stayed a little longer, fussing around him, urging him to try the sandwich, moving blankets and stroking his hair, but eventually the demands of the group outside drew her attention and Annie melted away to join the others.

Kip rolled onto his side, turning away from the noise outside and felt something sharp dig into his thigh. Reaching into his pocket he felt the metal blade of the shucking knife. He closed his eyes and ran his fingers over its sharp point. Secret treasure.

'Hey,' said Felix, sticking his head through the open doorway, 'how are you feeling?'

Kip didn't know what to say.

'Look, I'm sorry, about what I said yesterday, on the beach. You're not a weirdo.'

It was a peace offering, of sorts – or maybe someone had told him to apologize. Either way, it didn't make much difference to him. He didn't really care what Felix Davies thought of him. The boy looked as though he was about to leave when he turned back to Kip. 'I don't suppose you've seen Scarlet?'

Kip shook his head.

'Strange.' He shrugged. 'Dad and Tanya are having a massive argument about something up at the car and I can't find her anywhere.' He rolled his eyes. 'Still, she can't have gone far. Her phone's still in the tent.'

Felix left and through the open flaps Kip saw Juniper and Willow turning cartwheels across the grass, a dejected-looking Kira nursing Asha and Max clearing away plates and cups. Suze seemed to be gathering items of clothing and assorted belongings, perhaps packing for the drive home. Further away he could see Josh folding the tarpaulins that had been used to protect the communal shelter from the worst of the storm, laying them in a pile at the far end of the table. Kip watched as Josh glanced round at the group, before sliding Max's penknife off the table and dropping it into his pocket. He gathered up the folded tarpaulins and made his way towards Max. 'If you don't need me for anything else,' he called, 'I think I'll head home.'

Max gave Josh a friendly wave. 'Course,' he said. 'You must be exhausted. Thanks for staying on last night. You've been a great help. We'll pay you overtime, of course.'

Josh shrugged. 'Least I could do. I'm just glad everything worked out. Shall I take the rubbish up to the farm?'

'Sure thing, buddy. Take the truck.' Max had already

turned away, distracted by Annie calling out about a problem with the gas bottle on the BBQ.

As Josh began to make his goodbyes to the rest of the
group, Kip saw his chance. If he moved fast, he could
be up at the farmhouse before anyone could stop him –
before anyone had even realized he'd gone. None of
them would miss him and that way he could be sure to
avoid Dominic.

He slid off the bed and left the tent, limping to the
buggy as quickly as his ankle would allow, where he
crawled into the rear trailer and burrowed beneath its
tarp cover until he was lying curled on his side, pressed
up against the back of the tray. He lay as still as he
could beneath the heavy fabric, breathing quietly. Josh's
footsteps drew close. Something – the rubbish bags,
he presumed – landed beside him on the trailer with
a thump, then he felt the shift of the vehicle as Josh
climbed into the driver's seat and the judder of the engine
surging to life.

He had to grip the sides of the trailer tightly as the
vehicle took the steep hill up to the farmhouse. The jolting
ride sent shockwaves of pain through his ankle, but he was
relieved to be leaving behind the noise and the celebration
at the campsite. He'd already decided that he'd wait for
Josh to park the truck in the barn and head to his own car,
before he risked slipping out and sneaking into the house.
If the power was on, he'd go straight up to his room. They
passed through the gateway leading to the yard, the bump
of the old cattle grid alerting him to their progress, when
Josh surprised him by veering in the wrong direction,

away from the barn, away from the farmhouse, heading out towards the headland.

Confused, Kip lifted the edge of the tarpaulin and saw that they were travelling along the coastal trail. He couldn't understand it. There was nothing out that way except the cliffs, the ocean and, in the far distance, the stone ruins of the old engine house. Kip held his breath, hoping that Josh would come to his senses and turn the vehicle around, but the truck kept going.

After all the rain, the trail was muddy. Once or twice the vehicle lost its grip on the track, skidding and sending dirt flying out from the rear wheels in a great spray. Josh swore loudly in frustration. The further they went, the more Kip began to wonder whether he should reveal himself, tell Josh about his failed escape plan and ask him to divert back to the farmhouse, but something about Josh's energy – the agitation, the swearing – kept him hidden. He'd never seen Josh angry before. It made him afraid. What if he discovered him in the back of the trailer and got mad? He knew what happened when adults got mad.

He'd have to ride this one out, wait for Josh to complete whatever job he was doing, and hope he could slip away undiscovered when the vehicle eventually returned to the farm.

A little further on and the buggy came to a jerking halt. The engine fell silent. Kip held his breath beneath the cover as Josh jumped from the vehicle, his feet landing with a splash in a puddle. He fumbled for something at the rear of the trailer, the tarpaulin rustling, Kip holding himself as still and quiet as possible, before the man's footsteps began to fade away. Kip waited a minute before looking out. Josh was already some distance away, weaving down between the thick gorse and bracken, making for the engine house. In his hands he held one of the folded tarpaulin sheets from the campsite.

Kip knew he could have stayed in the trailer and waited for Josh to return – it certainly would've been easier on his ankle – but something about Josh's purposeful stride made him curious. He was up to something. He wanted to know what. Sliding out from the trailer, he crouched low and began to limp after him.

The sky was clearing after the storm, clouds breaking apart like fragile grey eggshell to allow streaks of orange and yellow to slant across the pastel sky. A stiff breeze still blew off the ocean, but it was nothing like the gales of the previous night.

As he neared the engine house, Josh hesitated and glanced back. Kip ducked behind a burst of bracken, wondering if he'd been spotted, but when he looked out again, Josh was already striding away, disappearing behind the tall stone walls of the ruins. Afraid of losing him, he limped onwards, surprised, as he drew near, to hear Josh's voice. He sounded angry.

Drawing closer to the thick, stone wall, Kip tried to slow his breathing, worried he might be heard. Pressing one eye up to a crack, he could just make out Josh inside. He was leaning over something on the floor. There was a flash of silver in the darkness, metal glinting in the light falling through the roof above, and Kip realized it was the blade of Max's penknife.

It took a moment for his eyes to adjust, but as he began to focus on the scene inside the ruins, Kip's breath caught in his throat.

Scarlet was lying at Josh's feet, her head bloody, her hands and legs tied. Josh seemed to be trying to drag her onto the tarpaulin sheet which was now spread out across the floor. But Scarlet was moaning and struggling, resisting him. 'For fuck's sake,' Josh shouted.

Kip stifled his cry and turned away as Josh bent over her, the knife flashing purposefully in his hand.

SCARLET

Monday morning

Recounting her ordeal to the police has taken it out of Scarlet, so they stop the interview for a few minutes, at her mother's suggestion. While the police wait outside in the hospital corridor, making calls and checking notes, Scarlet sits up in bed and sips water from a plastic cup. She studies the red marks on her wrists where the restraints have sliced into her skin.

'I know this is hard, but you're doing so well,' says her mum, brushing her hair from her face. 'You're very brave.'

Scarlet doesn't feel brave. She feels stupid. Stupid for liking him. Stupid for thinking she could make Lily and Harry jealous. Stupid for being a dumb, self-obsessed teenager with no clue about anything.

'It's okay, Scarlet,' says her mum, reaching out to wipe her tears from her cheek. 'None of this is your fault.'

They keep telling her this, but she doesn't believe them. Somehow it all feels like her fault.

Tanya re-enters the room. She stands at the end of the bed and throws Clare a glance.

'What is it?'

Tanya shifts uncomfortably. 'There's a special nurse. She needs to check Scarlet over. Take swabs. Scrape under her nails. Gather evidence. That sort of thing. The police need to know if he . . . if he . . .'

Scarlet shakes her head. 'He didn't rape me. He didn't want that. He wanted something else.'

Clare leans back in her chair and releases a heavy sigh. 'Right.'

Scarlet squeezes her eyes shut and tries to control the trembling in her legs. She can still hear it. The sound of the sea pounding against the cliff.

She knows she must've slipped back into sleep, still affected by the drugs coursing through her veins, because when she next opened her eyes, Josh was standing over her, the knife in his hands flashing silver as he lunged for her. Scarlet let out a cry of fear and tried to twist from his grip.

'For fuck's sake. Stay still,' he muttered as he cut through the ties on her ankles and wrists, releasing her from the restraints.

She wriggled herself up to a seating position, her head swimming as she rubbed her sore wrists. There was a tarpaulin sheet stretched out on the ground beside her that hadn't been there earlier.

She didn't know if it was the effect of the sedatives or the injury to her head that was making her feel so woozy but when she touched her head she could feel the dried blood matted in her hair and a fresh trickle begin to slide down her temple from the wound. She groaned. 'I don't feel good.'

'Get up,' he said, nudging her with his foot. 'Just do as I say. It'll be easier that way.'

'Why are you doing this?' Her voice was hoarse, little more than a whisper.

He let out a hollow laugh. 'It's a certain kind of person who thinks they can march through life untouched, using people, crushing them for their own amusement and advantage.'

She didn't understand. 'Whatever I did to upset you,' she said, trying to appeal to his better nature, 'I'm really sorry, okay? Just please, don't hurt me.'

'You think this is all about *you?*' He gave a hollow laugh. 'Maybe you are a chip off the old block after all. No doubt Dominic Davies is used to everyone knowing who *he* is. He's less invested in remembering us mere mortals, those of us whose lives he's shattered.'

'Dad?'

'It's ironic, don't you think? Your dad changed my family for ever, but I doubt he even remembers my sister's name.'

'This is about my dad ... and your sister?' Her head swam so sickeningly she thought she might vomit. 'Amber,' she said, the name returning to her. 'This is about Amber?'

'No more talking. You need to come with me now.'

Scarlet shook her head and Josh, sensing her reluctance, flashed the knife again. 'I mean it. Get up.'

She scooted on her bum until her back pressed against the damp wall of the engine house. 'Listen, let me go and we can talk to him. If Amber wants a career in music . . . a job . . . he'll find a way to help her. But this isn't the way to go about it. Dad won't respond well to blackmail. If anything happens to me—'

'Blackmail?' Josh shook his head. 'You think that's what this is?'

'Does she have a demo tape? Something we can play him? Maybe she could go on his show?' Scarlet was talking fast, the desperation evident in her voice, but Josh ignored her, hauling her to her feet. She cringed at his touch, staggered awkwardly, her legs buckling beneath her. 'I won't tell anyone about this, if that's what you're worried about.'

'I told you,' he said, his teeth gritted, 'just do as I say.' He gave her a shove, pushing her towards the open door.

'Maybe you've got this all wrong? My dad's a good guy, I promise.'

'A good guy? Is that right?' He shook his head and gave her another forceful shove.

Scarlet stumbled through the doorway, the sudden shock of daylight blinding her, so that she tripped and swayed, Josh dragging her with one hand, the knife still held in the other. She was so weak she could barely hold herself up.

Now they were outside, she could see that they stood on a barren promontory, a steep shard of land falling away dramatically into the thundering sea. The grey stone building in which he had kept her captive towered behind them and that melancholy sound – the one that had haunted her inside the engine house – was louder now. Her vision blurred. All she wanted to do was close her eyes and let the nightmare be over, but she knew she had to hold on. If she passed out now, he could do anything to her. She had to hold on.

'You know, Amber was convinced your dad's show would get her in front of the right people, that it would be the platform she needed to "make it big". I begged her not to go,' Josh said, pulling her down the pitched slope, 'but she took herself up to London, got singled out by the producers and bundled up onto that stage in front of the cameras, the judges and the jeering crowd. She was nothing but a piece of meat to be shot out of the reality TV cannon.'

Josh's rant came to an abrupt halt at the sound of rocks shifting and tumbling from somewhere behind them. He glanced back at the engine house, distracted, and Scarlet saw her chance. She wrenched herself free of his grip and ran towards the path. It was like running through quicksand and she had only gone a few metres by the time he caught her. 'Oh no you don't,' he said, dragging her back towards the cliff. 'We're going this way,' he said, pointing to where the cliff face sheered away, to where the waves crashed onto the rocks below.

She stared at the cliff edge in horror. He couldn't be serious? She shook her head, dizzy at the thought, the churn of the ocean and the strange wailing chorus filling her mind. 'That sound.' She gazed about, bewildered. 'Can't you hear it?'

He tilted his head and listened. 'The seals. There's a colony of grey seals out on Morvoren Rock, across the bay. They're singing ... or crying. I imagine a few were washed away in the storm.'

Scarlet didn't know whether to believe him. Seals could make that noise? It was so eerie – it sounded almost human.

'The locals used to believe it was the mermaids.'

Scarlet shivered. 'Tell me what happened,' she said, hoping to buy more time, thinking if she kept him talking, she might be able to stall him from whatever he was planning. 'With Amber. Tell me.'

Josh gazed out at the grey horizon. 'She would've been the best thing they'd heard all day, if they'd given her a proper shot, but Amber was nervous. She got up on stage and they asked her all the usual questions, where she was from and what she did. She told them she was a student and that she worked weekends in a Cornish bakery. She told them that she wrote her own music. She said she was going to play one of her original songs. As she hoisted her guitar onto her shoulder, your dad looked her up and down and stage-whispered, "I'd say someone's been enjoying her Cornish pasties just a little too much."'

Josh turned back to her and she could see the hurt and the rage in his eyes. 'With one cruel comment he took the wind out of her sails. Amber stood there under the spotlight and she froze. Stage fright hit her like a freight train. She opened her mouth to sing and nothing came out. And you want to know what your dad did?'

Scarlet shook her head, utterly miserable.

'He said, "Sweetheart, I really don't think this business is for you. The star we're looking for needs to have the right look *and* the right voice. It seems you have neither."

'Amber began to cry. She pleaded for a second chance. She literally begged him to give her another go, but the damage was done. Her song – when she eventually managed it – came out all wrong. Her voice was shaky. They cut her off after a single verse. Your dad said he was "bowled over by her mediocrity". He told her to "go back to the pasty shop and find another dream".

'Of course, the audience booed him, it was all part of the pantomime, but Amber wasn't strong enough to rise above his comments. She came home a different person. She thought the whole world was laughing at her, and when some arsehole turned her crying face into a cruel meme and began to circulate it across social media, I suppose it was.'

'That's awful.' Scarlet felt sick. Josh's story conjured an uncomfortable memory of a young, red-haired girl crying on stage in front of her father. It must have been a season or two ago, for she hadn't really thought of that moment since, certainly hadn't given the girl another moment's thought.

'Can you imagine how it feels to be reduced to a single, humiliating meme? To go "viral" for your most shameful moment?'

Scarlet stared at Josh in dismay. 'I know Dad can seem cruel, but it's not real. It's the show. The producers need him to be the villain. The audience expects it.'

Josh cut her off, his eyes narrowed, his fist gripped around the knife. 'You want to talk about real life? Amber refused to pick up her guitar after that. She stopped singing. My dad and I tried to help, but she'd shut down. I told her that she couldn't let one man's opinion change the course of her life. I told her that we still believed in her, but nothing we said got through. He'd crushed her. Made her feel completely worthless.'

Scarlet shook her head. 'I'm sure my dad would want to help, if we explained how—'

Josh gripped her tightly, pulled her closer so that she had to look right into his furious gaze, his breath hot on her cheek. 'She left the house early, before the sun was even up. Neither of us heard her go, but it was Dad who found the note. She said she couldn't make music any-more – all she could hear was *his* voice, his cruel words echoing in her head.'

'Where did she go?'

Josh squeezed her arm so tightly she had to bite her lip to stop herself from crying out. 'It took the police three days to find her body. She was here all that time, lying at the bottom of these cliffs.'

Scarlet gasped. Josh dragged her closer, Scarlet's feet trailing across the grass, until they were standing at the very edge, staring down into the swirling ocean frothing and smashing against the rocks below. 'This is where she jumped from.'

Scarlet's eyes darted to the small wooden cross at the edge of the headland. 'I'm so sorry.'

'You have no idea. It wasn't just Amber's life he destroyed. Her death broke my dad. His health has suf-fered ever since. It was bad enough when we lost Mum, but it was as if all the light left him when Amber died.'

Josh narrowed his eyes. 'I knew I had to do something. I knew I had to make your dad pay for what he'd done. But it wasn't until I saw that article in Dad's Saturday paper, lying right there on his lap, the one about Max and Annie's plans for Wildernest, that I knew how. There was a mention of the glamping site, but it was their friendship with Dominic Davies that had clearly got the journalist wetting her knickers. She couldn't stop banging on about him, saying how lucky we'd be to see such a "big television star" visiting his friends on the peninsula. All it took was a carefully orchestrated meeting with Max out on the headland, a few hints about how much I'd like to help, and here I've been ... waiting ... for the *infamous* Dominic Davies to show his face.'

'Why didn't you talk to Dad?' Scarlet asked. 'Tell him what happened? Make him understand ...'

Josh looked through Scarlet, unseeing. 'I'd fantasized endlessly about what I'd say to him, but that first afternoon at the campsite, when your dad finally reached out to shake my hand, I couldn't find the words. How do you define such a great loss with words alone? It was then I realized I'd have to *show* him the pain he's caused. It would be wrong, don't you think, for Dominic Davies to go through life without any understanding of the damage he's done?'

Scarlet felt fear rising from the depths of her belly, prickling across her skin. She glanced about, looking for something she might be able to use to protect herself, wondering which direction she should run in. She didn't fancy her chances.

344

'I think your dad needs to learn exactly how fragile life can be ... needs to know what it feels like to lose a precious daughter.'

'He knows,' cried Scarlet. 'You've seen him this weekend, searching for Phoebe. He's beside himself.'

There was something in Josh's eyes, something wild and desperate. He shook his head. 'It's not enough.'

He took a step towards her, the knife in his hand. Scarlet felt her feet at the edge of the cliff, heard a handful of stones skittering away down the rock face. She understood. He was going to force her over. He was going to make her jump, like Amber. 'Don't do this,' she begged. 'It won't bring her back. You'll go to prison. Who will be there for your dad then?'

She saw a flicker of doubt pass across his eyes, a split second of hesitation, before it was gone, replaced by a sneer. 'But that's the beauty of it. Who's going to know? An unstable girl out wandering the cliffs. Searching for her little sister. Upset because her boyfriend kissed someone else. A few sleeping pills in her system. Trust me, the police won't give a toss. *Death by suicide*. That's what the coroner ruled when Amber died. I thought it would all come out at the inquest. I was waiting for it to hit the news, the truth about your father's cruel comments, how he'd crushed the life out of Amber. But the inquest was a sham. No one wanted to delve any deeper. No one wanted to question why a perfectly healthy sixteen-year-old girl – a girl with dreams and talent and a future ahead of her – would end her life. They didn't care. They claimed she was unstable, but she wasn't. She hadn't been. Not until she came face-to-face with your dad. It'll be the same . . . when they find you.'

Scarlet gasped as the heel of one of her trainers slipped at the edge of the cliff, felt a sickening vertigo as she teetered momentarily, the roar of the ocean rising from below, the seals calling out in the bay. She thought of her family back at the campsite, her mum at home in London, her best friend Lily. She didn't care about any of that stupid business with Harry anymore. She just wanted to go home. To be with them all. A single tear slid down her cheek.

'Turn around,' Josh said, his voice cold. 'Look at the horizon. I want you to see what Amber saw.'

Scarlet shook her head and let out a low moan. 'I can't.'

'Do it.' He lunged at her with the knife and she shrieked as the blade slid into her thigh. She didn't feel it at first, just stood, shocked, looking down at the rip in her jeans and the dark stain spreading across the fabric. Then it came: a searing pain shooting along the nerves of her body and rattling in her foggy brain. She staggered slightly, regained her balance, moaning in fear and agony.

'Turn around.'

With tears streaming down her face, she turned towards the ocean, her toes at the ledge. Below her, waves smashed against jagged rocks, granite shards rising like decaying teeth from the foaming, grey water. The loud, too-fast thump of her heart competed in her head with the roar of the sea and the gusting wind.

He was a dark presence behind her, urging her on. 'Do it,' he said. 'What are you waiting for?'

The ledge shifted beneath her toes. A fragment of earth crumbled and dislodged, disappearing into the swirling water far below. Carried on the wind, mingling with the seal's chorus, came the shrill cry of a bird. She lifted her gaze and saw a white gull turn in the sky above. Free.

'Do it now.' His voice again, louder, closer, goosebumps rising as if his words curled through the air and grazed the back of her neck. There was no escape. Nowhere else for her to go.

With a final breath she closed her eyes and stretched out her arms, spread them wide like the wings of the bird above her, praying for a miracle to catch her.

KIP

Sunday morning

Kip crouched in the shadow of the old ruins and watched as Josh wrestled Scarlet towards the cliff face. He hadn't been able to catch Josh's every word through the crumbling walls of the engine house, but he knew Scarlet was in danger. Josh was strong – much stronger than him – and he didn't know what he could do, but he knew he couldn't just stand there and watch him hurt Scarlet. He had to do something.

Josh was talking and gesticulating wildly, the penknife flashing in his hand as Kip crept round the side of the ruins. Awkward on his swollen ankle, he tripped and sent several loose rocks skittering away, ducking back behind the stone wall just as Josh spun round. Kip's heart leapt like a caged cat in his chest. He was certain he'd been spotted, but when he peered out next, he saw that Scarlet had seized her chance. She had broken out of Josh's grip and was staggering towards the cliff path.

She didn't get far. Josh caught up with her easily, hauling her back. 'Oh no you don't. We're going this way.'

Kip frowned. Which way? There was nothing in the direction he'd gestured but the high bluff and the ocean thundering below. From far away he could hear the cries of the seal colony echoing across the water from Morvoren Rock, their strange song carried on the wind.

Josh hauled her towards the edge. He was talking in a low monotone, on and on. Scarlet looked terrified. Kip could see how her legs trembled, how she seemed to struggle to keep her balance, the blood still oozing from the gash on her head, shocking red against her ashen skin. She looked grotesque, like one of the zombies from the game Annie hated him playing.

With Josh's back turned, Kip crept ever closer, fragments of his words coming to him. '... The police won't give a toss ... it'll be the same when they find you.'

Scarlet was precariously close to the ledge.

'Turn around,' Josh said, his voice cold and harsh. 'Look at the horizon. I want you to see what Amber saw ...'

Scarlet shook her head and let out a low moan. 'I can't.'

It was the anguish in her voice, the sob catching in her throat that told Kip he had to act. He had to do something, and he had to do it *now*. Josh lunged. Scarlet shrieked. Slowly, she turned to the ocean. Kip saw his only chance.

He rushed at Josh, adrenalin carrying him forward, his swollen ankle forgotten as his feet thudded across the cliff. He saw Scarlet stretch her arms wide, as if she were about to take flight.

'Stop!' he cried, his voice so loud and strong that the sound of it surprised him as much as it surprised Josh.

Josh spun round and Kip knew he only had one chance. He hurled himself at Josh. Scarlet teetered on the edge, unbalanced, and for one horrible moment Kip thought she was going over, but then she swayed and fell, sprawling backwards onto the cliff ledge.

Kip barrelled into Josh's legs, trying to knock him sideways. If he could give Scarlet a fighting chance, maybe she could get away. But Josh was too strong. He seized Kip easily as they collided, grabbing him around the waist and lifting him high off the ground. For a split second, Kip was weightless. He saw the sky and the ocean, saw his legs dangling over the precipice, his stomach plunging at the realization he was hanging in mid-air over the ocean drop, but then he was spinning back towards the ground, Josh hauling him round and slinging him down onto the rocky ledge. 'What the fuck, Kip!' he said, panting. 'What are you doing here?'

Scarlet was sobbing. She was crawling across the ground, her hands clawing at the mud as she tried to put as much distance as she could between herself and the cliff's edge, between her and Josh.

Josh saw her and dragged Kip up, holding him tight against his chest, pinning his arms easily at his sides. Kip was gripped by a cold panic. He knew he should wriggle and kick, fight with everything he had, but he was flooded with memories. Fragments of a time years ago when he had been held and hurt, kicked and hit by the people who were supposed to love him – supposed to be his family. The betrayal came spinning back and paralysed him. He'd thought Josh was his friend, but

350

Josh was no better than anyone else. He went rigid, all fight leaving him.

'That was a dumb move, Kip. You shouldn't've followed me. You shouldn't've got involved.' He turned to Scarlet. 'And where do you think you're going?' he called, his voice almost amused.

Scarlet looked back. She glanced between Josh and Kip. He could see how weak she was. For a second, she held Kip's gaze, the two of them locked in a terrible nightmare. Kip tried to tell her with his eyes that he was sorry – that he'd tried his best.

'Come on now, Scarlet, you don't want to be responsible for me hurting Kip too, do you?' Josh's arm tightened and Kip felt the cold blade of Max's knife against his throat.

Scarlet moaned.

'You don't want me to hurt a little kid, do you?'

Scarlet closed her eyes and Kip knew then that he had failed. He hadn't helped her at all. He'd only given Josh another way to leverage Scarlet and put them both in danger. He wanted to shout at her to run. He wanted to tell her to look out for herself. He didn't think Josh would let him go, but he might be able to convince Scarlet. If only he could find the words. But his lips remained frozen, the words trapped in his body, stifled by fear.

Scarlet rose unsteadily to her feet and held out her hands. 'Please,' she begged, 'please don't . . .'

'I'll do it,' Josh hissed, shaking him fiercely. 'I swear.' The point of the blade dug into Kip's flesh just below his ear. He gasped as a warm trickle of blood slid down towards his collarbone. Josh shook him again and Kip felt something sharp digging through his own shorts pocket into his leg. 'Get back here!' Josh yelled.

Scarlet stumbled towards them, tears streaming down her face. She didn't look right, as if she might collapse at any moment.

'Do it,' Josh urged. 'Do it now or Kip goes over too.'

Josh tensed, squeezing Kip even tighter in anticipation. The sharp digging sensation in Kip's leg increased. Kip closed his eyes and reached down, stretching his hand, reaching desperately until his fingers found his pocket, until his fingertips grazed rusted metal, cold and sharp. The shucking knife. His treasure. It was their only chance.

With a cry, Kip withdrew his hand and jammed the blade as hard as he could into Josh's side.

Josh yelled out in pain. His arms instinctively released, and as they did, Kip shoved him towards the cliff's edge. He heard scuffling sounds at the ledge, Scarlet's scream, a loud cry. Kip fell to the ground and squeezed his eyes shut, curling into a tight ball. For a long moment there was nothing but the sound of sobbing, the waves crashing onto the rocks below and the mournful, faraway call of the seals.

'Kip,' he heard. 'Kip, it's okay.'

When he opened his eyes, he saw Scarlet crouched before him, ghastly and blood-soaked, her face white as a sheet, her hands mud-caked and torn. She was shivering as she slumped down beside him.

'Where is he?' he asked, afraid to move. 'What did I do?'

Scarlet lay back, her glassy eyes gazing up at the gun-metal sky. 'See for yourself.'

Kip lifted his head. There was no sign of Josh on the bluff. Slowly, cautiously, he crept towards the cliff's edge and peered over. Far below, he saw a body lying in a motionless heap on the jagged rocks, red blood leaking into the foaming water as the indifferent ocean continued to hurl its waves against the shore and the seals sang on.

ANNIE

Monday morning

DC Haines' face is grim as she hangs up the phone in the farmhouse kitchen and turns to them both. Annie sees the look in her eyes. Fear rises and catches in her throat. She's known this moment would come eventually, but she's been hoping they'd have a little more time before it did. She nudges Max. 'They know,' she murmurs.

'Scarlet's in with my colleagues now. She's giving her statement,' Haines says.

Annie's stomach flips. 'How is she?'

'Well, she's talking. Scarlet's confirmed that Kip was involved in the incident on the cliffs.' She eyes them both closely and Annie can't help her quick glance at Max. 'Her statement suggests that you've both been covering for your son all this time.' Haines looks at them both in turn and Annie feels Max shifting beside her. He reaches for her hand. 'I think it's about time you told me the truth.'

'We didn't mean . . . we didn't know—'

Max cuts her off. 'Annie. Stop.'

Haines shakes her head. 'I'd advise you both that there could be significant consequences for not telling the truth now. Making false statements. Obstruction of justice. I'm sure you don't need me to warn you that they both carry a heavy penalty.'

Annie bites her lip. 'We just wanted some time ... to understand. Kip wouldn't have ...' She peters out. She doesn't want to finish the sentence. 'There's no way he would've hurt her.'

'Why don't we sit.' Haines gestures to the kitchen table. 'Tell me everything you know – the truth, this time.'

Annie turns her face away, burying it against Max's shoulder, trying to absorb some of her husband's strength for whatever lies ahead. 'Come on, love.' He guides her to the table.

Annie takes a deep breath and lifts her face to meet the detective's gaze. 'It was after Phoebe had been found and we'd cleared up from the celebratory breakfast that Max and I discovered Kip had gone. We didn't want to tell everyone. We didn't want to make a big deal of it, so we left everyone else down at the tents and walked up to the farmhouse together.'

'We'd specifically told him he should stay at the campsite,' adds Max, 'so to find he'd disobeyed us was disappointing. I know it had been a rough twenty-four hours for everyone, but just disappearing like that wasn't on, not after all we'd been through with Phoebe.'

Haines nods. 'What did you find at the farmhouse?'

'I expected Kip to be holed up in his bedroom.'

355

Annie remembers walking through the silent house, searching the rooms in turn, taking the stairs up to Kip's empty bedroom. 'The power hadn't been on long. I assumed he'd be playing Xbox, but there was no sign of him. We checked the whole house and the barns. Nothing. I couldn't believe it. I turned to Max in disbelief. "Where the hell has he gone?"'

'It was moments later that we heard the buggy,' Max added. 'I assumed it would be Josh. I thought he might've seen Kip, so we went down to the yard to talk to him, but when the truck appeared, it wasn't Josh who was driving.'

Annie shook her head. 'I don't think either of us could quite believe our eyes.'

Haines leans forward in her seat. 'Go on.'

'Kip was behind the wheel. The buggy was lurching and swerving but he was doing a pretty good job of driving it, all things considered. To be honest, I wasn't really looking at Kip. My eyes were drawn to the person slumped in the passenger seat beside him. I didn't recognize her at first. She was in a terrible state.'

Annie picks up the thread as Max composes himself. 'Kip cut the engine as soon as he saw us. I think the silence jolted us out of our shock. Max was first to react. He ran to the vehicle as Scarlet began to fall and caught her in his arms.'

Max winces at the memory. 'Her eyes were rolling back in her head and I could see she was badly injured. There was blood everywhere. She had a nasty head injury and a deep cut on her leg that looked . . . well, it looked like a stab wound.' He swallows.

'Max was holding her, but I was still frozen. And Kip

just sat there in the buggy. I wanted to go to him, but I'll admit,' she swallows, 'I was afraid.'

'What were you afraid of?'

Annie chews her bottom lip. She eyes the officer sitting across from her. She doesn't know how to find the words; doesn't know how to tell her about that one small gesture Kip had made that had chilled her to the bone. How, while Max tended to Scarlet, Kip, still holding her gaze, had reached into his pocket and pulled out the knife – his bloody fist curled around a small, rusty dagger. She wonders if now is the right time to tell them both, but Max saves her from sharing the memory by speaking next.

'I called out to Annie. I told her to hurry to the house and call an ambulance. Right away.'

Annie nods. 'Kip was staring at me. He had this look on his face – fear and need – and I wanted to go to him, but I knew Max was right. Scarlet was in trouble, so I left them in the yard, and I ran.'

'The ambulance seemed to take an age and it was while we were waiting that I talked Max into it.' She glances across at her husband and throws him a remorseful look. 'Scarlet was unconscious. She couldn't tell us what had happened, but the state she was in ... I didn't know if she'd even ...' she trails off. 'I thought if we just had a little time with Kip – to understand what had happened ...' She tries again. 'If you lot had come and hauled him away to a police station, there's no way he would've talked. Not given his past – all he's been through. I thought it was the best thing – for him, and for Scarlet – if we handled it here. We needed a little time.'

As she offers this explanation, Annie finds herself wondering how much of it is true. Had she really been motivated by uncovering the truth, or was it purely her maternal instinct, pushing her to protect Kip, at whatever cost? And how much had she been swayed by that bloody knife in Kip's hand? Had she really believed wholeheartedly in his innocence? She still wasn't entirely sure what she thought – and feared.

'You lied. You told the first responders you'd returned to the farmhouse and found Scarlet alone, collapsed in the yard.'

Annie nodded. 'While Max waited with Scarlet for the ambulance, I took Kip upstairs. I put him in the shower. Gave him clean clothes to change into. I told him to stay in his room.' She hesitates. She glances from Max to the detective and something stills her tongue. She doesn't mention the knife she had prised from Kip's hands, the blood transferring to her own as she'd wrapped it in an old towel and buried it deep beneath a pile of dirty clothes in the laundry basket, Kip watching silently, his eyes fixed on her. She doesn't tell them how it had felt to scrub the blood from her own palms, watching it wash away down the plughole. Not even Max knew about that.

Haines frowns. 'By doing all of that – showering, changing his clothes – you know you destroyed important evidence? Then you gave false statements and obstructed the police investigation by withholding important information. Information that might have helped our investigation – helped Scarlet.'

'It wasn't like that.' Annie's eyes fill. She wants to

justify her actions, show how she meant well, but in her heart, she knows that what they did – what *she* did – was wrong.

The police officer rises in her seat and shuffles her papers. 'I'll need to speak to Kip, as soon as possible.'

Annie bows her head.

'Given his age, a guardian will also need to be present. Do you think there's any chance he could be persuaded to speak to me?'

Annie shrugs. 'I don't know. Perhaps if we were there?'

DC Haines leans back in her chair with a sigh. 'Okay. I have one last question, if I may?' She eyes them keenly. 'I can't help wondering why you would keep all of this from us. I know how worried you've been for Scarlet. You both seem to want to help. Was the reason you kept Kip's involvement from us because you believed he was involved in some way? That he was the one who had hurt Scarlet?' DC Haines' face is grave, but she holds their gaze, her eyes darting between them as she awaits an answer.

Annie feels a great swell of emotion rising inside of her. Her boy. Her lovely, complicated boy. That bloody knife. She can't bring herself to say the word, so instead, she gives the smallest nod of her head.

A sound from the stairwell behind makes her turn. Kip is standing on the bottom step, his eyes fixed on Annie, a pile of paper in his hands. He is staring at her with such sorrow that Annie feels it like an arrow flying straight to her heart. As their eyes meet, Kip drops the papers, the sheets scattering in a cascade.

'Kip!' she says. 'Kip, come back.' But he has already gone, limping back up the stairs to his room, leaving her in the kitchen with nothing but her remorse and a collage of his pictures spread across the flagstone floor.

MAX

Monday morning

They spread the drawings across the kitchen table, a dozen of Kip's pictures drawn in felt-tip pen, laid out in the morning sun so that they almost cover the entire surface. 'My god,' says Max, peering at them in turn, 'it's all here. Everything that happened. Everything he couldn't tell us.'

DC Haines is taking photos of the pictures on her phone. She turns to them both when she has finished. 'I need to call the DI. She'll want to see this.'

'Who is that?' Annie whispers, pointing to the crude figure Kip has drawn, the one holding Scarlet at the cliff's edge, a silver knife in his hand. 'Is that . . .' she swallows, '. . . Kip?'

'No. Look.' Max points to the outline of a roughly drawn stone building. 'That's the old engine house out on the headland. Look at the chimney. It's quite clear. And just behind, do you see?'

Annie peers at the picture and sees what she had

originally missed: another small figure beside the stone wall.

'Look at the hair. The T-shirt and glasses. That's him. That's Kip.'

'If that's Kip,' she asks with a shiver, her finger sliding back to the taller figure holding the knife, 'who is that?'

As DC Haines talks on the phone, Kira and Suze enter the kitchen. Kira looks anxious and drawn. She glances about at the pictures spread across the table, seems about to say something, when the detective hangs up the phone and turns to them all. 'The forensics team have a positive ID on the body they found out on the cliffs.'

'Oh.' Kira lets out a small sigh. She reaches for the back of a chair. Suze steps forward and grabs her hand, giving it a gentle squeeze.

'The deceased is a local man. Joshua Penrose.'

'Josh?' says Max, alarmed. 'Josh is dead?'

Kira lets out a long, slow sigh. Annie gasps.

'Yes, I'm afraid so. Scarlet's confirmed that it was Josh who took her out onto the cliffs.'

'What? Why?'

Annie shakes her head. 'I don't understand. What would Josh want with Scarlet?'

'And why was Kip out there with them?' adds Max.

'According to Miss Davies' statement, Mr Penrose was upset with Scarlet's father. It appears Josh had been holding a grudge against Mr Davies for an event that happened to his family a couple of years ago.' DC Haines runs her hands through her hair, pushes her glasses back onto the bridge of her nose in a gesture that is now familiar to

Max. 'I'm afraid I can't say too much at this stage. It's all part of the ongoing investigation, but from what we can determine, Penrose learned about your friendship with Mr Davies from an article in the local newspaper. He sought a job with you here at Wildernest, hoping it would, eventually, offer him the opportunity to meet with the man.'

Max shakes his head. 'He used us to get closer to Dominic?'

'Yes. Mr Davies' appearance this weekend triggered a desire for revenge in the young man. He made Scarlet his target, as a way of getting to Mr Davies. Kip, it appears, was simply caught up in the attack. We think he might have travelled out in the back of the trailer. See. Here.' She points to another of Kip's drawings, one of the buggy bumping along the headland track.

'How did Josh die?' asks Annie. She can't help herself, still thinking of that rusty knife.

'The autopsy will confirm the exact cause of death, but I think it's safe to assume the cliff fall killed him.'

She nods. 'And Kip? Has Scarlet said anything about him?'

'According to Scarlet's statement, your son distracted Josh during the attack. He helped her onto the utility vehicle and drove her back to the farmhouse. He was very brave. He saved her life.'

Max reaches for Annie, squeezing her shoulder. 'I knew Kip was innocent,' he says. 'He wouldn't hurt anyone. I always knew it.'

Beside him, Annie lets out the breath she has been holding. When he turns to her, he sees tears streaming down her cheeks. He tries to pull her into his arms to comfort her, but she resists his embrace, the hurt and the regret evident in her eyes.

KIRA

Monday, midday

Max and Annie are still busy with the detective when the phone in the kitchen rings again. Suze answers it, a smile spreading across her face as she listens to the voice at the other end. 'Hang on,' she says, thrusting the handset at Kira.

'Kira, is that you?'

'Oh my god! Fred! Where are you?'

'Have they found her?'

'Phoebe? Yes. Yes, they have – she's fine.'

'Thank god.'

'Where are you?'

'Good question. The arse end of nowhere. If I give you the postcode, will you come and get me?'

Suze offers to look after Asha. 'Go,' she says. 'You two need to talk.'

Kira follows her sat nav out to a tiny hamlet about six miles inland, pulling up outside a pebbledash cottage with a faded

B&B sign swinging in the breeze. A lace curtain twitches at the window, and seconds later, the front door opens and Fred is loping out with his hands jammed in his raincoat pockets and a sheepish smile on his face. 'Perfect timing,' he says, sliding into the passenger seat beside her. 'The landlady was force-feeding me bacon and black pudding. Mountains of the stuff. I thought I was going to explode.'

She turns and studies him. 'Fred, I'm so—'

'I'm so sorry—'

Their words overlap each other. They both fall silent, then laugh.

'You go first.'

The lace curtain twitches again. Kira grimaces. 'I think we've got an audience. Let's find somewhere more private to talk.'

She turns the car round and heads in the direction of the farmhouse, pulling onto an unmarked side road, then parking in a layby with a sweeping view across the Atlantic. The stormy skies are a distant memory; all is now a placid blue, smoke-white clouds drifting in the breeze above a silver sea, tall fronds of ferns rustling against the car. She turns to face him. 'I thought something dreadful had happened to you. I was so worried.'

'I'm sorry. I had to go. I had to get my head straight.' He throws her a glance. 'I have to tell you something. Something bad.'

'What is it?' She braces, waiting for him to tell her that he's done. That it's all over between them.

Fred runs his hands through his hair, 'I told Tanya. I told her about you and Dominic. About Asha.'

Kira lets out a breath. 'I know. She told me.'

'Shit. I'm sorry. I was so angry.'

'Dom knows too. They were having a huge row up by their car yesterday, but then we got the news about Scarlet being taken away in an ambulance and I haven't seen either of them since. They've been at the hospital with the police.'

'Scarlet? What on earth happened?'

Kira fills Fred in on everything she knows. She tells him how Phoebe was found safe and well, and about Scarlet's ordeal with Josh.

'He seemed like such a sound lad.' He shakes his head.

'It's awful. They found his body at the bottom of the cliffs.' Kira bites her lip. 'I thought it was you.' She lets out a small sob.

Fred seizes her hand. 'You eejit. I'm right here.'

'He was wearing a blue hoodie. I heard the police talking and I thought . . .' She shakes her head. 'It was him. Josh was the one who took your rucksack. I knew I'd heard something – someone – outside our tent that first night. The police think he used our sleeping pills. They think he drugged Tanya, then when she'd fallen asleep, he tricked Scarlet into going off with him.'

'God.' Fred shuddered. 'That's . . . dark. Poor Scarlet.'

She studies him for a long moment, then punches him on the arm. 'Where did you go? Why didn't you call sooner? I was so worried.'

'I was drunk. I just started walking. I needed to clear my head. I didn't really think about where I was going. I was only thinking about you and Asha, about how much

I love you both. How I didn't want to lose you. I thought about how I would feel if it had been Asha that had gone missing.'

Kira reaches out and touches Fred's sleeve, grateful to have him sitting safely beside her.

'I was wet and miserable anyway, so I started to think I should have a crack at getting help. I walked and I walked, and I kept checking my phone and then a little before daybreak, I saw I had a weak signal. I had no idea where I was, but I called the emergency services and asked them to send a search party out to the farmhouse. I couldn't remember the address. I kept telling them "Wildernest" but they didn't know where I meant. Then I remembered that weird dude. Kellow. They knew about his dairy. They said they'd send help.'

'So that was you?'

He nods. 'I was wrecked,' he adds, 'and a tad hung-over. When I saw that little cottage with the B&B sign, I thought I'd stumbled on an oasis.' He grins. 'The landlady wasn't too happy to have me banging on her door at 5am, but I offered her everything in my wallet, and she came round pretty quickly. Quite the rip-off.'

'But you should've called me earlier. You could've let me know you were safe.'

'Babe, I was done in. I didn't wake up till the early evening. My phone was dead. I was out of cash. No phone charger. Edith said I should stay another night while we figured it all out.'

Kira raises an eyebrow. 'Edith?'

'The landlady. She's eighty-nine. Half blind. Can

talk the hindleg off a donkey. I think she took a bit of a shine to me.'

'You still could've called.'

'How? I knew your mobiles didn't work at the campsite. I didn't have the landline number, and the last I knew it was down anyway. It took half the morning to track you all down.' He tilts his chin, 'I was angry too, Kira. I needed time to cool off. My hot head, you know how it is.' He throws her a sheepish look. 'Maybe I wanted you to miss me.'

'Miss you? I was going out of my mind with worry.'

'I'm sorry.'

Kira leans back in the driver's seat, suddenly exhausted, all the fight leaving her. White caps lift on the ocean ahead of them, galloping towards the shore. 'I'm sorry too.' She shakes her head. 'What a weekend.'

'Kira.' He squeezes her hand. 'I love you. I love Asha. I love our life together. I walked all night through the storm, praying that I wouldn't lose you both.'

Kira sighs. 'What will we do about Dom? Things could get tricky. There are going to be some difficult conversations ahead, if you still want to be a part of them?' She eyes him keenly. 'I love you, Fred. As far as I'm concerned, you're Asha's dad – if you still want to be?'

'It's not about *want*, Kira. Don't you see? Not anymore.' He leans over and kisses her. 'Let's go back and get our daughter, pack up our stuff and get out of here.'

She kisses him back, long and hard. 'Yes, let's go home.'

DOMINIC

Monday afternoon

Tanya and Dominic sit at a table in the hospital café, two cups of coffee cooling between them.

'Take the car,' he says. 'There's no point us all staying. Clare wants Felix back in London with her. You and Phoebe can return to Harpenden. I'll remain with Scarlet until they're ready to discharge her. Barry knows I'm unavailable. I've told him no more work for a while.'

Tanya nods. She's wearing very little make-up and with her blonde hair tied-up in a ponytail, she looks younger, softer. He'd tell her she looks beautiful, but he knows it's not the time.

She reaches for her coffee cup, then pushes it away. When she lifts her gaze, he sees something new in her face, something cold and resigned. 'I want you gone, Dominic. As soon as Scarlet is home safely.'

Dominic stares at her. 'Gone?'

'I'm done. I don't want to be with you. Not anymore.'

Dominic frowns. He tries to reach for her hand, but

Tanya snatches it away. Panic rises in him. 'You don't want this, Tanya. Trust me, I've done it before.' There's a lump rising in his throat. 'Separation is ugly – painful for everyone. No one comes out of it better off. Emotionally it's difficult and financially, well, it's a disaster.' He trails off, seeing the expression on her face.

'I don't think you're in any position to tell me what I do or don't want. I don't even know that myself.' She narrows her eyes at him. 'But if you think I care about any of that other stuff right now – the money, the house, the cars, the luxuries of our life – then you're mistaken.'

'I didn't mean—'

She holds up her hand. 'This weekend has opened my eyes, Dominic. Not just to you – and your affair with Kira.'

'It was hardly an affair! It was *one night*. Not even a night. It was a mistake.'

'Mistakes have consequences.'

He drops his head. 'I can fix this.'

'Fix it? We nearly lost Phoebe this weekend. Scarlet's lying in a hospital bed. I see what's important now. Family. Loyalty. Love. Trust. Can you offer me that?'

He meets her gaze. 'I can, Tanya. I wish you'd believe me when I say it didn't mean anything. It was just one, crazy moment. A weakness. I swear, it's you I love.'

'Maybe,' she shrugs. 'But it means something to me, Dominic. It's *your* weakness. And there's a child now, too ... and she also means something. The kids – Scarlet, Felix, Phoebe ... and Asha too now – they mean everything.'

He hangs his head, awash with shame. 'I know. I'm sorry, Tan. Don't you think I know now how much pain I've caused? This weekend – this nightmare we've been living – it's all my fault. Don't you think, every time I close my eyes, I remember how close I came to losing my girls? How close that psycho came to – to . . .' He can't finish his sentence. He pushes the palms of his hands into his eyes to try to stop the tears that have begun to fall. 'I know I've fucked up. Not just Kira, but the job, everything. I'll move out. I'll give you whatever space you need. I'll wait, while you decide.'

They sit in silence as Dominic composes himself. 'This weekend has changed me too,' he says, after a time. 'This place – everything that's happened – it's done something to me. I can feel it.' He *could* feel it. It was as if the elemental wildness of the place had got under his skin, altered him. All his emotions rising to the surface. A stopper loosened. All his love, his fear, his rage. Out on the headland in the storm he had come face-to-face with his true nature, his worst self, and now he had to deal with that man – all his desires, all his anger, all his failings and the consequences of his actions. It wasn't just Tanya he owed apologies to. There were his children, Jim, all his friends, Kip, and that poor man – Penrose – who the police told him had lost his daughter, and now his son. His actions had created ripples he was only just beginning to understand.

He looks for a sign of softening from Tanya, a relenting, but he finds only anger.

'I won't be treated that way. Never again.'

She is reaching for her handbag when a shadow falls

over their table. Dominic glances up to find a young man hovering beside his chair, a phone in his hand and a familiar, hopeful look on his face. 'Sorry to interrupt but aren't you—' He grins, and gestures to his phone. 'My mates will never believe me. Could I get a quick selfie?'

Tanya rises from her chair with a sigh.

Dominic seems to consider the man's request, then shakes his head. 'I'm not him. Just a bad lookalike. Sorry.'

The man frowns and looks doubtful. 'Oh. Okay. Sorry to disturb.' He glances once over his shoulder as he walks away.

When Dominic turns back to the table, he finds that Tanya has already gone.

He slumps low in his chair. He wants to believe he can talk her round, that he can convince her to give him another chance, but there was something in Tanya's eyes that makes him deeply afraid, that makes him realize that maybe this is one mess that Dominic Davies isn't going to be able to talk his way out of, not this time.

SCARLET

Five days later

Sitting next to her father in the front passenger seat of their hire car as they pull out of the hospital car park, Dominic suggests she chooses some music. Scarlet flicks through the radio stations until she finds a track she likes. For a while, they sit in silence, Dominic's fingers tapping in time on the steering wheel as Scarlet watches green hedgerows skim past the window, a ribbon of cobalt blue ocean visible beyond.

Her mobile phone pings on her lap. She lifts it and reads the message from Lily. *Have you left yet?*

She hesitates. It still stings to think of Lily and Harry together, but they've been best friends since primary school. She doesn't want to let a boy come between them. There's nothing like facing the cliff edge to make you see what's important to you ... and what's not. After a moment, she types her reply. *Yep. Dad says I'll be back at Mum's by 4pm.*

The reply comes almost immediately. *Can't wait to see you.*

She smiles. *Me too.*

She lays the phone in her lap and turns back to the window. 'What do you think is going to happen between you and Tanya?' she asks. Her father hasn't told her what's going on yet, but she knows it's something serious.

Dominic sighs. 'I don't know, love. I think I might have blown it.'

She thinks about her and Lily, about Lily's daily phone calls to her in hospital and her tearful apology. 'Sometimes you have to find the strength to forgive.'

'I'm not sure,' Dominic says, clearing his throat, 'that Tanya considers what I've done forgivable.'

'So you're not going back to the house in Harpenden?'

'Not right now, no. I've booked a hotel.'

Scarlet shakes her head. 'Wow. You really did mess up.'

A moment passes before he speaks again. 'I'm trying, Scarlet . . . trying to be a better man.'

She reaches out and squeezes his hand.

'Tell me when you need to stop – if your leg starts hurting, I'll pull over.'

She rolls her eyes. 'Stop fussing. I'm fine.'

He throws her a rueful smile. 'Someone's feeling better.'

'You know what the police said about talking to someone about all of this?'

'Uh-huh.'

'Are you and Mum *really* going to make me see a counsellor?'

'Yes, we really are.'

She shrugs and falls silent for a moment. 'By the way, Dad . . .'

He turns and looks.

'Remember that bet we made in the car coming down?'

Dominic frowns, then smiles.

'I think you owe me a tenner.'

As they come to the now familiar turning, her father slows the car. 'Are you sure you're up to this?'

'They know we're coming, right?'

'Yes. I squared it with Max.'

She nods. 'I still want to.'

He turns the car off the road, jolting them down the trail leading back to Wildernest. As they draw closer to the farmhouse, she feels a tightening in her chest, a tremor in her hands. She closes her eyes and focuses on her breath, counting slowly, calming herself, just how the doctor showed her back in the hospital. 'Scarlet,' says her dad, concerned. 'I can turn round.'

'No,' she insists. 'Keep going.'

When she opens her eyes, she sees Max and Kip standing out in the yard in front of the farmhouse. There is a chopping block in front of them and a pile of split wood at their feet. Kip appears to be wielding the axe, under Max's close supervision. As their car pulls up, she sees Kip visibly stiffen. He lays the axe carefully onto the block and takes a step closer to his father. Beside her, Dominic lets out a deep exhale before switching off the engine. He seems as nervous as she is. He turns to her. 'Give me a minute with him first, will you?'

'Sure.'

She watches her father step out of the car and exchange a few polite words with Max. There is a figure standing at the kitchen window. Scarlet doesn't know if Annie can see her behind the windscreen but she raises her hand in greeting and Annie returns the gesture. She doesn't blame Annie for wanting to avoid her dad.

Dominic is turning to Kip. He takes a step forward, then stops, keeps a careful distance as he addresses the boy. Kip's head remains bowed. She can't hear what her father is saying but she knows the gist of it. *I'm sorry. Thank you.*

Then he is turning, nodding at her, and Scarlet opens her car door and gingerly rises from the seat. Seeing her struggle, Dominic rushes over and tries to press the hospital crutches lying across the back seat on her, but she doesn't want them. Gently, she pushes him away, before hobbling over to Kip. She throws him a smile. 'Hey,' she says.

Kip lifts his head and meets her gaze, his cheeks flushing pink, his eyes tracking to her hair. 'Hey.'

She reaches up and touches the side of her head, where the nurses had to shave her hair. 'I know. Looks weird, huh?'

'I think it looks sick.'

She smiles. 'Thanks. I wanted to say thank you, too. You saved my life.'

Kip shrugs.

'You were very brave.'

She reaches out a hand. Kip hesitates, then lifts his own and Scarlet, sensing his acquiescence, pulls him into a gentle hug. Her lips graze his ear. 'I won't tell,' she whispers, so that only he can hear. A final reassurance. He nods and when he pulls away she sees it in his eyes, his silent promise in return: *I won't tell.*

She feels lighter as they drive away, the farmhouse and the ocean and the cliffs receding, winding lanes turning to dual carriageway, which in turn fades until there is nothing to see in the rear-view mirror but the reassuring asphalt of the motorway stretching endlessly behind them.

She still wonders why Kip hasn't shared the exact details of Josh's death with the police. The nurses at the hospital had told her that shock can act like an emotional muffler, protecting you from things your brain finds too painful to think about. Maybe he found it too hard to think about? Maybe he doesn't remember. Or maybe, it's something else. Maybe he thinks he is protecting her? Either way, they share their secret now. A secret that binds them to that one moment with Josh at the cliff's edge.

Josh's autopsy had revealed the knife wound on his torso. She and Kip had both been asked about it in their interviews. It had confounded the police. The wound didn't match the penknife they'd found at the site of the crime, the one with Josh's fingerprints on, the one that matched the wound he'd inflicted on Scarlet. Yet no other weapon had been found at the scene, despite their careful search. The police had circled the matter with both kids in their interviews, but Scarlet had kept her silence. Kip had saved her life. For whatever reason, he didn't want to mention the knife. She wouldn't either.

She tries hard not to think about it now – that moment, with Kip curled at Josh's feet and Josh teetering at the edge of the cliff, his hands clutching his side, the bewilderment on his face as he'd lifted his palms and seen the blood smeared on his hands; that look as Josh had turned to her with something soft and imploring in his eyes, a look, she thinks now, that could've been defeat.

Who knows what might have happened if she hadn't acted? Maybe there was a chance they could've all survived. Josh would be locked up in prison, but still alive. Instead, standing at the cliff's edge, staring into his stricken face, she had felt something powerful rise in her. A wild fury. A force of nature she couldn't deny. She had rushed at him and, using every ounce of her remaining strength, she had shoved him over the lip of the cliff, watching as he'd twisted in the air, his body falling and bouncing like a rag doll off the cliff's sharp overhangs until it came to rest, an inert, bloody mess, caught in the jagged rocks below. Between them, she and Kip had made sure that Josh could never hurt anyone ever again.

Scarlet closes her eyes and takes a long breath.

Breathe in.

Breathe out.

As she focuses on her breathing, she tells herself that she is strong – and she is here – and that no one is going to hurt her again.

ANNIE

After the hire car has driven away, Annie remains at the kitchen window a while longer. Max and Kip return to chopping the fallen branch of the wych elm, Max watching intently as Kip swings the axe against the block.

She hadn't wanted to face Dom – hadn't known what to say to him, hadn't needed to hear the exact words that were shared in the yard, the apologies and the thank yous. There have been so many words – both spoken and unspoken. Kira's secret finally revealed. Jim and Dom's argument out on the headland that it seems neither man has quite recovered from. Kip's trauma held silently inside himself. And those cruel words spoken by Dom all that time ago to Josh's sister, which had escalated the whole nightmare. Maybe, she thinks, Max had got his wish, unintentionally. Maybe their reunion weekend had brought the wildest, truest sides out in all of them – one way or another.

Her gaze tracks back to Kip, to the focused expression on his face as he wields the axe. He's been having nightmares again, calling out to them in his sleep – Annie and

Max, Scarlet, Josh – and another name too, one that she hasn't heard from his lips before: *Evie*. His baby sister.

Max has found a private child psychologist in Truro, someone specialising in childhood trauma. He'd explained their situation and Kip had been given an emergency appointment. The counsellor, a calm, studious young man, had seemed a good fit with Kip. At the end of their first session, he had ventured out behind their son with a warm smile, handing Annie a pamphlet about a small school on the peninsula, one with limited classrooms and specialist support. She and Max are going to talk to Kip about it, when the time feels right.

In the meantime, their plans for Wildernest continue. There are workers out on the headland sealing the mining adit and erecting new signs, warning tourists and hikers to stick to the paths. Just yesterday, an envelope with a council stamp had landed on their doormat. She'd guessed what it contained even before she'd slipped her finger beneath the seal and pulled out the paperwork confirming the permits for their glamping site. They've invested in a fancy satellite phone and back-up generator. Even John Kellow has been round, gruff as usual, but muttering about the 'terrible business with the kiddies' and pushing a packet of butter wrapped in greaseproof paper and a glass bottle of whole milk into her hands, a peace offering, she'd assumed, though he hadn't said as much.

On the surface of things, they are in full recovery mode, doing everything they possibly can to ensure nothing untoward will affect their future guests. Below the surface, Annie knows the scars run deep. There are wounds that will take time to heal – not just for the three of them, but amongst their friends.

She still hates herself for doubting Kip. She knows it's going to take time to rebuild the trust, but they are getting there. Last night, before he went to bed, Kip had hesitated on the stairs, then returned to the kitchen and flung his arms around her waist, squeezing her tightly for the longest time. 'I like it here,' he'd said simply, before heading up to his room. Annie hadn't been able to reply, too moved by his unprompted display of affection.

His bedroom is where she heads now, while Max and Kip are still busy outside. She pushes open his door and stands for a moment, surveying the room, running through all the possible hiding places.

The axe meets the block with a steady, rhythmic thump as she moves swiftly and decisively about the room, lifting the mattress, checking behind the books lining his shelves, feeling into the corners of his desk drawer, rummaging amongst his clothes. She comes up empty.

The knife isn't there.

Just as it wasn't there when she returned to the laundry basket to retrieve the bloodstained weapon the day after the terrible events out on the cliffs. She had foraged frantically, sure she must be mistaken . . . but it had vanished and the only person she knew who'd seen her hide it there had been Kip.

She leans back on her heels and sighs. She tries to visualize it again – the flat, bloody blade clutched in his fist. The look in his eyes. It's all starting to feel like a terrible dream . . . as if she might have imagined the weapon there in his hand. Like a nightmare, vanished with the breaking day.

The axe has fallen silent now. Annie stands and moves to the bedroom window. Max is talking to Kip, gesturing to the pile of logs they have cut, his hand resting lightly on their son's shoulder. Watching them below, Annie is overcome with emotion. For the first time since they have moved here, she feels the stirrings of a feeling she has been craving: a sense of rightness, of settling, a feeling that maybe they are in the right place after all – even after everything that has happened. And maybe, just maybe, she doesn't need to worry about having all the answers – all the right words. Not right now. Maybe, she realizes, all she really needs to tell her family, today and always, is that she loves them.

ACKNOWLEDGEMENTS

The first seeds of this novel were sown in 2017 on a Cornish camping holiday with my friends, Marthe and Joel, then later blossomed on a glamping expedition with the 'Hodder girls' and their families. Thank you for the friendship, the fun and the memories, most of which I'm glad to say did *not* provide inspiration for this novel!

I wrote *The Search Party* out of contract, which was both freeing and terrifying. Sarah Lutyens, my agent, was a calm and patient voice throughout the writing and submission process. She seized on this new direction with excitement and is the reason this novel found a wonderful publishing home. I'm grateful to Sarah and the Lutyens & Rubinstein team, as well as David Forrer at Inkwell Management, for matching me with such enthusiastic publishers around the world.

Working with Simon & Schuster in the UK, Australia and North America is an incredible privilege. Thank you to the editorial dream team that is Clare Hey, Cassandra di Bello, Anthea Bariamis, Kaitlin Olson and Adrienne Kerr. Your vision for this novel was impressive from the get-go and your expertise and advice have helped to make this a far better book. Huge thanks to everyone across the group in Sales, Design, Production, Marketing, Publicity, Finance and Distribution. So many people have helped to bring *The Search Party* into the world. I know I'll have missed names, for which I'm sorry, but I'd like to mention Dan Ruffino, Louise Davies, Sabah Khan, Amy Fulwood, Rebecca McCarthy, Genevieve Barratt, Rosie Outred, Anna O'Grady, Fleur Hamilton and Ifeoma Anyoku. For the copyedit, my thanks go to Clare Wallis. For the map of author dreams I thank Jill Tytherleigh. For the sensational book covers, all gratitude to Craig Fraser, Christa Moffitt and Min Choi.

Librarians and booksellers are the heartbeat of the book industry and I think it's fair to say any writing career would be non-existent without them. I'm thankful for their magic ability to press the right book into the right reader's hands and I'm even luckier to call some of them my friends. My special thanks to Juliette and Nic Bottomley, who have been supporters of my books and cherished friends since I moved to south-west England. If you love exploring beautiful, independent bookstores, a visit to Mr B's Emporium in Bath should be at the top of every book lover's bucket list.

Professionally, Kelly Weekes offered me a post-pandemic boost of confidence through her brilliant author mentoring service. I also received a welcome creative re-set through author Kathryn Heyman's Immersion course for writers, which helped pull me out of the writing doldrums. Anna Barrett at The Writer's Space offered invaluable editorial insights on an early draft of this novel. I highly recommend all three to any writers finding themselves at a perplexing crossroads.

I wrote a section of this novel on an Arvon Foundation retreat in Shropshire where I found myself, serendipitously, in the company of Katy Schutte and Amy Rosenthal, both of whom provided encouragement, laughs and inspiring conversation. Likewise, fellow authors Cesca Major, Kate Riordan, Katherine Webb and Emylia Hall always help to put the creative life into perspective and the world to rights. Thanks for the Whatsapps, emails and lunches.

I thank Hachette for the ongoing stewardship of my backlist, their continued friendship, and the work they do with the excellent Emerging Writers' Festival each year on the Richell Prize, the writers' award established in my late husband's name.

I write for many reasons, but perhaps my biggest motivation is to make my kids, Jude and Gracie, proud and to honour their dad, Matt, who was the first person to encourage me to put pen to paper. I now have two wonderful Matts spurring me on, the Matt who lives on in my memory and heart, and Matt Poynter, who swept me off my feet in 2019 and has brought love and joy back into my days. Our blended family is one of the most unexpected and wonderful outcomes of the last few years. Thank you, Matt, for finding us.

My sister, Jess, is the best first reader I could hope for and the only person I ever want to show my first drafts to. She never fails to take my writing seriously or offer helpful feedback, even when I send her a first draft titled *'pile of poo'*. She is the best. Love you, Jess. Our three-way 'favourite siblings' chat may have fallen silent, but you and Will are forever my favourites.

Finally, this book is for my mum and dad, Gillian and John Norman. I cannot remember a time when I haven't felt supported by them. Dad often has a wonderful take on something I'm struggling with, or a helpful pep talk when I need a boost, and Mum has gifted me endless encouragement and countless days of time and space away to focus on my writing. This book is dedicated to them both, on their respective sides of the world, with my love and appreciation.

Hannah x